Race to the Bottom

By

John T. Hackett

authorHOUSE

1663 LIBERTY DRIVE, SUITE 200
BLOOMINGTON, INDIANA 47403
(800) 839-8640
www.authorhouse.com

© 2004 John T. Hackett
All Rights Reserved.

First published by AuthorHouse 07/07/04

ISBN: 1-4184-5672-1 (sc)
ISBN: 1-4184-5671-3 (dj)

Library of Congress Control Number: 2004094114

Printed in the United States of America
Bloomington, Indiana

This book is printed on acid-free paper.

Chapter 1

The dark blue Lincoln Continental was parked near the entrance of a modern office building in lower Manhattan, engine idling and parking lights glowing in the late afternoon shadows. The driver, a large man clad in a black raincoat and chauffeur's cap, recognized his passengers as they emerged from the building. He stepped out of the limousine, signaled to them, opened a large black umbrella, moved quickly to the other side of the vehicle, and opened the rear door nearest the sidewalk. The two men sprinted to the car to avoid the rain. The driver shielded them with his umbrella as they entered the limousine. As soon as they were seated, he closed the door, lowered his umbrella, and returned to the driver's seat.

The rain was heavy and cold, as it often is in New York City in mid-November. It started in the early afternoon and increased in intensity as evening approached. A wedge of gray sky appeared above the buildings. White, red, and amber vehicle lights reflected and whirled in the cold, damp air. Emergency sirens seemed more intense as the rain and wind whipped across streets and sidewalks. Pedestrians attempted to shield themselves with umbrellas and newspapers as they hurried to reach subway entrances or bus shelters; others stood along curbs or between parked vehicles vainly attempting to attract unoccupied cabs.

Before moving the limousine, the driver informed his passengers that weather and traffic would prolong the trip to the Teterboro Airport. He offered to call ahead and inform their pilots. It was unnecessary; they had called at the conclusion of their meeting, and their flight plan had been

1

adjusted. He then eased the vehicle into the westbound traffic and headed for the Lincoln Tunnel. The conversation in the back seat excluded any discussion regarding the day's activities. There were many stories—some true, some pure fiction—regarding limousine drivers acquiring sensitive information by eavesdropping on passengers' conversations and cell phone monologues.

Thirty-five minutes later, the limousine emerged from the west end of the Lincoln Tunnel engulfed in the drone of heavy tires on damp pavement, the odor of diesel exhaust, the intermittent hiss of air brakes, the piercing sound of aircraft ascending and descending in the Newark International Airport flight pattern, intermingled with the rhythmic thump of windshield wipers. As the limousine ascended the ramp from the tunnel exit, the Hudson River and lower Manhattan came into view, illuminated by an orange glow as lights reflected off low clouds and mist, creating silhouettes of an uneven skyline, a reminder of a nation's tragedy.

Forty-five minutes later, they arrived at Teterboro Airport. The driver lowered his window and spoke briefly into a speaker box attached to a security gate. After a brief delay, the gate slid open, permitting the limousine to enter a private aircraft parking area. The driver slowly maneuvered the Lincoln near the stairway of a gray and blue Falcon 50 executive jet. As the limousine stopped, an airport security vehicle pulled alongside. A few seconds later, the aircraft door opened, and a young man descended the stairway and opened a large, blue umbrella with a gray W embossed on each panel. The limousine driver disembarked and opened the rear door nearest the aircraft, allowing his passengers to board the aircraft quickly. As they entered the aircraft, the man with the umbrella walked to the security vehicle to assure the occupants that the men boarding the aircraft had been properly identified. He then re-entered the aircraft, retracted the stairway, and closed and sealed the door.

The aircraft's passenger compartment contained six spacious gray leather seats: a row of four located on the right side of the cabin, the remaining two seats located in a row on the left rear side. A gray leather sofa that seated three or converted into a single bed occupied the remainder of the left front side of the cabin. A door at the back of the cabin shielded a toilet and sink. A small, elaborate galley was located near the entrance. The cabin floor was covered with a plush blue carpet with a large gray W woven into it at the entrance. On the forward wall, facing the passengers, a color video screen displayed alternately the time, altitude, outside air temperature, air speed, expected arrival time at their destination, and a map of their route and current location. The last seat, located on the right side of the cabin—referred to as the "command seat"—contained an instrument panel in the left armrest that permitted the occupant to control cabin lighting, temperature, wireless telephones, audio/visual equipment, and communication with the flight crew.

After hanging the passengers' coats in the cabin closet, the young man returned to the cockpit, occupied the copilot seat, and began to assist with the preparation for takeoff and communications with ground control, tower, and radar control personnel.

Immediately after occupying the "command seat," Harris Stevenson, president and chief executive officer of Wiemer Industries, executed his standard pre-flight routine. He removed his shoes, stood up and pivoted the seat in front of him, returned to the "command seat," placed his feet on the seat facing him, fastened his seat belt, folded his arms across his chest, and closed his eyes. Stevenson was 57 years old, a large man with broad shoulders and a barrel chest, nearly six feet tall, with a full head of hair and a military-style haircut. His business suits always appeared one size too small. He wore oxford cloth dress shirts with button-down collars, which accentuated his double chin. His collar was buttoned only on formal occasions, and his tie always appeared to be a random choice, bearing no relationship to the balance of his attire. As always, he wore badly scuffed brown loafers and ankle-length cotton socks. His reading glasses, attached to a short nylon cord, rested below his double chin.

Bruce Kramer, chief financial officer of Wiemer Industries, occupied the seat parallel to Stevenson. He secured his seat belt, opened his briefcase, removed his PDA, and secured a pair of half-lens reading glasses from a small aluminum case. After placing the glasses on the midpoint of his nose, he began reading his e-mail messages. Kramer was 44 years old, medium height, and balding. Unlike Stevenson, he was acutely aware of his appearance. Despite his collection of fashionable suspenders and custom-made French cuff shirts, he rarely appeared without his suit coat while in his office. In contrast, few other executives at Wiemer Industries were seen wearing their suit coat, with the exception of board of directors meetings. His wardrobe and formal bearing reflected his previous career in investment banking, a source of sarcastic humor among his Midwest colleagues.

Within minutes, the plane began rolling along the taxiway. The pilot executed a 90-degree turn to position the plane on the assigned runway. A warning bell sounded in the cabin, alerting the passengers that the plane was in position to takeoff. As the pilot advanced the throttles, the roar and vibration of the two jet engines increased rapidly. Within thirty seconds, the plane was airborne, followed by the sound of the landing gear retracting in the underside of the aircraft. The lights of northern New Jersey disappeared quickly as the aircraft was engulfed in heavy clouds and the pilot sought the initial compass heading and altitude assigned by the Newark air controller.

As the plane ascended to its assigned cruising altitude, the passengers were silent. It had been a long and difficult day. It began with a 5:30 A.M. departure from Indiana, a turbulent two-hour flight to Teterboro, a one-hour limousine ride to Manhattan, and a series of meetings from mid-morning to late afternoon, saturated with legal and accounting hyperbole.

The purpose of the meeting, as defined by Bruce Kramer, was "corporate hygiene." The senior management of Wiemer Industries, like other publicly owned corporations, periodically met with legal, accounting, and banking advisers to review their capital structure, evaluate defenses against corporate raiders, and assure that they had complied with Securities and Exchange Commission (SEC) and New York Stock Exchange regulations. At today's meeting, the discussion focused on three interconnected and controversial subjects: plant relocations, labor contracts, and financial problems.

The meeting began with accountants and lawyers, exploring the conundrums buried in Wiemer Industries' loan agreements and labor contracts—specifically, the protection they provided and restrictions they imposed on management. That meeting was followed by a carry-in lunch and two-hour discussion of recent changes in accounting rules and standards, their impact on financial reporting, and the protection or exposure they provide in the event of a struggle for control of the company. The day ended following a prolonged synopsis of SEC regulations and NAFTA legislation that might be used to defend against what the investment bankers referred to as "the phantom aggressor." All of the resulting advice and counsel was provided with appropriate professional aplomb, despite the fact that none of the participants, with the exception of Stevenson and Kramer, had more than a rudimentary understanding of the operations or products of Wiemer Industries.

Less than ten minutes after takeoff, the plane reached its assigned cruising altitude. The engine noise was suddenly reduced as the pilot adjusted the throttles to reduce the air speed.

Harrison Stevenson opened his eyes, placed his hands behind his head, exhaled loudly, and exclaimed, "By God, I don't know if that was a productive meeting, but I know it was expensive."

Kramer laughed, but did not respond.

"You know, I'm convinced they tell each client the same thing," Stevenson continued. "It's all accounting and legal gobbledygook and investment banker bullshit."

Kramer removed his glasses, opened his briefcase, returned his PDA and glasses to their assigned location, closed the briefcase, and placed it beside his seat. He spoke softly, hardly audible above the roar of the jet engines.

"Well, it's similar to buying insurance. We may never need the advice, but if we do, it's important to have access to them. If they're obliged to represent us, they can't represent the other side." Kramer sounded more like an advisor than an associate.

Stevenson loosened his seat belt, removed his feet from the seat in front of him, leaned forward, and rested his arms on his knees.

"That argument probably makes sense until you start contemplating who they'll be working for when our need arises. They move from job to job like nomads. And they get paid, and damn well, regardless of whom they represent, the sheep or the wolves. The lawyers and the accountants claim they're restrained by ethical conduct codes." He paused. "Now that's a true oxymoron: legal and accounting ethics. Hell, the bankers don't even attempt to hide their intentions; they're 'free agents'."

He paused again, looked at Kramer. "What would you guess the average age of the people attending that meeting?" he asked.

Without waiting for Kramer's response, he continued, "I think we spent nearly eight hours listening to a bunch of kids less than ten years out of business or law school, telling us how to fend off the phantom aggressors, who are probably advised by their ex-colleagues, partners in other deals,

5

or old friends from graduate school or some prep school. In actual practice, the whole damn industry operates like a private club."

He leaned back in his seat. After a brief pause, his voice became more intense.

"You could damn near smell the ambition in that room today. They all expect to make big bucks, and they want it tomorrow. Their lifestyles require it, and they'll do whatever is necessary to make it. Who knows, next year they may be working for the phantom aggressors. It wouldn't surprise me to find one or more of them advising the other side in a hostile takeover or a labor negotiation."

After a long pause, and no response from Kramer, Stevenson unfastened his seat belt and stood up. "Want something to drink?" he asked.

"No thanks," Kramer responded.

He watched as Stevenson made his way to the small galley at the front of the cabin. He was surprised at Stevenson's blunt criticism of the afternoon meeting. He was frequently criticized for exhibiting too much patience and avoidance of confrontation.

Harris Stevenson grew up in a small town in northwestern Indiana. His father owned a local business that supplied new tires and tire repairs. During high school, he worked in the tire repair shop; a tough, dirty job. After high school, he attended Purdue, studying mechanical engineering. He was a serious student with a strong academic record. But at the end of his third year, without explanation to family or friends, he enlisted in the Marine Corps. At the end of "boot camp", he volunteered for Marine reconnaissance and was transferred to the West Coast for additional training. Eight months following his enlistment he was a member of a Marine Corps recon unit stationed in Vietnam. Seven weeks later, he was wounded while on a reconnaissance patrol. A friendly grenade went astray, resulting in shrapnel wounds to his right arm and shoulder, and a significant loss of hearing in his right ear. The fact that he was naturally left-handed helped disguise the wounds.

Following his recovery, he returned to Purdue and completed his undergraduate studies. He joined Wiemer Industries as a manufacturing manager. He rose steadily from manufacturing manager to vice president of manufacturing to executive vice president of operations, and after 25 years of service, he was appointed president and chief executive officer. There was little question about the depth of his understanding of Wiemer's products, customers, and technology. His leadership skills, however, were better demonstrated when he was conversing with foremen and hourly employees on the shop floor, and he enjoyed interaction with customers. He disliked the pretentious formality of the board room, and avoided meetings and presentations to security analysts, bankers, and institutional investors. He assigned those tasks to Kramer.

Stevenson returned from the galley with a can of beer and a large bag of pretzels. Before sitting down, he looked at Kramer and smiled. "You think I am paranoid on this subject, right?"

Kramer laughed. "Maybe a little, but I understand your concerns." It was a diplomatic response.

Following graduation from Kenyon College, Kramer was hired by Morgan Stanley as an investment banking trainee at their New York City office. Three years later, he enrolled in the Stanford University MBA program, then returned to Morgan Stanley following graduation. A strong, confident personality with a quick mind, he was promoted rapidly to vice president, and among other client assignments, he was the senior manager on the Wiemer Industries account. Following the birth of their second child, he and his wife decided they would prefer to live in the Midwest, where their families continued to reside. Although they sought an opportunity to return to the Midwest, the flat rural landscape of northeastern Indiana was not what they had envisioned, but the professional opportunity at Wiemer Industries outweighed the disadvantages of the location. Kramer was completing his sixth year as CFO.

Stevenson sat down, placed the beer can in a holder in the armrest, and opened the bag of pretzels.

"What really pisses me off," he continued, "is their arrogance and condescending attitude. We've been working with them for years, yet they've less than a basic understanding of our business. When I looked around that room today, I didn't recognize anyone who had ever visited one of our plants, looked at one of our products, or asked a question about our business that didn't pertain to their narrow interest. The only exception was the lady lawyer. At the afternoon break, she asked me about current business conditions. I couldn't tell if she was really interested or only sucking up to a client."

Kramer sensed that a response was required, but he wanted to avoid sounding defensive. Stevenson frequently expressed his contempt for lawyers and bankers. Kramer had always assumed that his background and demeanor rendered him suspect.

"It's the nature of the beast" he said. "They'll argue that they deal with too many businesses to acquire a deep knowledge of any single client's operations. They're trained to interpret the law, accounting rules, banking regulations and capital market behavior. They assume we only want counsel and assistance on those issues and nothing more. Offering opinions on other issues may offend a client."

He paused momentarily, attempting to measure Stevenson's reaction before continuing.

"What really scares the hell out of those guys is the knowledge that the loss of a client can result in the loss of a job, loss of one hell of a big income, and loss of traction in a very tight business society. It's all about attracting and retaining clients, billable hours, and underwriting fees. The rainmakers attract the clients and the rest of the organization services them. The more clients you attract, the more fees you generate, the bigger your slice of the annual bonus."

He paused again, smiled at Stevenson. "That's what buys the Ferrari, the second home on Nantucket, and pays the alimony."

Stevenson nodded his head. "Oh, I understand what motivates them, but what I don't understand is why the hell we depend on that pompous Jack Perkins to counsel us about labor contracts and plant relocations. I'll bet the sonofabitch has never met a union member, let alone negotiated with one."

Kramer was well acquainted with Perkins, having dealt with him several times while at Morgan Stanley. He often described him as a brash young lawyer who was "full of himself," but, in fact, he made every effort to assure that Perkins was consulted regarding Wiemer Industries' labor contracts and relocation plans. He admired Perkins' "take no prisoners" approach to labor negotiations.

He responded with appropriate sarcasm, but no criticism of Perkins.

"I doubt if Jack believes there's any subject that falls completely outside his radius of expertise. But he only focuses on what our labor contracts allow and don't allow, what we can and can't do under NAFTA, and how we might slip around some of the restrictions. He doesn't give a damn if we manufacture steel or chewing gum. It's all generic to him. I am not sure he even knows where we're headquartered. He assumes all of that is irrelevant. He knows the law and interprets contracts. He doesn't want to be burdened with any other issues. They all adhere to that narrow, cautious approach. Here's the law, here's our options, do what you have to do, and pay my fee."

He paused before continuing, "Perkins and the other people in that room don't want to get drawn into discussions about job replacement, community relations, benefit extension, wage differentials, or Mexican labor conditions. They don't give a damn."

He laughed. "If we push those issues, you'll have to endure another lecture about the need to remain competitive in a global economy, the worldwide benefits of free market economic policy, and our obligation to our shareholders."

Stevenson was silent. He appeared to be focused on the cold, dim lights 30,000 feet below.

Kramer elected not to pursue the conversation any further. He had always been cautious with Stevenson on this subject. He assumed that Stevenson had not supported his selection as the CFO. When he was with Morgan Stanley, he had met Stevenson on two occasions, but nearly all of his dealings had been with Gus Arnholt, the CFO he replaced. A few months before his retirement, Arnholt recommended to the chairman of the board of directors that Kramer be selected as his replacement. He opined that Wiemer Industries needed a CFO with Wall Street connections. He didn't inform Stevenson of his conversation with the chairman

Arnholt and Stevenson had a stormy relationship. Arnholt had mounted a strong campaign to become the CEO. The board of directors decided he was too old to assume the responsibilities. It was his final attempt to secure the top job. He had also failed on several previous occasions. It was not until the next board of directors meeting that Stevenson learned of Arnholt's recommendation regarding Kramer, At that meeting, it was agreed that the chairman and Gus Arnholt would meet with Kramer to explore the opportunity. Kramer had one interview with Stevenson before being hired. It was short and stiff. Three days later, Stevenson called and offered him the job, with something less than unbridled enthusiasm. The Wiemer financial staff was surprised and disappointed. It was assumed that the corporate controller would move up to CFO. As the chief accountant and a 15-year veteran with Wiemer Industries, he was respected and well-liked. Despite Stevenson's efforts to retain him, he resigned.

After a few minutes of silence, Stevenson turned and spoke directly to Kramer, his voice lower, resonating less anger. He spoke as a mentor addressing a younger man.

"Bruce, they're parasites. They don't create value, they consume it. I've watched them for 30 years. Each year they become greedier. They recruit the best and the brightest from the elite business and law schools, pay them incredible salaries, and promise them they'll be super rich in less than ten years. They drain millions of dollars from corporate clients. Look at the increased amount of fees we've paid them over for the past ten years, and show me the increased value we've received."

"You can't," he said, answering his own rhetorical question.

"But that's not enough for them. They've convinced themselves that if they don't break the law, or get caught at it, it's O.K. to engage in any transaction that generates more income, irrespective of the ethics involved, or the impact on their clients and financial markets. Some of those kids make more bonus money in one year than a master machinist in our plant makes in a lifetime. And now, that same greedy behavior has begun to show up among corporate executives. They've seen Wall Street grab the gold and they want part of it."

"It's wrong," he declared.

"I'm not an economist or a political scientist. I'm a mechanical engineer, but I've spent enough time on factory floors among hourly workers to know that if the greed doesn't stop, they'll change the system. They won't tolerate it. They'll go for radical change. They'll throw the baby out with the bathwater. All the talk about the benefits of world trade, free markets, and shareholder value is so much garbage when all they see is lots and lots of people losing their jobs, savings, and pensions, and a handful of people becoming unbelievably rich. It has to stop. When the system works, everyone has a chance to benefit. It doesn't work when it becomes a zero sum game; where all the benefits go to a few and the rest lose."

The quiet intensity with which Stevenson had just spoken was uncharacteristic. Despite his background and physical appearance, he did his best to avoid confrontation, even at the cost of his reputation as a leader. His current demeanor was a caution signal for Kramer. He sensed it would be unwise to disagree, but he felt compelled to respond.

Although unintended, his response was condescending. "I don't disagree with anything you've said, Harris, but I'm not sure we can change the system. If we don't accept the new environment and adopt appropriate business practices, we may lose the entire company. It's a lot bigger issue than Wiemer Industries. It's a worldwide economic trend. I think the cost of resisting can be devastating, many times greater than accepting the new economics."

Kramer's response appeared to heighten Stevenson's belligerence. "Bruce, I've listened to that bullshit for years. The only performance measure they use is a rising stock price. Those sonsabitches don't care about anything else; the employees, the community, they don't count. It's all about stock prices and getting rich. They're pushing us to move more operations to Mexico because it would reduce costs, increase our stock price, and protect their financial investments. There wasn't one goddamn word today about the effect on employees in Indiana or the community."

Early in his tenure with Wiemer Industries, Kramer became convinced that Stevenson was guilty of what he referred to as "naïve rejection of reality." He had told several old friends at Morgan Stanley that Stevenson lacked the vision to lead the company; although an outstanding manufacturing executive, he was wed to old ideas and customs. He'd been promoted above his skill level; he lacked the sophistication to lead a public corporation.

Kramer's evaluation of Stevenson was widely accepted on Wall Street.

"I don't believe they're totally unaware or uncaring about the employees and the community, but it's economic reality," Kramer replied. "A lot of manufacturing companies are leaving the United States to take advantage of lower wages and costs in Mexico and China. They're only suggesting what needs to be done if we're going to remain competitive, if we're going to survive."

"No, no, no." Stevenson raised himself up in his seat and punched the air with his left forefinger for emphasis. "What they really believe is that our employees are a bunch of stupid rednecks who will find some other job, maybe stock boys at Wal-Mart or cleaning crews at Wendy's; and Hammelburg is just another goddamn bump on the map that you fly over on the way to California."

"Well… that's an ugly reality, Harris."

"Reality," Stevenson barked, "I'll tell you what reality is. It's going home and telling your wife and three kids that after 20 years of working for a company, it's over, flat-ass gone. No negotiation. No other jobs. The mortgage, the car payments, the hopes for the kids' education are still there, but the company just told you that despite the fact that you're a qualified machinist or assembly worker, you're too expensive. They can hire someone in Mexico for 30 percent of what you cost. You can either accept lower wages or lose your job. Reality is having your wife and kids try to disguise what they really think: you're a loser. Your wife wonders if the family can make it on her salary and your unemployment benefits. That's reality"

"Well, there are other jobs, especially for skilled workers."

Stevenson's anger suddenly achieved a level that Kramer had never witnessed before.

"What fucking jobs are you talking about, Bruce?" he barked. "What other jobs in Hammelburg? What jobs did they find when we moved the foundry and forge shop to Juarez? Goddamn it, go down to Muncie and Anderson and ask about the jobs they found when those auto components plants closed."

Kramer was stunned by Stevenson's response. It was totally out of character. He attempted again to soften the conversation. "What's our alternative, Harris?" Kramer asked in a quiet voice. "The banks and the investors expect us to protect their interests. I don't think it's possible to save those jobs and compete in this market."

Stevenson took a long drink from the can of beer, jammed his hand into the bag of pretzels, turned, and looked out the cabin window. He didn't respond.

Chapter 2

Wiemer Industries' corporate headquarters and largest manufacturing facilities were located in the city of Hammelburg, in northeastern Indiana—a small city with a population of approximately 75,000, the county seat of Alamost County. The city had been founded in the early 1800s by several German families, including Adolf Lauterbach, a farmer and Lutheran minister. Most of the early settlers were immigrants from the northeast section of Bavaria and Hesse; farmers, artisans, and merchants. Lauterbach was credited with establishing a spirit of civic pride, generosity, and progress in Hammelburg

The original settlement sat on a high, wooded bluff above the north bank of the Wabash River, surrounded by rich agricultural soil. The Lutheran, Catholic, and Amish churches were the first community institutions, and created the first educational institutions, long before other Indiana communities had primary and secondary schools.

Beginning in the early 1900s, Hammelburg emerged as one of the most progressive small cities in the Midwest, as a result of the philanthropy and vision of its leading citizens. The main streets of Hammelburg had been designed by a local architect who created broad avenues and boulevards lined with oak, maple, and sycamore trees. Other outstanding architects were hired to plan public buildings, and city planning became a formal part of Hammelburg city government. A hospital, sanitary sewers, public recreation facilities, and a unique education system were established long before other similarly-sized Indiana cities were even contemplating such projects. The city's parks, public buildings, schools, and infrastructure were the envy of neighboring communities.

Wiemer Industries' corporate headquarters, however, was an unexceptional two-story brick building with a large plaza at the entrance. It was located in what had been the commercial center of the city, before the development of several large shopping centers on the city's perimeter. As visitors entered the building, they immediately encountered a large portrait of the founder of the company, Jacob Augustus Wiemer, painted nearly 20 years after his death. The artist's model was an old family photograph that included Jacob—a stern-looking man with penetrating eyes, a well-trimmed goatee, narrow celluloid collar, and a dark tie. He appeared to be a small, slight man in his sixties. He wore a GAR campaign ribbon in his left lapel. His granddaughter suggested that the artist exclude a scar over Jacob's right eye, a permanent remembrance of his military experience.

It was believed that Jacob Wiemer was born in Melsungen, Germany, located near the Fulda River south of Kassel. The year of his birth had never been clearly established. According to incomplete and rather unreliable family records, he was the second of three children, an older brother and younger sister. His father was a merchant and his mother was the daughter of a music teacher According to verbal history, Jacob had few physical attributes. He was small and ordinary in appearance, with little interest in athletics and few of the requisite skills. However, he was exceptionally intelligent, and it was assumed that he had been an outstanding student.

German tradition dictated that the oldest son would acquire the family business; therefore, according to Jacob, his mother was concerned about the opportunities for her second son. Germany was not a unified nation, but a collection of sovereign states. Opportunities for young men of middle class families were limited. Even greater obstacles existed for a second son.

His descendents believed his mother and maternal grandfather encouraged Jacob to travel to the United States to visit his father's relatives. Jacob apparently never commented on his reasons for leaving his homeland. But sometime between the ages of 17 and 20, he sailed from Hamburg to New York, accompanied by an aunt, his mother's youngest sister, Martha Gerstel, a young English teacher. After landing in New York, Jacob and Martha continued their journey west; north on the Hudson River to Albany, and the Erie Canal to Buffalo. From Buffalo, they traveled by train to

Cleveland, Ohio, where they parted. Martha traveled to Canton, Ohio and was met by relatives. Jacob continued on to Indiana. His father's younger brother, Hans Wiemer, met him upon his arrival at Fort Wayne. Hans and his wife, Eva, had immigrated to the United States ten years earlier and lived near Hammelburg. They had two children, Wilhelm and Sophia. Hans was a farmer and a blacksmith. Jacob became the fifth member of a hard-working immigrant family and learned to speak English, to farm, and to be a blacksmith. Although not a robust man, he developed a skill working with metal.

Two years later, the United States became embroiled in the Civil War. Despite the objection of Hans and Eva Wiemer, Jacob and his cousin Wilhelm enlisted in the 47th Indiana Infantry Regiment of the Union Army. Wilhelm was killed at the Battle of Vicksburg. Jacob was wounded. He returned to Indiana to assist his Uncle Hans with his blacksmith business. He became the surrogate son.

Five years later, he married Marie Scheid, the only child of a prosperous Alamost County farm family. The Scheid family had immigrated to the United States from Germany in the 1820s. Although intelligent and relatively well-educated, Marie was not attractive. She was tall and big boned with large features, and considered by many as too assertive and outspoken. She was four years older than Jacob. Prior to her marriage, she was a teacher in Hammelburg and active in establishing a small library in the community. After several years of marriage, Marie gave birth to four children. The first was stillborn, and the three surviving children were Hans, Frederick, and Anne.

According to Wiemer Industries history, Jacob was intensely ambitious and entrepreneurial. Soon after he returned to Hammelburg, he began planning to build a larger business from the foundation of his uncle's blacksmith shop. He had observed forge shops and small foundries at Union Army ordnance facilities. The forming and creation of products from molten metal fascinated him. With Marie's assistance, he studied all the English language material he could find on metal forming and metallurgy. He also wrote his family in Germany, requesting any books they could acquire on metallurgy. He attempted to work with other metals, as blacksmithing was largely confined to iron. Within a short while, he began experimenting with casting and forging gray iron products. He traveled northeastern Indiana and northwestern Ohio seeking opportunities to supply small quantities of forge and foundry products to small manufacturers and blacksmith shops.

Hans Weimer's primary interest was his farm. He helped Jacob when he had time and never attempted to discourage his ambition. However, he worried about Jacob's health and family relations. Jacob had no social life and few close friends. His only activity outside of his business was the church. He was a devout Lutheran. Despite the demands of her children and her home, Marie encouraged and supported Jacob's plans and ambitions. On several occasions, when the expansion of the business began to exceed the available resources, she convinced her father to advance the required capital.

Jacob had several detractors in the community, but none more vocal than his cousin Sophie. She had married a struggling farmer, and they required her family's assistance. Sophie resented Jacob's dominance and ambition, and the attention and support he received from her father. She would not accept Jacob as a surrogate brother, nor did he attempt to play that role. She deeply resented his decision to name his first child Hans. Sophie believed Jacob had cheated her father and that the Scheid family had acquired too large a share of ownership of the metal business. She also resented Marie. She criticized her assertiveness and appearance, described her as too ambitious for her husband and her children. Sophie discussed her resentment with family and friends. In time, the entire community was aware of the bitter relationship. Others may have shared her resentment and envy, but none were as vociferous as Sophie.

Following two decades of struggling and planning, Jacob had established a successful gray iron and brass foundry and a forge shop in Hammelburg. The business that evolved from the small blacksmith shop employed approximately 25 people.

As water and sewage systems were adopted in larger communities, they required larger and more sophisticated processing systems. Jacob, with the assistance of several other German immigrants, had acquired sufficient knowledge of metallurgy and mechanical engineering to enable him to design and manufacture globe, gate, and check valves.

In the early 1890s, Hans Wiemer offered to sell his remaining interest in the business to Jacob. Jacob was receptive. Again, Marie approached her father to obtain the necessary financing. With the exception of Sophie, the community approved of the transaction. It was assumed that Jacob would grow the business and the community would prosper. By the close of the century, the business employed more than 50 and the facilities had been enlarged several times.

By the end of the century, Jacob's sons, Hans and Frederick, joined their father in managing the company. By 1900, the management included Jacob's son-in-law, William Rieff.

In 1910, both of Marie's parents died. As the only surviving family member, she inherited the Scheid family estate. Thus, Jacob and Marie became the sole owners of the business and the Scheid farms. They elected to call the combined enterprise Wiemer Industries.

During the early 1900s, the agricultural sector of the U.S. economy experienced one of its most prosperous periods. The price of agricultural products stabilized, exports expanded, and increased mechanization reduced cost. The food processing industry expanded rapidly and the demand for large industrial valves and metal filtration systems increased. By 1915, Wiemer Industries was also manufacturing valves for the emerging oil and gas industry. The growth of automobile transportation had resulted in a significant increase in demand for petroleum products, and refining plants required large numbers of industrial valves.

By the time the United States entered World War I, Wiemer Industries was a regional supplier of industrial valves and metal filtration systems for the food, petroleum, and chemical industries. The demand for products to support the war effort created additional growth for the company.

By 1917, Alamost County contained a large community of German immigrants and descendents. Many were skilled machinists, forge and foundry workers at Wiemer Industries. Following the U.S. entry into WW I, German families became targets of discrimination and suspicion. In an effort to counteract the bitterness toward Hammelburg's German community, Wiemer Industries published periodic reports describing the support the company and its employees contributed to the war effort. In addition, the Wiemer family also sponsored celebrations highlighting German cultural traditions and events, and invited the entire community to attend.

As a result of their German ancestry, Jacob's three oldest grandsons volunteered to serve in the U.S. Army. Seventeen-year-old Alfred Rieff, the oldest of Anne Wiemer Rieff's three sons, died in the flu epidemic at an army hospital in Georgia. Hans Wiemer's two oldest sons, Martin and Stefan, both served in France. Following their discharge, Martin returned to Hammelburg to join the family business. Stefan enrolled at the University of Michigan to study engineering. By the end of the war, Wiemer employees numbered over 400, and nearly all were of German ancestry.

In the decade following World War I, the company continued to expand as the demand for its products escalated. The company was an early exponent of elaborate valves and filtration techniques for the food processing industry. As the country experienced increased urbanization, municipal governments began acquiring Wiemer products to equip water and sewage systems. Increased demand for electric power provided opportunities to sell their products to hydroelectric and steam power producers.

In 1920, the family incorporated the business. The common stock of Wiemer Industries, Inc. was distributed among the immediate family members. Although both were elderly and less active in the family business, Jacob and Marie retained the majority of the shares.

Jacob was also the majority shareholder and chairman of the board of the Alamost County Bank. Marie retained sole ownership in the Scheid farm properties, among the largest in the Alamost County. The Wiemer family was the major contributor to the construction of the First Lutheran Church. At the suggestion and encouragement of his wife, Jacob financed and helped plan a building and a small park for the Alamost German-American Society. Although it was never publicly acknowledged, it was widely known that the Wiemer family assumed the cost of higher education for several promising young men in the community. Marie contributed a portion of her inherited wealth to help finance the original Alamost County Hospital.

In 1922, Jacob Weimer died. It was believed that he was in his 80s. His sons, Hans and Frederick, had become the senior executives in the company. Hans assumed his father's role. William Rieff served as the senior sales executive. The two grandsons, Martin and Stefan, formed the next generation of management. Jacob's share of Wiemer Industries' common stock was placed in a trust managed by his wife, Marie, and her two sons.

19

By 1928, the Wiemer Industries annual sales totaled $83 million and the company employed nearly 600 people. Martin Wiemer was being groomed to replace his father, Hans, as the senior executive. Stefan had assumed responsibility for engineering. Frederic Wiemer retired from the company and assumed the direction of other family businesses, including the bank and agricultural properties. He also became active in public affairs, serving two terms as the president of the Indiana Chamber of Commerce, chairman of the Alamost County Republican Party, and was a leader in the Indiana German-American Society.

The roaring twenties left some tarnish on the Wiemer family name. Hans Wiemer III was expelled from Princeton University during his second year as a result of inappropriate behavior with a young woman in a dormitory room. In September of 1925, two weeks after his enrollment at the University of Wisconsin, he and a female companion were killed in an automobile accident. Phillip Rieff, the second son of William and Anne Rieff, a student at Northwestern University, was badly beaten in a public restroom in Chicago . Two men were apprehended, but all charges were dismissed. The police were unsympathetic, accusing Phillip of soliciting sex. He denied the accusations, but was severely traumatized by the event.

In the spring of 1927, Marie Wiemer died. Before her death, she requested that her two sons use a portion of her estate to establish a trust fund to support the Alamost County Hospital and the German-American Culture Club. She also bequeathed a large gift to the Alamost County Library.

The Great Depression took a heavy toll on Wiemer Industries and Hammelburg. The depletion of private and public investment resulted in a sharp decline in the financial fortunes of the company and its employees. By 1934, annual sales had fallen to $43 million, less than half the amount recorded in 1928, and the company had incurred operating losses for three years. Martin Wiemer was urged by his father and his aunt, Anne Wiemer Rieff, to retain local employees as long as possible. Consequently, wages were reduced in an effort to maintain income for a greater number of workers. Nevertheless, employment declined from nearly 700 in 1928 to less than 300 by the end of 1934.

Despite these economic setbacks, Wiemer Industries had established a solid reputation in the design and production of industrial valves and filters. The company was well respected for the quality of its products and labor force. In early 1936, new orders increased in response to government spending for water reclamation, municipal sewage treatment plants, and hydroelectric power systems; part of a widespread effort to stimulate economic recovery. In the following nine months, nearly 150 employees were asked to return to work in Hammelburg.

Management was also expanded to include the next generation of family members. Jacob Wiemer Rieff, the youngest member of the Rieff family—referred to as J.W.—joined the finance staff after graduating from Wabash College. With a degree in mechanical engineering, Benjamin Wiemer, Frederic's only son, was hired as a supervisor in the valve assembly plant. Max Arnholt joined the staff as a sales executive following his marriage to Katherine Wiemer, Frederick's oldest daughter. After a delayed graduation from Northwestern University, Phillip Rieff reluctantly returned to Hammelburg. A job was created as editor of Wiemer Industries technical manuals.

Following the premature death of Hans Wiemer III, J.W. Rieff was considered the most promising leader of the new generation. A handsome, bright, and energetic young man, he had studied economics, served as president of his fraternity, played on the varsity tennis team for three seasons, and was awarded a Phi Beta Kappa key. Soon after joining Wiemer Industries, he demonstrated exceptional ability at financial management.

Chapter 3

Will Heider was frustrated by the confusion and delays that he always encountered after landing at Chicago's Midway Airport. He was tolerant of delays at the beginning of a flight; the security checks and passengers cramming all of those incredible objects in the overhead storage bins, but he could not understand why so much time was required to offload. The widespread elimination of first class seats aboard regional airlines had eliminated the assurance of a seat close to the exit. Even when first class seating was available, he refused to pay the outrageous premiums, particularly on flights of less than two hours. Because he always requested an aisle seat, he was usually assigned to row 20 or higher. He complained about being seated in the "FOLO section"—first on and last off.

Will was a lawyer and partner at Cutler Earl and Levin, a midsize law firm located in Chicago. It was not a "white shoe" firm, but was respected by its peers and retained a strong corporate clientele. The firm limited its practice to corporate, tax, labor, and environmental law. Most of the clients were Midwest-based corporations supplemented by a small number of other U.S. and foreign-based clients with business operations in the Midwest. He had served two years as a summer intern while a law student, and joined the firm as an associate following graduation. Now in his mid-forties, married and divorced. His ex-wife was a travel editor for a women's magazine. There were no children.

His youthful appearance sometimes became a temporary obstacle with a new client. He was of medium height with an athletic appearance.

Handsome, but not glamorous; he had acquired his mother's dark hair and eyes. Other than his professional life, he was devotee of the Chicago Bulls, Chicago Bears, and the Chicago to Mackinac Island yacht race. His devotion to the Bulls had diminished with the departure of Michael Jordan. His associates avoided any mention of the Chicago Bears. Will did not suffer defeat gracefully. He lived well, but rarely discussed his private life. He had expensive, but not ostentatious tastes. Although he made friends easily, he made few attempts.

His social life was described as semi-active. He dated several women, but none seriously. He followed a firm rule: no dating in the firm or other lawyers. He was attracted to female business executives that were fashionable and focused exclusively on career goals. He avoided people who talked about past or present marriages, and he harbored an irrational dislike for people who "dramatized" restaurant menus and wine selections. Following his divorce, Will purchased a condominium with a splendid view of Lake Michigan, near the city center. Not being an automobile owner he walked to work: rain, shine, or Chicago snowstorm. His only material obsession was his 40-foot sailboat, *The Affliction.*

After finally exiting the airplane, he began his usual search for a vacant payphone. Much to the consternation of his associates, he refused to carry a cell phone or pager. He was weary of listening to other people's private conversations in public facilities. His decision had been reinforced when a man standing next to him at a urinal at an O'Hare men's room initiated a conversation on his cell phone.

Finally securing a payphone, he called his office. Shirley Kovac answered. She had been Will Heider's administrative assistant for seven years.

Shirley was admired and appreciated by the senior members of Cutler Earl and Levin. She understood the meaning of clear and unambiguous communication. No long answers with unnecessary detail. You asked a question. You got an answer, or an immediate "I don't know" or "I didn't ask." A plain but intelligent woman dressed in functional clothing, fifty-one years old, married to a high school math teacher two daughters, one in college, the other a computer programmer. Among her closest friends, Shirley described her relationship with Will Heider as "an affair, but like a mother and son."

Her pattern of relaying information to Will was crisp and linear: important phone calls, important e-mail messages, a brief synopsis of FAX messages, anything in the mail that she thought he should be aware of before he returned to the office, a review of tomorrow's appointments and promised phone calls, and finally what she classified as unimportant phone calls.

It was in the middle of the last category that he interrupted her. He asked her to repeat the name of the first caller.

"Jimmie Hudson," she answered.

"Jimmie or Jim?" he asked.

"Jimmie. I asked him to spell it; J I M M I E. Jimmie."

"Really, what did he want?

"He asked for you... said you would remember him... requested a call back... and left his number."

"Yeah, I remember him... went to high school with him in Hammelburg. What did he want?"

"Didn't ask... he left his number," she repeated.

"God, I haven't talked to him in 20 years. I'll call him tomorrow. Remind me."

"I can give you the number if you want to call him now."

"No, I'll do it tomorrow... can't be that important. I hope it isn't some damn high school reunion." He paused and laughed, as if recalling something humorous. "On second thought, I doubt if Jimmie would be involved in arranging any reunions."

On occasion, when friends inquired of Paul Heider about his youngest son, Will, he would respond with humor: "He's a scab lawyer."

For nearly 40 years, Paul Heider had managed and later owned Bernard's Men's Store in Hammelburg, better known as Bernie's. In 1935, Will's maternal grandparents, Bernard and Wilma Stein, and their two children,

Peter and Ruth, emigrated from Germany to Chicago. Three years later, the family moved to Hammelburg and established Bernie's. They catered to working men in Hammelburg and Alamost County. Bernie's was where men bought heavy flannel and denim shirts, cotton and corduroy work pants, cotton and flannel underwear, work shoes and gloves, fleece-lined jackets and hooded sweatshirts. If your daughter was getting married and you needed a suit, you didn't go to Bernie's. There were no suits, neckties, white shirts, or dress socks in Bernie's inventory.

Later, there were hardhats, safety glasses, and steel-toed boots. The store was popular among farmers, factory and construction workers, and truck drivers. Despite religious prejudices and anti-Semitism, the Amish, Mennonites, Catholics, Lutherans, and Fundamentalists bought their work clothes and shoes at Bernie's. They were popular merchants who offered fair prices and good merchandise, and spent little for advertising or store decoration. As the business grew, the store was enlarged, but nothing ostentatious was included in the expansion. Initially, Bernie and Wilma were the only employees, but as the business prospered, they hired a few employees. In their early teens, Peter and Ruth began working in the store.

In the early 1940s, Paul Heider's father disappeared, following one of his frequent binges. He deserted a wife and two children. Paul's mother worked for Bernard Stein as a seamstress. During his second year of high school, Paul began working at Bernie's on weekends and after school as a stock boy and clerk. The employment lasted throughout high school. Following graduation, he became a full-time employee. In 1951, he was drafted in the army. Twelve of his twenty-four months of military service were spent in Korea. Following his discharge, he returned to work at Bernie's.

Paul Heider and Ruth Stein attended school and worked together. Ruth was an excellent student, but very shy. Although she occasionally helped her parents, she dreaded her time in the store. The customers were frequently rough and occasionally foul-mouthed. Her mother termed it "barnyard language." In time, Paul Heider became her shield. He would assume responsibility for a customer when he believed she was being harassed. Occasionally, she would overhear an anti-Semitic remark. Despite her parents' attempts to persuade her to disregard them, she found the experiences distressing. Paul became the person she turned to when these incidents occurred. By the end of high school, they were deeply committed to each other. Two years after his return from military duty, Paul and Ruth were married

Outwardly, the Steins expressed pleasure with their daughter's decision to marry Paul. Privately, they were disappointed. They would have preferred a Jewish son-in-law, not a Lutheran. Her older brother, Peter, had graduated from dental school and established his practice in Cincinnati. He married a Jewish girl. Growing up in Hammelburg, Peter and Ruth had limited exposure to Jewish religion or customs. There were occasional trips to Fort Wayne to participate in Jewish youth activities. As children of a Jewish merchant in a predominantly Christian community, the Christmas season was the most difficult. They were required to work in the store during the holidays. Their parents reminded them frequently to extend the usual Christmas greetings to their customers. The phrase "Happy Hanukkah" was not a part of their vocabulary, and only on rare occasions would a customer offer the greeting. Few customers were familiar with Jewish holidays.

Following their marriage, Paul gradually assumed the responsibility for the operation of the store as his father-in-law's health deteriorated. Ruth was rarely seen in the store. They became joint owners following Bernard Stein's death in 1965. The business continued to prosper as the community and industrial employment expanded. Paul was careful to maintain the character of Bernie's. His customers were comfortable with him. He was more attuned to their tastes and habits than other merchants. After so many years of exposure to his customers, he developed a unique ability to anticipate their needs and manage the inventory to accommodate them.

When work clothing became popular among clothing designers and younger customers, he refused to change his merchandising plan. He enjoyed conversing with men and women who earned hourly wages in manufacturing and construction jobs and farming. He belonged to the American Legion and the Elks, but not the Rotary Club or the Alamost Country Club. Ruth and Paul avoided involvement with any church or religious organization. Their marriage was conducted by a Circuit Court judge in his chambers. They contributed generously to local fund drives and helped sponsor cultural and educational activities, but maintained a low profile in the community. Their circle of friends consisted of a few couples who lived in their middle class neighborhood and friends they made while participating in philanthropic activities. They were not, nor wished to be, viewed as community leaders.

Will and his older brother, Tom, worked in the family store during high school and college. Their Christmas vacations were devoted to helping manage the Christmas rush. Their sister, Marilyn, was excluded, much to her disappointment. Ruth Heider insisted that her daughter not be exposed to the problems she had experienced at Bernie's. Tom was two years older than Will. He enjoyed the interaction with customers. He loved listening to the customers' outrageous stories, practical jokes, and gossip He was responsive to their petty complaints. The customers admired the similarity between Tom and his father. It was widely acknowledged, however, that Will was "different." A good student, an average athlete, well-accepted among his peers. But unlike Tom and his father, Will was not attracted to retailing and interaction with customers. Although diligent in carrying out his responsibilities, he was impatient to put Hammelburg and Bernie's behind him.

Following his brother's path, Will enrolled at Indiana University. When Tom graduated, he returned to Hammelburg to join his father. The family assumed that in time Tom would replace his father as the store's owner and manager. But for Will, there was too much family at Bernie's and too much history in Hammelburg; he confided in a friend that he "mentally suffocated whenever he returned to Hammelburg." During his senior year, he applied to several law schools and chose the University of Illinois.

The offices of Cutler Earl and Levin were located in the heart of Chicago's financial center on LaSalle Street. Will arrived at nine the following morning. From his lakefront apartment to his office was a brisk 20-minute walk. As expected, Shirley Kovac had prepared his single sheet "to do list" and placed it on his desk. The list was always prepared in order of priority and scheduled events. In open time slots, when he was not scheduled to meet with staff members or clients, Shirley would schedule return phone calls or suggest responses to correspondence. They appeared in order of importance. Her judgment was excellent. He relied upon her and rarely, if ever, questioned her priorities. However, as he surveyed the current list, he was surprised to find that the first item was a return call to Jimmie Hudson. He studied the list for a few moments before stepping out of his office and appearing at Shirley's desk.

She looked up and smiled. "Surprised by the first item, right?" she asked.

He frowned. "Yeah! It's been more than 20 years since I laid eyes on Jimmie Hudson. Is he in some kind of trouble?"

"I don't know. He didn't tell me why he was calling. All he said was you knew him and he needed to talk to you. But he sounded like a fellow with a problem."

She paused before continuing. "Sometimes I have premonitions. I had one about him. I think he needs to talk to you. When I came in this morning, I was still thinking about his call. I decided it should be first on the list."

"Well, any premonitions why he called?" he asked with a chuckle.

"Nope, not a glimmer... just a premonition," she said.

Will studied the list again and shrugged. "O.K., I'll get him on the phone."

"Want me to place the call?" she asked.

"No. Jimmie would think I was putting on the dog if I didn't call him direct." He glanced at the phone number on the sheet, walked to the kitchen for a cup of coffee, and returned to his office.

A female voice answered his call, "Metal Workers Union."

Will was surprised; he assumed that he was calling Jimmie's home. "Hi, this is Will Heider returning Jimmie Hudson's call"

Her response was swift and informal: "O.K., hang on. I'll try to find him. I know he's here."

A few moments passed "This is Jimmie."

The voice sounded different from the one he remembered. "Jimmie, this is Will Heider."

Jimmie was obviously surprised and pleased, "Will, how the hell are you?" It's been a long time. I appreciate your calling back."

His cheerful response puzzled Will.

"No problem, Jimmie. What can I do for you?"

"Well, before we dive into that, tell me what's happened to you in 20-plus years. Are you married? Any kids? Understand you live in Chicago... a lawyer."

He was surprised by Jimmie's knowledge and interest in his personal life. They were classmates at Hammelburg West High School, but not close friends. He wasn't sure Jimmie had close friends. He was tough kid and a loner. He wore his long black hair combed straight back and coated with a substantial amount of Vitalis hair tonic. His primary wardrobe was all black: T-shirt, pants, work boots, and black motorcycle jacket with a crude drawing of a coiled snake on the back. His parents were divorced. His father was a long distance truck driver. It was rumored that upon returning from a trip, his father routinely beat the hell out of Jimmie and his older brother. During his third year in high school, Jimmie purchased the shell of a 1938 Ford coupe from a salvage dealer in Fort Wayne and completely rebuilt it in the family garage. The car, like his wardrobe, was solid black. If the car had a muffler, it was hard to detect. Jimmie would drive to school every morning, the big V8 engine rumbling menacingly as he pulled in the school parking lot.

As early as his second year in high school, the teachers and staff decided Jimmie was trouble, despite his good academic record. They finally found a reason to expel him midway through his senior year. A manual arts teacher who enjoyed bullying students while acting as a hall monitor had made the mistake of taking hold of Jimmie's neck while disciplining him for some minor infraction of hallway conduct. Every kid in Hammelburg West High School avoided physical encounter with Jimmie Hudson. He was tough. Jimmie responded by grabbing the teacher by the lapels of his jacket, raising him off the floor, and slamming him several times against a row of student lockers. After his expulsion, he never returned to school

"Yeah, I am a lawyer. No kids. My ex-wife is a journalist. I wanted children. She wanted a career. It happens."

Will was surprised at his own candor. His sudden response was uncharacteristic. He was usually very cautious when commenting on his personal life and failed marriage. Somehow, with Jimmie, it didn't matter.

"How about you?" Will asked.

"Well, you won't believe it, but I finally got myself straightened out. After two years of working low-pay construction jobs and damn near starving to death, I realized I needed a high school degree. I passed the GED test and earned the diploma. Landed a job with Weimer as an apprentice machinist. Nearly 20 years later, I am a fully certified, card-carrying machinist, a vice president of the Independent Metal Workers Union, and a senior tool and die man at Wiemer."

"Congratulations." Will paused, creating a silence, hoping Jimmie would seize the opportunity to explain why he had called earlier.

"You're probably wondering why the hell I am calling you after 20 years... well, a couple of months ago, I ran into your Dad and asked about you and... "

Will interrupted. "Did he tell you that I am a 'scab' lawyer? That's what he tells everybody else."

Jimmie laughed. "No. He said you were a labor lawyer in Chicago"

"He's gone soft," Will responded.

Jimmie paused for a moment. "Last week, I called your Dad... talked with him about the Wiemer problem. He may have told you, I asked for your phone number."

"No, haven't talked with Dad in several weeks "

Jimmie paused again, searching for where to take the conversation. He had little history with Will. There were few common experiences or past friends to discuss. There were no connections or shared moments in the lives of the two men.

"As you have probably guessed, Will, I didn't call to catch up on your life. I guess you would describe my reason for calling you as professional. As I told you earlier, I am a vice president of the IMU. It's been a tough row the last few years. Job by job, Wiemer is leaving Hammelburg. First it was the foundry, than the forge shop, now they want to relocate machining and assembly. They've moved damn near a thousand jobs to Juarez, Mexico, just across the river from El Paso. The fancy Mexican name for those border town plants is *malquiladoras*. Damn near 400 of em have been set up by U.S. companies in and around Juarez. Our labor contract has a relocation clause in it that is supposed to protect us, but management keeps finding legal loopholes. Our lawyer doesn't seem to have any answers. We're getting screwed, along with the rest of Hammelburg."

There was a brief pause, followed by a short, blunt statement: "Will, we need a good labor lawyer."

Will didn't like the sudden change of direction of the conversation. He decided to respond quickly and decisively

"Jimmie, I'm a labor lawyer, but my firm and I have never had a labor union as a client. We've always represented management in labor negotiations and contract disputes. That's the reason Dad jokingly refers to me as a 'scab' lawyer. I hope you're not offended, but representing a union would create some real consternation at this firm."

"I know, he warned me that you might have an issue about working for a union," Jimmie replied. "But your Dad understands our problem. He said he decided to close his store after the foundry and forge shop were relocated and the Wal-Mart store moved in. He told me your brother left town, took a job as a sales rep for a men's clothing company. He said you might be willing to give us advice, but probably not represent us."

Will grimaced. He was annoyed. Talk about putting him in a bad spot. What was the old man thinking, for Christ's sake? How goddamn many times had he told him that he didn't represent unions, only management?

Jimmie continued. "Will, our lawyer is a local loser. We're the only union client he has; Wiemer management and their lawyers scare the hell out of him. If we were an international union, we could bring in some heavyweight lawyers. Your Dad remembers when this union was formed. We're an independent union because the members didn't want to pay national dues and be required to contribute to nationwide strike funds. There was also management influence. J.W. Rieff decided not to oppose a union. He pissed off a lot of his management team and some union haters in the community, but he made it damn clear he'd accept and work closely with a local union. He didn't want an international."

Will tried again. "Jimmie, I can recommend some good labor lawyers who represent unions."

31

"I know, your Dad mentioned that possibility. We've considered that, but we don't have the bucks to hire a big-time union lawyer. They won't come to Hammelburg to defend some local blue collars who think they have a complaint against a multinational company, unless it's big bucks and a sure thing."

He knew Jimmie was right. This had all the markings of a pro bono deal. Good old Will, Paul's son, Tom's brother. They all remember Bernie's and the family connection. Go back to Hammelburg, have a piss up with the Wiemer management, and come back and explain that to your partners. No goddamn way, he thought.

"Hey, Will," Jimmie continued, "I know we weren't close friends. But you grew up here. You played ball, drank beer, and raised some hell with a lot of guys who've already been screwed, and others who are going to be if this relocation happens. They're already hurting. We've offered big concessions to keep the jobs here, but management says it ain't enough. They have to meet competition. For several years, we've watched Hammelburg begin to fall apart. Stores are closing, home prices are declining, kids leave as soon as they can, and they don't come back. Businesses like your Dad's are gone. Twenty years ago, this was a great town. Wiemer did some wonderful things for Hammelburg. It was a model community. But today, it's a different company. The family's gone. Who the hell knows who owns the company? I don't, but I know they don't give a damn about Hammelburg."

He paused. "All I'm asking is take a look at the contract and see if we have any ground to stand on."

Will's thoughts focused on his partner's potential reaction. Risk a partnership in a successful law firm by doing pro bono work for a union and not bothering to inform your managing partner and ethics committee. No matter how good you think you are, you'll lose big time on a deal like that. What the hell was the Old Man thinking about?

He finally responded, "Look, Jimmie, this is tough. Today is Wednesday; give me a couple days to consider some options and I'll call you on Friday."

His voice revealed his disappointment "O.K. Will, all we're asking you to do is read the contract and tell us if we have any chance to stop this move. That's all. We won't ask more than that."

Will placed the phone in the cradle, picked up his coffee mug, walked to his office window, and looked down at the traffic on LaSalle Street. The conversation puzzled him. One of the toughest guys he had ever known pleading for help. Not for himself, but for something bigger. Maybe bigger than Jimmie could adequately describe or even understand. Jimmie wasn't a bully, but he remembered him as a tough kid. Muscular and menacing in a tight black T-shirt and heavy boots. He was both smart and scary. Never looked for fights, but everyone knew he could take care of himself. Not an athlete, but the athletes didn't play "big jock" around Jimmie. He didn't do much with girls, but he never gave them a reason to dislike him. Strange, he hadn't seen him in 20 years, and today, this tough kid with the black leather jacket and more balls than anyone else in school had asked him for help.

Will turned away from the window and walked out of his office intending to replenish his coffee. On the way, he passed Shirley's desk, stopped, and smiled at her. "Give me some advance warning the next time you have a premonition," he said.

"Was I right?" she asked.

"Yeah, he needs help," he shrugged. "But why me?"

Chapter 4

In 1940, as the nation prepared for war and assisted those already engaged in the struggle, the demand for Wiemer industrial equipment accelerated. Large industrial valves and filtration systems were required for installation aboard merchant and military vessels. Chemical and refinery operations were expanded, increasing the need for valves and filters. Annual sales totaled $93 million, and 30,000 square feet of space had been added to accommodate increased manufacturing and inventory. Employment at Wiemer Industries surpassed the record level achieved in 1928.

Martin Wiemer retained his position as president and chief executive officer. His father, Hans, although no longer active in the company on a daily basis, continued to serve as chairman of the board of directors, a perfunctory role. The five additional members of the board were family members and officers of the corporation. They included Hans Wiemer, Stefan Wiemer, J.W. Rieff, Max Arnholt, and Ben Weimer. The board met once each year during the second week of January to review the results of the past 12 months, approve the operating and capital budgets for the coming year, and most important, declare a dividend for the shareholders, comprised exclusively of family members. The meetings rarely exceeded three hours. The only other business discussed was the engineering report. As vice president of engineering, Stefan Wiemer supervised 12 engineers and several draftsmen. He was an outstanding engineer and had recently designed and supervised the construction of a product testing lab to assure that the company's industrial valves and filters would withstand the enormous pressure that they were exposed to in various applications.

J.W. Rieff was responsible for preparing all financial documents for the meeting. He was also considered the heir apparent to Martin Weimer. Frederic Wiemer had resigned from the board in order to allow his son-in-law Max Arnholt to take his place. He continued to be involved with other family properties and active in community development projects and state politics. Max Arnholt had assumed responsibility for sales, following the early retirement of William Rieff.

After the United States entered WW II, Wiemer Industries was required to focus primarily on war production, as their products were essential to the war effort. The management of the company also underwent changes. J.W. Rieff enlisted in the navy as an ensign. Max Arnholt joined the army and was sent to flight school. Ben Wiemer became vice president of manufacturing. He was classified 4F because of poor eyesight. Phillip Rieff was drafted into the army.

The increased demand for Wiemer products imposed enormous pressure on the company's workforce and management. By the end of 1944, the company employed 1,500 and sales exceeded $250 million. Despite the increase in sales, the company realized only moderate profits. Martin Wiemer had begun to suffer ill health as a result of his increased responsibility. Labor problems began to surface as the company attempted to obtain more production from a limited labor force. The rapid growth in Wiemer employment and activity also began to create problems within Hammelburg. The demand for housing, education, and medical services grew rapidly. Farmers abandoned their farms to seek high-wage jobs at Wiemer Industries. A number of small companies were formed to provide services and products to a growing community, further exacerbating local labor and cost problems. While labor costs accelerated, the Office of Price Administration (OPA) would not permit Wiemer Industries to offset all of their additional costs with price increases. Profits and cash flow shrank and the company began to experience difficulty financing maintenance costs and machinery replacement.

Heavy drinking further impaired Martin Wiemer's health and leadership. By 5:00 P.M. on weekdays, he occupied his favorite bar stool at the Alamost Country Club, consuming martinis, Scotch and club soda, or gin and tonic, depending on the day of the week and season of the year. Weekends were doubly difficult. He usually began drinking late Saturday morning and continued into Sunday evening. The leadership of the company began to drift. Hans Wiemer avoided the problem by denying that his son was

35

impaired. Stefan and Ben Wiemer attempted to assume many of Martin's responsibilities. Both men were stretched beyond their capacity. Stefan was a brilliant design engineer, but lacked management skills.

Ben Weimer had reached his pinnacle of ability by assuming responsibility for manufacturing. He was comfortable with direct involvement in the manufacturing process. He was uncomfortable in an office.

Confusion and frustration emerged as the organization attempted to determine who was responsible for the decisions Martin was neglecting. Manufacturing and quality control deteriorated, resulting in costly rework and repair. The company was forced to borrow $5 million from an Indianapolis bank to finance its capital budget. This was the first time Wiemer Industries had ever borrowed money; even during the darkest period of the 1930s they had avoided incurring any debt.

In February of 1945, Martin Wiemer suffered a severe stroke. The entire right side of his body was paralyzed. His speech was severely impaired. His father, Hans, himself in poor health, remained as chairman of the board. It was decided that Frederic Wiemer would return and replace Martin as the temporary CEO until a permanent management change could be established. However, Frederic had been absent from the daily responsibilities of the company too long, and at an advanced age, he did not possess the energy to provide the leadership required by a company experiencing the twin problems of rapid growth and insufficient profits.

By the end of 1945, a new set of problems arose. As the war ended, the company suddenly experienced a large decline in sales as the market was flooded with a government surplus of competitive products. Large layoffs were required, and the company suffered financial losses. As the management struggled with rapid expansion followed by abrupt contraction, Hammelburg reflected the turmoil. Unemployment rose, local businesses suffered declining sales, and agricultural prices sank. It was widely expected that without the stimulus of wartime demand, the depression of the 1930s would resume.

By 1946, J.W, Rieff, Max Arnholt, and Phillip Rieff had been discharged from the service. J.W. served as an officer aboard a navy supply ship in the Atlantic. Max had been trained as a pilot and flew B-29 bombers in the Pacific. He had accumulated 18 missions and was discharged with the rank of major.

Both J.W. and Max returned to Hammelburg and Weimer Industries.

Phillip Rieff, who had studied German at Northwestern, served with an army intelligence unit in Europe. Following his discharge, he elected to take advantage of the G.I. Bill of Rights and enrolled as a graduate student at the University of Chicago to study European history with the intention of pursuing a university teaching career

Hans and Frederic Wiemer, both elderly men, decided that J.W. should resume the management succession path he was pursuing before he entered the navy. He was slated to become the next president and chief operating officer of Wiemer Industries. But Martin's physical handicaps and Frederic's lack of energy required an acceleration of J.W's ascendancy. Nine months following his return to Hammelburg, it was decided to elevate J.W. to the leadership role, albeit with occasional mentoring by his uncles.

The company and community were surprised by the management realignment; J.W. was only 34 years old. Although a handsome and personable young man who had demonstrated significant skill as a financial manager, it was assumed that he would be given a longer period to prepare for the assignment. There were questions about his long-term commitment. He was also considered the community's most eligible bachelor.

Max resumed his role as vice president of sales. Both men were reelected as members of the board of directors. Although Hans continued to serve on the board, he agreed that J.W. would become chairman. Martin Weimer, who had not attended a board meeting since suffering a stroke, was replaced by Frederic Wiemer, who returned to the board. Once again, the board was comprised of six members of the extended family.

J.W. did not hesitate in taking command of the ailing company. His skill at financial management helped him evaluate the dilemma. With the help of the existing management and several new additions, he launched a program to reduce operating costs, increase sales, and introduce new products. Before introducing the changes, he convened an unscheduled meeting of the board of directors to inform them that the company could not continue to make dividend payments, and management salaries were being reduced, all to conserve cash for improvements in manufacturing facilities and new product introductions. Within days, the entire community was made aware of J.W's decisions. With the exception of several family members, his actions received widespread approval. The community had grown accustomed to layoffs and reductions in hourly wages, but this was the first time the family and management had been asked to participate in the pain.

When Frederic Weimer died in 1948, J.W. took his seat on the board of directors of the Alamost County Bank. The Weimer family remained the largest and majority shareholder. Alamost County contained five commercial banks and three savings and loan associations. The Alamost County Bank had been conservatively managed and survived the banking crises of the 1930s.

The third largest bank in Alamost County was the Hammelburg National Bank. The board of directors had recently recruited a young bank executive from Chicago to replace the retiring president. Henry Brinson was a rising star with one of Chicago's largest banks. J.W. Rieff quickly befriended Brinson and was impressed with his banking knowledge and marketing skills. Within a year, the two men had convinced their respective boards of directors that the two banks should be merged. With J.W.'s support, Henry Brinson became the president of the consolidated company, Alamost National Bank, the largest bank in the county and among the largest in northeastern Indiana. The Wiemer family remained the single largest shareholder in the new bank and J.W. became chairman of its board of directors.

Soon after Henry Brinson assumed his new duties, J.W. requested that Henry accompany him to Chicago and introduce him to lending officers in several of Chicago's largest banks. The trip was successful, and Wiemer Industries received a loan from The Chicago National Bank in the amount of $10 million to finance improvements in manufacturing facilities and new products.

Following the death of Hans Wiemer, the Wiemer board had two vacant seats. J.W. decided that it was time to install an outside director on his board. Following a lengthy discussion, it was agreed that Henry Brinson would be invited to fill one of the seats. Consequently, the two men formed a deep friendship and important business affiliation that would have a significant impact on Hammelburg during the next 40 years.

By 1950, Wiemer Industries' sales exceeded $300 million, and profit margins were significantly improved. Total employment was approaching 1,700. Under the leadership of Stefan Wiemer and his engineering department, a line of stainless steel valves was introduced for use in the food processing industry. In addition, hydraulic and pneumatic valves and cylinders were designed and marketed for widespread application in manufacturing and construction equipment. Sales of the traditional Wiemer products were also increasing. The growth in suburban residential areas required the expansion of municipal sewage systems and electrical power plants. As automobile production increased, so did the need for oil refining facilities.

In July of 1950, Henry Brinson and his wife, Eleanor, invited J.W. to an informal patio dinner at their home. Among the guests was an attractive young widow who was spending the weekend with the Brinsons. Mary Pinnay and Eleanor Brinson had been sorority sisters at Stephens College. Mary was 26 years old and employed by the Chicago Public Library as a genealogy research librarian. She had recently relocated from Houston to her original home in Chicago, following the death of her husband in an automobile accident. He had been a sales executive with a large chemical company.

Mary was dark-haired, petite, and rather quiet. In her informal attire, she had a youthful, co-ed appearance.

The seating plan at dinner placed J.W. next to Mary. They conversed the entire evening, almost to the exclusion of the other guests. As the party ended, J.W. invited her to be his dinner guest in Chicago the following week. Graciously, but not eagerly, Mary accepted the invitation.

Chapter 5

The primary purpose of J.W.'s trip to Chicago was to visit with his brother Phillip to discuss family financial affairs—primarily their mother's estate planning.

Anne Weimer Rieff was the last of Jacob and Marie Wiemer's children. in her mid-seventies, a widow for nearly 10 years, a devout member of the Lutheran Church. She had recently been diagnosed with dangerously elevated blood pressure. Anne had inherited many of the physical characteristics of her mother: she was tall and big-boned, but more graceful. She was a handsome woman, penetrating blue eyes, soft-spoken, never wore makeup, and her gray hair was always worn in a French bun. Although intelligent and socially active, in public she was always deferential to her two older brothers. In private, she commanded their respect.

She retained her ownership in Wiemer Industries, the Alamost National Bank, and the agriculture property, which had been divided between her two brothers and herself. Like her mother, she had been generous to Hammelburg, and talked at length with her two sons of her intention to leave a substantial portion of her estate to support the community and the church. As children and young adults, Phillip and J.W. were lectured by their mother regarding the family responsibility to the community and the church. She insisted that "responsibility" was the appropriate term, not charity or gifts. She believed that the community had played an important part in the success of the family businesses, and that it should be acknowledged more openly.

"Supporting the community is not charity or private welfare," she argued, "it is equitable sharing."

On several occasions, she addressed church gatherings and informed the congregation that support of the community and the church was "equitable sharing among all those who have helped create the value." Among the more conservative and wealthier citizens of Hammelburg, Anne Rieff was respected, but considered "too liberal." Her husband enjoyed teasing her about becoming "the family Marxist" and "Hammelburg's comrade for economic justice." Other members of her family, including her sisters-in-law and nephew, Martin Wiemer, were openly critical of her.

J.W. suggested that his brother meet him for lunch at the Chicago Club, which he had recently joined at the suggestion of Henry Brinson. The Chicago Club was a new experience for Phillip. Although he had resided in Chicago for several years, he had never experienced this aspect of Chicago society. He arrived before J.W., dressed in a corduroy sport coat, denim shirt with tie, and well-worn khaki pants—accepted academic attire, but a bit short of satisfying the Chicago Club dress code. When he announced that he was meeting a club member for lunch, the staff sniffed appropriately, but said nothing. When J.W. arrived a few minutes later, they were seated in a remote corner of the spacious main dining room by a proper but disapproving head waiter.

Phillip Rieff was handsome, thin, and almost fragile in appearance, a few inches shorter than J.W. Both his speech and demeanor were soft. His nearly gray hair was cut short in a military style. His horn-rimmed glasses and casual clothing identified him as an academic. Yet, beneath the soft intellectual veneer, he occasionally revealed a hard surface. In his late thirties, he was older than most graduate students, older than many junior faculty members. He was in the final stages of completing his Ph.D. dissertation: "The Causes and Ramifications of the German Immigration to the United States in the 19th Century." He had recently returned from a three-month visit to Germany, where he had completed the research for his dissertation.

The brothers never shared a close relationship. J.W. assumed the distance between them was a combination of age difference and Phillip's reticence to returning to Hammelburg following graduation from Northwestern. J.W. was five years younger. He was in high school when Phillip was attacked and later accused of homosexual behavior. His parents were deeply concerned about Phillip's physical and emotional health, but he had never heard either of them suggest that Phillip was a homosexual; nor had he ever done anything to suggest a preference for a gay lifestyle . He was attractive and had female friends, but there were no romantic liaisons.

The tragic loss of his oldest son, Alfred, and the obvious question about Phillip's lifestyle resulted in William Rieff focusing his attention and adoration on his youngest son, J.W.

At the close of the war in Europe, Phillip was transferred from London to a military intelligence unit in Berlin, and later to Washington D.C. On several occasions, J.W. had attempted to encourage Phillip to discuss his experiences during the war. Phillip would always find a smooth segue to J.W.'s military experience, revealing little of his own activities. Following his discharge, he enrolled at the University of Chicago, but continued to make occasional visits to Washington. It was assumed he was engaged in academic research or visiting friends. His infrequent trips to Hammelburg were confined to visiting with his mother and brief conversations with J.W.

Over a bottle of Rhine wine—selected by Phillip—and lunch, they discussed Phillip's recent academic research in Europe, postwar progress of West Germany, and business conditions at Wiemer Industries. After lunch was completed, J.W. raised the subject of their mother's wishes regarding the disposition of her estate. Phillip listened carefully as J.W. described recent conversations with their mother and the condition of her health.

When J.W. concluded, Phillip requested more coffee. After the waiter had delivered a fresh decanter of coffee and a small plate of cookies, Phillip resumed the conversation. His opening declaration surprised J.W.

"You may have surmised, J.W., that I intend to spend the rest of my life in research and higher education. You've already secured success. Neither of us is going to require Mom's estate to achieve our goals. By leaving a substantial part of it to the community and the church, it's her opportunity to make a permanent statement regarding her concept of the contract between the family and the community. I needn't describe it; we're both familiar with it," he smiled.

J.W. nodded approvingly.

"Consequently," he continued, "I've given some thought to Mom's requests and how we can help her achieve them."

"Spoken like a man who has already developed a plan," J.W. responded.

"Well, you may not have time to listen to my rambling this afternoon."

"I have until seven-thirty this evening, is that sufficient time?"

"What momentous event occurs at seven-thirty?"

"I'm meeting a very attractive widow for dinner at the Palmer House."

Phillip laughed. He suddenly appeared more relaxed.

He began to describe his vision of how they might help their mother fulfill her objectives. He dismissed conventional approaches: single large donations to selected organizations and institutions, grants for buildings bearing the donor's name. He envisioned broader projects with longer-range implications for the entire community.

"I believe we can achieve much more in the community by forming a permanent foundation that provides long-range assistance for those who pursue creative ideas, ideas that benefit a wider spectrum of the community. More than a single church or school can affect. The foundation could remain in existence for a much longer period of time. Perhaps attract others who wish to participate in support. It could become a catalyst for progress and change in Hammelburg."

J.W. observed Phillip's enthusiasm as he described his concept.

"Phil, I think I follow you, but give me a concrete example of what you envision."

"O.K., instead of financing a new wing for the hospital, we provide the funds for a group of MDs who want to pioneer new methods of practicing medicine. If they're successful, they might attract others; perhaps the community becomes a center for a new field of medicine. Sounds impossible? Maybe. But it's happened in other communities, and it generates lasting change and progress. It isn't investing solely in brick and mortar. It's investing in ideas that broaden the community and create new opportunities, a lasting impact on generations of people in Hammelburg, creating a much more diverse community."

J.W. sensed that Phil expected a response, but he struggled with it.

"Phil, what you have described is exciting, really exciting, but do you believe that is what Mom wants to achieve?"

He realized that he had phrased his question badly. He feared that it sounded like a challenge. He was still considering how to rephrase it when Phil responded.

"Let me share some things with you that we've never discussed."

Phil looked directly at J.W. for a moment and cleared his throat before continuing.

"When I came home from Northwestern, you were between your second and third year of college. Except for a few weeks each summer, you and I hardly knew each other. You were the kid brother, five years younger, popular, the male pride and joy of the Wiemer/Rieff clan. You replaced young Hans Wiemer. Had he survived, Hans would outgrow his reputation as a stud, a horny college kid. There would have been lots of lusty, male humor about his escapades at Princeton, and with fast women and fast cars. Despite the initial embarrassment he caused, his indiscretions would have become nothing more than humorous macho episodes.

Phillip looked down at the table, drank some coffee, and brushed cookie crumbs from the tablecloth. He again looked directly at J.W. for a moment before continuing

"But, I was the family *bete noire*. No jokes, no acceptance, only quiet contempt."

His voice tightened as he continued.

"Coming back to Hammelburg was the hardest decision I ever made. I isolated myself in Wiemer Industries training and maintenance manuals. I could have disassembled and reassembled a Wiemer valve blindfolded. Even the engineers came to me on occasion for advice. I decided to live at home, because I was sure that if I had lived alone, the community would be watching to see who visited me. I never entered a bar alone, went to a movie alone, and entered public restrooms only on rare occasions when there was no other choice. When I visited Chicago or Cleveland on weekends, there was a lot of conversation and probably some raunchy jokes about what I was doing. Martin Wiemer was my nemesis. Any time we engaged in conversation, he found a way to put the knife in."

He paused to evaluate J.W.'s reaction before continuing.

"That was my life for seven years with one very important exception… that exception was Mom."

He spread both hands on the white tablecloth. His long, tapered fingers reflected the tension he was experiencing.

"For seven years she protected my sanity. She is the only person I could talk with. Night after night, we sat and discussed and explored every conceivable subject, except me. She never asked what happened, never expressed concern about my life. She loved to recall her visits to Chicago and St. Louis and Cleveland; the art museums, the music, the plays. She loved to read and discuss the ideas she encountered in books."

J.W. was stunned. This conversation marked the first time that his brother has ever mentioned these incidents and his relationship with their mother.

After a brief pause, Phillip continued.

"As you know, Mom, like the rest of the family, has always been a loyal Republican. But as the Depression continued and she observed the impact on Hammelburg, she began to sample a few of the liberal authors: Dos Passos, Hemingway, Steinbeck. She wanted to discuss books and ideas. Other than myself, she was afraid her family and friends would discover that she was the reading these books and criticize her. She didn't even tell Dad. That may sound silly, but many of her closest friends in Hammelburg were, and still are, more than a little conservative."

J.W. laughed and nodded his agreement.

"To express it in a more theoretical sense, she never lost faith in capitalism, but in the mid-thirties she began to question outcomes. I remember one evening, she asked me if I thought there was too much economic disparity in Hammelburg. Did I think the economic rewards were too heavily skewed in favor of too few? She was deeply troubled by the suffering she observed among people she knew, grew up with; members of her church. She began to talk about the need for a more gracious and less harsh society. It never became a question of political philosophy. She focused on what individuals and communities might do to foster change."

He paused momentarily.

"I think it was then that she began to think about what she wanted to do with her own wealth. I was the only person who realized that she was going through this transformation. Everyone else thought of her as a good, generous, Christian woman, but naïve and over-generous. When the war started, our conversations occurred less often. Her two remaining sons were eligible to participate in the war. She had already lost one in the first war. He was so young, a boy, barely 18; died alone in an army hospital in Georgia. She couldn't bear the thought of losing another. I wanted to enlist, but I was afraid I'd be rejected. I was deeply depressed by this inner conflict. She sensed what I was experiencing. Without telling me, she went to the local draft board and told them 'My son wants to be drafted.'"

He removed his right hand from the table and momentarily placed it over his mouth before continuing.

"She wanted so much more than Hammelburg, but she also wants Hammelburg to continue to be more than just another town in Indiana."

J.W. sat there with the realization that he was unable to respond to his brother. This was the first time that Phillip had ever confided in him about his life. He wanted to reach out to him, but he struggled to gain control of his own emotions.

Phillip sensed his dilemma. He leaned forward and rested his hand on J.W.'s arm. "You can trust me, J.W.; I know what Mom wants. I've known for a long time."

Chapter 6

Harris Stevenson's work habits required that he depart his home on the north side of Hammelburg at approximately 7:15 A.M. The drive from his home to Wiemer Industries headquarters required 20 minutes. The traffic in the downtown section of the city was light. The retail store windows featured the expected array of winter clothing and sports equipment, with decorative references to the current football season. However, many of the retail businesses that had occupied the downtown section when Harris first joined Wiemer Industries no longer existed. A few had relocated to shopping centers on the edge of the city; most had closed. The abandoned buildings were a sign of the declining local economy, castoffs of a deteriorating business environment. They detracted from the feeble efforts of the few remaining downtown merchants and local chamber of commerce to stem— or at best delay—the inevitable shift from local merchants to large national chain stores. Initially, a few of the owners had attempted to maintain the appearance of their buildings in the hope that new occupants could be attracted. However, the relentless increase in the number of abandoned storefronts was accompanied by an accumulation of trash in doorways and torn and faded rent and lease signs. A few businesses that struggled on were primarily family-owned enterprises, managed by elderly owners contemplating retirement with little prospect of sale or family succession. Improvements or expansion were not a rational consideration.

The contrast between the Wiemer Industries headquarters and the slow decay of the buildings and neighborhood which surrounded it became more visible each year. The growth of strip malls and the rapid emergence of superstores with their huge asphalt parking lots and shopping cart corrals had replaced the downtown section as the hub of local commerce. The shopping malls and their national brand stores reminded Harris of the traveling street carnivals that annually visited small Indiana communities during his youth. They appeared overnight, setting up their tents and rides in the downtown streets. The local residents, farmers, and families spent their evenings at the carnival—riding the rides, playing the games, eating the corn dogs and cotton candy. But after a few days, the carnival disappeared as quickly as it had appeared. The local merchants who had encouraged the carnivals in hopes of attracting the customers to their stores ultimately discovered that local people spent their money at the carnival, not with the local merchants. The "carnies" took all the money and left a few pleasant memories.

By mid-November, the faint morning sunlight required that Stevenson turn on the overhead lights in his office and conference room. He detested the harsh glare and unnatural color of fluorescent lights; convinced they were the cause of his recurring headaches. He wanted to replace them with softer indirect lighting, but he knew the expenditure would generate satirical remarks among employees about cost reduction. When he was alone in his office, he didn't use the lights. With the exception of cloudy days, natural light was sufficient. When visitors to his office commented on the absence of lights, he would jokingly refer to his contribution to the cost reduction program.

As the fluorescent lights flickered, he could feel his body tighten in anticipation of what he was about to learn during the next three hours. His reaction was intensified by the knowledge that there were less than eight weeks remaining in the calendar year, and no hope that the company could avoid a third consecutive year of operating losses; even worse than the dismissal performance of the previous year. The stock market had already anticipated the results. During the past week, the price of Wiemer Industries common stock had declined to its lowest level in 14 years.

For as long as the staff could recall, the senior management of Wiemer Industries had reserved Monday morning for executive staff meetings. Those attending included the chief executive officer and five corporate officers. They met in a small conference room adjacent to Harris Stevenson's office. It began promptly at 8:30 and usually ended before 11:30. The atmosphere was informal. With the exception of Bruce Kramer, none of the men wore a jacket. But the agenda was well-established. It began with a report of the year-to-date operating results, a detailed listing of the amount and value of products produced and shipped during the previous week, the value and product mix of new orders received, and a comprehensive review of the year-to-date financial results. The remainder of the three-hour meeting was devoted to an informal discussion of programs to correct deficiencies in the company's operating performance and two ten- minute bathroom breaks with an agreement that no one would return phone calls or respond to e-mail messages.

None of the attendees looked forward to the recent Monday morning meetings, but no one dreaded them more than Stevenson.

The previous year, total sales sagged to $3.5 billion, 25 percent below Wiemer's best year in 1997. They also incurred a $127 million operating loss. The decline in sales and profits was primarily the result of increased imports and severe price competition. During the past four years, the company had laid off 4,500 employees as a result of plant relocations or reductions in production. The current employment level was approximately 6,000, of which nearly 4,400 were based in Hammelburg. The remainder were employed in Mexico. As recently as 1995, Wiemer employed more than 10,000 in Hammelburg.

There were rumors that the Independent Metal Workers Union was planning a walkout and might seek a court injunction to stop the relocation of machining and assembly operations from Hammelburg to Juarez, Mexico. Three years earlier, Wiemer had relocated both its foundry and forge operations to Juarez. Closing the foundry and forge operations resulted in the permanent reduction of 850 hourly and salaried employees. It also provided a significant reduction in labor costs and avoided the need to invest several million dollars in new equipment required to comply with EPA and OSHA regulations. It was forecast that the relocation of the assembly operations would eliminate no less than 1,100 additional jobs in Hammelburg. It would require six months to move the machinery from Hammelburg to Juarez.

A new building for valve machining and assembly was being constructed with Mexican government financing. It was adjacent to the foundry and forge shop 20 miles south of Juarez. Machining and assembly operations were labor intensive, and the cost of labor in Juarez was less than 30 percent of the cost in Hammelburg. In addition, there would be no medical insurance or pension expense. The NAFTA agreement would permit a duty-free import of fully-assembled products from Mexico to the United States. But the IMU was intent on blocking the relocation, and the community was angry. The relocation would result in additional economic hardship and loss of tax revenue for Hammelburg and Alamost County.

As usual, Jon Pertoski was the first member of the executive staff to arrive for the meeting. Pertoski was the vice president of manufacturing operations. In his early forties, medium height, with the appearance of an ex-athlete who had maintained his training habits, he wore a white shirt, dark tie, no coat, and a tie clasp displaying a blue W. His shirt sleeves were rolled up below his elbow. His heavy black shoes, like all the factory labor force, had reinforced steel toes. In his shirt pocket, he carried a pair of plastic safety glasses and a ball point pen. The large file folder tucked under his right arm contained the information he was required to provide at the meeting. He had already made his daily tour of the manufacturing facilities. Appearing frequently on the shop floor, nothing in the manufacturing process escaped his attention. He conversed frequently with workers, without condescension. The union stewards talked openly with Jon and he reciprocated.

He occasionally questioned the wisdom of his strict obedience to routine. He feared it limited his ability to become a more effective executive. However, following each attempt to alter his daily schedule, he experienced a feeling of disorientation and quickly returned to the familiar daily work pattern.

Pertoski's father and grandfather had spent their entire adult lives as members of the Chicago Fire Department. Both had achieved the rank of captain. His mother was a teacher in a Chicago elementary school. Jon and his two siblings represented the second generation of the Pertoski family born in the United States. His older brother was also a fireman. His sister had become a nun in the Order of the Sisters of Providence.

The Pertoski children attended Catholic schools from kindergarten through high school. As a member of his high school wrestling team, Jon competed twice in the Illinois State High School Wrestling Championship, winning fourth and second place honors, consecutively, in his weight class. After graduating from high school, he received an athletic scholarship at Iowa State University, studied mechanical engineering, and competed on the varsity wrestling team. Despite a heavy academic and athletic schedule, Jon became an active member of the Newman Center, a campus organization serving Catholic students. In the spring of his junior year, he met Maureen Cogan at a Newman social gathering. Maureen was a bright, saucy, redheaded native of Cork, Ireland. She had been awarded a Bank of Ireland Scholarship to support her graduate studies in agricultural economics. Jon and Maureen were married in Ames, Iowa one week after his graduation.

General Motors recruited Jon from Iowa State as a trainee in manufacturing management, and the newlyweds immediately relocated to Lansing, Michigan. The manufacturing process fascinated him. The coordination, teamwork, and planning involved in producing a product appealed to his engineering training and the self-discipline he acquired as an athlete. But following one year as a trainee, Jon was assigned a job in materials purchasing, where he was responsible for helping coordinate the purchases of automobile components from independent suppliers. During the next seven years, management decided that Jon was a promising purchasing executive, and his rapid promotions reflected their opinion.

But Jon yearned for a direct involvement in manufacturing. When he learned from a college friend about an opportunity at Wiemer Industries as director of valve assembly, he applied, and Maureen, their two children, and Jon moved to Hammelburg.

He acquired a positive image among the Wiemer hourly employees soon after his arrival. During his first week on the on the valve line, he overheard a foreman remark to another employee, "First we got the niggers, then the goddamn women, now were gonna be supervised by a fuckin' Polack."

The foreman, Charlie Knight, was six-feet-three and weighed in excess of 250 pounds. He was not popular. His nickname was "Three B's," an acronym for "bully, bigot, and bigmouth." He displayed a large tattoo on his upper right arm, which included a drawing of the Crucifix and the inscription "Jesus is my Boss."

Upon hearing Knight's remark, Jon turned around and approached him. He paused for a moment to observe Knight's nametag.

Without a trace of emotion, he said, "Mr. Knight, I gather from what I just heard, you have a low opinion of Afro-Americans, women, and people with Polish surnames."

Knight assumed a defiant posture with his large arms crossed tightly across his chest, which exaggerated the protrusion of his gut and enlarged his tattoo.

"My opinions are my business," he responded, without looking at Jon.

Jon stepped closer to Knight and spoke a bit louder. "Well, Charlie, let me tell you my opinion. Men who display their religion on their arms and let hate come out of their mouths confuse me. If you want to talk that trash, I suggest you wear long-sleeve shirts."

He stared at Knight for a moment, providing time for a reply; there was none. He turned and walked away.

As Jon departed, Knight smiled sheepishly and sneered, "What's his fuckin' problem?"

The other employee chuckled, "Don't know, Charlie. I ain't got no dog in that fight, but I think you better clean up your act when he's around."

Before the first shift clocked out that afternoon, nearly all the hourly workers had heard various renditions of the encounter between Jon and Charlie Knight. Charlie had met his match.

Elizabeth Brinson was second to arrive for the meeting. She had been the company's general counsel for nearly eight years, but never attended executive staff meetings until Harris Stevenson became CEO. Everyone except her widowed mother referred to her as Beth. She was small, in her mid-forties, divorced, and the mother of two adult sons. She retained her married name. Her clothing was expensive, but tastefully conservative. Her gray hair was cut short. Her tenure at Wiemer Industries was approaching 20 years. She conducted herself with a cool, professional demeanor. Beth was described as a lady who could and would provide a lot of help and good advice. Frequently referring to her as a "damn smart lawyer," her staff members were quick to warn people that "She's damn good, but she doesn't suffer fools."

Her early years were spent in Pittsburgh, an only child. Her father was a civil engineer who spent his entire career with a large electric utility. She displayed her intelligence at an early age, graduating from high school two months following her seventeenth birthday, and enrolled at Penn State

University to study metallurgy—perhaps, as she occasionally boasted, the only female metallurgy major in her class. In her senior year, she arrived at the painful realization that metallurgy was not a promising career path for a young woman. It was then that she prepared applications to several prominent law schools. To her surprise, she received a letter of acceptance from the Yale Law School.

Her first year at Yale, she fell in love with a classmate, Ted Brinson, the son of Henry and Elizabeth Brinson. Ted was a graduate of Amherst College. He was intelligent and equally handsome. They were married during the summer following their graduation from law school and returned to Hammelburg. Beth joined the Wiemer Industries law staff as a patent attorney.

Ted was the assistant vice president for legal affairs at the Alamost National Bank, until their divorce.

Soon after Beth arrived for the executive committee meeting, the remainder of the staff arrived: Bruce Kramer, Paul McLean, and Finn Sullivan. Following a few minutes of idle discussion about weekend events and college football scores, Harris Stevenson asked Jon Pertoski to review the previous week's manufacturing results.

His initial response was succinct: "It's ugly." He then distributed a single-page report to all the participants.

"Let me sum it up real quick. At current production levels, we're using less than 65 percent of our manufacturing capacity in Hammelburg. My numbers on the Juarez operations are a week old. I didn't get their e-mail this morning. Foundry and forge operations in Juarez are not great, but our operating costs are so much lower that we continue to operate above break-even."

Stevenson was shading his eyes from the fluorescent lights with his left hand.

"What about incoming orders, Jon, any hope for increased production in the short run?"

"No," Pertoski responded, "the further you look out over the next six months, the nastier it gets. Based on our current orders, we could produce nearly all of our orders in the next 90 days with no increase in production rates. The only orders we couldn't fill are a small number of nonstandard products. In time, we could source that production from Juarez at significantly lower costs."

He paused to permit everyone to absorb the impact of his response.

"To put the problem in perspective," he continued, "if our total production were restricted to the Hammelburg manufacturing facilities, we would require less than 70 percent of Hammelburg capacity. Three months from now, using only Hammelburg facilities, we would require only half its capacity. However, for the same production in Juarez, our forecast savings, if correct, would approach 53 percent."

Everyone was fixated on the middle of the conference table, except Pertoski, who was attempting to gauge the reaction to his report. There was no eye contact.

Stevenson had enormous confidence in Jon. He considered him the best manufacturing executive he had ever known. He wished, however, that he would develop a technique of reporting bad news with a somewhat softer touch; a little more finesse, a little less emphasis on negative comparisons. For a moment, he considered injecting some humor into the grim proceedings by suggesting that they all take the elevator to the roof, hold hands, and jump.

He elected to forgo the humor and move on. "Well, with that cheerful news, how are we doing with sales?"

He stopped shielding his eyes and looked at Paul McLean, vice president of marketing, who had positioned himself at the far end of the table, his favorite seat. At an earlier meeting, Stevenson had teased McLean about his seating preference. He asked him if he chose it because it was nearest the exit. Everyone thought his remark humorous, except McLean.

"Well, Paul, what's happening with our customers?"

Paul McLean was a quintessential salesman. He had an excellent knowledge of the Wiemer product line, but was not an engineer. He was a cheerful, slightly overweight extrovert who had earned the respect and admiration of Wiemer's customers by solving most of their application problems and entertaining them on golf courses. Both his son and son-in-law were also employed by Wiemer as salesmen, or "technical application representatives", a title Paul had bestowed on all the members of his immediate staff. His wife had also been employed as a secretary at Wiemer before marrying Paul. Both had been hired following their graduation from Hammelburg North High School.

Paul's response was defensive. "They're not our customers. They're still there and they're buying, but not from us. I know… they tell me they are. They also tell me our prices are too high. Unless we lower our prices they won't even accept our quotes. Last week, Justin Chemicals ordered seventeen hundred, 24-inch gate valves from Maddox Engineering. At our current prices, that order is worth roughly 1.2 million dollars. The rumor is that Maddox got the order at a price of less than 1 million. I got pretty good confirmation of that rumor Friday afternoon from their purchasing department. They told me Maddox will supply the finished valves from Mexico… casting, forging, assembly, everything from their Monterrey plant."

There was no response, no rebuttal.

"Last week I told you about the Reliance Equipment request. We gave them a price for 3,000 hydraulic valves and pistons for replacement parts. We quoted them less than 1.3 million dollars."

"Less than 1.3 million!" he repeated. "Bruce Kramer damned near strangled me."

He looked around the room before delivering his dramatic ending.

"Fidelity Fluid Power won the bid at less than 1 million. Again, finished valves and pistons… supplied from their Nuevo Laredo plant."

After a long silence, Stevenson asked, "You gotta solution to this problem, Paul?"

"There's only one solution. We've got to reduce cost and prices. We can't meet competition unless we reduce prices and, according to Bruce, we can't make any money unless we reduce cost," he answered.

"Paul's right," Kramer interjected, "at the prices that Maddox and Fidelity quoted on those products, we would lose nearly 250,000 dollars. I'm sure that both of those companies are making money with those bids because they're producing the entire product in Mexico. We can't continue to absorb Hammelburg's labor cost and compete with Mexican-made products. Our customers know it. Our bankers know it. And our current stock price suggests that the market knows it."

Paul McLean and Finn Sullivan nodded in agreement.

"Assuming you're both correct," Stevenson responded, "tell me how we break the impasse with the IMU regarding moving more operations to Mexico. I gather you're suggesting that we move the entire manufacturing operation out of the country."

"We can't continue to pay Hammelburg wage levels and compete," Kramer insisted. "The bankers aren't going to make any more credit available unless we convince them we can reduce cost and generate profits. You know that, Harris, they have made that point painfully clear last week. The stock price is a pretty good measure of their attitude. And we can't continue to operate unless we can renew our existing debt and raise additional capital."

"So we're between a rock and a hard place," Stevenson remarked sarcastically.

With a rather defiant tone, Kramer responded, "Yes, in my opinion that is exactly where we are. There is no other choice than relocation of manufacturing out of Hammelburg. We can retain engineering, marketing, and other administrative activities here, but we can't continue to absorb Hammelburg direct labor costs and survive."

"Survive is a hell of a strong word, Bruce."

"Harris, I am not engaging in hyperbole. The bankers have put us on notice. Once we've exhausted our current line of credit, the banks won't loan us more until we can demonstrate a significant improvement in cash flow and lower operating costs. That was the message we heard last week in New York. We both heard it. We can't survive without the availability of bank loans. Our cash flow is too small. We have to demonstrate to the banks that we can generate enough profit and cash flow to retire our current debt before they will extend more."

Stevenson looked hard at Kramer. He realized that he was about to have an open argument with a staff member. He had to respond, but he wanted to avoid a confrontation.

"Bruce, I didn't hear anyone at that meeting tell us that we had to relocate the assembly operation to Juarez. I heard a lot of talk about our need to improve cash flow and repay debt. I heard a discussion about what we probably can and cannot do with our existing labor contract if we want to make that move. But I didn't hear anyone tell us to move assembly operations to Juarez. Moreover, I don't intend to allow bankers and lawyers to dictate… "

Beth Brinson interrupted him. "It appears to me that's not the only rock and hard place we find ourselves lodged between," she said. "We're not going to walk away from a labor contract with the IMU for free. Before we make any final decisions, we better consider how much a negotiation with the IMU is going to cost, and measure it against the saving we hope to derive from the relocation."

Kramer responded, "Last week, Jack Perkins told Harris and me that we can probably relocate without violating the labor contract, based on the business hardship clause. That suggests a very small, if any, settlement with the IMU."

Beth was obviously annoyed with Kramer's response. "Well, Jack Perkins may be a hell of a smart labor lawyer, and I am aware that he inserted that clause in the contract, but I believe the financial failure or hardship clause is vaguely worded, and it would require a court interpretation and probably be subjected to a lengthy appellate process, regardless of how the initial ruling came down."

"Beth, you may be correct. I am not a lawyer," Kramer answered. "But the local lawyer for the IMU may not read the clause as carefully as you have."

Beth laughed. "Is that what Jack Perkins is basing his opinion on? Never build your case on the assumption that your opponent has a dumb lawyer, Bruce."

"Nobody said anything about a dumb lawyer, Beth. But I am betting on a very experienced New York law firm versus a small law firm in Hammelburg."

Fenn Sullivan joined the discussion. "There's a rumor on the plant floor that an international union may attempt to organize the IMU on the basis that they can stop the relocation."

His voice revealed his apprehension; his eyes darted around the room, attempting to read the group's reaction to his remarks.

Sullivan was vice president of personnel for Wiemer Industries. He had held the job for 22 years, following a short career as a health insurance executive. He was considered adequate. His skills were political, rather than technical. He had lobbied Harris Stevenson for two years to change his title to vice president of human resources. Stevenson refused, He detested pretentious titles and he displayed little patience with Sullivan's political machinations. Sullivan was capable of changing sides several times in a single meeting, depending on how he read the potential outcome of a dispute. In private, Stevenson referred to Sullivan as the "corporate windsock."

"Which international union, Fenn?" Stevenson asked impatiently.

"I don't know."

Stevenson could not disguise his annoyance with Sullivan. "Goddammit Fenn, I have heard that same goddamn rumor for 20 years. Every time there is a labor dispute, it's reported that the IMU is going to vote in favor of joining an international. When we closed the foundry and forge shop, there was a rumor about the UAW and the Teamsters coming in. It never happens. The union members don't want to pay international union dues. It would be a hell of a lot cheaper for them to hire a good lawyer."

Beth Brinson nodded in agreement.

Jon Pertoski thought a little humor might ease the tension before re-entering the discussion. "There's an old saying on the plant floor: 'If you don't hear a new rumor by ten o'clock, start one'."

Everyone laughed. Sullivan shrugged his shoulders. "Just reporting what I've heard."

"Seriously," Pertoski continued, "there is more dissatisfaction and anger out there than I have seen in a long time. People are threatened. They're frightened. You back people into a corner, they tend to fight. It's becoming a survival issue."

Kramer resumed his argument. "Jon, were only talking about moving hourly jobs. The higher-paid employees will remain in Hammelburg. The engineers, marketing people, the IT group aren't going anywhere. They're the highest paid. The community isn't going to lose them. It's only hourly jobs that will be lost. They've already experienced that with the relocation of the foundry and forge operations."

"I wish it were that simple," Pertoski responded. "We're talking about several generations of families that have worked at Wiemer Industries. They've bought homes, educated their kids, paid property taxes, supported churches, invested in the community, retired with some security. The IMU and the community believe that their last offer included enormous concessions. They accuse us of not being responsive to their proposal."

Bruce Kramer stared at the ceiling, signaling his impatience with Jon Pertoski's remarks.

"There's also another major issue that has to be addressed," Jon continued. "Several weekends ago, someone from the IMU traveled to Juarez. They visited the cement block single-room houses that the Mexican employees live in... saw the lack of running water... communal baths and toilets... open sewers... and the polluted Rio Bravo on the Mexican side. They took lots of pictures... came back and passed them around, displayed them in the plant, local bars, American Legion, churches. It's more than a labor negotiation... people in Hammelburg can't believe Wiemer Industries would allow employees to live like that. Now, it's a Hammelburg issue. We're not gonna pacify a lot of people in this community by telling them the higher-paid employees stay here while the hourly jobs go to Mexico."

Kramer could no longer contain his exasperation with the conversation. "Jon, I am aware of all of that, and I agree those issues need to be addressed, but if we don't move those jobs to Juarez, there aren't going to be jobs in either location... high-paid or low-paid. This company can't survive with Hammelburg hourly labor costs, even those offered in the last IMU proposal. We're talking about saving jobs by relocating. The alternative is losing all the jobs. Moreover, if the stock price keeps plummeting, the bankers will begin holding discussions with smart money managers who won't wait while we struggle with relocation decisions. They'll buy this company on the cheap, restructure the balance sheet, bail out the bankers, and close Hammelburg... Believe me, the money managers and the bankers don't give a damn about Hammelburg... the tradition of community progress. Paternalism plays no part in their management policy. Moreover, the current Wiemer shareholders, including people in this room, will also lose."

He paused before making his final point. "Our first obligation is our shareholders and ourselves."

Chapter 7

J.W. Rieff entered the Palmer House lobby 30 minutes before the scheduled time. Mary Pinnay arrived five minutes late. It was obvious that she had taken time to change clothes. She was dressed in an elegant burgundy dress with a white silk scarf wrapped loosely around her neck and trailing over one shoulder. Her short, dark hair was attractively fashioned. She carried a tan raincoat and small black purse. As she crossed the lobby to meet J.W., she attracted polite attention among staff and guests. The co-ed appearance at the Brinson dinner party was not in evidence. J.W. observed a very attractive, intelligent lady with elegant taste.

As they were being seated in the main dining room, Mary commented on her familiarity and fondness for the Palmer House dining room. It was one of her father's favorite restaurants. He frequently brought his family to the Palmer House for holiday dinners.

After making their menu selections, J.W. attempted to learn more about her career.

"I think I understand the meaning of genealogy, but what does that have to do with the Chicago Public Library?" he asked.

She laughed. "A good question. I was surprised that you failed to ask me at Brinson's dinner party."

"It wasn't tact, it was an attempt to disguise my ignorance,"

"To put it simply, I help people discover their roots," she said.

"Their roots?"

"Yes, I'm sure you're aware of the enormous ethnic diversity we have in Chicago. There are many neighborhoods where Polish, German, Yiddish, Czech, and other European languages still prevail. The migration from Eastern Europe began in the early part of the century. Many immigrant families maintained communication with their relatives in Europe until the beginning of the war. However, after the devastation of Europe and the Soviet occupation of Eastern Europe, many of the contacts were lost. There's a growing interest in family history in Chicago, particularly among second and third generation eastern European families. Fortunately, the Chicago Library is an excellent genealogical research center."

"That sounds like a job that requires some intense training, particularly languages and history."

She hesitated before reacting to J.W.'s comment. "My father was born in Prague and immigrated to Chicago in the early 1900s. When he arrived, Chicago had more citizens of Czech decent than the entire population of Prague. He insisted that his children learn to speak his native language. We didn't live in a traditional Czech neighborhood; therefore, our only opportunity to use the language was at home. But I became interested in language and European history, and studied those subjects in college."

"You have much in common with my brother, Phillip."

"What does he do?"

"He's completing his Ph.D. in modern European history at the University of Chicago. His thesis is a study of German immigration to the United States during the last century." He laughed. "You now have exhausted my knowledge of Phillip's thesis."

"That would interest me," she said.

"Phillip is very fluent in German. At least, fluent enough that the U.S. Army assigned him to an intelligence unit in London during the war, and he served in Berlin and Washington following the end of the war, before he was discharged."

Suddenly, she changed the direction of the conversation. "I understand that your family has lived in Hammelburg for several generations."

"I am sure with your knowledge of European languages and history you recognize Rieff and Wiemer as German names. My grandfather immigrated in the 1850s. He was the founder of Wiemer Industries."

"Yes, the Brinson's told me a great deal about your family and the success of your business. Elizabeth and Henry are very fond of you. They told me about the recent success of Wiemer Industries and progress in Hammelburg. Henry credits you with much of the success. Elizabeth also admires your mother"

J.W. was caught off guard by her response. Mary had obviously taken more than a modest interest in J.W.'s background, and was not shy about revealing her acquired knowledge.

The conversation during the remainder of the evening focused on J.W.'s plans for Wiemer Industries, and an extended discussion of his earlier meeting with Phillip and the suggestions regarding the distribution of his mother's estate. Mary expressed a strong approval of Phillip's ideas.

It was very late by the time J.W. arranged for a taxi to deliver Mary to her apartment in Evanston. They were nearly the last guests to vacate the dining room. Mary was cautious, but it was obvious that she had enjoyed the evening and his company. He suggested another dinner and she agreed.

Upon returning to Hammelburg, J.W. invited Elizabeth and Henry Brinson to join him for dinner at the Alamost Country Club. The invitation provided the opportunity to return their hospitality, but his real purpose was to learn more about Mary Pinnay. He was always a gracious host and both Brinsons enjoyed his company. He made a special effort to include Elizabeth in the conversation. As the evening progressed, he described how much he had enjoyed meeting Mary at Brinson's party and later in Chicago. Elizabeth recognized that despite his attempt to be nonchalant, he was strongly attracted to Mary and was attempting to become better acquainted with her.

"We were roommates and sorority sisters," she volunteered. "Mary grew up in Evanston. Her father is an architect. I've meet her mother on several occasions. She is a lovely lady. Mary had a brother, Milton, a few years older. I believe he was also an architect, or a scientist. He graduated from Washington University in St. Louis before he was drafted. He visited Mary occasionally at Stephens. Mary was very fond of him. He was killed at Normandy."

"I gather she retains her married name. What was her maiden name?" he asked.

"Mary Kosick," she replied. "She married Harold Pinnay during the war. They met in Washington D.C. Mary was working in Washington at some military agency. She had language skills. Mary has never discussed her work, but I believe it was military intelligence. Harold Pinnay was a Lieutenant, assigned to the OSS. When Mary met him, he was a junior aide to Wild Bill Donovan, who ran the OSS. They began dating, and it became a serious affair, at least for Mary. Up until that time, she had limited experience with men. Stephens being a women's college, the students saw men occasionally on weekends. Pinnay received an overseas assignment soon after Mary learned of Milton's death at Normandy. Mary was crushed. She was emotionally off balance. Pinnay proposed marriage before he left. Her parents had never met him. They were married in a civil ceremony a few weeks before he left. Neither family attended. It was the classic wartime marriage."

She paused for a moment and lowered her voice. "He was an asshole."

Henry Brinson laughed. "Elizabeth can never bring herself to express her true feelings."

I'm sorry. I'm not in the habit of using crude language, but there is no other way to describe Harold Pinnay," she said.

"Mary told me the whole sad story after she returned to Chicago. Harold Pinnay was the only child of a successful opthalmologist in New York City. His mother was a moderately successful artist. After graduating from a private school in New York City, he enrolled at Trinity College. He was a mediocre student. He shared his mother's love of art, but none of her creative skills; nevertheless he decided to study art and history. In the spring of 1942, he enlisted in the army. He was sent to OCS. For reasons that aren't very clear, he was then assigned to the OSS.

"An unusual assignment for a new officer," J.W. remarked.

"After they were married, Mary learned that he had requested a transfer to the London office of the OSS. When the war ended, he was stationed at Nuremburg to assist with the preparation of evidence against the defendants at the Nuremburg war trials. He was scheduled for discharge, but volunteered to remain in Germany for an additional year. Mary didn't know that he had volunteered. He told her they refused to discharge him, that his work was too important"

"What was his assignment?" J.W. asked.

"His primary job was locating the valuable artwork that the Nazis had stolen from Jewish families and synagogues in Germany, Poland, France, and Austria. He was able to arrange this assignment because of his knowledge of art history. When the Nazi leaders realized they were losing the war, they arranged for most of the stolen art treasures to be hidden in various locations in Germany. It was their intention to sell the art and buy their way out of Germany and prosecution. Harold Pinnay was appointed the officer in charge of a small group of American, British, and French military personnel assigned the responsibility of recovering the stolen property and transferring it to a central location in Nuremburg. It was to be used as evidence in the trials and then attempt to locate the original owners, many of whom perished in the death camps."

"Was Mary aware of his assignment?" J.W. asked.

"No, he never discussed it with her; even after he returned, he never mentioned it," Elizabeth replied. "In order to learn where the stolen art had been hidden required intensive interrogation of high-ranking Nazis. The prosecutors promised some leniency in exchange for the information. Once the art had been found, a careful inventory was taken and recorded by art experts. It was moved, under heavy security, to a central location in Nuremburg. When the collection arrived in Nuremburg, several of the most valuable pieces listed on the inventory manifest were missing. There was a full investigation."

Elizabeth paused for a moment before continuing. "Harold Pinnay and two of his French colleagues swore that the manifest was incorrect and nothing was missing. Several others disagreed. There was no resolution, but Harold was under suspicion. He was transferred back to the United States and given an honorable discharge. But the event was recorded in his military record. He tried to obtain a civilian job in military intelligence, but was turned down."

"Why did he attempt to obtain a job in military intelligence with that record hanging over his head?" J.W. asked.

"They suspected that he wanted to stay in intelligence to maintain communication with his accomplices. There was also a suspicion that Harold had received a large amount of money before returning to the U.S.; there were transfers of money from a bank in New York to a Swiss bank in Geneva. The transfer was initiated by an Argentine company. But given Swiss bank secrecy laws, none of it could be traced."

"Was Mary aware of the money?"

"No, nor was anyone else in his family, but that's not the end of the story. His father realized something was amiss. Harold was drinking heavily and carousing. He hoped that his son was merely suffering from the transition from military to civilian life. He called a good friend of his, a senior executive with a large chemical company in Houston, and arranged for Harold to be hired, and Mary landed a job in the library at Rice University. Harold convinced his new boss that he should help develop new markets in Latin America."

She paused. "His real reason for seeking the assignment was to maintain contact with several Nazis living in Argentina, Paraguay, and Bolivia who wanted to buy the art that Harold had stolen and transported to Switzerland. The Nazis created a phony business to buy the art from a blind company that Harold and his French accomplices had established in Switzerland. After the Nazis purchased the art from Harold, they sold it to a legitimate Swiss art dealer at a much higher price. All the transactions were subject to Swiss banking laws."

"Why didn't he sell the art to the Swiss dealer himself? He would have made more money." J.W. responded.

"Selling to the Nazis rather than directly to the art dealers was safer, it couldn't be traced to him. He knew the Nazis didn't want to reveal their whereabouts; therefore, their dummy corporation kept no records, except a secret Swiss bank account."

"How was all of this discovered?"

"From the beginning, Army Intelligence was suspicious that Harold was involved with the missing art. When he applied for a U.S. passport, the State Department notified Army Intelligence. They arranged to have him monitored on all of his trips to South America; probably by personnel in the American embassies."

"Why wasn't he arrested when he contacted the Germans in South America?"

"The Latin American authorities knew about the Nazis; they were protecting them. On his return to the U.S. from his last trip, Army Intelligence was waiting to grab him. However, before he arrived, they learned that he was also serving as a courier for the Nazis, and he was he was going to meet someone in the United States who would assist him in illegal currency transactions. That was who he met in California. The woman who was injured in his car accident was not a casual pickup. She was involved in international money laundering. Army Intelligence thought that if they waited, they could nab both of them."

J.W. was puzzled. "Was he really killed in an auto accident, or was that just a cover story?"

"Army Intelligence told Mary he was much more valuable alive, but he was drunk when the accident occurred."

"What happened to the money in the Swiss bank?"

"It's now part of the funds that the State of Israel and the Swiss banks are quarreling about."

"Was Mary ever under suspicion as an accomplice?" J.W. asked.

"No, thanks to her experience in Washington, and to Dr. Pinnay."

"His father in law?"

"Yes, after Harold returned to the United States and moved to Houston, Army Intelligence decided to have a talk with Dr. Pinnay. They shared their suspicions with him; very unusual, but they did. He didn't respond as

67

they might have expected. He told them that Harold had engaged in some unsavory activities while in college and that he might have been involved in the art theft. He also told them that although he had met Mary on only a few occasions, he was convinced that she was not involved."

J.W. spoke softly "Well, I've observed from my own family experience that one of the great cruelties in life is to have been associated with something in which you didn't participate, yet, never be able to rid yourself or others of the memory."

Elizabeth and Henry failed to comprehend the meaning of his remark but didn't comment.

"It must have been very hard for Mary, but why does she keep the Pinnay name?" J.W. inquired.

"After the accident, his family was very kind to Mary, particularly his father. He was also candid with Mary. He told her that had he known about their plan to marry, he would have advised her against it. He provided Mary with financial assistance for an extended period of time, but requested that she not give up her married name. He is very fond of her. I guess he wanted her to remain in the family. Mary got out of Houston as fast as she could. She loved her job at Rice, but didn't want to live with Harold's reputation. He had acquired a bad one in Houston. She returned to Chicago and took the job at the Chicago Public Library. I think Mr. Pinnay may have even assisted in arranging that job. It's only recently that Mary seems to have recovered from a tragic marriage and the death of her brother. With the exception of her immediate family and occasional visits with us, you may be her first attempt to re-establish a social life."

During the following three months, J.W. spent nearly every weekend in Chicago with Mary. They attended theatre, concerts, museums, art exhibitions, and sampled scores of good ethnic restaurants. J.W. insisted that Mary select the restaurants, so that he could become better acquainted with the diverse Chicago menus. Their conversations centered on Wiemer Industries, Hammelburg, and the interesting insights that Mary was acquiring regarding Chicago's ethnicity. Other than the initial mention of her husband's death, there was never a discussion of Harold Pinnay or his family.

By the end of three months, they had fallen in love. On one of their weekend meetings, J.W. suggested that Phillip Wiemer join them for dinner. J.W. assured her that she and Phillip would have much to talk about, given their common interest in European history.

Despite some anxiety on J.W.'s part, the dinner was an enormous success. Phillip arrived in an appropriate dark suit and tie and, at J.W.'s insistence, agreed to select the wines. Mary was obviously pleased with Phillip and the wine. There were lively discussions of Phillip's Ph.D. dissertation, which was in the final stage of approval; Mary's research at the Chicago library; and problems in Western Europe, but neither of them referred to their experiences in Washington. Phillip entertained them with several humorous stories about events at university faculty meetings.

As the evening ended and they were departing the restaurant, Phillip totally surprised J.W. by suggesting that Mary visit Hammelburg and meet their mother.

"She's an exceptional lady," he said. "You'll enjoy talking with her and I know she'll enjoy meeting you."

After Phillip departed and J.W had secured a cab, Mary recounted Phillip's suggestion.

"I've heard so much about your mother from you, Elizabeth Brinson, and now Phillip. I really would enjoy meeting her."

J.W. was delighted. Upon his return to Hammelburg, he called Elizabeth Brinson to tell her about the invitation and ask if she would be willing to invite Mary to stay at the Brinsons' during her visit to Hammelburg. It was arranged.

Anne Rieff was as excited as J.W. Phillip had already informed his mother that he had made the suggestion and added, "You are way past due as a mother-in-law, grandmother, and spiritual advisor to another good woman."

The weekend was an enormous success. J.W. had prepared his mother by telling her much about Mary's past and current activity. He suggested that she call Elizabeth Brinson to obtain suggestions regarding entertainment. It was decided that Mary, J.W., and the Brinsons would have a catered dinner at Anne Rieff's home. J.W. escorted Mary from the Brinsons' to his mother's home one hour before the Brinsons arrived.

At the close of the evening, Anne Rieff asked Mary to join her for Sunday brunch at her home, but excluded J.W. When J.W. arrived to collect Mary late Sunday afternoon, both women appeared radiant.

In the summer of 1951, J.W. Rieff and Mary Kosick Pinnay were married in a small church wedding in Evanston. Both families were in attendance. Phillip Rieff served as best man, and Elizabeth Brinson was matron of honor.

In October of 1952, Mary Rieff gave birth to a son, Alfred William Rieff.

Two months later, the Wiemer/Rieff Foundation was established. The Foundation was a source of both family and community controversy from the outset. Other family members objected to the fact that a significant share of the ownership of Wiemer Industries, Alamost National Bank, and a large amount of real estate in Alamost County now rested in the hands of a charitable foundation. Many of Hammelburg's leading citizens were suspicious of what Anne Rieff might elect to do with the Foundation's substantial resources.

Two years following its formation, she confirmed her critics' expectations by establishing and financing a preschool program for underprivileged children. In 1954, Hammelburg had ten public primary schools, four middle schools, and two public high schools: Hammelburg Central and Hammelburg West. There were also two small parochial high schools: Concordia Lutheran School and St. Ignatius Catholic High School. Although the public schools were integrated, less prosperous white students and nearly all black students attended Hammelburg Central High School.

During the war and the immediate postwar period, black families migrated to Hammelburg to take advantage of job opportunities at Wiemer Industries' foundry and forge shop. As the company grew, so did the black population. It was apparent that the quality of education among the public schools was uneven. Hammelburg West High School was considered the college preparatory school, whereas, Hammelburg Central offered only vocational studies.

Anne Rieff was told by members of the Hammelburg School Board that the difference reflected the lack of basic educational skills among the less privileged black and white students. According to an extensive study and evaluation, financed by the Foundation and conducted by Ball State University, many of the less privileged black and white students were unable to master college preparatory courses by the time they reached high school. The primary cause was traced back to a slower pace of learning from the beginning of their educational experience, associated with a lack of preschool training. Many of the children of more prosperous families attended private preschool programs and had achieved modest reading and mathematics skills before entering public school.

The Wiemer/Rieff Foundation underwrote the establishment of the Hammelburg Preschool Preparation Program. Seven churches on the east side of Hammelburg were provided funds to hire staff and purchase equipment and supplies required to conduct pre-schooling for underprivileged children. In addition to teaching fundamental skills, the children were also introduced to art and music. Unlike public schools, the preschool program did not have an extended summer vacation, and students could attend for a maximum of two years. The cost to the families who participated was $10 a year, regardless of the number of children. It was enormously popular in East Hammelburg. However, it was viewed with suspicion by many of the community leaders. It was another of Anne Rieff's "do-gooder" ideas. One of the arch conservative leaders in the community cautioned that this was the first step toward a "Socialist society."

Chapter 8

For several years, Cutler Earl and Levin had reserved Thursday for a simple buffet lunch for all the partners of the firm. It was held in the main conference room, which contained a large rectangular table and buffet. Had all the partners elected to attend, there would have been insufficient seating, but that never occurred. It was an informal gathering, providing opportunities for camaraderie and occasional enlightenment. There was only one rule: alcoholic beverages and cell phones were forbidden.

Will Heider was delayed. When he arrived, most of the partners had been through the buffet line. After acquiring a chicken salad sandwich, a small bag of potato chips, and a soft drink, he found a vacant seat next to Sam Thomas, a senior partner. Thomas was one of the firm's most experienced litigators and a recognized expert on labor law. For many years, he had served as an adjunct professor of labor law at the Northwestern University Law School. He had recently announced his intention to retire from the firm the following year.

One of the younger partners, Kevin O'Neal, was seated directly across from Thomas. They were discussing a recent decision by a client to close an automotive components plant in Anderson, Indiana and move the operation to Mexico.

As Will occupied the seat beside Sam Thomas, O'Neal was pursuing his favorite argument. "I don't understand why the union and community leaders object. U.S industry must outsource manufacturing jobs if we want to remain competitive in world markets. The companies have to reduce labor costs to compete. A worldwide market actually results in a fundamental rebalancing of the world economy. The developing countries are gaining the manufacturing jobs and the U.S. benefits from a shift to higher value added technology and service employment. It's a win-win situation."

Thomas reached in his pocket, withdrew a small pocket knife, and used the scissors to open his bag of potato chips. He carefully emptied the bag on his plate, folded the bag, placed in on the table, and replaced the knife in his pocket before responding. "That's the classic argument, Kevin. It's tough to refute. Even the liberals buy it."

O'Neal laughed. "You sound like a skeptic, Sam."

"A little more each day" he responded.

"That surprises me. I would have thought you would endorse open markets and free trade."

"Oh, I believe in open markets and free trade, Kevin, but I am less and less convinced that's what we're accomplishing."

"O.K., what do you think is being accomplished?"

"How many times have you traveled to Anderson, Kevin?"

"A lot, I can't count how many times I've flown to Indy and driven to Anderson."

"Have you ever taken time to drive around the city and look at the residential areas, schools, churches, commercial buildings?"

"Well, I haven't made a special trip, but I have seen a fair amount of Anderson during the past seven years."

"Seen any changes?"

"Hell, I know where you're taking this, Sam... Anderson and other industrial cities in the Midwest are deteriorating. They're losing manufacturing jobs. It shows up in the physical condition of the communities. Abandoned plants, empty retail space, deteriorating infrastructure. But that's an inevitable part of the transition from a manufacturing base to a technology and services base. In ten years, Anderson may be a showplace of electronic technology."

"Maybe," Sam responded. "Have you traveled to Mexico?"

"Yeah, I've also heard this argument before. Working conditions and the environment are atrocious. The U.S. companies are taking advantage of the poor. But nobody talks about what it was like before the relocations occurred and Mexican labor had a chance to acquire those jobs."

"Well. I know what it was like. I've traveled to Mexico for the past 20 years. It's as bad or worse than it's ever been. The air quality in Mexico City is deadly. The street crime is beyond description. The government is riddled with corrupt plutocrats. The border towns, where the *maquiladoras* are located, overflow with people attempting to find jobs that pay three to five dollars a day; twenty-five to thirty dollars a week for a five-and-a-half-day week, in order live in shacks surrounded by raw sewage."

"But in time, that will change. The market economy will bring about a balance." Kevin persisted.

Sam shook his head. "I've heard it that argument over and over. I want to believe it. I have spent most of my adult life writing and interpreting labor contracts. I've wrestled with labor leaders and their lawyers. I've watched the Midwest towns prosper and expand and I've watched them decline. I've seen people go from good jobs in well-maintained factories to bad jobs in chain restaurants. I've also been told by my conservative and liberal friends—most of whom have never set foot in a manufacturing plant—that it's only a transition from manufacturing to technology, and everybody will be prosperous again. I hope so, but I don't see it happening."

He paused. "I've come to realize that any profitable market strategy, regardless of how much it is driven by greed, is always defended as being good for the world economy and society by those who stand to gain the most. People tend to confuse ethics and morality. Ethics has to do with measuring the public good; morality focuses on ideology, and devotion to an ideology often requires a willingness to abandon any doubt."

Kevin, having finished his lunch, prepared to leave the table. As he departed, he forced a smile and said, "I believe you're wrong, Sam."

"No one could hope for that more fervently than I do, Kevin."

Will sat quietly for a few moments before resuming the conversation. "I gather you aren't a free trade advocate, Sam?"

Thomas looked directly at Will " I support free trade and market based economics, if they achieve the intended objectives. According to the current advocates, Anderson loses manufacturing jobs to Mexico or China or some other country with substantially lower labor costs. Over time, Anderson workers are reemployed in better jobs in new industries and the workers in developing countries receive the old jobs and a better standard of living. Everyone wins."

"That's the rationale for supporting NAFTA," Will responded.

"Yeah, I agree, and I supported I NAFTA when it was introduced. But I don't see the expected results emerging. In the past few years, unemployment in Midwest communities, like Anderson, has risen substantially. Nearly all of it represents the loss of manufacturing jobs. But I don't see any evidence of the emergence of high-tech industries absorbing these workers. And I don't see any improvement in the lives of Mexican workers."

"In other words, you don't see any net value?"

"No, a substantial amount of value can and has resulted from free trade. As a lifelong conservative, I believe that free trade and free markets have been the primary sources of our economic growth, but the current version of free trade troubles me; none of the value appears to be accruing to the workers in Anderson or Mexico. I would bet that the average income in Anderson has probably shrunk in the last five years. God knows, the living standard of factory workers in Mexican border towns is dismal. Now, someone is profiting when you reduce labor costs from twelve dollars an hour with health and retirement benefits to five dollars a day with few benefits. But if the quality of life in Anderson is deteriorating and the quality of life in Mexico isn't improving, that sure as hell can't be labeled progress."

"Isn't it a matter of time? It's not going to happen overnight," Will asked.

75

Sam rose from his chair, collected his paper plate, cup, and empty potato chip bag, and looked down at the table before responding. "Will, I'm an old man... probably too impatient and skeptical... I still believe in the concept, but I'd like to see more evidence of success... I've also come to recognize that the best of us occasionally invest in illusions, and these illusions can blind us to our own inconsistencies."

Will spent the remainder of the afternoon reviewing an outsourcing amendment to a client's labor contract. Shortly before five o'clock, he came out of his office and stopped at Shirley Kovac's desk. "I'm going to take a long weekend. I haven't seen my folks in a long time. I'm going down to Hammelburg to visit them. I'll need a plane ticket to Indy and a rental car. I want to leave tomorrow and return very early Wednesday morning. Will my schedule allow that?" he asked.

She smiled. "There is nothing that can't be rescheduled, but I think you might be very lonely here next Thursday and Friday unless you prefer to celebrate Thanksgiving by yourself."

He laughed. "I gotta start paying attention to the calendar. In that case, I'll spend the entire week in Hammelburg and my folks will be so tired of me I won't need to return for a long time. Schedule me back on the Saturday after Thanksgiving and I'll avoid the Sunday travel jam."

"I'll call the travel agency before I leave and they can deliver the tickets in the morning," she responded. He was about to return to his office when she spoke again. "Any chance you might say hello to Jimmie?"

"Shirley Kovac, you are shameless," he chuckled.

Before departing the office he called his parents' home in Hammelburg. He was sure they had nothing planned that would prevent him from visiting, but he wanted to alert them about his plans for an extended Thanksgiving holiday.

His mother answered the phone and was delighted to learn he would join them for the holiday. Neither his brother nor sister were coming home.

He mentioned that he had received an unusual phone call that he wanted to discuss with his dad during his visit. His mother inquired if the call was from Jimmie Hudson. He was surprised by her question, but confirmed that it was Jimmie, .

On Friday morning he called Jimmie. He was not at the IMU office. Will left a message for him suggesting that they have a beer on Saturday afternoon. He asked that Jimmie call his parents' home and leave a phone number, Will would call him again on Saturday morning.

Will caught a Friday afternoon flight from Chicago Midway to Indianapolis at 1:30. Because of the time difference between the two cities, the plane landed at 3:35 in Indianapolis.

It was a cold, cloudy day with a strong wind. The drive form Indianapolis to Hammelburg was 75 miles. The first 15 miles consisted of the I-465 outer belt with its myriad of shopping centers, office buildings, and light industrial complexes. Will left the outer belt at the I-69 connection to travel north. The initial ten miles of I-69 was comprised of several off ramps for expanding residential communities in northern Marion County; the remainder of the trip was flat agricultural terrain with occasional exits for small cities, preceded by advertisements for service plazas, fast food restaurants, and motels. The interstate highway traffic was comprised largely of heavy-duty trucks with cargo for Fort Wayne, Lansing, Detroit, and other Midwest locations, and newly-harvested grain being delivered to regional storage and rail sidings.

The harvest season was in its final stage. The air was crisp with the scent of the late fall harvest; mechanized equipment, resembling huge insects, devoured the few remaining corn and soybean plants. Trailing the harvesters were flocks of migrating birds feeding on spilled grain, swirling in amazing, intricate, synchronized patterns as they flew from field to field; patterns so perfectly coordinated they appeared choreographed. The harvested fields were flat with only a few inches of stubble remaining about the surface. Remnants of dried cornstalks whipped across the barren terrain and occasionally lodged in the highway median. The small wooded areas that remained on Indiana's once totally forested landscape appeared in random patterns among the flat harvested fields. They bore the last trace of autumn colors—deep brown and burnt red. The orange, crimson, and yellow colors had achieved their peak in late October. The dull colors and gray sky announced the onset of the winter season.

The fields and equipment were occupied by full-time farmers with big farms and part-time farmers with fewer acres who worked second shifts in factories and farmed during the daylight hours and weekends. Local manufacturing companies wanted to hire farmers. They understood machinery, weren't afraid of it, and had a natural ability to produce and repair it. Farmers drove pickup trucks because they needed a truck; nothing exotic or macho about their trucks. They were used to haul feed, equipment, and other farm supplies; American flags and NRA stickers displayed on the rear window or bumper. Farming was a family effort. Kids learned how to drive tractors and harvest equipment before they had driver's licenses. Wives drove corn pickers or larger trucks loaded with grain or soybeans to the local elevator__ a narrow, confining life; animals to feed, breed and care for; spring and fall plowing; spring and fall planting; and spraying and fertilizing.

Farm families went to church, high school athletic events, and an occasional movie. Most of the kids graduated from high school, left the farm, and never came back. The work was too hard, life too narrow, income too uncertain. As a result, farming became more mechanized; capital requirements increased. Farms became much larger and fewer people occupied farm homes. Hourly jobs in local manufacturing plants became the primary source of income for increasing numbers of rural men and women. They left the farms and moved to the local towns and cities, where they occupied cramped quarters in mobile home parks, monotonous, look-alike dwellings. The transition from living in an isolated farm house to a congested mobile home park was difficult. Family stress and domestic violence increased. Old, once prosperous farm homes were abandoned or rented by poor families who did not farm.

Despite the heavily mechanized farming activity, Mennonites and Amish families continued to maintain small family farms throughout northeastern Indiana, working without modern equipment. For generations, they had earned their living as farmers and skilled carpenters. Their farm houses and buildings, nearly always painted white, were neat and well-maintained. Many, primarily the old Amish, refused to use any power equipment, and continued to plow and harvest with horse-drawn equipment. Some drove cars and trucks, but many maintained horse-drawn buggies for family transportation, creating occasional traffic jams and accidents on secondary country roads; reflective orange triangular signs were attached to the back of their buggies when driving after sunset. The bearded men wore simple shirts and pants with large dark suspenders and round-brimmed hats; dark felt hats in winter, straw hats in summer. The women wore simple ankle-length cotton and flannel dresses, sometimes with decorative aprons, and white or dark bonnets, depending on the season and the occasion. The children, dressed much like their parents, were quiet and well-behaved in public. As a boy, Will was often attracted to the blue-eyed, blond-haired girls with long pigtails who occasionally entered his father's store with their Amish or Mennonite parents. His attention was never acknowledged. During recent visits to Hammelburg, he had observed young Amish and Mennonite women with their long dresses and bonnets emerging from manufacturing plants during shift changes. Many Amish farms were now too small to support the families.

His father related stories about attacks on Amish men by servicemen home on leave during WW II. The Amish were pacifists and conscientious objectors. It became a sport to search country roads for young Amish men. It was always a one-sided fight; the Amish men refused to fight.

At end of the harvest season, rich with cash from the sale of their produce, the farmers arrived at Bernie's to buy winter work clothes. Will remembered , weather-worn, hard men, with scarred hands and rural savvy. They were usually in a good mood, another year of hard work complete. Their conversations focused on harvest results, agricultural prices, and their expectations and plans for the next growing season. It was the time when they spent freely, with the exception of the occasional years when inadequate rain or cold weather delayed the planting season and reduced grain production. The farmers liked Bernie's. Paul Heider understood their problems and anticipated their needs. He frequently lectured Will and his brother that farming was the toughest business in the world. There were so many variables that farmers couldn't control: weather, agricultural prices, material costs, crop disease, insects, and worst of all, personal injury. Every year, there were reports of men and boys killed or badly injured attempting to repair farm equipment, or crushed in a rollover.

One evening, while in junior high, Will attempted to entertain the family with the latest "dumb farmer" joke. His father scolded him severely. It was uncharacteristic of Paul Heider, who usually disciplined his sons with a mild reproach. Recalling his father's admonishment, Will had recently taken a young associate aside and gently told him that he found little humor in his frequent "redneck" jokes.

At the start of the exit ramp at the first Hammelburg interstate turnoff, three signs appeared. The first, an older sign, proclaimed that Hammelburg was the "Center of Civic Progress in Northeastern Indiana: All-American City 1988." The second celebrated the fact that in 1996, the North Hammelburg High School football team won the Indiana Class A State Championship. The third recognized the West Hammelburg High School Lady Tigers as Indiana's Class A volleyball champions in 1999.

The four lane highway from the interstate exit to Hammelburg was a three-mile commercial zone comprised of a large factory outlet center featuring several national brand name stores; a Wal-Mart Superstore; a large movie theatre complex; several recently-constructed hotels, including a Marriott, Holiday Inn Express, and Ramada Inn; two older, single-story independent motels where guests parked their cars directly in front of their respective rooms; many familiar fast food franchises; several large gas stations and convenience stores that advertised low prices for fuel and cigarettes; two large mobile home parks and a low-cost apartment complex. It was the familiar unplanned commercial and semi-residential sprawl that occupied the entrance of most small cities in the Midwest.

Within a quarter mile of the city limits, property on both sides of the highway had been acquired by the Hammelburg Planning and Zoning Board and landscaped to provide a brief but pleasant entrance to the city.

Until Will entered high school, with the exception of the older motels, nearly all of this property was corn and soybean fields. The primary shopping, dining, and overnight accommodations were located in the center of the city, surrounding the Alamost County courthouse.

It had been several months since Will had visited his parents. On these infrequent occasions, he avoided the commercial and industrial sections of Hammelburg by following the most direct route to his parents' home, located on the west side of the city. Despite the diminished daylight, he decided to take a quick look at Hammelburg's downtown section before continuing to his parents' home.

He drove north on Wayne Avenue for two miles toward the historic commercial center of Hammelburg. During his childhood, this section of Hammelburg had been an attractive middle class residential neighborhood. It had changed. He passed several small retail shopping centers; strip malls featuring branch banks that advertised ATMs and drive-up teller services;

loan companies that made short-term loans against future paychecks at near-usurious interest rates; pawn shops; drug stores advertising liquor sales; beverage stores advertising special sales on brand-name beer; jewelry stores offering instant credit; two windowless adult bookstores; and several national brand shoe stores with their perpetual seasonal sale signs. The spaces between the strip malls were occupied by used car lots with large garish signs advertising one-stop car sales and zero-interest financing. There were few remnants of the old residential neighborhoods. Nearly all the remaining houses had been converted to offices for insurance agents, real estate brokers, and personal liability and injury lawyers. .

Upon arriving at the center of Hammelburg, the gracious Alamost County courthouse, came into view, occupying the middle of the historic roundabout traffic pattern. Erected in 1895, its dark limestone façade was overdue for cleaning and repair, but new lights had been installed to illuminate the copper dome and statue atop the dome. The municipal offices were located directly across from the courthouse on the north side of the city center. It was a was an unremarkable modern building, well landscaped, with distinctive signage. These two public buildings stood in stark contrast to the balance of the once attractive and admired center of Hammelburg.

The downtown section of Hammelburg was approximately seven blocks in length and four blocks wide. In that space, Will counted 20 vacant stores. Kimberly's Fashion Store, a four-story building which had been the leading department store in Hammelburg for several generations, was abandoned, with the exception of the first floor, which was occupied by a shabby-looking antique store and a used clothing boutique. Gang graffiti appeared on nearly all the abandoned buildings and even a few that were still occupied.

He recalled that three of the vacant buildings had housed a drug store, shoe store, and sporting goods retailer. An empty lot was all that remained of McPherson's Restaurant, a victim of a winter fire nearly a decade ago. Graffiti covered the facing walls of the adjoining buildings. At six-thirty on a Friday evening there was little traffic, the few retail shops remaining were closed, and the only activity appeared to be taking place at three small bars, one of which advertised "live dancing." Several motorcycles were parked vertically in front of each bar. He encountered two police cruisers within three blocks of each other, moving slowly, observing what little activity existed on the streets; several young men dressed in hip-hop and gang attire; a few shabbily-dressed men and women who represented the recent outcropping of homeless people in Hammelburg.

He noted, however, that the Old Bavarian Garden Restaurant seemed to be active and appeared somewhat larger than he had remembered it.

During his youth, Friday and Saturday nights in downtown Hammelburg were busy with families having dinner in the local restaurants; the movie theaters had early and late shows, and parking places were difficult to find. The sidewalks were crowded. After the high school football or basketball games, the downtown came to life a second time. But the familiar teenage hangouts no longer existed: Louie's Soda Shop, Parson's Drive-In Restaurant, the Varsity Grill, the abandoned Rialto, Embassy, and Indiana theatres all displayed empty, dilapidated marquees.

Located on the edge of the downtown section, Bernie's original location was unlighted and empty. A faded For Sale sign, posted by a local real estate broker, appeared in the front window.

Both surprised and disappointed with the condition of the city center, he resumed his journey to his parents' home. Approximately one mile west of the downtown area, he passed a familiar, well-lighted complex of modern buildings—the Hammelburg Regional Health Center. The facility was comprised of a complex of buildings, including the original, but vastly expanded, Alamost County Hospital, modern outpatient clinic, children's medical facility, cancer and cardiac center, hospice, and two large buildings that housed branches of the Indiana University Medical and Nursing School. It was designed as a campus with modern buildings and a large parking garage; an impressive facility for a city of 75,000 inhabitants. He was familiar with the facility as his mother had played a prominent role in helping establish a free health clinic for indigent and migrant families. Friends in Medicine was a unique facility, much admired by other communities, but rarely emulated.

Fifteen minutes later, he arrived at his parents' residence, a two-story colonial style brick home located in an older but moderately prosperous section of Hammelburg. Originally a heavily wooded rural area outside of the city limits, it became a residential area in the 1950s, and was now well within the municipal boundaries. Paul and Ruth Heider built the home in 1958. They had selected that neighborhood because of the short walking distance to a complex of public schools, including a primary, middle school, and Hammelburg West High School. So near to the schools that they could hear the Hammelburg West High School Marching Band playing at halftime during the football season.

The first floor contained conventional living, dining, and kitchen space, and a half bath. Four bedrooms and two baths were located on the second floor. Several years after construction, they had carpeted and painted the basement to encourage their three children to entertain their friends at home. Neither Will nor his brother had used the remodeled basement for its intended purpose. Their sister, Marilyn, had used it to host several slumber parties with her high school friends.

Ruth Heider had prepared a light supper. Friday evenings, an important period among traditional Jewish families, had never been recognized in the Heider family. It had been agreed early in their marriage that religion would play a minor role in their lives. As a family, they recognized Christmas and Easter, but did not participate in the religious celebrations. Ruth informally recognized Jewish holidays before Tom, the first child, was born. After that, there was little recognition. The only exception was the seasonal display of small Hanukkah candles on the mantle. However, all three of the children were fully aware of their Jewish heritage.

The dinner was informal, only Will and his parents. They discussed family matters: the four grandchildren;, Tom's job with the clothing manufacturer and his new home in North Carolina; Marilyn's career as a primary school teacher, wife, and mother in Toledo; and Paul's disappointment with the real estate broker's failure to find a buyer for the vacant building that Bernie's had occupied for more than 50 years. There was no mention of Jimmie Hudson.

As was the family custom, coffee was served in the living room. Shortly, after completing her kitchen duties and returning to the living room, Ruth Heider asked Will about his conversation with Jimmie Hudson.

He quickly summarized the conversation.

His mother asked, "Is that the reason you're here this weekend?"

"It's not the only reason, or the primary reason. It's been awhile since I've visited you and Dad." His response sounded defensive.

"I'm sorry," she said. "My question was not intended to be sarcastic."

She studied Will for a moment before continuing. "The reason I asked is because Jimmie Hudson called this afternoon. He said he received a message that you'd like to meet him this weekend He left a phone number and suggested that you call tomorrow morning to arrange a place and time," she said.

Will nodded his acknowledgement.

"It's the first time I have ever spoken with Jimmie Hudson," she continued. "Your Dad has, but I never have. I remember stories about his behavior as a teenager and being expelled from school. But he sounded like a rather intelligent, decent man."

"Don't know, Mom. I haven't seen Jimmie since high school. I gathered from our phone conversation that he has changed. But I was never sure there was that much wrong with Jimmie. His appearance didn't please the faculty at West, but I am not sure he ever did anything wrong except bang Doc Wright against the lockers a couple of times. Had a vote been taken by the male student body, nobody would have considered slamming Doc against the lockers a wrongful act, only a long overdue, deserving act."

Paul Heider laughed. "Jimmie was a tough kid from a troubled family, but he got himself straightened out. I'm the one who owes you an apology. I volunteered you. I probably should have told Jimmie not to call you. I did tell him you don't represent labor unions."

"You were polite. You didn't refer to me as a scab lawyer," Will laughed.

"I wish your father wouldn't use that vulgar term."

"Oh hell, Ruth, it's a joke, Will knows that. But he's right; I didn't say that to Jimmie. In retrospect, maybe I should have. It might have convinced him not to call you."

"Just as a matter of interest, why did you encourage him to call me?" Will asked.

"I don't think I encouraged him. I told him you didn't represent unions. He said he understood that, but still wanted to talk to you. I gave him your number. I guess I was wrong. But let me say a couple of things before you chew me out. This town and the Wiemer workers have gone through some pretty tough times. We lost hundreds of jobs to Mexico because the Wiemer management saw an opportunity to avoid spending money to meet new air pollution and OSHA standards and hire cheap labor. I've spent most of my life selling clothes and safety gear to hot metal workers in foundry and forge shops. It's tough, dangerous work. I've seen a lot of bad burns. They were well paid, but believe me, they deserved to be."

He looked at Will to measure his reaction before continuing. "I never thought I would hear Wiemer management tell a lie, but when they said they couldn't afford to meet the new air pollution standards, everyone in this town knew it wasn't true."

"How do you know that, Dad?"

"Will, a lot of wives, sisters, and girlfriends work in the Wiemer offices, and they type memos, send faxes, and overhear conversations. Wiemer moved the foundry and forge operations to Mexico to take advantage of cheap labor and avoid new EPA and OSHA regulations. They walked away from men who had worked for years in those shops. That would have never happened when J.W. Rieff was the CEO."

"Dad, they couldn't have walked away. There had to be some form of compensation. There must have been a negotiation with the IMU."

Paul Heider leaned forward abruptly in his chair, nearly toppling the coffee cup and saucer on the adjoining table.

"Sure there was a negotiation. Byron Hinkle negotiated for the union. Byron is probably a hell of a good divorce and estate lawyer, but he's out of his league attempting to negotiate a labor agreement with the Wiemer lawyers. They cut a deal that provided an early retirement benefit for the workers with more than 20 years of service. The guys with ten to twenty years got seven months pay and medical benefits; those with less than ten years got four months pay and medical. The retirement benefit paid to those with over 20 years is 75 percent of what they would have received at retirement, with significantly reduced medical benefits. So the older workers came away with something, but those with less than 20 years were left high and dry after the termination benefits ran out; no salary and no medical. If they'd worked at Wiemer for more than ten years, their retirement benefits were vested. So, they can retire at age 65 with a very small pension. Not much help for a 30-year-old with two kids."

"Dad, I don't know anything about Hinkle, but I've got to believe the IMU got something more than that."

"Well, the union voted against the first offer. Some of the younger IMU members criticized the bargaining committee and insisted on a clause that no more jobs could be moved out of Hammelburg without a much more generous settlement. The management refused. They finally settled on a clause which prevents Wiemer from moving any more jobs unless they can demonstrate that the company can't survive financially without relocation. That's the rub. That's what their fighting about now. The management claims that if they can't move machining and assembly to Mexico, the company will fail. The IMU calls that bullshit. Someone rewrote the clause in the final agreement. Apparently, it's wobbly, and Hinkle's wobbling."

"What happened to the forge and foundry workers; any new jobs or training?" Will asked.

"You gotta understand, Will. Very few of the workers had 20 years' service. It's damn tough to work in a foundry or forge shop for 20 years. The human body wasn't designed for it. Probably no more than 20 percent of the workers qualified for the pension. I don't know what your going to train hot metal workers to do that will get him another job. There are few, if any, manufacturing jobs available in Hammelburg, even in Indiana. They aren't going to become computer programmers. If they had those skills, they would've never ended up working in a foundry."

"What about other, smaller operations that hire experienced foundry and forge workers?"

"Wiemer workers aren't the only ones who lost jobs. There were three independent foundry mold and pattern shops in Hammelburg that supplied Wiemer. Collectively, they probably had more than 300 employees. We have one left. They have about 25 on their payroll. They're scrambling to stay alive. These are skilled workers who probably made 15 to 20 dollars an hour. Small businesses, no unions, no retirement fund. The layoffs started two months after Wiemer moved to Mexico. Lots of other businesses also felt the loss. Not many new jobs in Hammelburg, unless you're good with computers or wanta sell fast food."

"Is that why you closed the store?" Will asked.

"It was kind of the final blow. After Wal-Mart came to town, things began to get progressively worse."

"Your Dad couldn't handle the store without Tom," his mother added.

"Tom did the right thing," Paul responded. "He saw it coming. He knew with the loss of factory jobs, the decline in farming, and the big superstores coming in, there wasn't much future in Bernie's. We watched Kimberly's and several other businesses close. It was a matter of time."

"I know it's tough for both of you to watch what's happening in Hammelburg," Will interjected, "and I know how much confidence you had in the Wiemer management when J.W. Rieff was the leader, but its not just Hammelburg. It's a worldwide economic phenomenon. If J.W. was alive and the CEO of Wiemer, I am not sure that he could do anything differently than the current management. The competitive environment for manufacturing companies is intense. They have to find methods to reduce cost, and labor is probably their single largest cost. When they can cut labor cost by half by moving to Mexico, China, or Thailand, they have to do it, regardless of how much they dislike it. It's a matter of business survival," Will argued.

The room grew quiet. His mother began collecting the empty coffee cups before she spoke. "Will, I am not as well-educated as any of my children, but I was taught that there are certain fundamental issues of fairness and respect for the rights of others. The Rieffs demonstrated respect for those issues in the way they conducted their lives in this community. It was more than generosity. It was the leadership they provided. They convinced many others to help create a community that cared about the lives of all its citizens. We haven't done everything perfectly, but we have certainly, until recently, exceeded any other community I am familiar with. Somehow we've lost that leadership, and it's a tragedy."

She took the china cups and saucers to the kitchen and began putting them in the dishwasher.

Paul and Will sat quietly, saying nothing. After a few moments, Will stood up.

"Well, if I am going to talk to Jimmie Hudson tomorrow, I guess I'd better get a good night's sleep. He was always a tough one."

"He's not the boy you knew in high school, Will," Paul responded. "Jimmie's a leader, a mature man. He's every bit as smart as he ever was, but he's dropped the macho image."

Will awoke at 7:00 the following morning. He was always surprised how quiet the neighborhood was compared with his apartment on the Chicago lakefront. Though his apartment was on the 27th floor, he could still detect traffic and aircraft noise in the morning. After showering and shaving, he dressed in khakis, a long-sleeve shirt, cashmere sweater, and comfortable shoes. His parents were already seated at the kitchen table, awaiting his arrival. Both were reading sections of the local paper. His father held the front page which bore a headline, "IMU lawyer believes Wiemer Industries relocation dispute resolved soon."

His mother asked what he would like for breakfast.

Will had always admired his mother's housekeeping. It was difficult to discover dust or an untidy room in her home. Ruth Heider was rarely seen inside her home without an apron, and she was meticulous about cleanliness, particularly the kitchen and bathrooms. But her family knew she did not enjoy cooking.

"How about a toasted bagel, orange juice, and some coffee," he suggested.

"Is that all you want? she asked.

"That's my normal breakfast."

Following breakfast, he asked his mother for Jimmie Hudson's telephone number. Aware that they were interested in hearing the conversation, he placed the call from the kitchen phone.

Jimmie and Gloria Hudson lived in one of Hammelburg's older residential neighborhoods. They bought the house one year after their second child was born. It was a small, two-story brick house with three bedrooms, built in 1925 by a local newspaper editor. He died seven years later, in the midst of the Great Depression. His family, unable to meet the mortgage payments, lost the home. It was now classified by local real estate agents as a "starter home"; a small house, in a stable, middle class neighborhood with convenient school locations. It had been purchased and sold several times, before being acquired by the Jimmie and Gloria. During the nine years they occupied the house, Jimmie had devoted countless weekends and vacation periods to remodeling, rewiring, and replacing the plumbing. Laura, their oldest child, was twelve years old, and Irene was ten. Both were bright, attractive girls and, like their parents, excellent students. Gloria was the senior accountant at the Alamost County Treasurer's Office. Following the birth of her two daughters, she had earned an associate's degree in accounting, attending night classes for several years at the local community college. Gloria was two years younger than Jimmie and had been a secretary and bookkeeper for a local insurance agency at the time they were married. Gloria's father and grandfather were hourly employees at Wiemer Industries. Her father, a widower, had worked in the foundry and retired before the facility was closed. One year later, he relocated to a modest retirement community in northern Florida. Her older brother was a maintenance foreman with Citizens Power & Gas in Hammelburg. Her younger sister, twice divorced, was an elementary school teacher in Fort Wayne.

Jimmie Hudson and Gloria Kiel were considered an unlikely couple before they were married. Jimmie still bore his reputation as a maverick hell raiser. Gloria, an attractive, quiet young lady, was expected to transition from high school to college. It was her intention to work two years and save enough money to enroll at Valparaiso University, a Lutheran school in northern Indiana. They began dating soon after Jimmie had completed an introductory machinist's course and landed his first job at Wiemer Industries. A serious motorcycle accident and Gloria's influence appeared to make a significant change in Jimmie's lifestyle. They were married on the second anniversary of his accident.

Will's call was answered by a child. "Hudsons' residence."

"This is Will Heider. Is Mr. Hudson available?" he asked.

"OK."

The sound of the receiver being laid on a table was followed by, "Daddy, its for you."

There was a pause of a few seconds before he responded, "Hello."

"Hi, its Will Heider. I'm calling about buying you a beer."

Jimmie laughed. "Great. Where and when do you want to meet?"

"Hey, you know this town better than I do. You name the time and place," Will responded.

"Well, I suggest that we meet someplace quiet and not so popular. How about the bar at the Hammelburg Inn about one-thirty?"

"Fine. Meet you there at 1:30," Will replied.

"I really appreciate this, Will. I know you're a little reluctant, but I'll keep my promise. All I am asking is, read the contract, give me your opinion."

"Sounds good," Will answered.

Jimmie concluded the conversation. "Just you and me at the Hammelburg Inn," he laughed. "I'm buying the beer and don't be surprised if we're the only customers."

Will hung up, turned to his father and said, "It's the Hammelburg Inn at 1:30."

Paul Heider laughed. "My God, I haven't been in that bar for at least ten years. I am surprised it's still open."

Will decided to make a brief tour of other parts of Hammelburg before meeting Jimmie. Two blocks north of the downtown section, he passed the Hammelburg Public Library, which had been completed in 1985. A remarkably large and attractive glass and steel structure designed by a leading architectural firm from Boston, it was a gift to the city from several families and local businesses, including the Wiemer/Rieff Foundation. Many children, escorted by adults, were entering the building to attend Saturday morning activities.

He continued north on Anthony Street for several miles before reaching the industrial section of the city. When he arrived at the corner of Anthony and Wabash Road he recognized the abandoned buildings that had housed the Wiemer Foundry and Forge Shop. A large commercial real estate dealer's sign advertised 250,000 square feet of space for sale or rent. It was covered with rust and graffiti, nearly illegible. A heavy wire fence, topped with concertina wire, had been erected in an attempt to prevent unwanted visitors from entering the buildings and adjacent parking area. Until the fence was erected, the property had become a hangout for derelicts and narcotics dealers. Nevertheless, gang graffiti appeared on all the buildings, and the discarded beer cans and wine bottles in the abandoned parking lot gave evidence that it was still accessible. Before closing, the foundry and forge shop employed nearly 800 workers on two shifts, and in 1994, employment had reached a peak exceeding 1,100.

The rusting real estate sign puzzled Will. Who the hell, he thought, would be nuts enough to buy property that had been used as a foundry and forge shop for God knows how many years. He could imagine what an environmental soil sample would uncover. The EPA cleanup requirements would cost ten times the asking price for the property. The property couldn't be given away. Moreover, under EPA regulations, the company could never avoid the environmental liabilities, no matter who bought it or received it as a gift. The buildings contained a huge festering environmental liability for Wiemer Industries. Even if someone acquired the company, the liability would come with the property. If they later sold the property, they would still have a liability__ like having chewing gum in your hair.

He turned right on Wabash Road, After proceeding one block, he saw the familiar quadrangle of four large single-story buildings that occupied four blocks; the Wiemer machining and assembly plants. Lights were on, but the parking lot contained only a few cars, indicating that there was no Saturday overtime. Directly across the street from the manufacturing facility stood the Stefan Wiemer Engineering Center, a three-story building constructed in the 1970s. When it was opened, it was equipped with the latest technology for mechanical engineering and metallurgical design and analysis. The building, although nearly unoccupied on a Saturday morning, was fully lit; the lobby was partially occupied by a display of chrome-plated Wiemer products. A security guard sat at the entrance behind a well-worn wooden desk, observing a few employees entering and exiting the building. Before the building was erected, the site contained low-income family homes, referred to as "shotgun houses." They were small, wooden, three- or four-room single-story homes built in the early 1900s; occupied by working families. Most contained three rooms connected linearly. The front entrance opened on the living room, which entered the kitchen, and, finally, bedroom and bath. Most baths were added long after original construction. They were all demolished to provide the site for the engineering facility. The mobile home parks that were located on the city's perimeter had replaced the shotgun houses.

One block east of the engineering building, Will encountered a building he had not seen before—a modern, single-story facility, with a large sign that read Wiemer Industries Information Technology and Processing Center. It was constructed in the early 1980s, replacing a low-income residential neighborhood, the last building that Wiemer Industries had erected in Hammelburg.

As he turned south, back toward the center of the city, he passed the Purdue University-Hammelburg campus. Until the construction of this regional campus in 1975, there had been no higher education facility in Hammelburg. Branches of Indiana University Medical and Nursing schools were built a decade later. Although not a residential campus, approximately 5,000 full- and part-time students were enrolled at the Purdue campus. A large group of Hammelburg citizens and business leaders had expended a great deal of effort and made significant financial contributions to establish this facility. During the past decade, the regional campus had expanded its curriculum to permit students to complete undergraduate degrees, and graduate courses and programs were being added.

Re-entering the downtown section of the city from the east side, Will passed the familiar First Lutheran Church, a magnificent glass and Indiana limestone facility, unique in both structural and acoustic design. Large contributions from the congregation, and a portion of the Anne Rieff Endowment financed the construction and acquisition of 100 yards of property bordering each side of the facility, creating a beautifully landscaped park and outdoor sanctuary. Teenage boys dressed in gang-style clothing were skateboarding on the sidewalks and benches in the sanctuary.

In daylight, the extent of the deterioration of the downtown section was even more visible; mounds of trash in the entrances of abandoned stores; grimy, empty display windows; new and old graffiti etched a deeper impression of economic decline.

He parked in an empty lot adjacent to the Inn. It appeared to be an abandoned building site that had become a parking lot. Much of the asphalt had disappeared and had been replaced by weeds, loose gravel, and potholes. Graffiti had nearly obliterated the old Hammelburg Inn sign on the side of the building facing the parking lot.

The Hammelburg Inn was built in the 1920s and remodeled in the 1970s. It featured small rooms, miniscule bathrooms, antiquated TV sets, a dining room with an infamous dinner menu, and a continental breakfast buffet that had never included bagels, croissants, or fresh fruit. Occasionally, the unfortunate and unforgiving guests who experienced overnight accommodations at the Inn were frequently told that Wiemer Industries had made their reservations at the Inn in an effort to arrest the decline of the city center. However, it was common knowledge that Wiemer's valued customers, members of the board of directors, institutional investors, and other special guests had never visited the Inn, and were probably unaware of its existence.

The entrance to bar was at the rear of a large, shabby lobby, a rectangular room, dimly lit, with a bare wooden floor. A horseshoe-shaped bar with unpadded wooden stools occupied the entire midsection of the room. Small tables and chairs were located on both sides of the bar. The odor in the room was a combination of the urinal deodorizers in the adjoining men's room and stale cigarette smoke.

Will arrived a few minutes before Jimmie. The bartender—a large, balding man wearing a well-worn short-sleeve shirt and denim work pants—looked at him suspiciously as he entered the bar. There was only one other customer seated at the bar. He took no notice of Will. His attention was focused on a football game on the small television set suspended from the ceiling at the end of the bar. Will selected a corner table near the entrance.

The bartender did not bother to approach his table, he merely shouted at Will, "Whataya drink?"

"What kind of beer do you have on tap?" Will asked.

"Everything served in this bar comes out of a can or a bottle," he snarled.

"O.K., what do you have in bottles?"

"Whataya drink?" he repeated in a louder, more confrontational voice.

"How about a Budweiser?"

"Is that whatya drink?" he snorted.

"Yeah," Will shouted, annoyance surfacing in his response.

"We could've saved some time if you'd asked for that at the start," the bartender responded as he turned his back and reached in the cooler to select a bottle of Budweiser.

The customer laughed and slapped the bar with the palm of his hand.

"What you laughin' about, Fred? Notre Dame's g'tting' their ass kicked," the bartender snapped.

A minute later, the bartender appeared at Will's table, grim-faced, his large fist wrapped tightly around the neck of a bottle of Budweiser. The first two knuckles of the index finger were missing. He set the bottle down firmly in front of Will.

"There's your beer. It's a buck and a half."

Will looked up at the bartender, and with more than a hint of sarcasm, asked, "Do you own any glasses?"

"Jesus, only a buck and a half and you want a glass."

The customer at the bar laughed again.

Suddenly, the bartender displayed a large smile and winked at Will. "O.K., I'll bring a glass."

Will than realized that he had been the victim of the bartender's macho humor.

As the bartender was returning to the bar, Jimmie Hudson appeared in the doorway. Will recognized him, but was surprised by his appearance. He wore faded blue jeans, a loose-fitting long-sleeve gray athletic shirt, and white and blue running shoes. His dark hair, which had begun to recede, was short. He appeared to be in excellent physical shape, but the angry appearance that had been his trademark in high school was absent. A thick manila file folder was tucked under his arm.

He recognized Will, smiled, and approached the table.

The bartender was surprised. "Well, I'll be goddamned, Jimmie Hudson, what the hell are you doing in here?" he smiled broadly.

The mention of Jimmie's name suddenly drew the attention of the man at the bar. His face also registered pleasant surprise.

"Having one of your expensive beers, Art," Jimmie responded. "Give me a Coors."

The bartender winked again at Will. "At last, a man that knows what he wants."

Will stood up, they shook hands, and Jimmie sat down across the table from Will and placed the manila file folder on the table. "You haven't changed much from high school" he said.

"That was like a long time ago, Jimmie."

"It was, Will, in many, many ways, a long time ago. The world has changed, Hammelburg has changed, even I've changed."

Will noted that Jimmie was more handsome than he had remembered him. He had learned how to smile. The absence of the tight black clothing that characterized his appearance in high school, improved his appearance. He was still strong, but the muscles were not on display.

The bartender returned with a bottle of Coors and two glasses.

He placed the beer and glasses on the table, with less bravado than the first time. "Still ridin' that red Harley, Jimmie?" he asked, with a hint of humor in his voice.

Jimmie laughed. "That was a long time ago, Art."

The bartender smiled at Will. "Jimmie decorated a tree with his Harley a few years ago."

"Like 15," Jimmie responded. "I not only decorated the tree, I also decorated myself."

He placed a finger on a long faint scar on the lower right side of his face.

The bartender said"You guys gonna take Wiemer Industries to the woodshed over this relocation? Or is everybody in machining and assembly gonna learn to speak Spanish, eat tacos, and move south?"

Jimmie's smile disappeared. He looked directly at the bartender. "We have a contract, Art, and were gonna live by it. That's what labor contracts are for. They aren't gonna walk away again. This community can't afford relocation like the last one. There's a lot more than profits and shareholder interests at stake in Hammelburg."

Art rested his hand on Jimmie's shoulder. "I'm with ya, brother. After 14 years in the forge shop, I walked away with seven months' pay, a puny pension, and nine fingers. Don't let 'em do it again, Jimmie."

He patted Jimmie's shoulder, turned away, and walked back behind the bar.

Jimmie poured some beer in his glass and shoved the manila file toward the middle of the table.

"I brought a copy of the entire contract, Will. I thought you might want to read it all. However, the dispute is over the relocation clause."

Will glanced at the file folder, but did not open it.

"When we bargained the agreement, it was our intention and understanding that the company would not relocate any more jobs out of Hammelburg unless they could demonstrate that the company wouldn't survive without relocation. They can still relocate, but without proof of financial failure, they'll have to pay a substantial termination bonus to union workers, retain a modified health care plan, and continue small contributions to the pension fund. In effect, if they can't prove financial failure, it will be too expensive to relocate. If they can prove financial failure, they can reopen negotiations with us and create a new contract. If we can't settle on a new agreement that satisfies them, they are permitted to relocate union jobs with much smaller termination payments, short-term medical benefits, and no additional contributions to the pension fund."

He drank some beer before continuing. "The issue is how to define financial failure. Our lawyer, Byron Hinkle, didn't read the final version of the contract close enough, and the Wiemer lawyers got away with modifying some wording. They changed the term 'financial failure' to 'financial failure or pending financial hardship'."

Will opened the file folder and looked at the first page of the contract. "How long do you have to negotiate a new contract before they can elect to relocate?" he asked.

"One year," Jimmie answered. "Management notified us last March that they were experiencing financial hardship—not financial failure, but financial hardship. We asked Hinkle to evaluate the contract to see if they really had a case. He came back and admitted that he had not seen the financial hardship term in the final draft. He said he didn't know how to define it, and recommended we agree to reopen the contract and start the renegotiation."

Will found it hard to believe that Hinkle had not challenged the definition of financial hardship before recommending that the IMU reopen the contract. It was bad enough that he failed to catch an amendment in the final draft; his negligence was compounded by failing to challenge the meaning of the two words.

"Are the negotiations still underway?" Will asked

"Barely. We made our best offer two weeks ago. It's a damn expensive proposal for the IMU. But we can't lose these jobs."

"How expensive?"

"We proposed a 30 percent reduction in hourly rates for two years; no increases for four years; increased the co-pay on health insurance to 40 percent from 20 percent; reduced the final pension benefit to 55 percent of the average of the final five years from 65 percent of the final two years; and capped the cost of prescription benefits on medical coverage after retirement. We only ask for complete elimination of relocation of the jobs in existence before March first of last year, with no financial hardship exceptions."

Will was surprised. What Jimmie had described was one of the most generous union concessions he had ever encountered. "Any response or counteroffers from management?"

Jimmie reached out and turned his beer glass several times before responding to Will's question.

"It was rejected in less than 48 hours," he said.

"Total rejection, no counteroffers, no requests for meetings?" Will's voice registered his surprise.

Jimmie looked at Will with his eyes narrowed. "Nope, we asked for a meeting and they didn't respond," he answered.

"According to the headline in the paper this morning, your attorney believes you're about to reach agreement on a contract," Will stated.

"That's bullshit. It keeps the local merchants and the mayor off his ass," Jimmie responded.

"Does Wiemer management use inside or outside legal counsel in labor negotiations?" Will asked.

"The lawyers that attend the meetings are from New York. The rumor is that the top lawyer is a guy named Perkins. Jack Perkins. We've never met him. He's never attended a meeting. Hinkle has met with him several times in New York. He has two assistants who attend the bargaining sessions: a young guy named Trent Baker and a young woman lawyer, Martha something... Martha... Martha Berman."

"They don't include any inside counsel in the meetings?"

"The only management representatives in the bargaining sessions are Fenn Sullivan and two of his assistants. Sullivan is the vice president of personnel. He rarely opens his mouth. Baker does all the talking."

"Who keeps the minutes and prepares the written material?"

"The woman lawyer, Martha Berman."

"Who represents the IMU in the bargaining sessions?"

"Five members of the IMU that are elected to serve on the bargaining committee. I am the newest member. This is my first time to be involved in contract bargaining. Byron Hinkle does nearly all the talking for the committee. We caucus occasionally, but Hinkle even controls the caucus meetings."

"Who keeps the minutes for the IMU and prepares the summaries?"

"Like I said, Martha Berman."

"You don't maintain separate minutes and summaries?"

"No, they give Hinkle copies and he reads them and approves them."

Will poured more beer into his glass and studied the bottle for a moment. "What's Hinkle recommending now?"

"He told us he wants to meet with Baker and Sullivan, alone."

The tone of Will's next question revealed his disbelief. "Meet management without any union representative?"

Jimmie looked at Will and shook his head before responding, "That's what the man recommended to us last week. The day before I called you."

Will stared at the document in the middle of the table. "What's your impression of Baker?" he asked.

"He's a smart, cocky sonofabitch. He scares the hell out of Hinkle and Sullivan. I took him on a couple of times, and Hinkle warned me that I was damaging our position. The other four members of the committee agreed with me, but they think it's best to let Hinkle do our talking. It's goddamn ridiculous. I've told them, Hinkle and Baker negotiated the last agreement and what the hell did we end up with? Hinkle sat there fat, dumb, and happy, while Baker, or more likely Perkins, put two extra words in the final draft that changed the whole meaning of the contract. I thought lawyers were taught to watch out for that kind of shit."

Will pulled the file folder toward him, opened the document and studied the index for a few minutes.

"Jimmie, give me the rest of today and tomorrow morning to read through the contract. Are you free tomorrow afternoon, Sunday?"

"Will, I'm free anytime you can meet me. We need help. I wanta fire Hinkle. The rest of the bargaining committee is opposed. They don't trust him, but they're afraid. He's all we got. But I know that if we keep him, we're gonna get screwed again."

Jimmie emptied the remaining contents of the beer bottle into his glass and slowly finished his drink.

"There's something else you ought to know, Will." He cleared his throat before continuing. "I'm the newest and the youngest member of the bargaining committee. The other four have a lot of seniority. Each one of them has more than 25 years with Wiemer. My support came from younger members of the IMU. They're worried that the older members may be willing to settle for the deal the foundry and forge workers got: a lot of money for those with high seniority and damn little for the rest of us. One of the bargaining committee members suggested that we settle for a generous early retirement benefit for those with high seniority and the younger workers get a small severance and government-supported job training and placement services. I can't prove it, but I think it was Hinkle's idea."

"This NAFTA job training and placement services is political bullshit," Jimmie continued. "We've looked at what happened in Flint and Toledo. They trained people for jobs that don't exist or jobs that people weren't well enough educated to handle. We've got lots of single parents on the plant floor, men and women. These aren't second-income families. They can't afford to take time off to be retrained and hope they can land a job when they're done. They've got mouths to feed and bills to pay."

Chapter 9

By the mid 1950s, Wiemer Industries' sales had exceeded $700 million, and the company was experiencing strong growth and profitability. Total employment exceeded 2,300. All of Wiemer's operations remained in Hammelburg. The company was the largest employer in the city. General Motors had built a large auto parts manufacturing plant in Hammelburg in 1953. Barker Packaging had doubled the size of its operations. Radio Components Corporation, a manufacturer of television and radio components, had doubled their floor space and employment in less than five years. Hammelburg was growing in population and newly-created manufacturing jobs resulted in increased prosperity. It was accompanied by a significant increase in new retail and service businesses.

In 1956, The United Steel Workers attempted to organize Wiemer Industries' employees. It was a closely-contested election. The USW was defeated by a very narrow margin. The attitude of the employees reflected the division of opinion. Immediately before and after the election, there were occasional fights in the parking lot, and the police were called several times to quell disturbances in local bars. There were handmade signs displayed near the Wiemer facilities, criticizing those who opposed the USW.

Despite the unrest among the hourly employees, the management had not become a target of those dissatisfied with the election, but J.W. Rieff sensed that unless something was done to eliminate the tension, it would become a major impediment to the productivity of the workforce. One month after the elections, he met with his executive staff and proposed that management encourage the Wiemer hourly employees to establish an independent union. He argued that sooner or later, Wiemer employees were going to organize, and management would be better off negotiating directly with their employees rather than a representative of an international union. Moreover, he thought the idea would appeal to the employees. One of the primary objections to the USW was the requirement to pay international union dues and contribute to strike funds. A local independent union would require much smaller union dues.

When J.W. presented his idea at a Monday morning staff meeting, Ben Wiemer, now the vice president of operations, barked his adamant opposition.

"This is insanity. For the last six months, the steel workers union have been telling our workers that management was abusing them and they would get them more pay and more benefits, and they didn't believe that horseshit, and they voted them down. And now we go out and help them organize a union. This is some goddamn fairy tale. What in the hell would this community think of us? Its nuts. The Chamber of Commerce would run us out of town on a rail."

Stefan Wiemer, approaching retirement as vice president of research and engineering, thought there was merit in J.W.'s idea.

"Ben, like you, I've always opposed having a union in Wiemer Industries. But I think J.W. may have a point. Wiemer is a big target for a union. G.M. and Radio Components have fewer employees, and both have a union. The steel workers lost by a small margin. They'll try again, and they may win. I think we ought to give J.W.'s idea a chance. It may not work, but it won't hurt to try."

"The hell it won't," Ben responded. "You open that goddamn door and you'll never get it closed. You put a union on that shop floor and you can kiss this company goodbye. The union will be running Wiemer Industries in six months. We dodged a bullet when the steel workers lost, and you wanta step in front of the gun again?"

Stefan smiled and shook his head. "C'mon Ben, the auto workers and the electrical workers aren't running the G.M. and Radio Components plants."

"It's a goddamn bad idea," Ben insisted. "What the hell do you think your brother Martin would say if he heard this conversation?"

Stefan spoke softly, but his anger was apparent. "Ben, I loved my brother. He had a tragic life. He did his best. But he lived and worked in a different time. There's no reason to raise that issue."

Max Arnholt had remained silent regarding the proposal. His son, Gus, was a student at Cornell University and planned to join the Wiemer finance staff following graduation. Max and Katherine Arnholt had great expectations for Gus. They hoped he would someday become the CEO of Wiemer Industries. Max had never had a good relationship with his brother-in-law, and there was political advantage in siding with J.W. and Stefan.

"Ben, I agree with Stefan. Let's see what the reaction is. We don't have to go forward if we decide it's a bad idea."

"Jesus, Max, how the hell can you sit there and say that? You deal with the customers, but I have to deal with the workers. You don't have to walk out on that shop floor every day and listen to that bullshit. I do. There are more assholes per square foot on that shop floor than you could ever imagine, and I don't intend to sit across the table once a month and listen to a goddamn grievance committee tell me that they want better quality toilet paper in the head and we've got the wrong brand of jelly beans in the vending machines."

Despite Ben's histrionics, it was decided that J.W. should explore the idea, but that meeting was only the beginning of the expression of misgivings regarding his proposal. The next source of resistance was several members of the personnel and manufacturing staff who issued dire warnings about loss of control, increased cost, and reduced productivity if the Wiemer workers organized. Nevertheless, J.W. requested a meeting with the three hourly workers who had been the most active in attempting to encourage an affiliation with the USW.

The meeting was held in a small conference room at the machining and assembly plant. The anxiety and suspicion of all three men was apparent when they entered the room. J.W had requested that they meet with him and Joe Gray, vice president of personnel, but hadn't informed them of the purpose of the meeting. J.W. had gambled; he thought the men might misinterpret the purpose of the meeting, but feared it would cause greater confusion if he attempted to explain it beforehand. There were angry rumors about the meeting throughout the company. The expectations were that the three men would be fired for attempting to organize a union. Even among those who had voted against the union, there was agreement that if anyone was disciplined for participation in the campaign, there would be a walkout the following day.

When J.W. and Joe Gray arrived at the meeting room, the three men were already seated on the far side of the conference table facing the door. None of them acknowledged the arrival of J.W. or Gray. Two of the men were in their mid-forties, both worked in the assembly operation. They were balding and slightly overweight They wore dark T-shirts, heavy denim work pants, and work boots. Their shirts bore permanent stains from the coolant in the machining operation. Both carried a package of cigarettes in their T-shirt pocket. The third man was a forge drop operator. He appeared to be in his late twenties. He bore several tattoos on his left arm. His cigarettes were tucked in his shirt sleeve. His face was heavily scarred from severe acne

The older men had come directly from their respective jobs. They were assigned to the first shift and were instructed not to clock out for the meeting. They would be paid while in the meeting. The younger man was a second shift employee. He was on his own time.

J.W. smiled, removed his suit coat, hung it on the back of his chair, and sat down. The men continued to stare silently across the table at J.W. The hostility was evident. J.W. attempted to lessen the tension by explaining why he had requested a meeting. He spoke softly and slowly, his arms extended in front of him, hands flat on the table.

There was no visible response from the other side of the table. The older men appeared apprehensive. The younger man assumed a defiant posture, his arms crossed tightly across his chest, his eyes narrow, but focused on J.W. He reminded J.W of a young petty officer that he had to discipline aboard a navy ship during the war.

"I requested this meeting for a very specific purpose. I want to learn—and I emphasize the word 'learn'—why you believe we need a union and why a significant number of Wiemer hourly employees agreed with you. I'm not here to criticize or argue with you. I'm not anti-union,' but I was surprised by the amount of support the USW received and I would like to understand why. To the best of my knowledge, I have never met any of you before, but I want this meeting to be informal and open. Again, I am here to learn."

The younger man now looked at J.W. suspiciously. The two older men continued to reflect apprehension.

"I'm aware that all of you played an important part in the USW organizing activity. I'm not critical of you. In my opinion, you've done nothing wrong or improper. I would, however, appreciate it if you would share with me why you believe Wiemer Industries' workers should be represented by a union."

There was a long silence as the three men glanced at one another, attempting to determine who would respond. Finally, the younger man spoke. His voice reflected anger. "Look, the company won. No one's arguing about that. We tried to bring a union here because we thought we deserved the right to a labor contract and collective bargaining, rather than be told to take it or leave it by the company... You won. We lost."

J.W. looked at the other two to see if there was any response. They were nodding in agreement.

He decided to speak directly to the younger man. " I don't believe the company would've lost anything had the election gone the other way. What I'm really interested in learning is what convinced so many of our employees that they should have a union after so many years without one."

The younger man's expression continued to reflect his skepticism. "O.K., Mr. Rieff. Let me ask you a question: If we had come downtown to your office and told you we wanted to organize a union, would you have said 'Sure, go ahead, I'm not anti-union'?"

"No, I wouldn't have said that. I would've asked you the same question that I am asking this afternoon: Why do you believe Wiemer employees need to be represented by a union?"

One of the older men finally responded "Well, that wasn't what we were told,"

"What were you told?"

" We were told plain and simple, if the Wiemer workers voted for the USW management would close the plant; move all the jobs to Birmingham, Alabama. You had already made arrangements to buy a foundry and forge shop down there, and would build machining and assembly operations next to it."

J.W. shook his head in disbelief. "Who told you that? That's nonsense."

The younger man answered angrily, "Every goddamn foreman in this company warned everyone that reported to them, over and over again. They said it was a decision that had been approved by the management and the board of directors. You vote union and you lose your job. That was the message."

J.W. did not respond immediately. He looked to Joe Gray, who shrugged to indicate he knew nothing about it. He then turned to the younger man and again spoke slowly and softly. "Let me assure you that there was never a plan to move any part of this company out of Hammelburg, regardless of which way the union vote fell. Second, even if the foreman told everyone that story, it appears they didn't believe it; a lot of employees voted for the union. Did the foreman tell you where they got that information?"

The second of the two older men elected to respond. "Mr. Rieff, they told us the vice president of operations held a meeting and told the manufacturing staff that Wiemer was going to Birmingham if the union vote passed. It made a lot of people mad. They trusted Wiemer Industries. They couldn't believe management would do that. Without that threat and the union dues associated with the USW, the vote would have passed. There's a hell of a lot of people mad at the company and each other. We've had fights in the plant, the parking lot, and a couple of bars. It ain't good."

The younger man spoke again. "That ain't all of it. There are lots of colored guys that work in the forge and foundry. They know that Birmingham, Alabama is not very friendly to colored people. They assume that Wiemer chose Birmingham for two reasons. First, it's a big iron and steel town, and second it's not a town where a colored man wants to live. They figure that's the best way to get rid of colored employees. They won't follow Wiemer to Alabama."

J.W. was dumbfounded. Struggling to find a response, he finally suggested that they take a five minute break and then continue talking. He asked Joe Gray to accompany him to a smaller, unoccupied conference room.

As they entered the room, J.W. shut the door and spoke directly to Gray. "Joe, what the hell is this all about? That is the wildest story I've ever heard. Were you aware of it?"

Gray was nervous. He was unaccustomed to meeting with J.W. He reported directly to Ben Wiemer. "I heard the rumor, J.W," he said, "but I thought it was just a dumb story no one would believe. I assumed the Steel Workers Union started it."

"Why the hell would the Steel Workers plant that rumor? They'd have to realize that it would hurt them, not help them. They can't be that dumb. If we knew about the rumor, did we attempt to correct it?" J.W. asked.

"I talked to Ben," Gray replied. "He told me to forget it. It would work to our advantage. If they really believed we were moving to Birmingham, they would think twice about voting for the union."

"But why did the foremen repeat the rumor if they knew it wasn't true? Why didn't they deny it rather than repeat it?"

Perspiration began to appear on Gray's forehead. He removed his handkerchief from his back pocket and pretended to blow his nose while wiping moisture off his forehead. "I am not sure I know," he replied.

J.W. stared at Gray for a moment before responding, "C'mon Joe, cut the crap. You have been with this company for 30-plus years. Nothing happens on the shop floor that you aren't aware of. Now, who the hell really started that rumor?"

Gray raised his hands, palms up. "All I know is that Ben Wiemer told the foreman that the rumor was in the plant and to talk about it with the workers."

"Did he tell them to deny it?"

"Not that I remember," Gray answered

J.W. was barely able to control his rage. His voice quivered with anger as he spoke. "O.K., Joe, you've answered my question. Let's go back in that room and talk with them."

When J.W. and Joe Gray reentered the conference room the three men were standing. They obviously had been engaged in a serious conversation.

They returned to their seats as J.W. sat down. There was no apparent change in attitude, although one of the older men appeared slightly less apprehensive.

"Before we go any further with this discussion," J.W. said, "I want to apologize to you. The rumor about moving the plant to Birmingham was a vicious lie." He paused, continuing to struggle with his anger. "Such a proposal was never discussed or considered by management. It's ludicrous. I don't know who started the rumor, but I am reasonably sure it wasn't the Steel Workers, and I am embarrassed and angry that the management of this company didn't immediately deny it when they first heard it."

There was a long silence in the room. The three men looked at Joe Gray. He avoided eye contact. His face reflected his discomfort.

Finally, the younger man spoke. "Well, Mr. Rieff that's all well and good, but it's done. The vote is over. We lost. We can't get the toothpaste back in the tube, can we?"

J.W. looked at all three men before responding. His reply was calm and deliberate. "I'm not sure we can't. At least we can try."

He then began to describe his idea regarding the formation of an independent union.

The meeting continued into the late afternoon. All three men showed skepticism regarding J.W.'s motives. But at the end of the meeting, they expressed a willingness to explore the concept of an independent union with the workers to determine if there was support for the idea. J.W. agreed that he would be the spokesman for management and would meet with the representatives whenever they requested a meeting.

Following the initial meeting, J.W. became a frequent visitor on the shop floor. He walked through the plants and engaged in conversations with workers. After six months of negotiation, an agreement was reached. The Independent Metal Workers Union was formed, and Wiemer Industries provided the funds to finance the organization until sufficient dues could be collected to allow the new union to become self-supporting. A three-year collective bargaining agreement was completed in January of 1957.

The reaction of the local community was mixed. The conservative element opposed any encouragement of organized labor and hoped that other employers would not adopt such a strategy. None did. Union supporters were divided. Members of the UAW at the General Motors plant and other local union members considered it a paternalistic strategy to create a weak union and block the entry of stronger international unions. But when the terms of the three-year bargaining agreement were revealed, the criticism evaporated. The *Hammelburg Sentinel* wrote several editorials that attempted to satisfy both sides. The articles praised Wiemer Industries for its innovative approach to labor relations but subtly suggested it was not a good idea for other companies to adopt similar policies.

There were only two people, other than J.W., that knew that the idea of an independent union had been suggested by Anne Wiemer Rieff: Mary Pinnay Rieff and Phillip Rieff. Had other members of the family learned that Anne was the source of the idea, it would have encountered even stronger opposition.

Anne Rieff proposed the idea to J.W. at a board of directors meeting of the Wiemer/Rieff Foundation at Anne's home, a few days after the USW proposal had been defeated. Mary and Phillip were present; Stefan Wiemer and Katherine Wiemer Arnholt were unable to attend.

Chapter 10

In February 1957, Mary Rieff gave birth to Susan Anne Rieff. Three months following the birth of her granddaughter, Anne Rieff suffered a severe stroke and died in route to the Hammelburg Memorial Hospital.

The family held a memorial service at the First Lutheran Church and a reception at a local funeral home. J.W. and Phillip were stunned by the number of people who attempted to attend both events. It was a warm spring day, and the line of people waiting to enter the church extended for two blocks. The church sanctuary and adjoining rooms could not accommodate them all. At the suggestion of Mary Rieff, the minister went outside and apologized to those who could not enter the church and invited them to attend the reception following the memorial service.

At the reception, J.W., Phillip, and Mary were overwhelmed with the number of people who came to them to express their admiration and affection for Anne. Many were dressed in work clothes and house dresses. Several black families attended both the memorial service and reception with their children. By the end of the day, her family realized that Anne Wiemer Rieff had known and helped far more people in Hammelburg than they had ever imagined, even her critics were astonished.

Mary Rieff and her brother-in-law, Phillip, were determined to continue the work that Anne had started with the Wiemer/Rieff Foundation. Phillip had completed his academic work at the University of Chicago and joined the faculty at Northwestern University. He was beginning to enjoy a modest reputation as a scholar of modern European history. Despite his teaching assignments, research efforts, and occasional trips to Europe and Washington D.C., he found time to work with Mary, evaluating proposals presented to the Wiemer/Rieff Foundation.

After her marriage, Mary Rieff became a close confidant of her mother-in-law. Anne Rieff was impressed with Mary's knowledge of European languages and culture. Shortly before her death, she asked Mary if she had time to help direct a research project on the German heritage and genealogy of Hammelburg. Phillip encouraged her to accept the challenge, and pledged his assistance.

Following two years of effort, Mary proposed that the Wiemer/ Rieff Foundation establish a Center of German-American Culture in Hammelburg. Her proposal encompassed a broad scope of activity for the Center, including an elaborate library for genealogical research with a permanent staff that would assist anyone who wished to research their family history, financial support for local students who wished to visit and study in Germany and Western Europe, and limited financial support for German artists and writers who agreed to present seminars and exhibits at the Center. She recommended that the Center be located in the home of William and Anne Rieff. It required expensive additions and renovations to the house, but it was an ideal location. With the assistance of Phillip Rieff, they were able to attract a well-respected professor of German history at the University of Wisconsin to serve as the chairman of the board of the Center and assist in recruiting a full-time staff.

The Wiemer/Rieff Foundation board met in January of 1959 to discuss the final proposal. It was agreed that it was exciting and would be an enormous asset for Hammelburg, but the funds required to finance the undertaking required too much of the assets of the Foundation. Mary and Phillip were deeply disappointed. Two years of effort evaporated in a single afternoon. J.W. was sympathetic, but understood the financial problem.

Later that week, J.W. was surprised to receive a call from Paul Michos, president of the family-owned Kimberly's Fashion Store. The Michos family had managed a dry goods business in Hammelburg since 1875. Paul was the third generation of family management. His grandfather, a Greek immigrant, had adopted his wife's maiden name, Kimberly, for the store. J.W. rarely encountered Paul. He was a very private man. Small, bald, and overweight, Paul had been one year ahead of J.W. in high school. He was an excellent student, but shy and lacking in self-confidence. His father was a large, gregarious man who frequently walked through the store greeting and visiting with customers. Paul was rarely seen by customers. He had wanted to study music in college, but his father insisted he study economics and return to the family business. He had married a local girl, but it was rumored that it was not a strong marriage. Paul's mother, Evelyn Michos, was a close friend of Anne Rieff, a quiet, handsome woman, devoted to the Catholic church.

The purpose of the call was an even greater surprise. Paul told J.W. that he was familiar with Mary's plan to establish a German-American Culture Center, and disappointed to learn that the Foundation had decided not to support it. He proposed that his family make a substantial contribution to support the Center, and he would personally solicit other business leaders in the community to raise additional capital, provided the Foundation reversed its decision.

J.W. immediately called the Foundation board members, and with the exception of Stefan Wiemer, they voted to accept Paul Michos' offer. Stefan thought it was unwise to focus on Hammelburg's German roots so soon after WW II.

Mary was ecstatic. Paul Michos requested that she help him organize a small committee to direct the fundraising effort. It was agreed that the Michos family would match the amount contributed by the Foundation. Consequently, their combined pledges achieved nearly two-thirds of the required capital cost and five-year operating budget. Donations from General Motors, Barker Packaging, Radio Components Corporation, Wiemer Industries, the Hammelburg Chamber of Commerce, other business organizations, and prosperous families provided the balance.

Hammelburg was suddenly a topic of regional interest. The *Indianapolis Star and News* printed a long article in their Sunday edition about the Center, describing its purpose and the broad community support. The *Fort Wayne Journal Gazette's* editorial page praised Hammelburg's citizens for their vision and generosity. The *Chicago Tribune* published a small article in conjunction with an interview with Phillip Rieff. Soon after the announcement, letters of interest and resumes began to arrive from those seeking employment. Others expressed interest in using the Center as a research base.

In addition to the praise, there was also mild criticism from the American Legion and Veterans of Foreign Wars for failing to include tributes to the American men who died in Europe in WW I and WW II. A series of letters to the editor of the *Hammelburg Sentinel* expressed fear that the inclusion of East Germany in its scope of information might result in Communists attempting to use the Center for propaganda purposes. Several religious organizations suggested an independent board be established to assure that no "inappropriate" material was included in any exhibits.

By the fall of 1960, the Center had opened and recruited its first staff members. A ribbon cutting ceremony was attended by representatives of several of Indiana's state and private universities, the lieutenant governor, and the president of the German-American Society of Indiana. It was the envisioned as the first step in establishing what would become an important research institute for German-American history and relations. In time, the Center expanded its mandate and began exploring current developments in Germany. With the assistance of Phillip Rieff, the Center attracted several advisors. Phillip devoted as much time to the project as his academic and travel schedule would permit. Two years after the opening of the Center, Jens Reichner was appointed the managing director of the Center. Reichner had managed a harrowing escape from East Germany while a professor of history at Leipzig University. He was selected, in part, for his ability to attract generous financial contributions from a select group of institutions and individuals As the number of staff members increased, so did the diversity of social and cultural life in Hammelburg. Seminars regarding German history and events were frequently open to the public. Other programs were specifically designed for Hammelburg's high school students. But the primary focus of the Center was shifting to the analysis of current sociopolitical issues in Europe. The Center also published a quarterly review devoted to current events in Germany and Eastern Europe.

Several months after the appointment of Jens Reichner, a letter to the editor appeared in the *Hammelburg Sentinel* suggesting that the Center was recruiting a research staff comprised of German expatriates who had been active members of the German Communist Party. The author of the letter, Thomas Damich, was a Hammelburg lawyer and member of the Senate of the Indiana General Assembly. Damich, a modestly successful lawyer who had inherited his father's law practice, had experienced some success in politics by identifying and denouncing what he considered subversive left-wing organizations and communist and socialist sympathizers. He had been a major critic of the formation of an independent union at Wiemer Industries and the most virulent antagonist of the Hammelburg Preschool Preparation Program. He earned much praise from the most conservative leaders of the community by labeling it as "a dangerous experiment in social engineering." His real, but unstated, objection was the mixing of black and white children.

He frequently referred to the Wiemer/Rieff Foundation as a "Socialist Think Tank" or "The Rieff family plan to run the city." Following the publication of his letter, he made a speech on the floor of the Indiana Senate denouncing the growing number of "left-wingers and fellow travelers nesting in the state's public and private universities and research centers." He proposed that the Indiana General Assembly establish a Joint Committee to Investigate Subversive Activities in Indiana. Following his speech, in an interview with the *Indianapolis Star,* he made reference to the staff of the German-American Culture Center in Hammelburg and declared that "it was plain for all to see that certain founders of the German-American Culture Center had played an important role in recruiting these people."

J.W. and Mary Rieff were well aware of Damich's objection to the Foundation and its activities. He had long been a spokesman for and a favorite of the ultra-conservative element in Hammelburg. But they were astounded at his recent remarks, and contacted Phillip to gain his approval of a statement to be released by the Center, denouncing Damich as a "brazen demagogue." However, Phillip suggested that before any response was made, he wanted to visit Hammelburg to discuss Damich's accusations.

The following weekend, Phillip drove from Evanston to Hammelburg to meet with J.W. and Mary. He seemed far less concerned about Damich than they had expected.

Mary had prepared a lunch for the three of them. As lunch progressed, Phillip began to explain what may have been the source of Damich's accusations. "When I served in London in military intelligence, my primary assignment was translation of intercepted German messages. Many of the men and women who served with me were German immigrants. Some were Jews who had fled in the late 1930s. Others were opponents of Hitler who left to avoid concentration camps. I know that some of them had been members of socialist or communist organizations in Germany," he explained.

"When the war ended, a few elected to return to Germany. One of the reasons I was sent to Berlin from London was to maintain contact with them, particularly those who had returned to East Germany. One of those who returned to East Germany was Jens Reichner."

J.W. appeared surprised and perplexed as Phillip continued. "His father was a senior officer of the *Reichsbank*, and a member of the Nazi Party. Jens and his father had bitter arguments about politics. When he was an undergraduate at the University of Heidelberg, he joined a student organization that had connections to the Communist Party. He continued to maintain his connections with the organization during his graduate studies at the University of Munich. In 1937, Jens was appointed as a junior faculty member in the history department at Leipzig University. That summer, he traveled to London to teach one semester at the University of London. A month after his arrival in the U.K., he received a private communication from his father, warning him that his membership in the student organization had been discovered and it would be best for him and his family if he did not return to Germany. He remained in the U.K. as a political refugee and taught in a private boarding school. When the war started, he volunteered for British Intelligence. I worked with Jens for three years. When the war ended, he elected to return to Germany. He discovered that his entire family had been killed in the Hamburg bombings. He went back to Leipzig, in East Germany, and joined the Communist Party in order to secure his teaching post at the University.

J.W. glanced at Mary in an attempt to measure her reaction.

"I continued to have contact with Jens for several years after his return to Leipzig." Phillip paused for a moment. "I can't tell you any more about that"

J.W. thought he detected a brief smile on Mary's face.

"Jens became disillusioned with what was happening in East Germany. The East German Democratic Republic became an oxymoron. The Soviet Union was transferring all of the German intellectuals in government and education to Moscow and replacing them with mediocre Party members. No one seemed to know what happened to the people who were sent to Moscow. The East German government and its leaders were comprised of dull people who took orders from the Russians. Jens decided he wanted to leave. A difficult decision, as you can imagine. He was able to make contact with me and we arranged to bring him out. It was a dangerous assignment and nearly fatal for Jens."

J.W. could no longer contain himself. "Who the hell is 'we', Phil?"

"I am sorry, J.W. I can't tell you that. I hope you believe me that it was in the best interest of our country. But let me assure you that I don't know anyone who harbors a greater rejection of Communism than Jens Reichner. To even suggest that he is a subversive is a crude joke. He has been a most useful source of information and insight for our government, and he is considered a scholar on current Eastern European affairs. God knows, Hammelburg, is fortunate to have Jens. He could join any major research university he desires."

"But how the hell does that help us with that idiot Damich? You can't tell that story to the *Hammelburg Sentinel* or the *Indianapolis Star.*" J.W. retorted.

Mary appeared annoyed at her husband's remarks. "I don't think Phil suggested that he intended to tell the story to the newspapers. So let's hear him out, J.W."

"I've known Tom Damich since high school," Phil said. "He was one year ahead of me. He was a fat bully who sat on the bench of the football team for three years. I'm not sure he ever played in a game. He was a poor student whose father got him into college and law school. He barely managed to graduate from both. After law school, he came back to Hammelburg and his father's practice. He wasn't considered the brightest young lawyer in town, so he decided to pursue a career in politics, and he set out to achieve that by glad-handing and sucking up to all of the right-wing reactionaries in Alamost County—and there were more than a few—and work his way up through local, state, and national politics. He made a couple of mistakes, however. He got too far to the right when he decided to join the German-American Bund and got cozy with Father Coughlin in Detroit. American Nazis didn't attract a lot of attention before the war. They do now. His second mistake was his military record. He didn't want to go fight his Nazi friends, so he arranged to get an army commission as a second lieutenant and was assigned permanently to a Richmond, Virginia supply depot as a procurement officer for military contracts. He got into some trouble when a supplier accused him of asking for a little money under the table. With the help of his father and a local congressman, he was able to avoid a court martial. But he never was promoted to first lieutenant. I don't think Tom is anxious to have all that revealed to his adoring constituency. He has bigger political plans. He still wants that congressional seat."

J.W. was amazed. "How the hell do you know all of this about Tom Damich? I've known him for years and never heard any of this"

Mary laughed.

"Hey J.W., remember, I lived in Hammelburg for a few years before the war, under a cloud. I took some pretty hard digs from Mr. Damich. He has always been a bully. Moreover, the information I just gave you is accurate. It's not my casual observations."

"Do you intend to confront him with this information?" J.W. asked.

"No, I have no desire to visit with Tom Damich. But I am gonna confide in you by telling you that Monday morning, he's gonna get a telephone call that will convince him that he doesn't want to continue his search for subversives, and that it's important that he explain to the newspapers that he must have been misunderstood or misquoted regarding the German-American Culture Center in Hammelburg."

"A call from whom?" J.W. asked.

Mary also appeared surprised at Phillip's disclosure.

"J.W., I can't tell you that, but I will assure you that it will be a call that he won't refuse and he will follow the advice he receives from the caller."

J.W. looked at Mary and then Phillip. He then tilted his chair back and looked at the ceiling before speaking.

"Phil, after this conversation, I am starting to suspect that the German-American Culture Center is involved in something a whole lot bigger than genealogical research for Alamost County, and that some of the generous donations that have been received by the Center may have been made surreptitiously," J.W. said.

Phillip began to reveal the hard edge that he so carefully disguised. "I'm not going to pursue that issue with you J.W. But let me make a few points.

First, the Center has been a godsend for this community. It has attracted international attention and brought enormous diversity to what was a sleepy Midwest city. Second, there is nothing being done at that Center that any member of the board of directors need be ashamed of or embarrassed by. Third, what is going on at the Center is also happening in nearly every social research center in the United States. Lastly, we are still fulfilling our original purpose of providing outstanding genealogical research, just as Mom wanted. Personally, I think she'd be very proud of what the Center has become."

J.W. turned to Mary and asked, "Did you know about all this, Mary?"

"About what, J.W.?" She seemed puzzled by his question.

"About Jens and Phil and all the research activity at the Center?"

Before Mary could respond, Phillip interrupted. "J.W, I've never shared anything with Mary that I haven't shared with you. Obviously, she has spent more time at the Center than you have and may have observed more. But the information that I have revealed this afternoon is the first time for both of you."

Mary suddenly stood up. "I think I am familiar with the organization that the mysterious caller represents, and after this afternoon's conversation, I suspect that Phillip has more than one employer, and that is as far as I want to pursue the subject."

She began to clear the luncheon dishes from the table.

Chapter 11

In the spring of 1964, J.W., Mary, and their two children vacationed for two weeks at Sea Island, Georgia. As neither of the parents were golfers, they spent most of their time on the beach watching and playing with Alfred and Susan. On the third day of their vacation, J.W. met another vacationer, a senior vice president of Wolverine Chemical Company, a large company based in Michigan. During one of their conversations, the chemical company executive described what Wolverine Chemical's management had done to support its community. He described the foundation that the corporation had established to take advantage of a recent IRS ruling which permitted corporations to donate up to 5% of before tax earnings to charitable activities. Much of the progress in the Michigan community was being financed by the chemical company, but it also encouraged other businesses and individuals to contribute to community projects by providing matching grants.

Soon after they returned to Indiana, J.W. arranged to travel to Michigan to learn more about how Wolverine Chemical organized and managed its foundation. He asked Henry Brinson to accompany him. They were both impressed by the progress that had been achieved. The foundation activities had helped fund education, medical facilities, recreational systems, a local symphony orchestra, and other cultural programs. The matching grant concept was perhaps the most innovative aspect of the program. It had resulted in millions of dollars donated from small businesses and individuals to support community projects.

Several months later, at a meeting of the Wiemer Industries board of directors, J.W. elected to discuss the trip to Michigan and Wolverine Chemical's impact on the Michigan community. The majority of the board was still comprised of a small group of corporate officers and family members, with only two outside directors.

Gus Arnholt had replaced his father, who elected to retire from the company. He had recently been promoted to chief financial officer. The promotion was both controversial and unexpected. Gus was 28 years old, overweight, and prematurely bald. Although no one denied his intelligence, it was his pomposity and self-satisfaction that made him unpopular. He was ambitious and aggressive, more aggressive than he could have afforded to be, had he not been a family member. His fondness for bowties and expensive double-breasted suits did nothing for his image in the organization. He frequently took random walks about the office, observing his staff in a somewhat imperial fashion, his head thrust backward, staring over the top of his heavy horn-rimmed glasses.

He had married his college sweetheart, the daughter of an Episcopalian minister. Cynthia Arnholt was tall, thin, and flat-chested, with a smile that radiated condescension. Her frequent public pronouncements regarding the lack of civility and cultural opportunities in the Midwest, and particularly Hammelburg, quickly earned her several unflattering nicknames. Arnholt's promotion to chief financial officer was received with derision and skepticism by the employees and the community. J.W. had serious reservations about his ability to handle a senior executive position, given his lack of experience and maturity, but decided he would surround him with an able staff and avoid a family quarrel. Max and Kathryn Arnholt had launched an aggressive campaign advocating his promotion immediately following his predecessor's retirement.

Ben and Stefan Wiemer made up the balance of the family members. Both of them had retired from active roles in the management, but Stefan served as a technical consultant to the research and engineering staff.

Henry Brinson and Peter Goldman were the two outside directors. Goldman was a bright, successful investment banker from Boston, a Cornell classmate of Gus Arnholt, and a Harvard Business School graduate.

Harry Achaffer was the seventh member. After being promoted to senior vice president the previous year, it was decided that Achaffer should serve on the board, as he was expected to replace J.W. as the president and chief operating officer. J.W. wanted to assume the role of chairman and chief executive officer, a less time-consuming task that would allow him to concentrate on other issues. Achaffer had been employed by Wiemer since graduating with an engineering degree from Ohio State University in 1947. He was a quiet but talented engineer who was highly respected for his understanding of Wiemers' manufacturing processes, but he had little experience in other aspects of the business. It was expected that he would acquire that experience with J.W.'s tutoring.

J.W. had spent no more than a few minutes describing what he and Henry Brinson had observed in Michigan, when Ben Wiemer interrupted him.

"Goddamnit, J.W. I know where you're going with this discussion." He was angry. "You want to set up another goddamn giveaway program with our money. I wanta remind you, it's family money, not your money."

"Wait a minute, Ben. I didn't say anything about a creating a foundation or giving money away. Let me finish before you tee off on me."

Ben interrupted again, "Bullshit! You and Hank Brinson didn't go to Michigan to look at the tulips. As a member of this board and a family member, I want to be on record that this company and our family have been plenty generous to this community. Your mother and our grandparents shelled out the equivalent of millions of dollars to Hammelburg. The rest of us have to subsist on salaries or dividends. There's a limit to the do-gooder mentality among the other owners of this company. You already reduced the dividend and there's no goddamn market for the stock of a family-owned company. So we all sit here with shares of stock we can't sell, and you want to start giving more of the profits away. I'll be goddamned if I'm going to agree to something like that!"

His anger reflected a combination of his past disagreements with J.W. in which J.W. nearly always prevailed, and many years of resentment of J.W.'s leadership role. Ben thought J.W. was given the top job much too early in his career, and despite J.W.'s success, Ben's resentment had not been mollified.

J.W. wasn't surprised by Ben's opposition, but did not anticipate his angry reaction. Other members of the board were embarrassed that a family dispute had surfaced at a meeting with outsiders present.

Before J.W. could respond, Gus Arnholt spoke. "J.W, I don't know what you were going to recommend, but Ben is right about dividends and the liquidity of our stock. Maybe its time to increase dividends before we do anything else."

J.W., with a calm voice, attempted to abandon the subject. "O.K. it was an idea that I wanted to discuss with the board. I think you have pretty well convinced me you won't support it. . So let's go on with the remaining agenda."

J.W.'s remarks were followed by an awkward silence. To everyone's surprise, Peter Goldman continued to pursue the subject. Peter rarely spoke at board meetings.

"Before you move on, J.W., I'd like to comment on a point that Ben made. Wolverine Chemical.is a public company, we've helped finance them. But there is still a substantial amount of family ownership in the company. The advantage is the family can sell their shares because Wolverine stock is traded on the New York Stock Exchange."

"I bet they sold a goddamn boatload of it before they let the company start skimming off five percent of their profits for charity," Ben growled.

Peter continued. "Maybe its time to consider making Wiemer Industries a public company, having an initial public offering of a small amount of stock. We're a fine company, profitable, well-established. I think there is a market for Wiemer stock. It would give the family some liquidity. In fact, those who need liquidity could sell some of their shares at the same time; a secondary offering combined with an initial public offering. Moreover, it gives the company the ability to raise additional capital by selling shares. The company's performing well and I think the market might pay a good price for some of Wiemer's stock."

Gus Arnholt was obviously pleased with his friend's suggestion. "I think Peter may have a good idea. We ought to look at a public offering. If we want to create a foundation and contribute a portion of the pre-tax profits, we could vote to do that simultaneously with a public sale. That way we don't have to worry about shareholder objections. Anyway, the family would still own most of the stock and we would still control the company."

Ben Wiemer continued to object. "I don't give a shit if we are public or private. I'm opposed to giving the company's profits away. If we've got that much money, increase the goddamn dividend."

Stefan Wiemer usually confined his comments at board meetings to technical issues, but he decided to weigh in on this issue. "Ben, you and I have been around for a long time, but we both have adult children who aren't ever going to be part of the company. They don't live in Hammelburg, and they never will. Phyllis and I want to leave our shares to our children. But the time will come when they will want to sell Wiemer stock. I think Peter has an idea we ought to evaluate, regardless of how we feel about charitable contributions versus dividends."

"You mean you wanta sell the goddamn company, Stef. Hell, if you wanta sell out, I might buy your shares. I might buy out anyone else that wants to sell their Wiemer stock. I've worked at this company my whole life. I'll be goddamned if I am going to sell out and have some East Coast sonofabitch come in and tell us how to run the company."

"Cool down, Ben," J.W. interjected. "No one's talking about selling the entire company. All Peter suggested was that we consider selling some shares to the public and create a market for Wiemer stock. We could sell ten percent of the shares and still control ninety percent. No one can tell us how to run the company if we own ninety percent, even if only one person bought the other ten percent."

He was embarrassed by Ben's reference to the East Coast. It was a thinly disguised anti-Semitic remark, and he assumed that Peter Goldman recognized it.

"I think it's worth exploring," Gus Arnholt suggested again. "Why not ask Peter to go back to Boston and discuss it with his organization and see if there's a market for Wiemer stock. It would give the family some liquidity and the company access to larger capital markets if we want to expand."

With the exception of Ben Weimer, the board approved Gus Arnholt's suggestion. J.W. attempted to pacify Ben by reminding him it was only an informal exploration; no decisions had been taken. No further mention was made of corporate donations and foundations.

In March of 1966, Peter Goldman's firm, Wolf and Feldman, underwrote a public offering of 100,000 new shares of Wiemer Industries common stock. It was a highly successful transaction. Despite the discussion at the board meeting, no one in the family elected to sell any of their shares. There was no secondary offering. The demand for the stock exceeded the offering fourfold. The company received $15.6 million after the payment of underwriting fees. After the sale, 87 percent of the ownership of the company was retained by family members. A large part of the success was attributed to J.W.'s presentations to groups of prospective investors, organized by Wolf and Feldman and other investment banking firms that participated in the underwriting. Presentations were held in New York, Boston, Chicago, Houston, San Francisco, and Los Angeles, all within ten days prior to the offering date. An executive jet aircraft was hired to transport J.W. and Peter Goldman to the meetings.

Following the offering, several articles appeared in the financial press heralding the success of the venture and praising J.W.'s presentation of Wiemer Industries to the investors. Two months after the stock sale, Wiemer Industries shares were listed on the New York Stock Exchange, and the share price had risen by 20 percent.

Wolf and Feldman also directed their public relations staff to seek publicity for Wiemer Industries to help bolster the market for the stock.

In July of 1966, a feature article appeared in *Business Week* magazine, bearing the title "Wiemer Industries: a Company and a Community." The article described the history of Wiemer Industries, its success and growth since its founding, and its recent transition from a private to a publicly-traded company. It praised the contributions that the company and the Wiemer family had made to the community. It described the positive relationship between Wiemer management and its employees and the community, and included brief interviews with workers and community leaders. Pictures of the German-American Culture Center and the recently constructed Hammelburg Preschool Preparation Center were highlighted. The article concluded with a description of the current construction and expansion of the Hammelburg Regional Hospital, an expansion from a county hospital to a regional hospital serving northeastern Indiana with both basic and advanced medical care.

Several weeks later, the financial section of the Sunday *New York Times* published a lead article regarding Wiemer Industries and Hammelburg.

The article praised the company and the community for its progress and commitment to the quality of life. The article also carried a a lengthy interview with J.W., in which he attributed the success of the company to the efforts of all of its employees, community support, and emphasized the need to share the economic benefits with all those who contributed.

At a board meeting in October of 1966, J.W. again proposed a resolution that would permit four percent of before-tax profits to be contributed to a company-controlled foundation, the WI Foundation. Ben Wiemer continued to protest strongly, insisting on larger dividend payments, but the board approved the resolution. At the annual shareholder meeting in April 1967, 80 percent of the shareholders voted in favor of the resolution.

In November of 1966, Ben and Stefan Wiemer elected to sell half of their shares. It was a secondary market transaction managed by Wolf and Feldman. As a result, the family ownershi declined to 65 percent. Max and Katherine Wiemer Arnholt elected not to sell. They continued to hope, that in time, Gus would become CEO. J.W. and Phillip Rieff's holdings of Wiemer shares were smaller than other family members, and a substantial portion of the Rieff family shares were now controlled by the Wiemer/Rieff Foundation. The increase in the number of shares publicly traded resulted in greater interest in Wiemer Industries, and the share price continued to rise.

Folowing the sale of their shares, it was agreed that Ben and Stefan would no longer serve on the board of directors and would be replaced with two additional outside directors. J.W. requested that Henry Brinson and Peter Goldman help select two new outside directors. After six months of interviews and discussion, two candidates were asked to join the board, and both accepted: Cyrus Brown, vice chairman of the National Bank of Chicago, and Quentin Phillips, senior vice president of Puritan Securities, a large Boston-based investment company . The Wiemer board of directors was now comprised of seven members, three inside and four outside directors.

Soon after the new appointments to the Wiemer board, J.W. experienced the reciprocity that exists between fellow board members; he was asked to join several boards of directors of other corporations. Creighton Scientific Laboratories in Cleveland was the first to enlist him. Quentin Phillips was also a member of the board. The company was engaged in research and manufacturing of electronic sensors and signal devices. It was considered a well-managed company that had grown rapidly due to its ability to provide cutting edge electronic equipment for the Defense Department. Seven months later, J.W. was asked to join the board of Banner Pharmaceuticals, a large drug company based in Chicago. Cyrus Brown had been on the Banner board for several years. The following year, he joined the board of trustees of Wabash College and the board of directors of United States Electric Power Company, a large public utility holding company based in New York City. The chairman and CEO of Creighton Scientific was also a board member and chairman of the nominating committee.

With the successful stock offering, the publicity regarding Wiemer Industries and Hammelburg, and the continued success of the company, J.W. had attracted the attention of the ubiquitous "business establishment," a small, informal coalition of senior business executives who had a long history influencing the direction of U.S. industry and economic policy. They associated and served together in many capacities—as directors of the largest and most prosperous corporations, trustees of prominent private universities, directors of well-established research institutes, and appointees to high-profile government committees. As an attractive, articulate, liberal Republican, graduate of a prestigious private college, and chairman and CEO of a successful company, J.W. had all the appropriate prerequisites. His inclusion was confirmed when he was asked to become a member of The Business Council, a select group of business leaders who gathered twice a year at an exclusive spa with the leaders of Congress, Cabinet secretaries, and the senior officials of the administration, including, on occasion, the President of the United States.

During the 1960s, Wiemer Industries continued to benefit from the rapid expansion of the U.S. economy. The demand for their conventional products, values, and filter systems was strong, but the market for the new hydraulic and pneumatic control devices had grown much faster. By the close of 1969, Wiemer sales totaled $3.7 billion and profits before tax reached $372 million. In January 1970, the Wiemer board of directors approved a two-for-one stock split and a ten percent increase in the cash dividend. They also announced that the 1969 donation to the WI Foundation totaled nearly $3 million, and they approved the purchase of a six-passenger executive jet aircraft at a cost of $4.5 million.

By the end of the decade, Wiemer Industries employed nearly 5,000 people in Alamost County. General Motors and the Radio Components Corporation had also created more jobs in Hammelburg; collectively, they employed 8,700. But the impact of Japanese auto and electronic imports had begun to negatively affect both companies. Barker Packaging, a glass container manufacturer, had failed to recognize the rapid shift from glass bottles to aluminum cans in the beverage industry, and their business and employment had declined. They now employed 800, down from a peak of 2,300 in the mid-1960s.

J.W. and Mary's family life was also in transition. Their son, Alfred, referred to as Al by family and friends, had elected to finish his final three years of high school at a private preparatory school in Connecticut. During his first year, he was required to repeat what had been his freshman year at Hammelburg West High School; therefore, he spent four years at the preparatory school. Although initially shunned as a small town Midwesterner, he established friends quickly as a member of the junior varsity lacrosse and varsity soccer teams. A diligent, but not brilliant student, late in his final year, he was accepted for admission at Middlebury College in Vermont. Influenced by his Uncle Phillip, he elected to study history and languages. His sister Susan, five years younger, was about to enter high school in Hammelburg. She firmly rejected the idea of following her brother's path, after listening to his tales of life at a boarding school. An attractive girl, popular among both male and female classmates, she had no desire to leave Hammelburg. She was an average student who enjoyed the social aspects of school much more that the academic.

Mary was deeply involved in the direction of the Wiemer/Rieff Foundation, spending much of her time reviewing proposals with the staff. She had also agreed to serve on the board of trustees of Stephens College, and as a member of the Indiana Commission on Higher Education. Her workload at the Wiemer/Rieff Foundation increased when Phillip Rieff agreed to spend a one-year academic sabbatical teaching at the Free University of Berlin. Both the Wiemer/Rieff Foundation and the WI Foundation were heavily involved in attempting to convince Purdue University to establish a branch campus in Hammelburg. Several million dollars had been set aside by the foundations to assist in financing the new campus.

However, several members of the Hammelburg School Board were promoting another plan. They urged Purdue to acquire Hammelburg Central High School, an old building in the middle of the city that was scheduled to be replaced by a new high school building currently being erected, Hammelburg North High School. There was considerable disagreement about this proposal. Those favoring the takeover of the old school believed that Purdue could establish a branch campus much faster and cheaper by occupying the old high school building, permitting the city to sell a building that would otherwise stand idle. Mary and others believed that Hammelburg should establish a campus that would provide an appropriate educational environment, with new buildings capable of attracting full-time faculty members and expanding to meet the community's growing demand for higher education. The argument raged around immediate cost benefits versus long-term objectives.

The issue was resolved when the WI Foundation offered to buy Hammelburg Central High School, renovate it, and establish The Hammelburg Learning Center. The purpose of the Center was to assist disadvantaged public school students and adults who had not completed their secondary education. Purdue would be located on a new campus, with the financial assistance of both foundations. Despite the community support for the proposal, there were several influential critics who believed that the two foundations and J.W. and Mary Rieff exerted too much influence in the community. They were criticized for using their money to achieve their own personal goals, regardless of the opinions of others in Hammelburg. Mary, in particular, was considered by critics as an outsider who used her husband's money and influences to achieve her liberal agenda. She was Anne Rieff reincarnated.

In the fall of 1971, shortly after Quentin Phillips became CEO of Puritan Securities, J.W. was asked to serve on the board of directors. J.W. was now in his late fifties and a member of eight boards of directors, including Wiemer Industries. At the end of the year, he announced that he would continue as chairman of the board of Wiemer Industries, but Harry Achaffer would assume the role of president and CEO. Achaffer would be responsible for the operation of Wiemer Industries. He also resigned as chairman of Alamost National Bank and requested that the bank's board of directors select Henry Brinson to succeed him. J.W retained an office and secretarial support staff at Wiemer corporate headquarters, but spent most of his time traveling, attending outside board meetings, and focusing attention on the WI Foundation. He had also become chairman of the endowment fund at Wabash College and served on The Presidential Commission to Evaluate Trade Relations with Developing Countries. The corporate jet had become his primary means of transportation.

The prosperity and growth that characterized the 1960s ended in the early 1970s. Wiemer Industries was not excluded from the slowdown. By late

1972, the company had experienced its first decline in annual sales in 20 years. Profits were less than half those reported in 1969. Management announced that significant layoffs would begin immediately following Thanksgiving. Despite the slowdown in demand, price inflation was exacting a heavy toll on both operating costs and the cost of living. As the Christmas holidays approached, layoffs accelerated and costs of living continued to escalate. The dissatisfaction among Wiemer employees was surfacing in the plants and the community. A strong working relationship between first line supervisors, the foremen, and workers began to unravel.

It became evident that the pace of work was slowing as people became uneasy about additional layoffs. The unofficial motto was "make the work last." The current three-year labor contract was due to expire on March 1, 1973. Preliminary negotiations had started, but both sides were reporting little progress. Wiemer Industries had never experienced a strike, but the word on the shop floor and in the local bars was that 1973 may be the year of the strike. The tension was exacerbated when General Motors announced a large layoff coupled with a decision to move a portion of the manufacturing activity from Hammelburg to a new plant in Louisiana, where operating and labor costs were lower. Radio Components Corporation was suffering severe price competition from Japanese and Taiwanese competitors who benefited from lower labor costs. Consequently, the management was insisting on wage and job reductions. The Electrical Workers Union accused management of bad faith bargaining and threatened a walkout. Returning Vietnam veterans were unable to find employment and the merchants in Hammelburg agreed that Christmas sales were going to be meager.

Less than one year after assuming the leadership role at Wiemer Industries, Harry Achaffer, the new CEO, was suddenly struggling to maintain control of the company. Gus Arnholt, the CFO—embittered at having been passed over for CEO—was not sharing vital financial information with Achaffer before sending it to the board of directors. Consequently, Achaffer was receiving frequent telephone calls from J.W. and other board members requesting explanations regarding information he had never seen. By early February, no significant progress had been made in establishing a new labor contract with the IMU. Although the proposals put forth by the IMU were not considered out of the range of settlement, the executive who represented management in the negotiations appeared to lack the experience and emotional maturity to direct a contentious negotiation. In addition, he was in the midst of a difficult divorce settlement. The union

129

was represented by a bargaining committee that had little, if any, previous experience in labor negotiations. In an effort to reduce operating losses, Achaffer had decided to institute a temporary ten percent wage reduction for all salaried personnel. He assumed it would demonstrate management's willingness to participate in the pain of a business downturn and encourage the union to settle before the contract expired.

Gus Arnholt elected to confront Achaffer about the ten percent wage reduction at an executive staff meeting.

"I speak for myself, Harry, but I am offended by being asked to accept a salary reduction. It makes us look weak in union negotiations. The union thinks that we're so desperate to settle that we're willing to cut management salaries."

Achaffer recognized what Arnholt was attempting to do. It was retaliation. The previous day he had requested that Arnholt discontinue sending financial information to the board of directors before he reviewed it with him and the executive staff. In turn, Arnholt had insinuated that Harry was attempting to hide important information from the board. He detested Arnholt. He considered him a legacy from the period of family ownership. In Achaffer's opinion, Gus was incompetent, but had been promoted to both CFO and director because he was a family member. There was no other apparent reason. Moreover, no matter how much he disliked him or how incompetent he became, there was no way to remove him as long as J.W. was chairman of the board and the family maintained significant ownership in the company.

"I don't understand your reaction, Gus. We discussed that decision at length in this meeting two weeks ago, and it was agreed. Why are you raising the issue now, after it's been announced and implemented?"

"Because it's wrong" Gus replied "It makes us look weak with the IMU. It looks like we are capitulating to their goddamn ridiculous demands."

Harry Achaffer grew up on the east side of Cleveland. His father was a master machinist at the General Electric components plant in Euclid, Ohio. He graduated from Latin Cathedral High School before attending Ohio State University, where he studied mechanical engineering. He was tall and thin, and his hairline was receding rapidly. While in high school, he broke his nose in an automobile accident, and it was set improperly. It was an attractive disfigurement for a senior executive in a tough industry. His wife, Jane, was a physical therapist at the local hospital. She continued to work despite the fact that her husband was the CEO of Wiemer Industries. They had no children.

"I still don't follow your logic, Gus. In my opinion, the IMU's proposals are not out of range of negotiation, and how does the salary reduction make us appear weak to the IMU?"

Gus continued to avoid answering Harry's questions. It was a technique he had adopted to permit him to make contentious speeches at staff meetings.

"The IMU knows we don't have to negotiate. We don't have to give 'em anything. Let 'em walk. See how long they like being on a picket line in March. They've never had that experience before. We need to be tough. Teach 'em a lesson. A couple days on the picket line and they'll be back with their tail between their legs. They've got no leadership and no support for a strike. We oughta put a minimum offer on the table and tell 'em to take it or walk. The negotiations have been going on too long. We need to show some steel. We don't run this company for the benefit of that goddamn union or the community. We are paid to run it for the benefit of the shareholders. The people on Wall Street think we're a bunch of pussies with all our corporate paternalism and do-gooder publicity."

Although no one voiced support for Gus, neither did anyone argue with him. Gus was, after all, a senior officer, a director of the company, and a family member.

By the end of February, little progress had been made in achieving a new contract. Despite Gus Arnholt's predictions, on Friday, February 28, 80 percent of the IMU membership elected to strike. It continued for 67 days before a settlement was reached and the original IMU demands were granted. But the length of the strike and its bitter residue created a permanent change in the relationship between the IMU and Wiemer Industries. It was the beginning of a deep division within the Hammelburg community.

By the end of June, business conditions were still weak and price inflation had accelerated. Interest rates were rising rapidly while stock prices and corporate profits continued to sink. Wiemer Industries was no exception.

In addition, the loss of sales and income during the 67-day strike had compounded the company's financial problems.

At the July board of directors meeting, Harry Achaffer made a presentation describing the potential for several new products and manufacturing techniques that had been developed by the Wiemer research and development staff. The adoption of new synthetic materials in their products, he explained, could both reduce the cost of manufacturing valves and hydraulic components, and improve their durability and life cycle. He explained, with specific illustrations, how the adoption of these materials could give the company a significant competitive advantage and reduce costs. He also conducted a plant tour to demonstrate new forging equipment that would reduce cost and improve their products.

At the conclusion of his presentation, he recommended that the board of directors approve a 20 percent increase in the 1973 and 1974 operating and capital budget to help finance the adoption of these programs. He explained, however, that cash required to finance the programs would require a reduction in the company's current cash dividend to shareholders. He proposed a reduction in the annual dividend from $2.10 per share to $1.25 per share. The dividend reduction would generate at least 40% of the increased cash requirement over the next 18 months. He stressed the importance of immediate implementation of his proposals to assure that the company achieved the competitive advantage and financial benefits. Any delays, he warned, would negate their advantage. Market intelligence indicated that their competitors were developing similar products, but their efforts were not as advanced as Wiemer Industries'.

Achaffer had discussed his proposal with Gus Arnholt several weeks before the meeting. Gus had agreed that the company could not generate enough cash from operations to finance the projects without reducing the dividend. He also recommended against borrowing, as interest rates were rising and the restrictions placed on the company by the lenders would be onerous. Both men concluded that selling new shares of stock to raise the capital was a poor alternative, given the recent sharp decline in the stock market. Achaffer had assumed that Gus would support his proposal. He had given no indication that he would oppose it.

As soon as Achaffer had completed his presentation and returned to his seat, J.W. asked if anyone on the board wished to discuss Harry's recommendation. Quentin Phillips inquired if there was any indication of how the stock market might react to a reduction in Wiemer's cash dividend.

Gus Arnholt responded quickly before Harry Achaffer could speak.

"The stock price will drop like a rock," he proclaimed. "A dividend cut is anathema in this stock market environment. It wouldn't surprise me to see a 50 percent reduction in the price in less than two weeks. A dividend cut sends a strong negative signal to the market. Particularly in a market as uncertain as the current one."

Harry Achaffer was stunned. He had no idea that Gus would raise an objection. "Wait a minute, Gus. I don't agree. I think we can explain to the market why we want to do this and the benefits that will result from making these investments. Investors and shareholders can understand the trade-off advantage of a dividend cut now for a significant improvement in future earnings. Other corporations have reduced dividends recently," he said.

Gus shook his head and smiled condescendingly, implying that Harry was naïve and uninformed.

"I am sorry, Harry. I wish the markets were that patient. But I've talked with several investment bankers about the impact of a dividend cut, and they all recommend against it. In this market, we're going to be crushed, no matter how nicely you attempt to explain the reason for lowering the dividend. Wiemer Industries has already demonstrated to the market that management doesn't know how to manage labor relations, and a dividend cut would suggest it knows even less about finance."

An icy silence prevailed. The edge on Arnholt's response was too sharp.

"Let me understand, Gus," J.W. said. "You actually called several investment bankers and told them we might reduce our dividend and asked them for advice?"

"Yes," Gus replied confidently

"I find that rather unusual, Gus. Did you explain why we might cut the dividend and what we intend to do with the cash savings?"

"I didn't think it was appropriate to reveal all of our plans to the investment bankers. I only inquired about their reaction to a dividend cut," Gus replied.

"Well, what the hell did you expect them to say if all you revealed was a possible dividend cut?" J.W.'s tone revealed his irritation.

Gus smiled and looked at the outside directors, suggesting he considered the question a reflection of J.W.'s lack of financial sophistication.

"J.W., the investment bankers aren't stupid. They know we aren't going to throw the savings out the window."

"When did you make those calls?" J.W. asked.

"Last week, in preparation for this meeting," he responded.

"Do you think those conversations may have had anything to do with the sharp decline in our stock price during the past five days?"

Gus removed his glasses, pinched the bridge of his nose, and put his glasses back on before responding. "It would be difficult to establish any correlation between those brief conversations and our stock price. After all, the market doesn't view the recent management decisions of this company as comforting." he replied.

The wince among the other board members was nearly audible.

"Mr. Chairman…" Quentin Phillips paused momentarily before continuing. "I am enormously impressed and encouraged by what Harry has shared with us today. I think his recommendations should be accepted, but I suggest that we table the idea of reducing the dividend until the recent confusion in the market can be cleared away. Perhaps there are other sources of cash that can be used temporarily until this problem is solved."

Everyone looked at Harry Achaffer. He looked at the chairman, and without any indication of emotion, he responded, "We'll see."

Thirty minutes later, the meeting was concluded. It was late afternoon, and board members who did not reside in Hammelburg were chauffeured to the local airport to board the corporate jet.

The following morning at 9:00, Harry Achaffer approached J.W.'s office. His door was open. he was studying the front page of the *Wall Street Journal*. Harry tapped lightly on the door to attract his attention. As soon as J.W. greeted him, he asked if he could spend a few minutes with him. Harry closed the office door before he sat down. J.W. recognized this gesture as an ominous sign.

J.W. decided to speak first. "Harry, I want to apologize to you for the outcome of that meeting yesterday. You made a splendid presentation. Very reassuring and convincing, and I want to assure you that the board supports you. I have no idea what the hell got into Gus. It was a ridiculous scenario."

Harry smiled. "I appreciate your confidence and support, and I have given a lot of thought to yesterday's meeting, as well as the events of the past year. Jane and I had a long conversation last night about our future. And we've a made a decision."

He paused for a moment and cleared his throat. "J.W., I'm resigning as president and CEO of Wiemer Industries effective the end of this month."

He paused briefly, but not long enough to permit J.W. to respond. "It's hard for me to express how much I admire you and how grateful I am for the opportunities you've provided me, but I am convinced that my resignation is the best course of action for Wiemer Industries and me."

J.W. frowned, looked down at his desk, and massaged the back of his neck with his left hand. "I know what this is all about, Harry. It's Gus. I'm aware that he has been attempting to undermine you, and I intend to put a stop to it, today. I am going to have a long and serious discussion with him at lunch. There is no reason for you to resign over this issue. You're too important to this company to allow this situation to be an obstacle to your leadership."

"J.W., I appreciate that," Harry said, "but no matter what you say to Gus or how hard you scold him, it won't change my mind. This situation has gone too far. I should have come to you months ago and discussed Gus and his behavior. I didn't think it was a manly thing to do. I was wrong. Sometimes we get confused about what constitutes manhood," he smiled. "Gus and I can't operate under the same roof. I can't work with a CFO I don't trust. I know and appreciate the fact that you can't fire him. He's a family member, and Wiemer Industries is still, basically, a family-owned company."

Their conversation continued for 40 minutes. J.W. was unable to dissuade Harry from resigning. They agreed that his departure would be announced within the company the following Monday morning, and a press release and statement to the New York Stock Exchange would be issued Monday afternoon.

J.W. spent the balance of the morning placing calls to outside directors to inform them of Harry's decision. Cyrus Brown, Quentin Phillips, and Henry Brinson also expressed deep regret and asked if they might help convince Harry to remain with the company. J.W. told them he was convinced that Harry could not be turned around. Peter Goldman expressed regret and wanted to assure J.W. that he was not one of the investment bankers that Gus had called regarding a reduction in the dividend. He suggested that Wiemer Industries would be best served by hiring an executive search firm to seek a new president and CEO. In Peter's opinion, there were no qualified candidates within the company. J.W. agreed. Not one of the outside directors inquired what J.W. intended to do regarding Gus Arnholt.

Shortly before noon, J.W. walked in Gus Arnholt's office unannounced, closed the door, and sat down before saying anything. Arnholt was obviously surprised.

"Where we gonna eat lunch?" he asked.

"We're not," J.W. responded. "Harry Achaffer walked in my office this morning and resigned. And you and I are going to sit here and talk about that very disappointing event and the role you played in it."

Gus registered no surprise. "Well, I am sorry to hear about Harry's departure, but I don't understand your assumption that I played a role in his decision, J.W."

J.W. wasn't attempting to contain his anger. "That knife you stuck in his back at that board meeting yesterday may have played some part in it. However, I'm quite sure that is only one of many knife wounds you have inflicted on Harry during the past year."

"I am sorry, but I find that remark very offensive. I have had disagreements with Harry, but never have I done anything to challenge his leadership or anything that would justify such an accusation."

"Gus, that performance you put on yesterday after Harry made his presentation to the board was one of the saddest events in the long history of this company. Everyone in that room recognized what you were doing, and they were ashamed and embarrassed."

"Now, wait one moment, J.W.... "

"No," J.W. interrupted him, "I am not going to lament about that sorry event any longer. But I am sitting here with the full realization that this company is facing a series of fundamental challenges. In the next 18 to 24 months, we have to develop several new products and manufacturing techniques to assure our future growth and profitability, and the man who was capable of leading that effort just resigned, and you played a large part in his decision to leave."

"That is ridiculous. I refuse to become the scapegoat or whipping boy for Harry's departure. Moreover, there are other people in this organization who can provide leadership"

J.W. glared at Gus before responding. "Gus, you're a member of a family and a community that has spent the past century working together to build a very successful economic enterprise. It happened because lots of people were willing to put their own personal ambitions aside and work together to achieve success. If Wiemer Industries hopes to continue to succeed, it's going to require the same amount of selfless dedication and support. I'm recommending to the board of directors that we hire an executive search company to help us identify the most capable leader we can find to serve as president and CEO of this company. There will be no inside candidates. If you find that unacceptable, I suggest you follow Harry."

By the close of 1973, the founding families controlled less than 40% of Wiemer Industries common stock.

Chapter 12

Will Heider and Jimmie Hudson left the Hammelburg Inn together and had a brief conversation in the parking lot. Before parting, Will again agreed to call Jimmie the following day. Will sat in his car a few moments before starting the return trip to his parents' home. He was in a quandary. Following his initial phone conversation with Jimmie, he assumed he would either avoid a meeting or visit his parents and treat the meeting as a perfunctory event. The brief luncheon discussion with Sam Thomas had modified that initial assumption. He admired Sam, and was surprised by the strength of his response to Kevin O'Neal. He never expected a senior member of the firm to defend those arguments. The discussion with his parents had also given him reason to approach today's meeting with more interest.

The meeting with Jimmie Hudson also softened his approach to the issue. His dad was right: Jimmie was an intelligent, mature leader. He appeared to understand the difficult situation the IMU faced in the current negotiations, but he wasn't a whiner or hypercritical of the Wiemer management. His criticism of Byron Hinkle seemed legitimate. It appeared that Hinkle had not protected his client's interests in past contracts and wasn't playing an appropriate role in the current negotiations. He was puzzled as to how a competent lawyer would allow the other side to insert the "pending financial hardship" phrase into the final contract without challenging it. Professional ethics required that such a change of wording be highlighted to draw attention to it. He couldn't believe a well-known law firm would commit such a breach of legal ethics. He also recognized that he should both read the contract and talk with Bryon Hinkle before drawing any firm conclusions, but it was that acknowledgement that triggered the realization that he was far more involved in this issue than he could have ever imagined four days ago.

He smiled as he recalled Shirley Kovac's premonitions.

When he returned to his parents' home, his father was seated in the living room, watching a college football game. "Well, how was the meeting?" he asked.

Will had anticipated the question long before he entered the house. "It was a good meeting. You're right about Jimmie. He's impressive. I'm going to go upstairs and spend sometime studying this contract. I agreed to talk with him again tomorrow."

His mother entered the room from the kitchen; as always, she was wearing an attractive flowered apron over her dress.

"Did I hear you say it was a good meeting?"

"Well, yes. I learned a lot and I was impressed with Jimmie. I've got some work to do and I'll talk with him again tomorrow. I have to be cautious; I don't want to be drawn into any negotiation or litigation. They have legal counsel. I intend to offer a little pro bono advice and depart," he smiled.

His parents smiled but offered no response.

"After you're done with your work, how about your mother and I treating you to dinner at The Bavarian?" his father asked.

"I accept. I haven't been to the Bavarian for years. Does the Berghoff family still own it?"

"You bet. Four generations, and as popular as ever," his father answered proudly "One of the great-grandsons converted the old brewery into a microbrewery. Once again, we have Berghoff Bavarian Beer and Ale. The first time they've operated the old brewery since 1963. Very popular. They had to buy some adjoining property and take down the old buildings to enlarge the customer parking lot. One grandson is manager, the great-grandson is the brew master, and for the first time, a lady Berghoff is

139

involved. Nora Berghoff Taylor is the chef, a great-granddaughter of the founder. She also manages the wine cellar."

Will glanced at his mother; she was smiling like a young girl anticipating an evening out.

Will went upstairs to his room, obtained a yellow legal pad and pencil from his briefcase, sat down in the reading chair, and proceeded to study the entire Wiemer Industries-IMU contract while making notes.

Two hours later, he rejoined his father in the living room. The college scoreboard television programs were in progress. Will noted that both Indiana University and the University of Illinois had lost to their Big Ten opponents, but Notre Dame had staged a comeback and won by nine points.

"No surprises," he commented to his father.

At 6:30 they departed for The Bavarian Garden. When they arrived, the enlarged parking lot was nearly full. The restaurant was located on its original site, one block east of the city center. It first opened in 1910 as The Bavarian Gasthaus. The owner was August Berghoff, a German immigrant from Wurzburg, Germany. He had been an apprentice brew master before deciding to immigrate to the United States. It 1920, the Berghoff family elected to change the name to The Bavarian Garden. The name change reflected the influence of WW I and the establishment of Prohibition. Throughout the Prohibition period, it remained one of the most popular restaurants in Hammelburg, serving authentic German food. When Prohibition ended, the Berghoff family immediately reopened the brewery. It was a popular decision in a town with a significant appetite for good German food and beer.

Upon entering, they were informed by the head waiter that a table in the dining room would be available in 30 minutes. Paul Heider had forgotten to call for a reservation. Ruth mumbled something about his obsession with football. They were invited to take advantage of the bar while waiting. Ruth and Paul entered the bar. Will elected to observe the main the dining room.before joining them The décor had changed very little except that the restaurant was larger and the Bavarian landscape scenes that decorated the walls had been repainted and repaired. The traditions had been preserved. There was no recorded music or electronic sound, although he was sure that if he were to enter the kitchen, he would find a computer-driven ordering system. When he entered the bar to join his parents, he had trouble locating them. He finally saw them, sharing a table with four other people; an elderly couple, a middle-aged woman, and a young man. The others had been served drinks and his parents were in the process of ordering.

"Will, over here," his father called to him.

As he approached the table, his father informed him, rather loudly, that he had already ordered for him, a large stein of Berghoff Bavarian Ale. He then began introducing Will to the other people at the table.

"You may not remember Henry Brinson and his wife Elizabeth." Will acknowledged that he recognized the name and shook hands with both of the Brinsons.

"You've not met their daughter-in-law and grandson," Paul continued, "Beth Brinson and her son Tim."

Will greeted and shook hands with both of them.

"Beth is the general counsel for Wiemer Industries," Paul added. He then winked at Henry Brinson. "Gotta be careful tonight, Hank, we've got two lawyers at the same table."

"Let's not have any lawyer jokes this evening, Paul," Ruth responded.

Paul laughed and continued, "Tim, you're a biologist with Eli Lilly in Indianapolis, am I correct?"

"Yes," Tim acknowledged.

"And your twin brother?" Ruth asked.

"Bob's completing his internship in family medicine at University Hospital in Pittsburgh," Tim responded.

Beth Brinson smiled. "I should be able to obtain a lot of good medical advice at a very low cost."

141

During his 30-year tenure as president and chairman of the Hammelburg National Bank, Henry Brinson had arranged the acquisition of three other banks in northern Indiana. At the time of his retirement, Hammelburg National Bank ranked among the ten largest banks in Indiana. Three years later, it was acquired by a bank holding company based in Cleveland. There were no longer any Hammelburg-based banks. They had all been acquired by Cleveland, Chicago, and Cincinnati bank holding companies and had become large branches of the acquiring banks.

Henry Brinson had grown up in Springfield, Missouri, and graduated from Amherst College. During his third year of college, he met Elizabeth Faulk at a party in St. Louis. She was a junior at Stephens College. After graduation, they were married in St. Louis and moved to Chicago, where he started his career in commercial banking. Ten years later, they moved to Hammelburg, and Elizabeth Brinson assumed the role of a civic leader's spouse and dutifully raised two children: Ted and his younger sister, Louise. Not a bridge player or active in social affairs, Elizabeth served as a leader and fundraiser for several charitable organizations

Their son, Ted was a bright, sensitive boy. As he matured, he became exceptionally handsome, almost delicate in appearance. A junior high school phys ed teacher joked with a colleague, "The Brinson kid needs a scar on his face, he's too pretty."

The year before Ted was scheduled to enter high school in Hammelburg, his mother insisted that he attend a private school. There were few alternatives in the Midwest. Over his father's mild objection, he enrolled at St. Paul's Academy in New Hampshire, the school his maternal grandfather attended. Four years later, he enrolled at Amherst College, his father's alma mater. His father had fashioned the compromise

At St. Paul's he was an excellent student, but shunned other activities, particularly athletics. He maintained close friendships with a small group of students. He was awarded a Phi Beta Kappa key at Amherst and applied for admittance at one law school, Yale, where he met Beth.

Between his second and third year of law school, Ted worked as an intern with a Boston law firm. By the end of the three-month period, his interest in practicing law had nearly vanished. Before returning to Yale for his final year, he traveled to Hammelburg to attend his sister's engagement party. At the same time, he had a lengthy conversation with his father regarding his career plans. After returning to New Haven, Ted called his father and agreed to join the Hammelburg National Bank following completion of law school. His mother was opposed to his career selection, but withdrew her objection as she observed the pleasure her husband derived from Ted's decision. A few weeks later, Ted proposed to Beth. She accepted, and cautiously agreed to live in Hammelburg, on the understanding that she would practice law. Two months after their graduation, they were married in Pittsburgh.

The task of finding a job opportunity for an inexperienced female lawyer in Hammelburg became Henry Brinson's responsibility. Despite his considerable influence in the community, none of the local law firms accepted his proposal, which included a clandestine return of salary, if necessary. A female graduate of an Ivy League law school was a tough sell to small Midwest law firms that focused largely on estate and family law. With the wedding day only three weeks away, Henry invited J.W. Rieff to lunch at the Alamost Country Club.

At lunch, Ted described his difficult assignment. Following a rather brief mention of Beth's background in metallurgy, J.W. suddenly displayed a genuine interest.

"Hank, a lawyer with a background in metallurgy is a rare bird. We pay, God knows, how many thousands of dollars a year to law firms to protect our patent rights. We could save lots of money if we did it in-house, but we have never been able to attract a lawyer with a technical or engineering background. The big corporate law firms pick them off. It's tough for us to compete against the starting salaries and big city locations. Your new daughter-in-law may be the answer to our problem."

Three months after her wedding, Beth became the third member of the law department of Wiemer Industries. The general counsel, Lee Guthrie, was not enthusiastic about his new employee, but as he explained to the other member of the law department, "Her endorsement by J.W. and Hank Brinson renders resistance hazardous."

Beth passed the Indiana Bar Exam in near record time, and was fascinated with the opportunity for interaction with engineers and technical personnel. The exclusively male members of the engineering department were initially suspicious of a woman lawyer preparing patent filings for new or redesigned products. However, within a short time, admiration and appreciation for her speed of comprehension and efficiency replaced suspicion. Within a year, she was invited to attend and participate in technical meetings and seminars, an invitation that had never been extended to consulting patent lawyers. She had passed muster with the engineers.

Elizabeth Brinson became very fond of her daughter-in-law. She was Beth's confidant. Over time, the strength of Beth's relationship with Elizabeth Brinson equaled the affinity with her own mother. Beth continued in the Wiemer law department for three years. When she became pregnant, Elizabeth supported and encouraged Beth's decision to continue working until the end of her second trimester. However, following the birth of twin boys, she elected to remain at home. Elizabeth was always available to help, but never overbearing. Their mutual admiration continued to grow.

In the fifth year of their marriage, Beth sensed that Ted Brinson was restless. Although the responsibilities of a vice president at Hammelburg National Bank required little travel, Ted made frequent trips to New York and San Francisco. His explanation, at home, was that regional banks required correspondent banking relationships with large money center banks. Their personal life also began to deteriorate. Ted showed less interest in intimacy with Beth. With increasing frequency, he resisted her attempts to arouse him. She tried to convince herself that he was experiencing the temporary transformation from the freedom of the unmarried student to the confinements associated with marriage, children, and job-related responsibilities.

On one of several visits to San Francisco, Ted rekindled a friendship with a prep school classmate. After graduating from St. Paul's, Jeremy Horning earned a degree in electrical engineering at Rice University and joined a small electronics firm in Dallas. After three years, he took a leave of absence and enrolled in the MBA program at M.I.T. His next move took him to San Francisco as an associate with a large venture capital company. Jeremy was excited about the wealth he expected to accumulate and the liberated lifestyle in San Francisco. He encouraged Ted to join him. A degree from Amherst and a law degree from Yale were important attributes in the world of venture capital, according to Jeremy. When Ted suggested that he lacked sufficient experience in technology, Jeremy assured him that his education credentials and banking experience would offset any shortfall in technical expertise.

After returning from a second trip to San Francisco in the same month, Ted told Beth they needed time to talk. Over a cup of coffee in the family kitchen, he informed her that during the last year, he had come to the realization that he had made a serious mistake in agreeing to return to Hammelburg. He could no longer abide going to the bank every morning and listening to the trivia. He had to leave. He knew his decision would wound his father, but he had no choice.

Beth was surprised, but assured him that she would support his decision. He did not comment. After a short pause, he announced that he had accepted a position with a San Francisco-based venture capital company. Beth again expressed surprise and inquired when he intended to start. He answered, "Immediately."

Beth was stunned by his response. She asked, "When do we move?"

Ted stared at his coffee for awhile and in a quiet voice answered, "We're not going to move... I am."

Beth was not sure she understood what he said. "What do you mean?

She noticed that his hand was shaking as he placed the coffee cup in the saucer.

 He was experiencing trouble swallowing and his hands were trembling. He placed his hands in his lap before continuing. His voice sounded unnatural. "Beth, I don't want to be married any longer! I want to start a new life!"

She didn't respond.

"I love you and the boys with all my heart, but I need to start again. It's more than just leaving Hammelburg. I need to start a whole new life in an entirely different location. I can't do it partway. I can't include remnants of my current life."

She was stunned and angry. "Remnants, remnants! Those two boys upstairs and I are remnants?" Her eyes filled with tears as she continued. "I strongly suggest you seek medical advice before you begin this new life of yours," she hissed.

145

"No, Beth, it's the other way around. If I don't do this, I am going to require a lot of medical advice."

She felt dizzy. "Are you telling me that you intend to move to San Francisco by yourself, assume a new job, and desert your family all in one fell swoop?"

"I think desert is a pejorative word," he answered, as if he were raising an objection in a courtroom.

She resented his tone. He used it frequently when they argued. "Well, how the hell do you describe it, counselor?"

"I assure you, I'm not attempting to escape my obligations. You and the boys will be taken care of. You may have any or all of our assets you want. I promise you, I will recognize and meet all of my obligations as generously as possible. I am not abandoning my family."

"Have you informed anyone else of your big plan?" She realized that she was rapidly becoming overcome with anger and anguish.

"No. How could I do that before I talked with you?"

"Well, I appreciate your courtesy and consideration," she responded sarcastically.

"I have a meeting with Dad this afternoon," he said.

"What about your Mother?"

"I could never make it home before he called and told her."

She scoffed. "Jesus, isn't that neat. Talk about duck and run. If you really believe what you're doing is O.K., then call your parents together and tell them."

"I didn't say it was 'O.K.'. You're angry and you have every right to be. But I really believe what I am doing is best for both of us, the boys, and my family. From your perspective, it's an incredibly selfish act. I walk in after being gone for three days and spring this on you."

She interrupted him. "Three days! How about five years and two children?"

His voice cracked. "Let me finish, Beth. I can't believe that during the past year, you haven't sensed my feelings about my job, living in Hammelburg, and our marriage. It's not an impetuous decision. I've thought about it for months."

"O.K., I'll ask one more time. Have you told anyone else about your big plan?"

"I told you, I wouldn't discuss this with anyone before we talked."

She stood up. She was shaking. Her emotions were swinging from rage to despair and back again. "I want to check on the boys. Naptime is nearly over."

She left the room. Ted remained with his elbows on the table and his hands covering his face, attempting to hide his anguish.

After what seemed an eternity to Ted, she returned, sat down, but there was no conversation for several minutes.

She ended the silence, speaking in a controlled but tight voice. "Ted, before this surreal conversation goes any further, I am going to ask you a question and I want a direct, honest answer." She paused momentarily. "Is there another woman?"

Ted shook his head no, continuing to shield his face with his hands.

"Answer me, Ted, yes or no?" she shouted.

He lowered his hands and looked directly at her with red-rimmed eyes. "Christ, Beth, I wish there was, it might make this whole thing easier. There is no other woman."

As the waiter arrived with the Heiders' beverages, Henry Brinson began to talk about how much they enjoyed the uniqueness of the Bavarian Gardens and how unusual it was for a family to maintain a successful local business for nearly 90 years.

"It's a rare thing in our current economic setting. The local banks have all been acquired. As Paul well knows, the local merchants are disappearing rapidly. Nearly all the restaurants and the hotels are national chains. You can't find a locally-owned drugstore, shoe store, or hardware store any longer. I am told that local auto dealerships will soon be owned by national and regional companies."

Ruth Heider nodded in agreement. "Everything is the same. The regional and local distinctions have disappeared. It's really a cookie cutter approach to merchandising. It's boring," she said.

Henry Brinson continued, "Now the plants are closing. For the past decade, Hammelburg and Indiana have steadily lost manufacturing jobs. According to the economic pundits, all these unemployed people were going to get new high-tech jobs. But where the hell are the high-tech companies? Thousands and thousands of jobs, gone, and the middle class communities are disappearing. They vanish with the jobs. As middle class neighborhoods disappear, mobile homes are growing by leaps and bounds, despite the fact that the tornadoes play hell with 'em."

He paused momentarily to sip his drink. "Wiemer Industries is downsizing again."

He decided not to stand for reelection to the Wiemer Industries board of directors following his retirement from the bank.

"This whole damn dispute between the Wiemer union and the management is about relocation. Good jobs going to Mexico."

He glanced at Beth Brinson as he spoke. "Beth tells us the union may have a strong argument, but not a good lawyer to represent them."

Beth Brinson frowned, her face flushed.

Elizabeth Brinson admonished her husband. "I don't think Beth intended for us to repeat that, Henry. I hope the Heiders will disregard it."

"You don't need to be concerned about it being repeated," Paul Heider said. "Ruth and I rarely see anybody," he laughed.

A few seconds of embarrassed silence passed before Ruth Heider spoke. "Elizabeth, have you seen Mary Rieff recently?"

"No, but Beth has helped her on several of her projects."

"Yes," Beth responded, "I've been assisting her with the community heath project. She's still as busy as ever, but it's hard for her to maintain her old pace. She visits both of her children regularly. Al still owns a software company in Burlington, Vermont. He also founded an Internet company that buys and sells rare books. Susan lives in Seattle, recently divorced. She wants her mother to live with her in Seattle, but Mary refuses to leave Hammelburg. She is concerned about the community. The WI Foundation is, of course, closed and the Wiemer/Rieff Foundation tries to support the community, but its assets are nearly depleted."

Ruth said, "She's done so much for this community. I enjoyed working with her when we established Friends in Medicine. It must be difficult for her to watch what's happening to Hmmelburg."

"It is," Beth said, "but she's bound and determined to find some way to turn it around and revitalize the community."

There was another brief pause before Henry Brinson directed a question to Will. "From Paul's earlier remark, I gather that you're a lawyer."

"Yes, I'm member of that maligned fraternity," Will answered while smiling at his father.

"Where do you practice?" Beth asked.

"I'm a partner at Cutler Earl and Levin in Chicago."

"What's your specialty?"

"Labor law and some environmental law," Will said.

"Oh my God, I really did open my big mouth a moment ago, didn't I?" Henry Brinson said.

Will laughed.

"It must be a difficult time to be a labor lawyer with all the changes like NAFTA and environmental restrictions," Elizabeth Brinson said.

"I've been at it for more than 20 years, and I can't remember any period as difficult. We're experiencing fundamental changes in our economy. As Henry mentioned, it's taking a heavy toll on manufacturing jobs and middle income families. Hopefully, we'll transition to the next phase when new jobs emerge. The economists and the politicians seem confident that will happen," Will said.

"Do you believe it will happen?" Elizabeth asked.

Will hesitated for a moment before answering. As he was about to provide a noncommittal response, the head waiter arrived to announce that the Brinsons' table was available in the dining room.

He elected to disregard Elizabeth's question.

As the Brinsons were departing for the dining room, Beth Brinson paused for a moment and spoke to Will. "Which side of the negotiating table do you represent in labor negotiations?"

"Our firm has always represented management," he replied.

She appeared about to ask another question. She hesitated, shook hands with Will, and joined her family.

Chapter 13

The following morning, as Will arose, he glanced out of the bedroom window to discover a light snowfall had occurred overnight.

The first snow of the season, like a huge white sheet, had covered the fading fall colors and announced the end of autumn. Some color continued to emerge among the trees, but the slate gray sky and snow on the tree branches dulled the last remnants of Indian summer. Northern Indiana and snow in November; the end of nature's spectacular panorama of color, sunny weather, and harvest season. He remembered the excitement he experienced as a boy at the sight of the first snow; sledding on the hill in Wiemer Park with his brother, sister, and friends; touch football on a snow-covered field at Hammelburg West High School on Sunday afternoons; the anticipation of skating and pickup hockey games on the Wabash River as soon as the ice appeared.

The first snow usually accompanied the start of the high school basketball season; Indiana high school basketball, with its unique role in community identification and unification. The local rivalry between Hammelburg West, Hammelburg North, and St Ignatius, and the tournaments in Fort Wayne and Muncie, were all part of a pattern of pleasant boyhood memories in a small Indiana community. But he knew that Hammelburg was not typical. It was special. So many of those pleasant memories sprang from the common vision and sharing that rendered Hammelburg an unusual community; a community that, as a boy, he had been anxious to escape. Now, as a man, it was the source of many pleasant memories.

As he stood gazing at the fresh snow, he wondered what would happen to Hammelburg, its sharing, and the vision. What would happen as the good jobs disappeared if the new jobs didn't materialize? What would happen when those who created the vision were no longer available to sustain it? How would those who remained in Hammelburg realize the benefits that previous generations had experienced? Without the jobs and the economic opportunities, who would remain or return to Hammelburg to share and nurture the vision? Who would generate the economic wealth to advance the vision?

He again recalled the discussion with Sam Thomas and his comment that this economic change is creating value and someone is realizing it. Is it reverting to a zero sum game, as Sam suggested, where only a few win and the rest lose? It was the shared value of the community that distinguished Hammelburg. Without the creation and sharing of value, how could the vision be sustained?

After showering and dressing, he went downstairs to join his parents for breakfast. His mother had prepared a full breakfast. His father, suggested that Will visit more frequently to allow his father the luxury of a full Sunday breakfast. His mother agreed and insisted that his father would prepare the meals.

After breakfast, he called Jimmie Hudson. He had considered limiting the discussion to a telephone conversation, but after reading the contract, he decided a brief meeting was more appropriate. Jimmie was obviously pleased and asked if Will would object if he invited two other people to attend. Will did not welcome the proposal, but ask Jimmie who he intended to include. Jimmie thought it was important that two other IMU board members be included in the discussion. He assured Will that they wouldn't violate the arrangements that they had originally established.

"Norma Landis is secretary and treasurer of the IMU, and Jerry Bentenhausen is a member of the executive committee. Neither of them are members of the bargaining committee," Jimmie explained.

"I understand your reluctance, Will," he continued, "and I suggest that we meet at the IMU office. No one else will be there on Sunday, and it'll be completely out of public view. You and I having a beer together at the Inn on Saturday afternoon is probably considered two old high school buddies revisiting their youth. Three members of the IMU and you in public on Sunday afternoon might be interpreted differently."

"Jimmie, I am assuming that your two colleagues understand that I am not acting as counsel to the IMU, and that we are having informal conversations that will not be discussed outside of our meeting?" Will asked.

"I haven't invited them yet, Will, and I won't if you object. If they don't agree to those terms, they won't be there."

There was a long pause before Will responded. "O.K."

"How about two o'clock at the IMU office?" Jimmie offered.

"Where is it? Will asked.

"On North Anthony Street, two blocks south of the old foundry and forge plant. It's a small building on the right-hand side of the street. Light blue aluminum siding," Jimmie responded.

Will arrived at the IMU office a few minutes before 2:00. Three cars were already parked in the small, unpaved lot at the side of the nondescript square building. The blue aluminum siding was badly faded. A small sign appeared at the entrance to the parking lot identifying it as the IMU Headquarters. The entrance was a glass and aluminum storm door shielding a single wooden door with a small, round window. There were two high, rectangular windows in the front of the building and three on the side facing the parking lot.

As Will entered, he was greeted by a large black woman standing in front of an open drawer of a bank of four olive drab metal filing cabinets. She had short, tinted hair that was beginning to recover its natural dark color. She appeared to be in her mid-forties, medium height and overweight, dressed in black wool slacks, red turtleneck sweater and white athletic shoes. It was obvious that she purchased the sweater before she acquired some additional weight. She looked up and removed her reading glasses from the end of her nose. They dropped to her chest, attached to a black lanyard around her neck.

"Hi, you must be Will Heider." She closed the file drawer and moved toward Will to shake hands. "I'm Norma Landis. Jimmie is in the kitchen making coffee. God only knows how that will turn out," she laughed. Her smile suggested that she may have been very attractive as a younger, less corpulent woman. But her handshake and eye contact gave no hint of lack of confidence.

In addition to the filing cabinets, the room contained three metal desks and two desktop computers and keyboards. The dark green carpet was badly frayed. There were several group pictures on the side walls and a large wooden union crest displayed on the far wall. A No Smoking sign was posted above the union crest.

"We're going to meet in the board room," she said, and began moving toward a doorway on the left side of the room. She stopped suddenly and turned back. "Sorry, I forgot my notebook. Give me a second."

As Will waited for Norma, he noticed color photographs posted on a large bulletin board adjacent to the entrance to the board room. He moved closer to look at them. They were photographs of a squalid neighborhood of small homes no larger than a single-car garage, surrounded by barren soil. One of the pictures showed two small children and a young woman standing near the doorway of one of the homes. The doorway was covered with a heavy curtain. The children were poorly dressed and unhealthy looking. Another picture displayed a larger building in equally squalid surroundings with a large sign above the door, written in Spanish. Will recognized one of the words as "toilet." The fourth picture showed a small stream strewn with trash; the small houses and larger building appeared in the background.

He suddenly realized that Norma was standing beside him. "Those pictures were taken a few weeks ago near Juarez, Mexico, across the river from El Paso. Wiemer employees live in those houses. The showers and toilets are in the large building. There are no sewers. They use the small stream to get rid of their waste." Her explanation reflected no emotion. She looked directly at Will, seeming to study his reaction.

Will turned and looked at the pictures again. He was reminded again of the conversation with Sam Marshall. He tried to recall what Sam had said as they were parting; something about illusions that blind us to our own inconsistencies.

"Who took the pictures?" he asked.

"You're about to meet him," Norma replied.

The board room was illuminated by overhead fluorescent lights. It had a strong odor of mildew. There were no windows. It contained a rectangular wooden table with four chairs on each side and one at each end. The table appeared to be too large for the room, leaving little space along the sides and the ends. A path had been worn into the green carpet around the perimeter of the table. A large blackboard was mounted on the wall at one end of the room. A second doorway, on the far side of the room, was the entrance to a small kitchen.

An older man was seated on the far side of the table. He arose, leaned across the table to shake hands with Will, and introduced himself as Jerry Bentenhausen; a small, muscular man with close-cut gray hair and a short beard. He had a weathered appearance, like a man who had lived a hard life. He wore a plaid flannel shirt and brown corduroy pants. As he extended his right arm across the table, a portion of a deep scar was visible on the lower part of his forearm. He held the handshake for a few seconds to allow him to visually evaluate Will. His eyes were intense; he appeared to take a hard but not hostile look at Will. As he returned to his seat, Jimmie Hudson appeared in the doorway of the kitchen.

"Hi, Will, I guess you've met Norma and Jerry. I've made some coffee. Anybody wanta take a chance?"

Will was the only volunteer. Jimmie went back to the kitchen and returned with two mugs of coffee, both bearing the crest of the IMU. He handed one mug across the table to Will and sat down beside Jerry Bentenhausen, facing Will and Norma, who occupied seats on the opposite side.

"First time in a union hall, Will?" Bentenhausen asked with a sardonic grin.

"Oh no," Will responded. "I've been in lots of union halls. But, like today, always as a guest."

Bentenhausen laughed and smiled. He appeared to admire Will's refusal to be intimidated.

"I know your Dad and was acquainted with your brother. I use to buy a few things at Bernie's. I liked that store. Can't find another store that carries the same quality. Wal-Mart's doesn't come close," he said.

"I was in high school with your brother," Norma said. She laughed. "Tom was a rascal. Not as big a rascal as Jimmie, but he was a rascal."

Both Will and Jimmie laughed. Will, however, was surprised. He had never heard his brother described that way.

"My younger brother, Luke Tyrone, played football with you. He was a linebacker," Norma continued. "As I recall, you guys didn't win many games."

"Sure I remember Luke. We played together. I was a defensive back. You're right, our team will not be awarded a place in the Hammelburg West Sports Hall of Fame, but Luke was a hell of a linebacker. Didn't he get an athletic scholarship?"

"Yeah, two years at Michigan State; a knee injury in spring practice of his sophomore year ended his career. No more scholarship. He joined the marines. After three years, they sent him to officers training. He's still with them… just made Lt. Colonel."

There was a momentary silence before Jimmie spoke. "I wanta thank you again, Will, for agreeing to meet with us. All of us understand that you are not acting in any official capacity, and that this meeting is informal and not to be discussed outside of this room."

He paused for a moment to assure that his colleagues concurred and to give Will a chance to respond. Will nodded, but didn't speak.

"I assume you've had a chance to read the contract. We'd be interested to hear any comments or suggestion you may wanta offer."

Will opened the file folder that Jimmie had given him and withdrew the copy of the contract and his penciled notes. "I don't want to beat the subject to death, Jimmie, but before I comment, I want to make sure everyone understands that my remarks are informal, not a professional opinion, and I won't be compensated in any way other than yesterday afternoon's beer and today's coffee."

Jerry Bentenhausen laughed. He seemed to be warming to Will.

"I read the contract yesterday afternoon. I have about four major comments." He paused for a moment as he arranged his penciled notes. "First, I was surprised at the absence of a definition of 'pending financial hardship' or even 'financial hardship' in the preface of the contract."

He paused again to study his notes. "Second, in the absence of a clear definition of either 'pending financial hardship' or 'financial hardship,' I was also surprised to find that the contract has no arbitration provision in the event of failure to agree on the meaning.

"Third, I am confident that at some point, a definition of pending financial hardship is going to be contested. It is a vague concept. There is no commonly accepted meaning. If the parties can't agree to a definition, and there is no provision for arbitration, it may require litigation. It could become a contentious issue. Again, I am surprised that the term is not clearly defined in the contract."

Will paused, waiting for a response. After a brief silence, Norma spoke. "You said you had four remarks."

Will nodded in agreement, placed his elbows on the table, and placed the palms of his hands together.

"I probably should have been a bit more specific. My fourth comment is really a question, and, frankly, a rather delicate question. I am not sure you can answer it today, but I think it ought to be asked."

"Jimmie told me yesterday that your lawyer said he didn't see the addition of the phrase 'or pending financial hardship' when he reviewed the final draft submitted by Wiemer's attorneys. When lawyers exchange drafts of contracts, it is legal protocol to use italics or highlighting to call attention to any proposed changes. It saves time and money by allowing the other side to immediately identify the proposed amendments without having to re-read the entire document."

Will paused to clear his throat. "I presume he has a copy of that draft in his files. I suggest that you ask him if the change was highlighted or italicized in the final draft."

"If you don't follow protocol, is it a legal violation? Does it invalidate the contract?" Norma asked.

"Neither one," Will responded, "but it's considered a violation of legal ethics, if it's done intentionally."

"Suppose Byron Hinkle tells us that it wasn't highlighted, or he tells us it was. What can we do?"

"If it wasn't highlighted, it should be called to the attention of the opposing attorneys. If they acknowledge the failure, one remedy may be to agree on a specific definition; another is to submit it to arbitration," Will answered.

"What if they admit it but refuse to discuss it?" Jerry Bentenhausen asked.

"I assume that your attorney would seek another solution, maybe litigation, whereby the court provides a definition."

Jimmie leaned back in his chair and placed his hands behind his head. "What if it was highlighted? What can we do?"

Will shook his head and studied the ceiling of the room for a moment before responding. "Not a hell of a lot, Jimmie, other than what I suggested earlier. Seek immediate agreement on a specific definition." He didn't want to pursue that question any further if he could avoid it.

"Couldn we sue even if it was highlighted?" Norma asked.

"There's really no basis for litigation, other than as a last resort to clarify the meaning of pending financial hardship. I would assume both parties would be willing to sit down and attempt to reach an agreement on an appropriate definition. You can always file a lawsuit. But if they did highlight it, the judge is going to wonder why the hell the plaintiff's attorney didn't insist on a specific definition before recommending that his client approve the contract," Will answered.

"How would you define pending financial hardship?" Bentenhausen asked.

"That's the crux of the problem. The definition could land anywhere across a broad spectrum of meaning. At one extreme, it can mean the company is forced to file for bankruptcy protection, or what is referred to as Chapter 11. At the other end, it could be as innocuous as having to amend the terms of a bank loan before getting a renewal."

"The original wording, 'financial failure,' is pretty straightforward. It probably requires that the company demonstrate that it may be forced to file for bankruptcy. It isn't cut and dried, but it has a much more narrow interpretation than pending financial hardship."

"I'm sure Wiemer Industries is not even close to bankruptcy," Norma said.

Will turned and looked at Norma. "How can you be sure?" he asked.

"I looked at their last quarterly report," she replied.

"Norma's our official number cruncher and a damn good one," Jimmie said.

"I review their financial statements every quarter," Norma continued. "When J.W. Rieff was still involved, they gave us the financial statements. In fact, J.W. insisted that the accounting staff meet with us every quarter and review the quarterly statements. He thought it would be easier to deal with the IMU if we understood the company's financial condition. I learned a lot about corporate accounting at those meetings. After J.W. was gone, their lawyers told them to stop the meetings and stop giving us financial statements. So, we bought ten shares of Wiemer stock so we could see their quarterly and annual financials."

"How do they look?" Will asked.

"Wiemer Industries was in great shape until Adam Fulton became the CEO. He and that overstuffed Gus Arnholt decided that Wiemer Industries wasn't growing fast enough; so they went out and borrowed a lot of money to make acquisitions. That's when the trouble started. Now the banks run the company," she answered.

"Well, in that case, the definition of impending financial hardship may depend on Wiemer's relationship with their banks. If they've violated a major provision in a loan agreement, the banks may refuse to renew their loans and require immediate repayment. Having to suddenly repay all the loans that you intended to pay off over five or seven years could become a financial hardship. But that isn't what usually happens. Unless the company is really in bad shape, the banks are inclined to agree to renew the loans after they renegotiate the terms. The new terms may require the company to adopt some tough cost reduction programs and pay much higher interest rates or higher fees," Will said.

"I can tell you that Wiemer's interest expenses have increased a lot in the past few years, and the amount of loans they show on their balance sheet is a big number," Norma added.

Suddenly, Jimmie leaned forward in his chair. "Let me ask my question another way, Will. What if Hinkle admits it was highlighted? What can we do to him?"

That was the question Will had hoped to avoid. His response reflected it. "I really don't want to go there, Jimmie. It's a complicated issue. The short answer is nothing, and I don't want to talk about the long answer because it won't give you any more satisfaction than the first one."

"Should we fire him and get another lawyer?"

"I can't answer that question, either. All I can suggest is that you ask him if those three additional words were highlighted in the final draft. You may want to revisit that question after you've heard his answer. From a professional standpoint, I can't say any more than that."

Jimmie didn't respond. He studied the back of his hands, which were placed palms down on the table in front of him.

"You've been a big help, Will," Jerry Bentenhausen said. "I'm sorry we can't hire you. Jimmie told us you couldn't do that. But if we called you, would you be willing to give us some more advice?"

"That's a difficult question, Jerry. As I explained to Jimmie, my firm has never represented a union. We only represent management. If I agreed to give you more advice, I'd be stepping over the line of my professional responsibility to my firm and my partners. I am probably too damn close to the line already. If I were to go any further, it would require that my partners agree that I could provide legal counsel to the IMU on a pro bono basis. I'm not sure I want to do that, and I am convinced that they wouldn't agree to it."

"I don't understand that," Norma replied. "I know for a fact that Byron Hinkle has been hired by Wiemer Industries on several occasions."

Will sat for a moment and attempted to think how he might respond to Norma. He was reminded of an old joke: How should one make love to a porcupine? Very carefully.

Jimmie looked across the table at Will and smiled. "Do you think Byron also has a code of conduct?"

"I can't answer that question, Jimmie. I don't know Hinkle or anything about his practice."

Jimmie wouldn't relent. "Are you surprised that he has worked for both Wiemer and the IMU?"

Will wondered how he could terminate this conversation. He knew that another evasive answer would only prolong the discussion. He finally responded, "Yeah, Jimmie, I'm surprised."

Will thought this was the appropriate time to end the meeting, and he was about to suggest it, when Jerry Bentenhausen interrupted him. "Will, I've worked at Wiemer Industries for more than 40 years, except for a short break in Vietnam. If I'd come here two years later, I wouldn't a got a job. I didn't graduate from high school. I was a kid. Seventeen years old. I was proud as hell to get a job at Wiemer. The company trained a lot of machinists and foundry and forge workers, like me, like Jimmie. We were cocky kids who used to talk about the products we made, how and where they were used, improvements in design and manufacturing. I'm not sayin' we agreed with everything that happened, but we were real proud of what we made and how we made it."

He glanced at Jimmie before continuing. "Two things happened that changed all that. The first one was the attitude of the IMU. The union was J.W. Rieff's idea. It was a good one. It worked real well, for a while.

The second was the management. The Wiemer family doesn't own the company anymore. I don't know who owns it. I've never seen them. I wouldn't know them if they walked through the plant. I don't know who they are or where they live. I don't know who the hell I'm workin' for, and they don't know a goddamn thing about me and probably don't want to."

"What do you think has happened?" Will asked.

"You heard Norma. When you talk about the company, you only talk about numbers. How much profit, how much cost, how much money is invested, how much wages have increased, how much benefits cost, how much money management makes. You gotta make the numbers every month, or the market, whatever the hell that is, won't like it and the stock price will go down. Product quality is important, so long as you make the numbers. It ain't about people, or products, its only numbers."

Norma nodded in agreement, and added, "

It isn't just management; the union's no damn better. For years, the company had a big Christmas party for all the employees. The kids all got presents, Santa Claus handed 'em out. Everyone got a turkey and trimmings. We all got together for one day a year and celebrated, kinda like a big family. Ten years ago, the IMU told the management we don't want the party anymore, just give us the money and we'll buy our own turkey. We figured how much the party cost and said to hell with kids, and Santa Claus, and the family fun, we'll take the money."

Will shrugged off the remark. "Well, Norma, a lot of unions and companies stopped doing that. It was considered paternalistic."

Bentenhausen suddenly moved out of his chair and leaned against the wall with his arms crossed over his chest. "Will, did you look at those pictures on the bulletin board before you walked in this room, the pictures from Juarez?"

"Yeah, I saw them."

"Do you think it would be paternalistic if Wiemer Industries decided to provide decent housing for those employees in Juarez, or created a sanitary sewage system?"

Will was growing increasingly uncomfortable with the direction of the conversation. Jerry was much more direct than Jimmie. He wasn't circling around the issue; he was going straight to the center of it.

"I guess not," Will responded.

Jerry studied Will for a moment before continuing. "But if they do, Will, it'll hurt the numbers, and the numbers are more important than the people. This union hasn't even taken on management about the conditions in Juarez. It never came up until management began talking about moving more jobs to Mexico. It was only then that some of us decided to look at how Wiemer employees live in Juarez. Until then, we didn't care. They weren't included in our contract and our numbers. We can't and don't want to communicate with them. There's a lot of smoldering hatred about Mexican workers. Walk out in our Hammelburg plant on Monday morning and start a conversation with some of the assembly line crew. It isn't just the management of Wiemer Industries that doesn't care. As long as we keep our jobs, the Mexican workers can fend for themselves."

"Why are you telling me all about this, Jerry?" Will challenged.

"Cause all we've talked about for the last half hour is legal issues and contracts, and who can represent who at the bargaining table. No one's talked about what happens to people in Hammelburg if another couple hundred jobs go south. Nobody's talked about the people in Juarez that get those jobs, how they live, and what happens to them. Who wins and who loses? So far, I only see losers, and that's what we ought to be talking about at the bargaining table, and we need someone who can lead that discussion."

Will didn't respond. An uncomfortable silence invaded the room.

"Will, I know you didn't come here to argue with me, but let me tell you a couple of things before you leave," Jerry continued. "First, we're not all dumbass factory workers... we know what's happening to this town and a hell of a lot of towns like Hammelburg. It's no damn different in Detroit or Toledo or Buffalo. The factory jobs are disappearing. The streets in this town aren't as safe as they use to be... peddlin' dope earns a lot more bucks than flippin' burgers. Dope peddlers don't pay taxes and burger flippers don't make much; so the amount of taxes collected by the city is way down. When you grew up here, there were a lot of after school activities for teenagers… can't afford that anymore. Besides, a lot fewer folks have time to work with kids… don't have time to coach or referee games when you're workin' two jobs, So the kids join gangs, hang around on street corners and in shopping malls, pick fights; some carry weapons. They've got no hope for decent jobs. It's a dope peddler's dream. The shit moves from Detroit, to Fort Wayne, to Hammelburg. All organized like a regular business. Sure, we arrest some of them. I've got a 19-year-old nephew doin' five years at Pendleton for sellin' that shit. Got out of high school… couldn't find a decent job… but made 700 a week movin' dope before they nailed him. It's gotten so goddamn bad that the local prosecutor has told the cops to go easy on narcotics violations, they can't handle 'em all."

Will had no response. Bentenhausen looked at Jimmie for support. Jimmie remained silent. Jerry continued.

"And I haven't talked about what's happening in Juarez. The stink, the poverty, the dirty sick kids, the filthy communal baths, the police corruption, the drug trade, those bodies that turn up in the desert every week. Hell, Wiemer Industries is small potatoes compared to what those guys pull in a week movin' that shit across the bridge. But we don't see that because we don't want to. It may screw up the numbers."

Bentenhausen returned to his seat. The room remained silent for a few moments.

"One more thing, then I'll shut the hell up. Someone needs to tell those trade organizations and world planners, whoever they are, that folks like us ain't buyin' that horseshit about high-tech jobs and the new economy. We got two big problems. First, none of us is trained for those jobs and our school system ain't educating kids for high tech jobs. Second, nobody's gonna get trained until we spend a hell of a lot of money that we don't have. They better wake up and realize that the pain ain't going to stop with us… sooner or later, everyone is gonna feel it, and then all hell is gonna break loose."

Will had no response.

Jimmie broke the silence. "I guess we've probably used as much of your time as we're entitled to, Will."

"Well, I hope I have been of some help."

"You have, and we appreciate it. But I have one more favor to ask. It may be too much, but I am going to ask it anyway… If we need some more advice this week, would you meet with us again? I know you're in Hammelburg for Thanksgiving."

Will laughed. "Jimmie, I think you've talked with my old man again."

"Nope, your mom told me when I called your home last Friday."

Will shook his head and smiled. "I've never been able to outsmart Mom."

Chapter 14

Immediately following Harry Achaffer's resignation, J.W. Rieff rearranged his calendar and assumed the role of CEO of Wiemer Industries. He immediately hired a large executive search firm to help identify candidates to replace Achaffer. The firm assigned one of their senior partners to conduct the search. He began by scheduling extensive interviews with J.W. and other Wiemer board members to determine the necessary qualifications and experience for a prospective CEO and president. J.W. informed him that there would be no inside candidates and his interview with Gus Arnholt should be considered nothing more than a formality.

Within three months, the search had been narrowed to two candidates, both of whom had senior executive experience with manufacturing companies. The first candidate was an electrical engineer who had been hired out of college by a large multinational manufacturing corporation and had been promoted several times. He was 47 years old and serving as executive vice president of domestic operations, and on the short list of candidates to replace the current CEO following his retirement. However, his retirement date was several years away. Therefore, the candidate was interested in immediate opportunities to achieve a CEO status, even though Wiemer Industries was a smaller company.

The second candidate had a more glamorous resumé. Adam Fulton graduated from Dartmouth, and worked two years with an investment banking firm in New York City, followed by two years at Harvard Business School, where he earned an MBA as a prestigious Baker Scholar. Following graduation, he joined an international consulting company as a member of a team that developed long-term business plans for clients, primarily large multinational manufacturing companies. Five years later, he was hired by one of the clients as vice president of long range strategy, reporting directly to the CEO. The company was headquartered in Minneapolis. Within 24 months, he was appointed senior vice president for international marketing, and based in London. Three years after arriving in London, he was contacted by a Harvard classmate, the vice president of an executive search firm. He relocated again as vice president of international operations of a much larger company, based in San Francisco.

While at Harvard, Adam had been well tutored regarding the career benefits of "networking." His "network" was comprised of Harvard classmates and past consulting colleagues. Hearing of the recent success of several of other classmates, he became restless and informed the network that he was ready for the next step in his fast track career. He was seeking a position as CEO of a company that offered an opportunity for restructuring and rapid growth.

When he was contacted by the search firm representing Wiemer Industries, Adam Fulton was 35, and had been recently promoted to senior vice president of marketing. The search firm executive and Fulton had been colleagues at the international consulting firm.

Adam was an impressive candidate. He was tall, handsome, articulate, and had learned all the appropriate issues to favor and reject in order to earn his place in the business establishment. He was also well-tutored in the art of corporate politics and corporate theatre. His Ivy League and Harvard Business School credentials appealed to Henry Brinson and Quentin Phillips. His father, now retired, had been a senior marketing executive at Proctor and Gamble in Cincinnati, and an acquaintance of Cyrus Brown. The only member of the Wiemer board of directors who expressed any reservations about Adam was Peter Goldman. He thought that Adam's nomadic business career made it difficult to determine if he was a qualified candidate, and he expressed reservations about the culture change he would experience in Hammelburg after residing in London and San Francisco.

Other board members and the search executive were quick to point out that Adam had lived in Cincinnati as a boy. The fact that he left Cincinnati at age 14 to attend a prep school in New Hampshire never arose. It was also assumed by other board members that Peter was merely objecting to Adam on behalf of his friend Gus Arnholt, despite the fact that Peter had been the first to suggest that there were no suitable inside candidates.

Adam's wife, Samantha, had acquired the nickname Chip, and it stuck. She was far from excited about relocating from San Francisco to Hammelburg. They had met and married in San Francisco. Both had previous marriages. Chip was the quintessential "trophy wife"; very glamorous and several years younger than Adam. She divorced her first husband, an Annapolis graduate, immediately after he announced his intention to become a career officer. With the exception of four years as a student at Smith College in Massachusetts, she had always lived in California. On Adam's second recruiting visit to Hammelburg, Chip accompanied him on a hot and humid early September weekend. Mary Rieff invited Chip and Elizabeth Brinson to lunch at her home. Chip appeared in chic California casual: expensive burgundy silk slacks, matching sleeveless blouse, and sandals. She did not attempt to disguise her lack of enthusiasm about a possible relocation, and made several unflattering remarks about the Midwest and its nasty weather.

J.W. had decided it was necessary that Adam meet Gus Arnold before he offered him the job. He invited Gus and Cynthia to join them for dinner. The three couples met at the Alamost Country Club. Chip drew the attention of all the occupants in the dining room, appearing in black silk slacks and blouse, black cashmere sweater over her shoulders, and bare feet with sandals. While J.W., Gus, and Mary visited with Adam, Chip listened attentively and sympathetically to Cynthia Arnholt bemoan the lack of cultural diversity in Hammelburg.

After returning home that evening, Mary told J.W. that she had some reservations about the Fultons' ability handle the transition from San Francisco to Hammelburg. She joked that if Adam accepted the job, Cynthia Arnholt and Chip Fulton would become inseparable and insufferable.

On January 1, 1974, Adam Fulton became president and CEO of Wiemer Industries. He immediately sensed that he needed to neutralize Gus Arnholt, and he recognized that feeding his ego was the best technique. After several long lunches with Adam—which always included a shameless stroking of his ego—Gus declared that Adam was an impeccable choice for CEO and swore his allegiance. Adam's next move was to hire his former colleagues at the consulting company to conduct a very extensive and expensive study of Wiemer Industries and assist in the development of a long-range growth strategy, a five-year business plan. He had already devised a name for the proposed growth plan: The Second Century Plan, recognizing more than 100 years of Wiemer Industries operations.

Gus was asked to coordinate the study, a perfunctory assignment. Nevertheless, Gus was ecstatic. Adam also convinced the board of directors to postpone the plan that Harry Achaffer had proposed. Consequently, new product development and manufacturing improvement programs were halted. He hired the same executive search firm that had recruited him to find a suitable candidate for a new position: vice president of strategy and long-range planning. He devoted considerable time and money to informing the financial community and shareholders that he was moving quickly to establish the Second Century Plan. He also announced that as soon as the consultants had finished their work, the new vice president of strategy and long-range planning was aboard, and the Second Century Plan was complete, a public relations firm would prepare a "state of the art" graphic presentation of the plan and help communicate it to the financial markets and shareholders.

At Wiemer's annual shareholders meeting in April, Adam Fulton was elected a member of the board of directors. Despite his role as CEO and board member, he had never been seen in the manufacturing facilities or the research and engineering center. Except for a picture in the *Hammelburg Sentinel,* few hourly employees knew what he looked like.

In early May, a two-day "management retreat" was held in Aspen, Colorado. Attendance was limited to Adam, Gus, and the consultants. The primary purpose of the meeting was to permit the consultants to review their preliminary recommendations. The discussion centered on a single recommendation: Wiemer's management should accelerate the growth rate of the company by making a series of "strategic acquisitions." This recommendation was to serve as the keystone for The Second Century Plan. Although never specifically stated, the recommendation also served the personal interests of all the attendees at the meeting. Adam Fulton was an ambitious young executive who wanted to become the CEO of a well-recognized growth company. It was a vital step in his long-term career plan. The consultants recognized that the recommendation was a virtual guarantee that they would continue to earn consulting fees assisting the Wiemer management with identifying and acquiring "target" companies.

Gus was pleased to accept any idea that Adam approved. He envisioned himself prospering in the wake of Adam's success.

By August, the new vice president of strategy and long-range planning was aboard. Ian Davis had been associated with Adam Fulton in London. He was employed by a U.K. consulting company that Adam had contracted to develop a marketing plan. Ian was a graduate of Cambridge University and The London School of Economics. He had spent the past 12 months at the advanced management course at Harvard Business School. Despite the fact that his employer, the U.K. consulting company, had borne the entire expense of his sojourn at Harvard, immediately following the completion of the Harvard program he resigned from the consulting company and announced his intention to seek new career opportunities in the United States. Ian and his wife thought the future was more promising in this country, and if they elected to start a family, the children would qualify for dual citizenships, U.S. and U.K.

By the end of the year, Adam, Gus, and Ian were making frequent trips to New York City to meet with investment bankers and attorneys. The visits served two purposes: the identification of prospective acquisitions and arranging access to necessary financial resources to acquire other companies, primarily borrowed capital. To facilitate their frequent trips to New York City, and the fact that J.W. scheduled most of the available time of the exiting corporate jet, a second aircraft was acquired; the same model but with greater speed, range, and advanced avionics, permitting the new plane to take off and land in Hammelburg in marginal weather conditions. The day-to-day direction of the company was assigned to a small group of second-tier executives, including a promising young manufacturing executive, Harris Stevenson.

At the July meeting of the Wiemer board of directors, Adam Fulton, with the assistance of the consultants and the public relations experts, introduced a 50-minute audiovisual presentation of The Second Century Plan. It was quintessential corporate theatre. The basic assumptions that underlie the plan were grand in scale. It was apparent that it was an exceedingly ambitious growth plan that would require a significant increase in borrowed funds and interest expense. But the promised profitability was dazzling. If successful, according to the visual and audio presentation, Wiemer Industries would be ranked among *Fortune* magazine's list of the 100 largest corporations in the United States by 1980. As Adam Fulton concluded the presentation and asked for approval by the board, he appeared to be bouncing with enthusiasm and confidence. Although several questions were asked regarding the feasibility of the plan, only one director opposed it, Peter Goldman. The Second Century Plan was approved by a vote of 6 to 1.

The following day, Peter Goldman called J.W. and resigned from the Wiemer Industries board of directors. He had served nearly 20 years as a director. Although Peter was a well-known and respected investment banker, the market registered no reaction when his resignation was announced.

Three weeks later, Clay Emerson, chairman and CEO of United States Electric Power, agreed to fill Goldman's seat. As a member of United's board of directors, J.W. considered Emerson a good friend and a prestigious appointment to the Wiemer board.

During the following two years, the senior management was busy negotiating the acquisition of five companies and making presentations to institutional investors and bankers in connection with a sale of $400 million of bonds and a $250 million revolving line of credit divided among seven large commercial banks. The proceeds were used to pay for acquisitions and finance Wiemer Industries' rapidly expanding operating expenses and inventory. Adam Fulton, Ian Davis, and Gus Arnholt continued to spend a significant amount of time in New York; therefore, it was decided that it would be appropriate for Wiemer Industries to acquire a small condominium in Manhattan to allow the executives more comfort and permit their spouses to accompany them occasionally. J.W. was not enthusiastic about the proposal. He argued that the second jet aircraft should allow day trips to New York without the necessity of a permanent overnight accommodation. If permanent accommodations were needed, he argued, a contract for a permanent room could be arranged with a good hotel. After several months of modest wrangling, he capitulated, and a condo was acquired on Park Avenue. Chip Fulton was asked to assume responsibility for the furnishings and decoration.

Adam Fulton was on a roll. With the assistance of the public relations firm, he began to attract the attention of the financial media. They portrayed him as a bright young executive building a dynamic company. Although not chairman of the board, which he considered an important near-term objective in his career plan, he was asked to join a few corporate boards, but he recognized that he was standing in the shadow of J.W., who was totally occupied with his expanding corporate and nonprofit board memberships. Adam began suggesting to other board members that J.W. had too heavy a schedule to continue much longer as chairman.

The day-to-day operation of Wiemer Industries, including the oversight of the newly-acquired companies, remained the primary responsibility of the second tier of management. When a staff member suggested that it might be a good idea for Adam to occasionally tour the manufacturing operations in Hammelburg and the newly-acquired companies, his response was direct and sharp: "My success in building one of the most dynamic industrial companies in this country has not been achieved by walking around shaking hands and shooting the shit with the Joe Six-packs on the shop floor."

By early 1979, a few cracks had begun to emerge in The Second Century Plan. Interest rates were escalating and the cost of Wiemer's heavy debt load had increased dramatically. The rate of inflation continued to escalate, and the cost of operations had risen much faster than the ability to initiate offsetting price increases. Foreign competitors and imports had also become an impediment to increasing sales and prices. Three of several large acquisitions were falling far short of the original expectations, and the capital investments required to support the acquired companies was well in excess of the plan. Finally, senior management's total preoccupation with The Second Century Plan had resulted in little attention to operating costs, which were escalating rapidly and drawing critical attention from the lenders.

In mid-February, J.W. was scheduled to attend a quarterly board meeting at United States Electric Company in New York City. He arrived the previous evening by corporate jet and stayed at the St. Regis. Early the following morning, he traveled by limousine to United's corporate headquarters on Sixth Avenue. He attended compensation and audit committee meetings the balance of the morning. As usual, the board meeting began with a lunch in the corporate dining room, and the balance of the afternoon and early evening were devoted to the board of directors' agenda.

It was a long-established custom for the board members and a few senior officers to conclude the meeting with cocktails and dinner at the Links Club. J.W. was not fond of the evening event. It resulted in a very late departure from LaGuardia Airport aboard the corporate jet, and arrival in Hammelburg past midnight, but he preferred that ordeal over the alternative: remaining in Manhattan a second night. When he had a convenient excuse, he managed to avoid the dinner meeting, but he had done that at the last meeting and thought it inappropriate this time.

Following the dinner, a limousine delivered J.W. to the FBO terminal at LaGuardia. It was 10:00 P.M.—a cold, windy evening, but dry and clear. The older Wiemer jet was visible from the lobby of the FBO. The pilots met him and arranged ground transportation to the plane. They had obtained the latest weather report for northeastern Indiana. The ceiling and visibility at Fort Wayne International Airport were marginal: one thousand foot ceiling and one mile visibility. They were expecting freezing rain after midnight. The control tower at Hammelburg closed every evening at 9:00 P.M. Therefore, there was no local report for Hammelburg. The pilots discussed the weather report with J.W. His response, as always: the pilots make the decisions, but he would like to go home, if possible. The pilots were unsure about attempting to land in Hammelburg, but assured J.W. they could land in Fort Wayne or Cleveland, if the weather worsened.

They departed LaGuardia at 10:35 P.M. The ascent was very bumpy, but the turbulence disappeared at cruising altitude. Fifteen minutes later, J.W. was asleep. Approximately two hours later, he was awakened by the co-pilot, who explained that weather conditions were about the same as reported at the time of their departure, but freezing rain might be encountered during their descent between the 5,000 and 3,000 foot level. With the assistance of Fort Wayne radar, they had decided to attempt a landing at Hammelburg. If the weather at Hammelburg was too bad, they would abort the landing and return to Fort Wayne where conditions were still marginal but instrument landings were facilitated. They would begin the approach to the Hammelburg airport in less than ten minutes. He should expect strong turbulence on the way down. J.W. acknowledged the information and tightened his seat belt.

At 1:05 A.M., the Fort Wayne International Radar Center reported the loss of radar contact with NWI-1. In addition, they had been unable to establish radio contact with the plane for ten minutes. At 1:20 A.M. the Alamost County Sheriff's Office received a call from a rural resident. He and his wife had been awakened by an explosion and fire in a field near their home. At 6:00 A.M., the Alamost County Sheriff contacted the security office at Wiemer Industries to report that a Wiemer Industries plane, NWI-1, had crashed and burned on what appeared to be final approach to the Hammelburg airport. The plane had impacted 400 yards short of the runway. There were no survivors. The FAA investigators were speculating that the accident may have been caused by a combination of wind shear and ice. The Wiemer security officer attempted to reach Adam Fulton at his home. There was no answer. Adam and Chip were in New York City. At 7:00 A.M., Mary Rieff met the Sheriff of Alamost County at her front door.

The family elected to conduct a small, private funeral service. Only immediate family members attended the gathering at the First Lutheran Church. A memorial service was conducted two days later. Many out-of-town visitors attended. The Hammelburg airport air traffic controller had a record day handling incoming executive jets as business and government executives traveled to Hammelburg to pay their respects to J.W. Both the *New York Times* and *Chicago Tribune* published extensive obituaries, as did the *Indianapolis Star* and the *Fort Wayne Journal Gazette*.

It was suggested that those who wished to make a bequest in his memory contribute to the Hammelburg Regional Medical Center Development Fund. Before his death, J.W. was in the final stages of completing an agreement with the Indiana University Medical School and Nursing School to establish a large facility in connection with the Hammelburg Regional Hospital. Mary Rieff was the chairman of the planning committee. A substantial amount of money had been pledged to the project by the Wiemer/Rieff Foundation and the WI Foundation. It had attracted much attention throughout the Midwest medical community. Mary had arranged for executives of The Mayo Clinic and Cleveland Clinic to serve as consultants regarding the physical structure and organization of the facility.

It was intended to become a unique center for medical education and research and the application of primary and advanced medical treatment. The combined new and existing facilities, designed as a campus, would occupy a redevelopment area consisting of 25 acres located seven blocks west of the center of Hammelburg. In addition to the existing Hammelburg Regional Hospital, the new facilities would include a medical school, nursing school, geriatric medicine center, children's hospital, cancer and cardiac treatment center, hospice, and a center for poor and indigent patients. It was Ruth Heider who suggested the latter facility be called Friends in Medicine. The donations to the project from corporate foundations in memory of J.W. totaled more than $1.5 million. It was suggested that the facility be named the J.W. Rieff Medical Center. Mary promptly rejected that suggestion. She assured the sponsors that J.W would not have approved of it. According to Mary, J.W. was always uncomfortable when the family name was directly associated with their philanthropy.

After Mary's children had departed, Phillip Rieff remained in Hammelburg to spend a few more days with her. He had recently retired from Northwestern University and had been appointed a senior fellow at the Institute for International Intelligence in Washington D.C. He was a well-recognized scholar of modern European history, having written several books and been awarded visiting scholar appointments at prestigious European and U.S. universities. He occasionally appeared on television news shows and roundtable discussions.

On the evening before his departure, Mary invited Phillip to dinner at her home. Following the meal, Phillip began to ask Mary a series of questions;

"How will Wiemer continue without J.W"

"I don't know," she replied. "he provided so much of the energy and vision for the company. But during the last few years, his focus shifted. He spent little time at the company, and his attention was centered on his board memberships, Wabash College, and various government panels and business leadership associations. When he first gave up the CEO post, he divided his time between the WI Foundation and the company. As he joined more boards and outside organizations, he attempted to maintain his interest in the Foundation, but less and less in the company. During the past few years, he appeared to have lost interest and energy. It became more and more difficult for him to keep up with all his responsibilities. He was beginning to grow frustrated and bored with board memberships. He told me that each meeting seemed like a repeat performance of every other meeting. He thought the formality of board meetings was stifling; he joked about the cookie cutter agendas. On several occasions, he had to remind himself which board meeting he was attending, He considered most of his fellow board members intelligent, successful people, but he suspected their primary purpose in joining the boards was to achieve greater social recognition. He began to question his own rationale for serving on the boards."

"Sounds like he though the meetings were dull?"

"He thought they were superficial, and wasn't sure the information the boards received was objective and candid. He believed many board members didn't want to delve too deeply into the corporation's performance. He laughed about the conversations at the cocktail hours following the meetings—

directors whispering about their misgivings and doubts concerning the company; important issues they'd never raise at the meetings."

"I've always assumed that these directors are powerful people. Why did J.W. think they were reluctant to raise issues at the board meetings?" .

"He attributed it to the fact that too many board members are CEOs or chairmen of other companies who don't want difficult issues raised by their board members, many of whom sat on the same boards."

She laughed. "He referred to it as the unspoken agreement among interlocking directorates."

Phillip suddenly changed the direction of his questions. "How strong is Wiemer's current management?

Mary paused before responding. "I don't know enough, Phillip. But I believe J.W. was beginning to have some misgivings about their vision and dedication. Whenever I asked him about Adam Fulton and the management, he adroitly avoided the subject. I was left with the impression that he was not pleased with their performance, but wanted to avoid getting involved. He may have doubted that he had the energy to challenge them. It may sound critical, and I don't intend that, but I think it would have been better for the company and the community if J.W. had devoted less time to expanding his radius of influence in the national business community and given more attention to the company and the community."

"I always assumed that J.W picked strong managers," Phillip said.

"He did. But I think the attitude and objectives of many corporate managers has changed, and J.W. may have failed to recognize and understand that transformation."

"What's changed?" he asked.

"Well, it's my impression that Wiemer Industries was built by men who had a deep understanding of the products, the manufacturing process, and the customers. They were devoted to the company and the community. Wiemer Industries and Hammelburg were intertwined, each an integral part of the other. It was a strong, healthy interdependence. The community wanted Wiemer to succeed and Wiemer wanted the community to prosper and progress. Today, the relationship between the company and the community is much different. The level of energy and support has declined. The community appears to be less interested in the performance of the company. To some extent, the union has assumed the role of the community. Their focus is much narrower: wages and benefits. Management appears to be pursuing other objectives—company size and prestige, personal recognition, a lot of pseudo-sophisticated management and lifestyles. They all seem to pursue the same nomadic career patterns: get a good business school pedigree, take a job with a high-profile company, attract attention and network, move on to something better, continue to attract attention and network, and move again. Their primary objective appears to be building successful careers rather than successful business. The companies and the communities simply become a means to achieve personal career goals.

"How does that impact Hammelburg?"

"Their lifestyles and attitudes seem to transmit a message: don't be concerned with this community or the next one; tomorrow there may be bigger career opportunities in Atlanta, and after that Dallas or New York or Chicago. After you're rich enough or retired, you can get involved in artificial communities like Hilton Head and Boca Raton. I think they view Hammelburg and Wiemer Industries as intermediate stops along their career path, way stations, or rungs on a ladder to God knows where," she said.

"What role does the family play in the management of the company?"

"Very little, without J.W. A few weeks ago, he told me that the entire family owns less than 30 percent of the company. Gus Arnholt is the only family member employed by the company. Unfortunately, Gus is a scheming sycophant, but he was the only remaining heir of Max and Katherine, and they left all their Wiemer stock in their estate. He's probably the single largest family shareholder. Nobody else in his generation or the next has shown any interest in joining the company, including my own children."

"How did J.W. feel about giving up so much ownership in the company?"

"He talked about it a lot. He wondered whether or not he made a good decision. When he elected to do it, he told me he had no choice. As the family expanded and more and more people held the stock who were neither employed by the company nor lived in Hammelburg, there was growing pressure to sell their shares. The company couldn't afford to buy them out. There were two alternatives, according to J.W.: sell the entire company or take it public and create a market for their shares. He thought the latter was the best alternative."

"Do you think it was a good decision?"

"In retrospect, I think it was. As the family expanded and fewer and fewer had any direct association with the company, there had to be some way for them to sell their shares. Inheritance tax was a big consideration. It was a much better choice than selling the entire company. I've seen what happens when family companies are sold to large corporations. Barker Packaging, as an example; a company that was an integral part of the community suddenly became a branch plant of a much larger organization. The decisions regarding operations, employment, and involvement with the community were made by someone hundreds of miles away. The loss of direct involvement with the community resulted in some bad decisions. Now the plant is closed and there are only a few members of the Barker family remaining in Hammelburg. Most of them collected their wealth, left the community, and left those who helped them build a successful company."

"Do you think that could happen with Wiemer Industries?"

She looked directly at Phillip for a moment before responding. "I don't know. I hope not. Nevertheless, we have to realize that with the exception of Gus, the entire senior management has no roots in the company or the community, and among the outside members of the board of directors, the only one who has any history with Hammelburg is Ted Brinson."

Mary left her chair, walked to the kitchen, and returned with the coffee server. She filled their cups and returned to her seat opposite Phillip. They both remained silent for several minutes, perhaps contemplating the previous conversation.

After a long silence, Phillip spoke softly. "I am very fond of you, Mary. I was overjoyed when you joined our family. I loved my brother with all my heart, but there were many times when I regretted that it wasn't me that brought you into our family."

Chapter 15

Shortly after J.W.'s death, Adam Fulton was appointed as chairman and CEO of Wiemer Industries. Eighteen months later, he urged the board of directors to approve the appointment of Ian Davis as president and chief operating officer and a member of the board of directors, replacing J.W. Rieff. Anticipating Gus Arnholt's objection to being passed over again, Adam inflated his title to vice chairman and chief financial officer. As soon as Gus appeared to be placated by his new title, Adam made some additional organizational changes, including having the corporate controller and chief accountant report to Ian Davis, rather than Gus Arnholt. Gus had a new title, but less authority. Ian Davis had a significant increase in authority and responsibility, but no relevant experience and less than a modest interest in overseeing the operations of the company. But he too enjoyed the prestige associated with the new title and significant increase in salary.

Adam also made some additional progress toward his personal career goals. He was invited to replace J.W. on the board of directors of United States Electric Company and Puritan Securities. Although J.W. had also served on the boards of Banner Pharmaceuticals and Creighton Scientific, there was no reciprocal seat on the Wiemer Industries board; therefore, Adam was not invited to replace J.W. on those boards. Nor was he invited to become a member of the business council; that honor would be bestowed later. He was invited to deliver an annual lecture at Harvard Business School regarding how to manage corporate growth.

But 1981 and the first half of 1982 were not a period in which the management of Wiemer Industries could proudly display good business performance. The Second Century Plan had undergone several substantial revisions. Projections of sales and profits had been deflated and 1980 had come and gone without Wiemer Industries' name appearing among the *Fortune* largest 100 companies. Interest rates were approaching near record highs, the prime rate for commercial bank borrowers had reached 18%, and interest rates on corporate bonds were also in double-digit territory.

The biggest problem the Wiemer management faced was an inadequate cash flow. Although the basic business was generating cash, the newly-acquired companies, corporate operating expenses, and dividend payments were absorbing substantially more cash than the basic business could generate. The banks were becoming increasingly unhappy about the inability of Wiemer to reduce the enormous debt load it had acquired to pursue its Second Century Plan, and the failure to correct its operating performance and outflow of cash was beginning to trigger occasional questions about the quality of management.

In July of 1982, the Wiemer board of directors held its regular third quarter meeting. The primary issue on the agenda was the financial problems facing the company. Following glossy presentations by Gus Arnholt and Ian Davis, designed to convince the outside board members that the cash flow problem was merely a short-term phenomenon, two of the board members, Ted Brinson and Cyrus Brown, voiced concerns about the growing outflow of cash and suggested that immediate action was required. Both men were senior bank executives and understood the bleak implications of Wiemer Industries' balance sheet and debt load. The stock market had also expressed an opinion regarding the severity of the problem; Wiemer's stock price had declined by 30% during the past seven months, the lowest level in more than 12 years.

Adam Fulton recognized that the outside board members were not buying the short-term phenomenon argument, and adroitly proposed some specific remedies. First, he recommended an immediate layoff of a substantial number of hourly employees at the Hammelburg plants. Second, the three-year labor contract with the IMU was scheduled to expire in October and negotiations were already underway; he proposed that management insist on a reduction in wages and medical benefit expense. Third, he suggested the elimination of the 4% pre-tax profit contribution to the WI Foundation.

Clay Emerson pointed out that it was the Hammelburg operations that generated cash, and inquired why Adam had not suggested layoffs and wage and benefit reductions at the companies that were not generating cash— namely, those companies that had been acquired under the Second Century Plan. Adam argued that the other plants were not represented by a union, and layoffs and wage reductions might encourage the workers to organize.

Several questions were asked about the advisability of reducing the dividend. Ted Brinson pointed out that a 50% reduction in the dividend would supply additional cash to help reduce bank loans and reduce the interest cost, which would further alleviate the cash problem. Gus Arnholt immediately took issue with the suggestion of a dividend reduction, arguing that it would further depress the stock price and unfairly punish the shareholders. Quentin Phillips supported Arnholt's argument.

Ted Brinson was annoyed with their self-serving arguments; Arnholt and Phillips were both substantial shareholders. He pointed out that the recent decline in the price of Wiemer stock was in anticipation of a dividend reduction; therefore, it was a dubious argument that the stock would decline further if the dividend was cut. The market had already adjusted to it. Arnholt continued to urge the other board members to oppose a cut in the dividend rate. He informed them, with lofty assurance, that as vice chairman and CFO, he was in close touch with the market, and that it would trigger another sharp decline in the price of the stock.

Still irked by Arnholt's arguments, Brinson asked why it was necessary to eliminate the policy of granting a 4% pre-tax profit contribution to the WI Foundation, given the fact that during the past 18 months, the company had no profits; therefore, no payments had been made to the Foundation.

Several outside members found his question both insightful and amusing.

Fulton appeared momentarily unable to muster a response.

But Gus Arnholt did not hesitate. "It's long overdue. The shareholders of this company are entitled to that money. If they wish to donate it to charity, let it be a charity of their own choice, not that of a select group of people in Hammelburg. Frankly, there are some programs that the Foundation has supported that are offensive to many shareholders."

Fulton immediately supported Arnholt's statement, employing his best rhetorical skills. "Gus is correct. The elimination of future pre-tax profit donations to the WI Foundation will be received with enthusiasm by the shareholders. It'll demonstrate the discipline that this management is willing to exercise to assure the success of Wiemer Industries."

"What about the response of the community and the employees?" Brinson asked.

Adam continued his rhetorical splendor. "Frankly, Ted, I consider the financial strength of Wiemer Industries and the support of its shareholders the most vital contribution this management can make to this community."

"I think that's going to be a tough sell, Adam. You're going to announce layoffs, but only in Hammelburg; a tougher bargaining position with the local union; elimination of the Foundation and at the same time convince the community it's in their best interest."

"Ted, I'm not suggesting that we eliminate the Foundation, only stop the contributions to it. The Foundation has assets."

"C'mon, Adam, you're proposing to turn off its only source of funds. Everyone in this community is going to read that as the end of the WI Foundation."

Clay Emerson spoke before Adam could respond. "Let me suggest that it might go down a lot better with the union and the community if they saw the management making some sacrifices at the same time. Maybe a temporary reduction in executive salaries and the sale of an airplane or the New York condo. You know, something that says management's going to share in the pain until the ship is righted."

Adam stroked his jaw and appeared to be contemplating the suggestion. His response reflected his lack of enthusiasm: "Well, maybe."

"Adam, how about getting rid of a couple of those unprofitable companies we acquired? They don't generate any profits and they use a lot of scarce cash. We could increase our cash and reduce its use by selling them," Cyrus Brown added.

Fulton was becoming increasingly apprehensive about the dialogue. His response was quick and reflected his annoyance with the board members' suggestions. "No, the market and shareholders would interpret that as a signal that we're abandoning The Second Century Plan. That would trigger a very negative reaction. We don't intend to slow the growth of this company."

"Well, if we don't solve the cash problem, it's going to slow down anyway," Cyrus Brown added sarcastically.

It was evident to Fulton that the meeting was not progressing as intended. He needed to regain control. He ignored Cyrus Brown's last comment. "Let's take a bathroom break before we move on to the next item on the agenda," he suggested.

As Ted Brinson had forecast, the combination of layoffs and bargaining for reduced wages and benefits backfired. The IMU rejected all of management's proposals and insisted on an inflation adjusted increase in both wages and benefits; the largest increase the IMU had ever proposed. The bargaining sessions continued through the summer and early fall with little progress. From the outset, an angry tone pervaded the negotiations.

In October, several days before the IMU contract was scheduled to expire, Ian Davis, who had no previous experience with labor negotiations and was rarely ever seen by the hourly employees, decided to assume responsibility for management negotiations. On his last day, he provided the ammunition the union negotiating team needed to assure a strike vote.

At the close of the meeting, with an angry voice, he pointed an accusing finger at the IMU representatives and shouted, "You're acting just like those freaking unions in the U.K. They wrecked my country with their idiotic socialist demands, and you're going to wreck this country with yours. It's a bloody shame what you chaps are doing, a bloody shame."

The following day, more than 80% of the IMU members voted to strike. The most popular sign on the picket lines displayed four words, "**It's a Bloody Shame.**"

Ian Davis never appeared at another bargaining session. The strike was a disaster for Wiemer management. It lasted 63 days; through Thanksgiving, Christmas, and the first four days of 1983. It ended when management capitulated and agreed to the union's original salary and benefit demands. Even among other unions in Hammelburg, it was considered a one-sided settlement on behalf of the IMU. The strike may have lasted longer or the ultimate settlement may have been less expensive, had it not been for Adam Fulton's ultimatum to his negotiating team: "This strike is creating problems for us in the financial community. Settle the goddamn thing; I don't care what it costs. Get 'em off that picket line."

Despite the generous settlement, the animosity between the IMU and Wiemer management remained. The community was divided by the strike and remained divided long after the settlement. Small manufacturing companies began to face demands from their respective workers that were comparable to the Wiemer wage and benefit agreement. Beauty and barber shops, dentists, lawyers, funeral homes, auto repair shops, and both skilled and unskilled craftsmen raised their prices and wage demands. Conversations at the Rotary Club and Alamost Country Club were critical of the IMU and its radical leadership. At the Moose, American Legion, and VFW, there was subtle recognition that the settlement was too generous, but unanimous agreement that Wiemer's management had inflicted it on themselves with their original demand for layoffs and wage and benefit reductions. There were IMU members and supporters who feared that the union had won too much and put the company at risk.

By 1986, Wiemer Industries had fallen from the list of attractive growth companies. Although its total sales advanced slowly, profits were sporadic, and it continued to suffer severe cash outflows. Bankers and bondholders were demanding repayment of loans and refused to extend existing loans. The management faced two bleak alternatives: renegotiate the loans and pay much higher interest rates and additional fees and accept much more onerous restrictions, or find some method to raise cash and pay off the loans and retire the bonds. In addition, the large mutual funds, pension funds, and insurance companies that owned Wiemer common stock were becoming openly critical of the management.

At a February 1987 meeting of the Wiemer board of directors, it was agreed —albeit over the objection of Gus Arnholt—that Wiemer Industries would sell three of its five acquisitions and issue $150 million of new common stock to reduce its debt. Gus reluctantly supported the resolution to issue more shares when an alternative motion to reduce the dividend rate was narrowly defeated. The decision to sell three unsuccessful acquisitions was applauded by the investment community, but the decision to sell such a large amount of common stock did not receive universal approval. The banks and bondholders favored the decision because it assured that the now very risky loans that they had made to Wiemer would be repaid. Wiemer Industries' institutional shareholders and large individual shareholders, like Gus Arnholt, were certain that the sale of additional shares would further depress the already battered stock price. Moreover, no one could be sure that there would be a receptive market for additional Wiemer common stock.

The Midwest economy remained stagnant. Its failure to participate in the nationwide economic recovery was blamed on its old industrial base that failed to keep pace with the growing high-tech economy. Wall Street pundits began to refer to the Midwest economy and its heavy manufacturing companies as the "Rust Bowl." Investors became reluctant to invest in these companies. Consequently, Wiemer stock prices did not benefit from the rapid rise in the stock market.

In the six-month period following the February board meeting, the management sold the three acquired companies for substantially less than they had paid for them seven years earlier, and the issuance of the new shares, as expected, further depressed the price of Wiemer stock. The proceeds from both transactions provided less cash than originally anticipated, but the total debt of the company was reduced, though it remained relatively high.

Following the sales of the additional stock, the Wiemer family share of ownership in the company declined to 12%, and Gus Arnholt remained the largest single shareholder in the family.

Wall Street no longer expressed its admiration for Wiemer Industries and its management. Any mention of The Second Century Plan triggered snorts of derision among security analysts and institutional investors. Ian Davis had proven incapable of managing the daily operating activities of the company, but retained Adam Fulton's support. After several quiet conversations with dissatisfied directors, Adam agreed that Harris Stevenson, vice president of manufacturing, would be promoted to executive vice president of operations, and assume responsibility for the day-to-day management of the company, but continue to report to Ian Davis. The organization cheered the appointment of Stevenson, a popular executive who was seen frequently in the manufacturing facilities and communicated easily with hourly workers. But the two executives had a rocky relationship. It was difficult for Stevenson to disguise his contempt for Davis, while Davis made little attempt to conceal his opinion that Stevenson was bereft of culture and refinement. Fulton dismissed Ian's objections by humoring him.

"Ian, we're sure as hell not going to take Harris along when we visit the investment bankers and institutional investors. But he knows how to get along with those rednecks on the shop floor. He talks their language, he's one of them. They love him. He knows how to go down their and shoot the shit with them. You and I don't want to do that, do we?"

Davis smiled and agreed.

Soon after the new shares had been sold and the three unprofitable companies had been disposed of, Adam Fulton hired an executive compensation consultant to determine if the senior management of Wiemer Industries was receiving adequate compensation. The consultant and Adam had been fraternity brothers at Dartmouth. The final study required three months to prepare. It was comprised of 73 pages of nearly incomprehensible comparative analysis and a two-page executive summary, and it cost the company $115,000.

It was presented to the compensation committee of the board of directors for approval in 1988. The chairman of the compensation committee was Quentin Phillips, CEO of Puritan Securities. Adam Fulton served as a member of Puritan Securities' board of directors and its compensation committee.

The committee members were aware that the compensation study had been approved by management. They had one brief meeting with the consultant, and received the final report two days before the special meeting scheduled to approve the recommendations. At the meeting, Quentin Phillips asked the consultant to present and defend his recommendations. The presentation required 20 minutes and was comprised largely of statistical analysis, most of which the compensation committee failed to comprehend. He concluded by asserting that his recommendations should be implemented if Wiemer Industries wished to maintain competitive salaries for senior management. There were few questions asked before it was approved by all three members of the committee. The resolution contained a 60% increase in salary for Adam Fulton, a 42% increase for Ian Davis and Gus Arnholt, and a 6% increase for four other senior officers of the corporation, including Harris

Stevenson. In addition, it recommended a 300,000-share stock option for Adam Fulton, and somewhat smaller options for the balance of the senior executives.

At the next meeting of the board of directors, the resolution of the compensation committee was presented for final approval. Quentin Phillips requested that Adam Fulton, Ian Davis, and Gus Arnholt recuse themselves from the meeting to facilitate the discussion by the outside directors.

After the three inside directors left the room, Ted Brinson immediately voiced an objection to the resolution.

"How the hell can we justify such a large increase in executive compensation for a company that has been unable to report a profit in four of the last seven years and hasn't achieved a positive cash flow for all seven of those years? I've always assumed that executive compensation was related to corporate performance. In addition, we just completed the sale of three companies that never made a dime, for a price that was less than we paid for them nine years ago. Have I missed something along the way?"

An embarrassed silence filled the room. Finally, Quentin Phillips responded. "Ted, it's not my recommendation. The consultant made a complete study of competitive salary structures. These are salaries we need to pay to remain competitive and retain this management. He reviewed them with the committee, the committee approved the resolution, and we recommend approval by the full board."

"Competitive with whom, for Christ's sake? Who would be interested in hiring them?" Brinson asked.

Cyrus Brown cleared his throat to gain attention. "I think Ted may have some valid arguments. I suggest that we trim a little off the stock options. But let's not fool with the salary proposals. I know the consultant that made these recommendations. He consults with several companies, including my own. He's very good."

It was decided to trim the stock option recommendations by 5%. The vote to approve the amended recommendation was 3 to 1.

By the end of 1990, under the leadership of Harris Stevenson, the company's manufacturing and operating performance had improved. However, the debt load remained high and the burden imposed by interest costs and corporate operating expense resulted in small profits and continued cash outflows. The banks remained concerned about the company's ability to meet their debt repayment, and the stock price continued to languish. The dividend was not reduced, but had not been increased in 12 years. The management elected to sell the remaining companies they had acquired in the early 1980s. They were also sold for substantially less than their original cost. By the end of 1991, Wiemer Industries had been scaled back to those businesses which existed before the adoption of the Second Century Plan. However, with a persistent shortage of cash and heavy debt service requirements, management had invested little in improving manufacturing facilities and designing and developing new and improved products in their base business. Wiemer Industries was struggling to remain competitive.

By mid-1994, Adam Fulton concluded that his career plan was modestly off schedule, and it was time to make the next big move. He contacted the public relations firm that had helped prepare the defunct Second Century Plan. He wanted to elevate his profile in the business world. With the assistance of Clay Emerson, he had recently been chosen to serve on the Business Council; an opportunity to occasionally meet and eat with leaders of the nation's largest and most successful corporations, albeit many of its members did not qualify for that distinction. After several weeks, the public relations firm presented their ideas. Adam Fulton would become the "poster boy" for the struggling industries of the Midwest. He would be portrayed as the hard- working, tough-minded, no-nonsense, roll up your sleeves industrial leader who was attempting to stop the economic demise of the Midwest, or the "Rust Bowl," as described by the *Wall Street Journal.*

He bought it. During the next several months, he spent an even greater proportion of his time in New York City doing interviews with the business media, arranged by the public relations firm. He and Chip established a near permanent residence at the corporate condo. When he returned to Hammelburg, the public relations firm arranged for a team of photographers to accompany him. They took still and motion pictures of Adam in the manufacturing facilities, shaking hands and talking with Wiemer employees and examining Wiemer products. He always appeared with shirt sleeves rolled above his elbows, and wearing safety glasses.

His face became a familiar sight on nationwide TV business news shows, financial publications, and regional newspapers. The public relations company encouraged the media to refer to him as "a leader of America's manufacturing recovery."

Wiemer employees were greatly amused by the pictures of Adam shaking hands with them. The articles and pictures were displayed on company bulletin boards with various sarcastic handwritten captions attached:

A lengthy article in a popular weekly business publication praised his ability to establish communication with "the little people." It described how he received daily phone calls from employees, "the little people," and always found time to listen to their problems or suggestions. It was later learned that the article was authored by the vice chairman of the public relations firm.

After a few articles had circulated throughout the community, a large crudely-printed sign was posted in the employee parking lot: **"The public statements of the officers of Wiemer Industries are not necessarily endorsed by the management of the firm."** The security officers were ordered to remove it.

All the expense associated with the public relations effort was borne by Wiemer Industries.

In October of 1994, Wiemer management and the IMU scheduled preliminary negotiations for a new labor contract. The existing contract was scheduled to expire in January 1995. The IMU bargaining committee presented a list of new contract provisions that, if accepted, would be prohibitively expensive. It was normal practice for the IMU bargaining committee to present a "wish list" at the outset of negotiations. It was expected that a month or more of negotiations would produce significant compromises. Harris Stevenson was chosen to represent management in the bargaining sessions. The respect he commanded among the hourly workers was considered a strong advantage. He was referred to by IMU members as a "straight shooter."

Following several preliminary sessions with IMU, he met with Ian Davis and Adam Fulton to review the IMU demands and his proposed response and negotiating strategy. Harris reported that the IMU's proposal far exceeded what they expected to achieve; they knew it was too ambitious and too expensive. He explained carefully to Ian and Adam that he intended to discuss each item on the IMU "wish list" and counteroffer a less expensive alternative. He was convinced that the IMU wanted to avoid a strike, but expected a reasonable contract. He expected both Ian and Adam to insist that he pursue a tougher bargaining strategy, given the difficult financial problems the company continued to experience.

He misjudged.

Adam was enjoying his growing reputation as "a leader of America's manufacturing recovery." He had received phone calls regarding his availability to serve on prestigious boards and panels and some hints of opportunities for greater career opportunities. He wanted to avoid anything that might tarnish his new image.

Adam sat at the head of the newly-acquired, marble-topped rectangular table in his conference room. Ian Davis occupied the seat on Adam's immediate left. Harris occupied a seat directly across from Davis. After Harris concluded his briefing, Adam leaned forward and placed his right hand on Harris's left arm. He looked directly at Harris and spoke in a low but determined voice.

"No goddamn strikes, Harris. I don't care what it takes. No strikes. If fact, I think it would be a real plus for this company and this community if we settled in the next two weeks."

Ian Davis laughed. "We've got more than two bloody months to settle this contract. We'd be bonkers to settle in two weeks."

Adam turned and looked at him; his face grew red and grim. "I want it understood, Ian, there will be no more strikes as long as I am CEO. I've had enough of the bad press and criticism that comes with a strike. There isn't going to be another one, and I am strongly suggesting that we settle before the end of this month and benefit from the positive community response."

Harris was amazed at Adam's reaction. "That'll be very expensive, Adam. We need at least until the end of November or early December to bargain the IMU requests back down to earth. They expect an extended negotiation."

Adam remained adamant. "No, I want it settled by the end of this month. Get as much as you can out of them in the next two weeks. But I want a new contract agreement by the first of November."

Harris was confused. He was sure that Adam didn't understand the cost increase they would incur if they limited the negotiations to such a short time horizon.

"That will cost us a bundle. How the hell do we pay for it? What do we tell the banks?" Davis protested.

Adam turned again and stared at Davis. His voice was intense with anger. "You're the president and chief operating officer of this company. I assume that you and Harris will figure that out. Try price increases. Let the customers pay for it. They understand the need to raise prices to meet increased labor costs."

Following the meeting Adam Fulton placed a call to his friend Jack Perkins and hired him to immediately assume responsibility for conducting the negotiations with the IMU. Harris Stevenson would assist him, but Jack and his staff would have primary responsibility and report directly to Adam.

He ended his conversation with Perkins with a short, explicit statement: "I know your reputation for tough negotiations, Jack, but I want it understood, no fuckin' strike."

During the first week of November, the *Hammelburg Sentinel* carried a series of articles about the generous three-year contract that had been initialed by Wiemer Industries and the IMU. The following week, the IMU membership voted to accept it. There were only a handful of negative votes.

The community was astonished. Wiemer employees were going to receive hourly wages and benefits that greatly exceeded any other industry in Hammelburg. When the leaders of the local UAW at the General Motors plant were told about the settlement, they refused to believe it. The prevailing attitude in the community was reflected in two common reactions: "How can the company afford that?" and "The IMU is gonna regret that. They're gonna lose lots of jobs."

In September of 1995, Adam Fulton announced his resignation as chairman and CEO of Hammelburg Industries to accept a new position as the CEO of a very large electronic research and manufacturing company located in San Jose, California. Chip was ecstatic.

Four weeks after his announcement, Adam and Chip invited a group of friends to join them at the Alamost Country Club, a combination celebration and farewell party. Chip, a self-appointed California wine connoisseur, had ordered several cases of champagne, Merlot, and Chardonnay for the occasion. As the evening passed, the noise level from the Fulton party suggested that the California wines were being consumed in substantial quantities. Among the guests, only Ian Davis, Gus Arnholt, and their spouses represented Wiemer Industries

In the main dining room, Harris Stevenson, his wife, Ellen, and Jon and Maureen Pertoski were dining together. As the evening was ending, Adam Fulton appeared in the main dining room, a bit wobbly, but not totally stoned. He stared momentarily at the Stevensons and Pertoskis, seemingly adjusting his focus, then walked directly to their table. He greeted them with great fanfare and—without being invited—borrowed an unoccupied chair from an adjoining table and sat down. He was obviously elated about the recent events in his life. Jon Pertoski made mention of the fact that four weeks had passed without any announcement regarding his replacement. Adam responded, loudly enough for everyone at the surrounding tables to hear, "It's a hell of a tough job, Jon. I hate to leave, I know it's a bad time for me to go, but that's life on the fast track."

"I am gonna tell you guys something." He spoke with a lowered voice as if about to relate some confidential information. "You're both really good manufacturing managers, and I have a world of respect for both of you. That's why I want to give you some straight from the shoulder advice."

As he paused, he leaned too far back in his chair and nearly fell before recovering his balance. "What I want to tell you," he continued, seemingly undeterred by his near accident, "is manufacturing jobs aren't going to get you to the big time."

Suddenly he became very animated and his voice rose. "Today, you need visibility." He raised both hands swiftly to express his point, nearly striking Maureen Pertoski in the face. "You have to be seen and heard out there in the executive market place. You have to let people know who you are and what you've done. You gotta make some news."

He looked at Jon Pertoski. "You know, Jon, I was smart that I didn't major in engineering in college. If I had, I would probably be stuck in some nowhere manufacturing job. My advice, guys, is break out, break out. Get some visibility. You're both smart guys, you can make it too."

Suddenly, Chip appeared dressed in a chic black miniskirted cocktail dress, revealing lots of breast and thigh. She placed her arm on Adam's shoulder, crossed her legs, and leaned against him. "Everyone having a big time in ole Hammelburg, tonight, huh?" she asked in a tone that dripped with sarcasm.

No one responded. She turned her attention to Adam. "What the hell are you doing here? All our guests have gone home," she said.

"I'm just doing a little coaching," he said, placing his hand firmly on Chip's shapely buttocks.

"Well, your coaching days are over here, Fulton. If these guys haven't got it by now, they're not going to… Let's go home."

She turned abruptly and walked away from the table. Adam stood up and, with appropriate stage presence, shook hands with all of them.

After they had departed, Maureen Pertoski declared, in her Irish brogue,

"For several years, I've been undecided about which of those two people I detest the most. I still haven't decided."

Two weeks after Adam Fulton's departure, the Wiemer board of directors met for the purpose of selecting his replacement. At the opening of the meeting, for which there was no chairman, Quentin Phillips recommended hiring an executive search firm and recruiting someone outside the company. Ted Brinson, Cyrus Brown, and Gus Arnholt preferred choosing someone from within the company. Everyone was suspicious of Arnholt's motive for endorsing that idea. It was finally decided that Clay Emerson,

Ted Brinson, and Quentin Phillips should meet as a nominating committee and return the following day with a recommendation.

The three men dined together that evening at The Bavarian Garden. After cocktails and dinner, they began to pursue their assigned task. Ted Brinson opened the discussion. "I have strong feelings on only one issue: I suggest that before we go any further with this process, we eliminate Gus Arnholt as a candidate. He was a pain in the ass for Harry Achaffer and J.W., and Fulton treated him like a toy. He wound him up and let him walk around as long as he didn't bump into anything."

"I agree, but we need to let him know immediately before he starts his campaign," Clay Emerson said.

"I don't disagree, but we have two members of the board who lust for that job, and I don't think either one of them is qualified," Quentin Phillips added.

"You're referring to Ian Davis," Emerson responded.

"Yeah, as president and chief operating officer, he would appear to be the natural inside choice, but he isn't even good at what he's doing now. Harris Stevenson is really the chief operating officer. Fulton kept Davis around for entertainment and companionship,"

Clay Emerson laughed. "O.K., what the hell are we going to do with these two guys if we don't pick one of 'em as the CEO? They're both on the board. No incoming CEO in his right mind would want those two guys sitting on his board."

"I'd recommend we give Davis a two-year consulting contract at his current salary and let him go. He'll take it. Tell Gus he can stay on the board for one more year, and give him a nice early retirement package. He can make it look like it's his decision," Phillips said.

"Christ," Emerson blurted, "with that strategy we lose three directors on a seven-man board. That means we've got a hell of a lot more than just a CEO to replace."

Ted Brinson nodded in agreement. "This company needs an independent board, comprised primarily of outside members. I suggest that the only member of management who can be elected to the board is the CEO. I also believe that the chairman of the board should be an outside member. Let the new CEO be a member, but not chairman. Fulton got away with too damn much that we didn't know about until long after it happened. An independent chairman provides more control."

"You really want to bring on a new CEO, a new chairman, and two new board members, and the only one who has any past experience with the company is, maybe, the chairman?" Emerson asked.

"It's going to take a long time to find that many qualified people," Phillips responded.

There was a long pause in the conversation.

"O.K., I am going to stick my neck out and make a recommendation," Brinson said. "I suggest that we promote Harris Stevenson to president and CEO and we select one of the existing board members to serve as chairman."

"Stevenson has the skills to run this company, but he isn't strong on finance. How do we solve that?" Emerson asked.

"We need a chairman with a good finance background who can coach him,and our colleague Ted is our our man," Phillips suggested.

Brinson laughed. "C'mon Quentin, stop hiding. You know damn well that I'm going to retire from the bank in a year, and when I do, I'm also going to retire from this board. It's you who has the appropriate financial experience. Not me, a regional banker from Indiana."

Phillips protested, "I don't have time to do that."

"You'll find time, and you'll do a damn good job," Brinson replied.

"So, we're agreed: we recommend Stevenson for president and CEO, Quentin as chairman, cashier Gus and Ian, and start looking for two new board members," Clay Emerson said.

"Jesus, hold on, Clay. You're way the hell ahead of me. I haven't agreed to serve as chairman. You're in one hell of a hurry," Phillips objected.

"Hey, we've got until tomorrow morning to go back in that room with a recommendation and make a decision. This entire company is expecting the board to come out of that meeting tomorrow and introduce the new leader. We can't afford to blink," Emerson replied.

"My God, but you're in a hurry," Phillips continued. "The rest of the board is going to be a little suspicious of how quickly we decided all this."

Ted Brinson interrupted him. "Quentin, there is only one critical vote that isn't sitting at this table, Cyrus Brown. Fulton is gone, Davis and Arnholt won't or can't stay if we don't pick one of them as CEO, and we just decided neither one of them is a candidate. If we don't announce our decision tomorrow, those two are going to start maneuvering to get the job, and they'll be disruptive as hell. I think the organization and the market will accept the idea of Stevenson as president and you as chairman. The organization knows Harris and has confidence in him. The market doesn't know him, but they do know you. It's our best alternative."

Phillips continued to reflect skepticism "How do you know the rest of the board will approve it?"

"Ted just laid it out," Emerson responded. "We've got three of six members sitting at this table, and I'm sure Cyrus will support us. Davis will go along with it so long as we cashier him with a long consulting contract. He won't fight to stay on the board if he isn't the CEO, and you know Gus isn't going to vote for him, and he isn't going to vote for Gus. And even if they get together and cook something up, we still have a majority of four out of six votes."

There was a long pause as Brinson and Emerson watched and waited for Phillips' response.

"O.K.," he finally replied, smiling, "I guess we don't have any other reasonable alternative, do we? But I want it understood that this is not a long-term commitment on my part. As soon as I think Harris is ready, he takes the chairman's seat."

There was a disingenuous tone in his response. But Brinson and Emerson nodded in agreement.

"Before we end this meeting," Ted Brinson said, "we ought to give some thought to new board members. We just jettisoned three of seven and I'm leaving in a year. That will leave three out of seven current members and four vacant seats."

"Maybe an executive headhunter can recruit some new board members," Phillips said.

"That takes a lot of time. We're down to five members, as of tomorrow. Gus will stay on for another year, but he won't be worth a damn. He'll just annoy the hell out of everybody, as he always has." Emerson said.

"Any better ideas?" Phillips asked rather impatiently.

Ted Brinson leaned forward, smiled, and lowered his voice as he spoke. "Yeah... I've got an idea. But hold on to your seats. I'm serious."

He studied his companions for a moment. "I suggest we invite Mary Rieff to become a board member."

He paused very briefly, but not enough time to allow a response. "Now, before you reject that suggestion, let me explain why I think it's a good idea... First, when Gus goes off the board, we lose the last member of the founding family, which still owns about ten percent of this company. Mary may not be a Wiemer, but she is considered part of the family... Second, she's respected in this community, and after Fulton's shenanigans, I think we need someone who is known and respected in Hammelburg. Third, she's a smart lady who understands more about this business than you'd suspect."

"Isn't she a little old to be joining a board?" Phillips asked.

"I don't think so. We don't have a mandatory retirement age, and she's in excellent health. Furthermore, she's a female, and it's time for Wiemer Industries to come out of the dark ages and get some diversity on its board."

Clay Emerson laughed. "I think Ted just shot down both of the traditional arguments."

Chapter 16

The Monday before Thanksgiving, two of Harris Stevenson's staff members had scheduled vacation to allow an extended Thanksgiving vacation. Consequently, he canceled the traditional Monday morning meeting. At mid-morning, he appeared at Beth Brinson's office door in his usual attire: no coat, loose tie, and shirt sleeves two rolls above his wrists. Beth waved him in while she completed a phone call. It was not unusual for Harris to visit with his staff members in their offices. He though it pretentious to request that they come to his office for informal and unscheduled meetings. He had earned Beth's respect long before he became the president and CEO. His knowledge and management style was refreshing. He wasn't the overly-ambitious CEO who employed corporate theatre to impress his subordinates. He treated her no differently than any other member of his immediate staff; sought and respected her professional judgment; but never hesitated to tell her directly when he disagreed. He had never referred to her gender, affirmatively or negatively.

"How was the weekend?" he inquired.

"My son, Tim, came home early for Thanksgiving. We spent the weekend together," she replied.

"Is he enjoying the life of a research scientist?" he asked.

"Yes, he's fascinated with his assignments. He believes it's the future. He has enormous confidence in what is being done in biotechnology.

It's wonderful to see a young person who is involved in a job where he continues to learn and is excited about his work."

"I wish we could establish that kind of an environment in Hammelburg," Harris said. "The argument that the old manufacturing jobs will be replaced with new jobs is losing strength. It hasn't happened; not in Hammelburg, or Indiana, only in a handful of communities in the entire Midwest. If we don't get on top it this problem, were gonna experience stagnation, not growth. When we lose the smart kids, we lose the chance to get the high-tech industries. It's a paradox."

"Anybody winning in this transformation?" she asked.

"I'm not sure. But it isn't who the economic planners intended. It sure isn't the Wiemer employees."

He shook his head and focused on something outside the office window. His voice softened. "Christ, I've begun to sound like a 1960s radical… I'll never forget those days. Coming back from 'Nam, being called a baby killer, never mentioning what happened for fear you'd be criticized."

Beth was surprised. She was aware that he had served and was wounded in Vietnam, but until now, she had never heard him mention it.

They were both silent for a few moments. For years, he had struggled to eradicate those memories, but they occasionally re-emerged. Finally, he turned and looked directly at Beth. "But that isn't what I came here to discuss. I need your opinion on a rather delicate subject, and I want this to be a confidential conversation; just you and me."

"O.K.," she responded. His request was not unusual for the CEO of a large corporation where senior managers share confidential information with the general counsel.

"Have you read our current labor contract?"

She was surprised by his question; he had never discussed the labor contract with her. "Yes, I've read it several times."

"Give me your opinion of our obligation to the IMU under the relocation clause."

As a well-trained lawyer, she attempted to organize her thoughts before responding. "Harris, I won't attempt to dodge your question by declaring professional disqualification. But, I'm not a labor lawyer, and I have never been invited to participate in labor negotiations or approve the contract. I think it's important that I say that before I respond."

"I understand that, Beth. That's why I said it was a confidential conversation."

She moved closer to her desk and placed her hands in her lap.

"O.K.... First, I believe the financial hardship clause is fuzzy and our interpretation might be challenged successfully... Second, I'm not sure that Byron Hinkle, the IMU lawyer, saw the inclusion of the financial hardship clause in the final draft of the contract. I'm not suggesting that it wasn't there, but I'm not sure he saw it... Third, if it was highlighted in the final draft and he didn't challenge it, it was a significant failure on his part... Fourth, if it was not highlighted in the final draft or slipped in the contract without his knowledge, our labor lawyers may have stepped over the line regarding ethical conduct... Finally, returning to my first point, regardless of whether or not it was in the final draft and whether he did or didn't see it, I can't understand why Hinkle hasn't challenged management's interpretation of the meaning."

"Did you see the final draft?" he asked.

"No. I've never seen a draft of a labor agreement. The only time I am asked to review a labor contract is after I receive a final signed copy from Jack Perkins, long after negotiations are concluded."

"Should you review them before they are signed?"

"Other corporations usually include the general counsel in the final review of a labor contract, before it's signed."

"Assuming you had seen it before it was signed, would you have suggested changes in the contract?"

"Yes... I would have suggested that a clear definition of financial hardship be included. The way the contract reads, financial hardship is open to wide interpretation. It could result in a long and expensive legal debate before an agreement is reached. It could delay the relocation issue for months or years. That's why I am puzzled that Byron Hinkle hasn't made the definition of financial hardship a major issue for the IMU."

"Does it work to our advantage to have the meaning of financial hardship remain ambiguous?"

"Harris, in my opinion, ambiguity in a contract is rarely an advantage to either side, but that assumes that both sides have competent and aggressive lawyers representing them."

"Do both sides have good lawyers?"

She laughed. "I feel like I'm slowly being led toward the edge of the cliff... Let me expand a bit on your question... From my perspective, during the past 20 years, the relationship between the Wiemer management and the IMU has deteriorated. When I joined the company, there was a strong spirit of cooperation between management, employees, and the community. When Adam Fulton became CEO, the relationship with the IMU and the community changed. He pursued a labor policy that gyrated between needless adversity and careless passivity; whatever best served his immediate objectives. At the same time, the IMU leadership stopped considering the impact of their demands on the company's financial strength. They grabbed for all they could get. By the time Fulton left, our relationship with the IMU was both adversarial and far too expensive."

She paused for a moment before continuing. "Today... our labor lawyers are very aggressive. They've earned a national reputation as tough opposition for union negotiators. There are times, in my opinion, when their negotiation strategy is too rigid, but that's how they maintain their reputation and clients. On the other hand, Byron Hinkle is way out of his league attempting to negotiate with Jack Perkins and his minions. It's David and Goliath, except David has no slingshot."

"What would you change?"

She shook her head. "That's a difficult question. It appears that we're determined to relocate machining and assembly operations to Juarez, regardless of IMU counteroffers. They've proposed some large concessions, but Bruce Kramer believes that it is still more cost-effective to relocate. The IMU's bargaining is weak. If they really pursued the issue of defining financial hardship, they would acquire more leverage. I have no idea why Hinkle doesn't pursue that issue."

He laughed. "You sound like an IMU supporter."

She pushed her chair back from her desk, crossed her legs, smoothed her skirt, and studied Stevenson for a moment before responding. "Yeah, I probably do... but that's not my intention. I believe the management of this company, like many others, is caught in a crossfire. According to corporate law and tradition, our primary responsibility is to protect the interests of the shareholders. So, if relocation to Juarez creates the most attractive results for the shareholders, we shouldn't hesitate. But what about the employees and the community? You described it... Hammelburg isn't creating new industries... there are few good jobs to replace those we've lost... the only employment opportunities are low paying service jobs. So, what happens to several hundred more people who lose their jobs when we relocate again? What happens to the community? Why would the smart kids hang around? A city that a few years ago was admired for its progress and vision is falling apart... but the NAFTA supporters tell us not to worry. We'll benefit from lower prices at Wal-Mart... high-tech companies will come to Hammelburg and hire people, despite their lack of adequate training and education... and they won't hesitate to move their management to a community that's experiencing a significant decline in the quality of life. Now, you tell me, who the hell really believes that fairy tale?"

Stevenson was surprised by her candid response. He stood up, walked to the window, turned to face her, and leaned against the window ledge with his arms folded across his chest. "I agree, but I'll be damned if I can figure how we can remain in business if we continue to manufacture here. We'll never convince the IMU to accept the wage and benefit packages that we've negotiated in Juarez. How can we stay in business if our competition relocates and we don't?"

"Is that becoming the new criterion for selection of manufacturing facilities?" she asked. "Relocate to any country that affords lower labor costs and less restrictive environmental regulations? Nicaragua or Guatemala may be less expensive than Juarez. They may have less restrictive environmental and labor regulations. Is Mexico going to reduce what few environmental regulations and labor standards they have to compete with those countries? Is that what the NAFTA proponents wanted to achieve?"

"Beth, I don't know if that was their objective, but from my perspective that's what's happening. What reason could there be for relocating facilities to Mexico other than lower labor cost and environmental regulations? Moreover, relocation isn't confined to manufacturing jobs; a lot of high-tech jobs are going to countries like India and China, where they can hire engineers and I.T. staff for less than half of what it costs in this country. God knows, that may be our next relocation issue. Nevertheless, the big shareholders support it. But they don't live in Hammelburg, or Fort Wayne, or Anderson, or Flint. All they want to hear is how much cost reduction we can derive by taking advantage of lower costs and fewer environmental restrictions."

"It sounds like a race to the bottom," she said. "Those countries that reduce labor costs and environmental restrictions attract manufacturing jobs, and the countries that insist on higher environmental and work standards lose. In a couple of years, we move our engineering and information technology jobs to Asia. What's left in Hammelburg?"

"I don't know. But if our competition relocates, and lowers its costs and prices, we have to find a way to match them. If we don't, we can't survive in a market economy. I'm not a financial expert, but I know if we're unwilling to achieve those cost reductions, the banks won't lend and the capital markets won't support our stock."

"Harris, do you ever worry about the public reaction to that scenario? It could become very ugly. It could lead to revulsion toward free market economics among winners and losers. Although, I'm not sure there are any real winners. If there are, it's a very small group."

"Hell, it's already started," he declared. "I've received calls from the mayor, the local and state chambers of commerce, the lieutenant governor, the local members of the Indiana legislature and two congressmen. Ironically, both of them voted for NAFTA. So far, they're only asking what they can do to prevent the relocation. I've no answers for them. They aren't going to pressure the IMU to reduce their latest offer, and the state and local government can't offer much. They've got their own financial problems, most of which stem from the loss of manufacturing jobs."

He returned to the chair in front of her desk. "Let's go back to the IMU contract. Tell me more about their lawyer," he said.

"Hinkle is probably a good small business and estate lawyer," she said. "He took over Tom Damich's law practice after he married Damich's daughter. A bit strange; Damich was never considered a friend of labor when he was in the state legislature and later in Congress. He was a far-right-wing politician. But Byron grew up in Minnesota and it is rumored that he has a different political orientation than his father-in-law. It's a small firm, maybe five partners. I suspect the IMU is their only union client. They've done some work for us in the past; small jobs, local lease and tax issues. Having both Wiemer Industries and the IMU as clients would probably be considered a conflict of interest in a larger law firm, but it's not that unusual among small, local practices."

"Has he done a good job for the IMU?" he asked.

"He probably would have when we conducted the negotiations directly with the IMU, but when Adam Fulton hired the New York law firm to conduct negotiations for management, the IMU hired Hinkle to represent them. It's no contest. Jack Perkins' young assistants devote all of their time to reviewing labor legislation and contracts, and they outnumber Hinkle's total staff by five to one. No matter how hard he works, he's always reacting to management's proposals. He ends up compromising or missing some clever move that Perkins has used in a myriad of other labor negotiations."

Stevenson again left the chair and walked to the window. "Beth, if you were asked to select counsel for the IMU, who would you choose?"

She laughed. "C'mon, Harris, a few minutes ago you accused me of being an IMU supporter. Now you want me to recommend counsel for them? Bruce Kramer would have me roasted over an open fire if I even suggested another counsel for the IMU."

He turned from the window and looked at Beth. "Forget about Bruce. He means well, but he spent too damn much time on Wall Street. I'm not suggesting that we somehow cave in to the IMU, like Fulton did, or neglect our responsibility to our shareholders. At the end of the day, we'll probably have to relocate machining and assembly to Juarez. But I've spent a lot of my life working with those people, and before I make that decision, I want to believe that they had good counsel and advice."

"Are you really serious about this? You want me to recommend another lawyer to represent the IMU? How the hell would I do that, even if I had any idea of who to recommend? I'm not a labor lawyer. I'd have to make inquiries, and that would appear very strange, the general counsel for Wiemer Industries attempting to recruit a lawyer for the IMU!"

He studied Beth for a moment. "I understand your reaction. But I've already had a similar conversation with Jon Pertoski. He can help and he's willing to. I told him I was going to have a conversation with you. I'd like to have lunch together. Assuming you're willing to become involved."

"Involved in what?" she asked impatiently.

"Beth, I'm not planning any clandestine activity. I'll say it again: I think our alternatives to relocating machining and assembly to Juarez are slim to none, but I want the IMU and the community to have someone who does a good job of representing their interests... I'm probably considered a naïve country boy on Wall Street, but I believe that the management of a corporation has an obligation to a wider group than just the shareholders... You as much as said it a moment ago, the shareholders may come first, but the interests of the employees and the community are also part of management's responsibility. I hope that's what you meant, but if you feel uncomfortable doing more, I'll understand, and our relationship won't be affected."

She smiled. "I really did talk my way into this arrangement, didn't I? Where and what time are we having lunch?"

"Our lunch is at 12:30 at Mary Rieff's home."

"With Mary Rieff?" Her response revealed her surprise.

"Well, sooner or later the board of directors has to become involved in this issue, and Mary is a director, and probably knows more about the operation of this company than anyone else on the board," he declared.

The Rieffs' home was built in the 1960s. Mary's father had helped design it; although nearly 40 years old, it appeared modern, with its geometrical angles, framed in cedar and glass. With the exception of the four outer walls, the first floor was entirely open, with half-walls dividing the living room, dining room, and kitchen. Several large Oriental and American

Indian rugs covered portions of the polished hardwood floor. The furniture was contemporary in design. J.W. had acquired a strong disdain for antique furniture. Anne Rieff loved antiques and had furnished her home with Wiemer family heirlooms. However, J.W. retained unpleasant memories of furniture that was neither functional nor, in his opinion, attractive.

The living room was very large. One side was comprised of floor-to-ceiling glass panels that looked out on a patio and beautifully landscaped garden, surrounded by a high cedar fence. Another wall was entirely devoted to bookshelves, which were nearly full. Visitors recognized quickly that the books were not selected for their decorative value. A fireplace occupied most of the third wall. A large portrait of Mary Rieff's paternal great-grandmother was displayed on one side of the fireplace.

A luncheon buffet had been arranged in the dining area with four settings for Mary and her guests. The dining room contained a large, oval-shaped, dark walnut table mounted on two pedestals, and three matching sideboards. A brass fixture of modern design illuminated the table.

Mary Rieff had recently celebrated her 80th birthday. Her natural white hair was cut short. She was thin, but her posture and mobility disguised her age. She wore a well-tailored dark wool slack suit and no makeup or jewelry.

Following a brief conversation in the living room, the party moved to the dining area for lunch. During the initial luncheon conversation, Mary and Beth discussed the events in the lives of their respective families. After several minutes, Harris Stevenson interrupted to explain to Mary why he thought it necessary to review with her, as a member of the Wiemer board of directors, the primary reasons that management had decided to relocate more of Wiemer's manufacturing facilities to Mexico, the status of current negotiations with the IMU, and the reaction of the community to yet another Wiemer Industries relocation.

Mary listened attentively without interruption as Stevenson described the financial benefits of the relocation and the pressure being exerted by the banks and institutional shareholders to pursue the relocation. At Stevenson's suggestion, Jon Pertoski described the growing resentment among the Wiemer employees and the adverse reaction of the community; in particular, the revulsion at the photographs of the living conditions of Wiemer employees in Juarez.

Mary admired Jon Pertoski. She had worked closely with Jon and his wife on several community programs to strengthen the Hammelburg public school system. Despite their active involvement in the Catholic church, Jon and Maureen had elected to send their three children to the Hammelburg Public Schools. During the past election, Maureen was a candidate for the board of directors of the Hammelburg School Board, but she was soundly defeated after her opponent falsely accused her of seeking a seat on the board in order to gain tax support for private schools.

Parochial and private schools were a sensitive issue in Hammelburg. Their enrollment had expanded significantly in the last decade, reflecting a growing dissatisfaction with the public school system. Many parents were convinced that the private or church-affiliated schools provided a more appropriate Christian education and social environment. Private schools sponsored by fundamentalist protestant denominations had experienced the most rapid growth. Issues surrounding school prayer, the Pledge of Allegiance, teaching of creationism rather than evolution, and the appropriate selection of books and authors all played a part in their popularity.

Consequently, state tax support for public schools—which was based on enrollment—had decreased; local property taxes had been increased to fund a part of the shortfall. Tax support for private schools was not on anyone's political agenda. In the final weeks of the campaign, the local teacher's union announced their support for Maureen's opponent. Because Maureen was considered a "liberal" on issues of diversity and women's rights, she had little support among fundamentalist religious groups that might have otherwise supported her based on the misguided assumption that she would seek public funding for private schools.

Following Jon's review of the IMU and community reaction, Beth described briefly the imbalance of negotiating skills between management and union representatives.

At the conclusion of Beth's remarks, Mary asked Harris if there had been similar discussions with any other members of the Wiemer Board. Harris said that he intended to, but had decided to talk with her first because of her long association with the community. She appeared to be surprised at his response.

"Do you have any idea how other members of the board feel about the relocation issue?" she asked.

"I think all of them are aware of the issue, but I haven't had an opportunity to discuss it with them," he responded.

"Well, what's your best guess ?"

Harris was surprised by Mary's questions. He had assumed that she would immediately express her opposition to the loss of more jobs in Hammelburg and the impact on the community.

"I guess that they would support what is best for the shareholders and the financial health of the corporation. The attitude of the banks and institutional shareholders has enormous influence on other board members."

It was obvious that Jon Pertoski was uncomfortable with Stevenson's response. Although he said nothing, Mary immediately turned to him.

"Jon, you spend most of your time in the plants, you talk with the IMU members frequently. What do you believe management should do?"

Beth was also surprised at Mary's initial response. She too had assumed that Mary would not hesitate to express her objection to further job losses in Hammelburg and the economic cost to the community. Mary was the last of the Wiemer family to have any influence on company policies; the last representative of four generations of the Wiemer family remaining in Hammelburg; the closest confidant of Anne Rieff, who had been the single largest influence for progress and generosity in the history of Hammelburg.

Jon glanced for a moment at both Harris and Beth before responding. "Mary, I'm not sure that the three of us even agree on an appropriate policy regarding relocation. There are several conflicting arguments. The financial advantages of relocation seem overwhelming: lower labor cost, avoidance of expensive environmental and OSHA regulations, no pension expense, lower cost for employee medical benefits, and probably some significant tax advantages. According to Bruce Kramer, the reduction in cost will permit us to pay down a significant amount of corporate debt over the next five years. That means lower interest cost, improved profits, and larger dividends for the shareholders, which should result in a higher price for Wiemer common stock. Of course, all that assumes that our competition, who are also moving to Mexico and other countries, don't lower the price on their products and further reduce our profit margins."

"Isn't it safe to assume that our competition might reduce prices regardless of our decision on relocation?" Mary asked.

"They already have," Stevenson responded.

"Does that mean we have no choice on relocation?" Mary asked.

"It tips the scale heavily in favor of relocation, but not all the way," Pertoski answered. "The IMU has made a counteroffer that dramatically lowers our cost in Hammelburg. It is a long way from matching the expected cost in Juarez, but it's a major concession. Moreover, we have a trained and experienced labor force in Hammelburg. If we relocate, we'll incur startup costs in Juarez. We don't know what will happen to quality and productivity when we relocate. It could be expensive. The Mexican government is not particularly stable. A new government could change the rules regarding environmental regulations and pension and medical benefits. I've learned that there is only one certainty in financial projections: They're either too high or too low."

"Well, you moved the foundry and forge operations down there. How has it worked out?"

"We achieved lower costs, but not as low as forecast. We suffered a big loss of productivity in Hammelburg when we announced the relocation. It took us two years to complete the relocation. In the intervening period, the Hammelburg employees lost their incentive. When we finally got the foundry and forge shop operating in Juarez our scrap rate jumped to 27 percent. It had been less than four percent in Hammelburg. That means that approximately one out of every four castings and forgings was rejected. A higher scrap rate was not included in the financial projections. The best scrap rate we've ever achieved in Juarez is nine percent and even the finished products are not as good as we achieved in Hammelburg."

"Are you saying that moving the foundry and forge operations was a mistake?"

"No, we have lower costs in Juarez, but nearly all the cost reduction is attributable to the avoidance of environmental and OSHA regulations and employee benefit costs. If those costs were equal in Juarez and Hammelburg, we would have made a mistake in relocating the foundry and forge operations. The Hammelburg workers were more productive. In time, the Mexican workers may catch up, but it will take a long time."

"Are you implying that our cost advantage in Mexico is entirely a result of avoiding anti-pollution and health and safety regulations in this country?"

Harris Stevenson offered a softer response: "Jon is correct that most of the cost reduction is a result of avoidance of U.S. regulations, but in time, the Mexican costs may be reduced as the labor force becomes more efficient."

"Do the bankers and institutional shareholders understand that is the fundamental reason we have lower costs in Mexico?"

Harris responded, "They probably don't understand it precisely. The big picture advocates for globalization and market-driven economic policies cruise at about 40,000 feet. When we look at the issues, we cruise at about 500. It's a much different picture at 500 feet."

"I suspect that even if they were aware, it wouldn't change their recommendations," Beth added.

Mary appeared amused at Beth's comment. "Is avoidance of U.S. regulatory requirements the primary reason we are proposing to move machining and assembly to Juarez? she asked.

Harris continued to respond, attempting to avoid having Jon offer his blunt answers to Mary's questions. "It's a part of the reason, but machining and assembly are much more labor intensive than foundry and forge operations; therefore, lower labor costs are a bigger factor in the second relocation."

"How much bigger?"

Jon quickly intervened. "That brings me back to the accuracy of financial forecasting. We know that it will require two years to complete the move. The building has to be finished, all the machinery has to be moved;

recruiting and training a labor force is a big job. The skill requirements are higher for machining and assembly. Therefore, the learning curve is steeper and longer. It's much tougher to forecast the total cost benefit. But the financial forecasters believe the relocation will generate major cost benefits."

"Do you believe the forecasts?"

Jon looked directly at Mary before answering. "No, I think they're too optimistic. They don't factor in the loss of productivity in Hammelburg during the two-year transition period, and its going to be a long, hard task to hire and train a labor force in Juarez that comes close to meeting the quality standards we've achieved in Hammelburg. The expected savings, in my opinion, are too optimistic."

Beth was amazed at the perceptiveness of Mary's questions. She had known Mary for more than 20 years and worked with her on many community projects. She had expected her to state her objection to the relocation at the outset of the meeting. Instead, she was exploring the issue carefully before committing herself.

"Have you discussed your reservations with the financial forecasters?"

"Yes, but they don't agree. They believe I'm too conservative"

Harris Stevenson attempted to recover the direction of the conversation. "I don't know who is right or wrong. Jon is the typical manufacturing exec who expects snafus in any big project, based on his own experience. On the other hand, Bruce Kramer and his staff are preparing the forecasts, and they tend to reflect the interest of bankers and institutional investors who want debt reduction, profit improvement, and higher dividends. But at the end of the day, regardless of who is right and wrong about labor costs, the avoidance of EPA and OSHA requirements will probably result in a substantial net savings and improved profits."

"So we're back to the issue of avoiding environmental and labor regulations as the primary reason for relocating to Juarez," Mary suggested.

The room was engulfed by an embarrassed silence.

Finally Harris Stevenson responded. "I won't deny that, Mary. The existing and proposed EPA and OSHA legislation places an enormous cost burden on older manufacturing facilities like Wiemer Industries. Now, if everyone had to meet these standards, we could probably compete, but when our competitors relocate to countries that don't require them, we can't absorb these costs and remain competitive. We have to follow them."

"What if you relocate to Mexico and the Mexican government adopts similar environmental and labor laws in the future? What do you do then?" Mary asked.

"I think there is little chance that Mexico will do that. They understand why many U.S. companies are relocating to the border towns. Secondly, even if they did, all of our competitors would be required to meet the new rules and we wouldn't be at a competitive disadvantage," Harris said.

"What about the employees in Hammelburg who are displaced by the relocation? What happens to them?"

"That's the primary reason we want to discuss this issue with you and other board members. We want to treat them fairly. We don't want the community to be torn apart by this issue. But it's difficult, given the inadequacy of the IMU counsel. They need better legal representation in the negotiations, and Wiemer Industries cannot represent both sides of the negotiating table," Harris said.

"Who have they hired to negotiate for them?"

"A local lawyer, Byron Hinkle," Beth responded.

"I don't think I've ever heard of him. Does he practice in Hammelburg?" Mary asked.

"Yes, he's Tom Damich's son-in-law. He took over Damich's practice after he retired."

"Oh my God, I hope he's more ethical than his father-in-law!" Mary exclaimed.

"I suspect his primary failing is lack of experience, rather than ethics," Beth said.

"All right, permit me to ask one additional question and I promise to give you my reaction to the problem," Mary said. She smiled. "I assume that's what you're really here for."

She took her napkin from her lap, folded it carefully, placed it gently on the table, and looked briefly at each of her guests.

"Wiemer Industries has a long history of treating its employees fairly and with respect. I realize that such policies are becoming unfashionable. Particularly among the neoconservatives who consider paternalistic management practices as regressive economic behavior. Nevertheless, you have already expressed your concerns about the impact of relocation on Wiemer employees and the Hammelburg community. Therefore, I assume that you still consider it an important part of Wiemer's management policy."

She paused for a moment and again looked at each of her guests before continuing. "So, my question is: What are you planning to do for our employees in Juarez to improve the quality of their lives, and how much will that cost?"

Her three guests were stunned. No one had discussed the Juarez employees, with the exception of Jon Pertoski's brief reference to the photographs. The entire discussion had focused on the financial issues involved in the relocation and the impact on the Hammelburg employees and the community.

After a long silence, Mary spoke again, very softly. "I've seen the pictures of Juarez that Jon referred to. She paused momentarily, aware that her next statement would surprise her guests. "I was with Jerry Bentenhausen when he took the pictures," she announced. "I've known Jerry for a long time. He and I fought several battles together regarding education and child care in Hammelburg. "

"Jerry called me about two months ago and told me he wanted to go to Juarez and visit the Wiemer employees. I decided to become one of those pesky, bothersome board members who want to see things for themselves. I had a trip planned to visit my daughter in Seattle. So, I flew from Seattle to

El Paso and met Jerry. We spent three days in Juarez. Not a very romantic location."

She smiled. "When you're an 80-year-old widow, you don't worry about the gossip that may result from accompanying another man to a strange city."

Beth laughed; she could no longer contain her amusement at Mary's revelation.

"Harris, I assume you have visited Juarez?" Mary asked.

"I was there for the plant opening."

"My, that was several years ago," she remarked.

Harris did not respond.

"How about you, Jon?" she asked.

"I've visited the plant several times, probably once every three months," Jon responded. "But I land in El Paso, drive to the plant in Juarez, and return to the airport. I've not taken time to visit the community or employee neighborhoods. I walk around the plant, but I don't speak Spanish, so I'm unable to have conversations with employees, like I do in the Hammelburg plant."

"Strange, isn't it?" Mary said. "We worry about the consequences of relocation in Hammelburg, but no one appears to be concerned about the environment and employees in Juarez. We move our manufacturing facilities from Hammelburg to Juarez to take advantage of lower wage, pension, and health benefits and avoid EPA and OSHA regulations. The result is a net decline in the combined quality of life and environment of both communities. But our leaders tell us that's economic progress, the benefits of a free market system, and globalization of the world economy."

"It's economic reality, Mary," Harris said. "It's worldwide competition. Ten years ago, we could increase our prices annually by five or six percent. In the past four years, we haven't been able to make a single price increase. Competition is too tough. Our competitors are taking advantage of NAFTA and reducing costs and prices. The economic advantage is lower prices for our products."

"Really," Mary responded. "What about the increasing damage to the quality of air and water in Mexico? The injuries and damaged health of our employees in Juarez? The loss of Hammelburg's middle class? The disproportionate loss of manufacturing jobs among Hammelburg's minority population? The quiet acquiescence of political corruption in Mexico?"

No one responded.

She continued, "Do the benefits of lower costs and stable prices for our products equal those costs?"

Harris Stevenson's voice reflected his frustration as he finally responded to Mary. "Most of our management feel as strongly as you do about the results of relocation on both communities, but we also have to consider the economic impact on our shareholders and our employees. If we don't achieve lower manufacturing costs, Wiemer Industries will not survive, and I don't know of any other method to reduce cost. What I'm most concerned about is how we cushion the effect of the relocation on Hammelburg and our employees. We want to be fair. We don't want to walk away from our obligations."

"I really don't intend to be contentious, Harris, but what obligations are you referring to?" Mary inquired. "If my reading of prevailing economic thought is correct, free market advocates and neoconservatives argue that management's primary, even singular, responsibility is to its shareholders. Anything else is paternalistic, a return to welfare economics or a mixed economy, rather than a true market economy. If Wiemer Industries leaves Hammelburg because labor and environmental costs are too high, free market adherents argue that it will result in lower labor costs in Hammelburg and generate new jobs. Simultaneously, the demand for labor in Juarez will increase, and the cost of labor will rise. Therefore, what they refer to as market equilibrium will occur. I gather that market equilibrium means lower wages in Hammelburg and higher costs and higher wages in Juarez. There is, of course, an absence of concern regarding the impact on the environment and the associated costs."

She paused, but there was no response.

215

"Am I correct in assuming that, as a society, we appear to be experiencing a fundamental transformation? Before the global market concept became vogue, many industrial companies, like Wiemer Industries, were owned and operated by people who had a direct connection with the company and the local communities. The economic success of the businesses was paramount, but there were also social objectives. Today, success is measured by a single parameter—the daily calculation of the market value of the enterprise. The companies are collectively owned by financial institutions that insist we must return to unbridled capitalism. Manufacturing pursues the lowest cost opportunities, regardless of language or cultural differences. Financial markets dictate that management pursue the lowest labor and operating costs."

She smiled at her guests. "Jerry Bentenhausen describes it very bluntly. He says its all about the goddamn numbers; nothing else counts. People are only financial obstacles to overcome."

Her tone of voice shifted from inquiry to declaration. "Following my visit to Juarez and a tour of that squalid community, I concluded that free market equilibrium has resulted in a significant cost reduction for Wiemer Industries, but it has also lowered the standard of living in Hammelburg, and provided little, if any, improvement in Juarez. I have little patience for their destructive behavior, but I must admit I have begun to understand the objections of that raucous minority of young troublemakers who insist that the vast proportion of the benefits of free markets and globalization are flowing to the small minority who already control a disproportionate share of the wealth."

She paused to study the response of her guests before continuing. "Now, the global market true believers tell us there is another scenario which envisions new high-tech industries emerging in Hammelburg, providing high value added jobs for our unemployed and modestly educated citizens, and thereby increasing the living standard of both communities, Hammelburg and Juarez... the magic of economic theory."

Again, there was no response.

"Well, I promised to try to be helpful, and I obviously haven't," she said. "You mentioned that you thought the IMU might be better served if they retained a stronger lawyer. Interestingly, Jerry Bentenhausen called me this morning and made the same suggestion."

Beth was the first to register her surprise. "Jerry Bentenhausen called you talk about Byron Hinkle and the IMU?"

"Yes, Jerry and several members of the IMU appear to share your lack of confidence in Mr. Hinkle. But Jerry didn't call me for advice. He wanted a favor. He asked me to call Ruth Heider, whom you know, Beth, and attempt to convince her son, Will, a labor lawyer, to assist the IMU."

"Who the hell is Will Heider?" Harris asked, reflecting his bewilderment at the direction of the conversation.

Beth responded. "Remember Bernie's clothing store? They sold most of the work clothes in Hammelburg. His grandparents started Bernie's, and his father and older brother managed it for years before the superstores put them out of business. He's a partner in a Chicago law firm. I met him Saturday evening at the Bavarian... with his parents."

She returned her attention to Mary. "How did Bentenhausen know about Will Heider?"

"I've no idea. But I've known Ruth Heider for years, a wonderful woman. We worked together on hospital projects. I remember Will as a boy, but I lost track of him when he left Hammelburg."

"Well, in my brief conversation with him Saturday evening, I gathered he has a lot of labor law experience, but I don't think he'd represent a union. He told me his firm represents management in labor negotiations," Beth said.

"That's what Ruth told me, but she didn't turn me down. Will is home for the Thanksgiving holidays and she agreed to talk with him."

"You've already called her?" Beth asked.

"Oh, yes. Jerry told me they had very little time to try to reach a solution and they need Will's help."

"But you don't know how he learned about Will?" Beth inquired again.

"No, but when Ruth called back later this morning, she indicated that he was neither surprised nor pleased by Jerry's request."

Both Harris and Jon sat silently, both puzzled by the conversation between Beth and Mary.

"She called back already?" Beth responded.

"Well, Jerry called early and I called Ruth immediately afterward. She called back just before the three of you arrived."

"I assume he declined the request," Beth said.

Mary laughed. "You don't know Ruth as well as I do. She's a quiet soul, but she can also be a very strong and determined woman. Apparently, she had a long discussion with Will. He finally agreed to meet with the management of Wiemer Industries, but not the IMU. He suggested that the initial meeting should be with Wiemer's general counsel."

"Me ?," Beth responded.

"Yes," Mary smiled. "Ruth said they visited with you at the Bavarian last Saturday. He suggested that if you want to meet with him, call him at his parents' home, and establish a meeting place and time, but he will not meet with the IMU."

"This isn't strange, it's bizarre," Beth said.

"Probably no stranger than having a member of the board of directors of Wiemer Industries establishing a liaison with a member of the IMU," Harris responded, smiling.

Mary turned, looked at Harris, narrowed her eyes, and asked bluntly, "Are you objecting to my friendship and communication with Jerry Bentenhausen?"

Harris laughed. "No, Mary, not at all. As a matter of fact, I think it is a unique and useful friendship." He paused momentarily. "And I hope you will take note of my concurrent use of the term 'friendship'."

"Thank you,"

"But, like Beth," Harris continued, "I'm a bit confused about how Heider is going to assist the IMU if he won't meet with their representatives, but meets with a representative of management. We already have outside legal counsel. It's the IMU that needs his help, not Harris Industries."

"I guess the only way to sort out this issue is for Beth to meet with Heider," Jon Pertoski added.

"Wait a minute," Beth objected, "I assume he wants to discuss the negotiation with Jack Perkins or some member of his staff, not me. I haven't been involved in the bargaining sessions."

"Beth, Ruth Heider was very specific. She said that Will was willing to meet with Wiemer's general counsel. He will not meet with the IMU or any other party to the negotiation," Mary replied.

"What about other members of management, are they also excluded from this meeting? What about Harris and Jon?" Beth inquired, reflecting her skepticism.

"I don't know, Beth," Mary answered. "According to Ruth, Will insists that it be understood that it would be an unofficial lawyer-to-lawyer meeting. He's not representing the IMU and he understands that the general counsel isn't directly involved in the negotiations with the IMU."

"How the hell does he know that?" Harris asked.

"Given the fact that he grew up in Hammelburg, his grandfather founded Bernie's, and his father and brother managed the store, I would guess he has a pretty damn good information pipeline in this community," Jon responded.

Beth shook her head. "I'm not sure this is a good idea."

"Why?" Jon asked.

"Because, like it or not, we have outside counsel that is representing management, and the IMU has counsel. It seems inappropriate for me to meet with another lawyer to discuss the negotiations, when neither one of us is directly involved."

"Well, we're not making a hell of a lot of headway with the current course of action. Meeting with Heider may provide some fresh insights," Jon said.

Harris appeared puzzled by the direction of the conversation. "Where and when is this clandestine meeting supposed to occur?" he inquired.

"Will Heider is leaving next weekend after the Thanksgiving holiday. I assumed that you would want to meet beforehand," Mary said.

Beth laughed. "You also assumed that I wanted to meet with him."

Mary smiled at her. "Oh, yes. I was sure you'd accept. Ruth and I agreed that such a meeting could be very beneficial."

Chapter 17

Following the lunch meeting, Harris and Beth returned to the Wiemer corporate headquarters. Harris intended on accompanying Beth to her office to discuss a possible meeting with Will Heider, but his secretary intercepted him and told him that Bruce Kramer had asked to meet with him as soon as he returned. It was urgent. Harris went directly to Kramer's office. As he entered, Kramer suggested that he close the door.

Before Harris was even seated, Kramer informed him, "We've got ourselves a nasty problem."

Harris sat down in a chair directly across from Kramer before responding. "O.K.... how nasty?"

He had grown accustomed to Kramer's dire predictions and warnings. He described them as "cover your ass" techniques. But he noted that Kramer appeared very nervous and rather pale.

"Late this morning, I got a call from the managing general partner of Jack Perkins's law firm. He told me that Jack has been placed on administrative leave and will be unable to represent any clients for the foreseeable future."

"Administrative leave, what the hell does that mean?"

Kramer's discomfort was obvious. His voice cracked slightly as he spoke. "Yesterday afternoon, Jack received a subpoena from the SEC which alleges that he and two other partners of the firm engaged in illegal insider trading of the stock of several corporate clients.... The firm has placed them on administrative leave until the matter is resolved."

"Wow! That's some serious shit. I thought Jack was smarter than that."

"Well, the managing partner assured me that a subpoena is not a conviction, but they've examined the SEC allegations and believe, as he phrased it, that it would be inappropriate for Jack and the other two partners to continue to represent the firm until these issues are resolved."

"Did he give you any specifics?"

"No, but it's already in the news. I pulled up the *Wall Street Journal* on the Internet and read about it. It's also on the *New York Times* Internet service. They'll both print hard copies tomorrow... But that's not the full extent of the bad news," he continued. "Trent Baker is one of the other two partners named in the subpoena."

"Holy Christ!" Stevenson exclaimed. "You mean both of the lawyers who represent us in labor negotiations are accused of illegal stock transactions?"

Kramer was having difficulty speaking; his face revealed his anguish. "Yes... both of them... both papers provide a pretty extensive description of the allegations. Perkins, Baker, and a third partner... established a hedge fund several years ago. They called it Urban Partners."

"What the hell is a hedge fund?" Stevenson barked.

Bruce sighed, moved his chair closer to his desk. "Large pools of private money managed by a few general partners. The investors are limited partners—limited in the sense that the legal liabilities fall on the general partners. They've become very popular in the last few years. You remember the recent scandal about Long Term Capital Management and the billions of dollars they lost? That was a big hedge fund. They're essentially unregulated. The money is provided by wealthy individual investors, pension funds, institutional investors. They take big, risky, long and short positions in stocks and bonds, and even foreign currencies. A hell of a lot of money has been made by hedge funds… and the general partners get a big slice for managing them."

"Perkins and Baker set up a hedge fund?" Stevenson asked.

"Yeah, Baker's wife is also a general partner and the chief investment officer. She managed the portfolio, and she's also named in the subpoena."

"My God" Stevenson exclaime

"The SEC claims that Urban Partners bought and sold shares of companies that Perkins and Baker worked for. According to the SEC, the trading was illegal because they used insider information that Perkins and Baker had access to."

"You mean like Wiemer Industries?" Stevenson responded sarcastically.

Kramer paused a moment, attempting to calm himself. "Yes." He cleared his throat before continuing. "The SEC claims that three months ago, they became aware of an unusually large transaction at Urban Partners. They bought 200,000 shares of a company that was about to announce a favorable labor contract settlement. Both Perkins and Baker were involved in the labor negotiations. The SEC claims they bought the shares five days before the public announcement for 39 dollars a share and sold in less than 60 days for 54 dollars a share. The size of that transaction triggered an SEC investigation, but the SEC claims there were several other illegal transactions over the past several years. They allege that illegal profits approached 20 million dollars."

Stevenson smiled and shook his head in disbelief. "So, old Jack got caught with his greedy hand in the cookie bowl. I thought he was too damn smart to do something like that. Apparently, those exorbitant legal fees weren't enough to cover the cost of the good life."

"Well, in all fairness, the managing partner is correct. They're accused, not convicted," Kramer protested.

"Listen, Bruce, you and I know that the SEC isn't going to issue a subpoena and tell the world about this fiasco unless they've got a ton of evidence."

"Well, if anyone understands the dangers associated with this kind of behavior, it's Jack. It's hard to believe he would do that, considering the potential penalties," Kramer replied.

Stevenson responded with a sarcastic laugh. "Bullshit, that sonofabitch will hire the best lawyers available, cop some rinky-dink plea, get off with probation and a fine, and he'll be back on Wall Street in a couple of years."

Kramer shifted the direction of the conversation. "Anyway, coming back to our problem, the managing partner told me that he's assigning two experienced senior partners to our account to carry on the current negotiations with the IMU."

Stevenson shook his head defiantly before responding. "No, Bruce. That firm isn't going to represent Wiemer Industries. There've been lots of rumors about Jack Perkins pulling a fast one during the last negotiation with the IMU. Now he's accused of securities fraud. I don't want anything to do with him or any of his colleagues. You can call the managing partner back, or I will, and tell him we no longer require their services."

Kramer's face grew red with anger. His voice became much louder. "Harris, you can't hold an entire major law firm accountable for the alleged misdeeds of three partners. They haven't been convicted of anything. I think the firm is pursuing a very appropriate and ethical policy by placing them on administrative leave. Moreover, who is going to represent us at this late stage of the IMU negotiations?"

Harris stood up abruptly, turned, and walked halfway to the office door before turning and responding to Kramer's question. His face was grim.

"You know, Bruce, my old man use to have a saying that really fits this situation. He used to say that when you find one skunk under your front porch, you can bet there's a whole family of 'em living under there."

He continued to walk toward the door, but before opening it, he turned again and looked at Kramer. "I don't know who the fuck were gonna use to help us negotiate with the IMU, but as long as I'm CEO of this company, it isn't going to be Jack Perkins or any of his associates. Do I call 'em, or you?"

Kramer, still flushed with anger, muttered, "I'll call them this afternoon."

Without responding, Stevenson turned and departed Kramer's office. He walked directly to Beth Brinson's office. He entered unannounced, closed the door, and sat down in front of her desk.

She smiled. "This is becoming a busy day for us, isn't it… Does this second visit have anything to do with a hedge fund and Jack Perkins?"

"When and how did you obtain that information?" His voice continued to reflect his anger.

"I've a few Yale Law School classmates who practice corporate law in New York," Beth said. "I had three separate e-mail messages when I returned from lunch. It's no secret that Wiemer Industries retains Perkins, and the news about his SEC subpoena is already common knowledge on Wall Street."

"O.K., what's your opinion of this mess?" he snapped.

"Well, we've got a couple of problems, Harris. First, I would assume that the SEC is going to examine trading patterns in all the companies that Perkins represented to see if the hedge fund engaged in any other illegal trading, and, if so, were the respective managements aware of it? That investigation will include Wiemer Industries, and it will attract some unpleasant attention. I've already called our specialist on the New York Stock Exchange and our registration agent and asked them to check and see if there is any record of Urban Partners as a Wiemer shareholder. I hope to have a preliminary answer in a couple of days. Second, the SEC action will get a lot of attention in the media, given the other corporate scandals that have surfaced in the last few months, and it will probably reinforce the IMU allegations that Jack and Trent Baker played dirty tricks in our previous labor negotiations."

"I've already told Kramer that Perkins's law firm will no longer represent Wiemer Industries. He's pissed, but he's probably informing the senior managing partner as we speak," Stevenson interjected quickly

"Well, I assumed we wouldn't rely on Martha Berman or Fenn Sullivan to complete the IMU negotiations," Beth said.

She looked directly at Harris and paused for a moment. "It appears we have two reasonable alternatives: We either hire new labor lawyers, or I assume responsibility for the negotiations."

Stevenson's attitude shifted from anger to surprise. "Jesus, Beth, are you serious? You take over the IMU negotiations?"

"I suggested two alternatives, Harris. There are advantages and disadvantages associated with both. I assume we would select well-established outside counsel with lots of experience. But they'll have a lot of catching up to do in a very short time, and they'll have to establish a working relationship with the IMU. On the other hand, I've never been involved in labor negotiations, and labor law is not my forte, but most of the IMU bargaining committee know me and have no reason to distrust me, and trust is going to be one hell of a big issue following today's news."

"How do we inform the IMU of these recent developments regarding Perkins and Baker?" he asked.

"I think it's a safe assumption they already know," she answered.

"I'm sure that one the senior members of Perkins's firm has already called Byron Hinkle. It's professional courtesy. Either Perkins or Baker was scheduled to meet with Hinkle this week. He's probably sitting there wondering what we are going to do and when. He'll probably call Fenn Sullivan and tell him about Perkins. God knows what Fenn might say, and then Hinkle will call a member of the IMU bargaining committee."

"You're suggesting we need to move rather quickly regarding selecting a replacement for Perkins and Baker,"

"Well, I don't think time is on our side. The IMU bargaining committee despises both of them. They've never understood why we hired them. They hired Hinkle in retaliation. Neither side ever used outside negotiators until Adam Fulton hired Perkins. Bringing the negotiations back inside the organization may reduce the tension in the bargaining sessions and the community."

Stevenson arose, walked to the office window, observed the corporate office parking lot for a moment, and then turned and looked at Beth.

"How would you manage the negotiations if I ask you to take charge?"

"Well, I haven't had a lot of time to consider that, and I only offered that as one of two alternatives, and at this point, I'm not even sure I'd recommend it. But I know that I would replace Fenn Sullivan with Jon Pertoski in the negotiation sessions. No other individual in this entire management team has earned as much respect among the hourly employees as Jon. Also, given my lack of familiarity with labor law, I would hire outside legal counsel, but I wouldn't include them in the meetings with the IMU."

"What about this guy Heider, that Mary was recommending at lunch?"

"What about him?" she responded.

"Could we hire him? He knows the community. He grew up here. His family is probably well-known among the IMU members. He's a labor lawyer."

"Well, the only time I've met him was last Saturday night at The Bavarian. It was hardly a professional meeting. I know his mother, and she is an outstanding lady, but I know nothing about his legal or negotiating experience, other than he told me his firm represents management exclusively. Given that small bit of information, I'd like to know why Jerry Bentenhausen decided to call Mary Rieff and ask her to intervene to convince Heider to become involved in this contract negotiation. That whole episode is downright bizarre."

"Any harm in calling and scheduling a meeting with him?"

"Probably not, but my first question is going to be about his relationship with Jerry Bentenhausen. We've had more than our share of obfuscation in our relations with the IMU."

"Would it help if I attended the meeting with you?"

Beth did not respond immediately. She realized that his question required a careful answer. She considered Harris a good CEO, but he had a tendency to be a little clumsy in meetings with third parties; particularly meetings that required some careful probing at the outset.

"If you want me to call him and arrange a meeting, I will. It would certainly be appropriate for you to attend the meeting, but Mary referred to his desire to have an informal lawyer-to-lawyer meeting. I'm not sure what he means by that, but it might be to your advantage if I met him alone the first time, briefed you following that meeting, and then you decide if you want to meet with him."

"When would you meet with him?"

"I'll call him this afternoon and arrange a meeting as soon as possible, probably tomorrow. He's here for the balance of the week, according to Mary."

"O.K. You meet with him tomorrow. Size him up. If you think he's right, I will meet with both of you this week. I agree with your suggestion about replacing Fenn with Jon. I want to wait until after the meeting with Heider to decide how we proceed with the negotiations."

Harris moved toward the door, but stopped abruptly when Mary spoke.

"Harris, I want to ask you a very personal question."

"O.K., ask it," he answered as he turned toward her.

"Are you hesitant about my leading the IMU negotiations because I'm a woman?"

He narrowed his eyes, pursed his lips, looked down at the carpet momentarily, looked up, and responded. "Beth, my evaluation of your strengths and weaknesses as an executive and a leader never included your gender as a consideration, and it never will. Does that answer your question satisfactorily?"

She smiled. "Yes. That's a very satisfactory answer. Thank you."

However, his response contained one surprise. It was the first time she had heard him include the word "leader" in describing her responsibilities at Wiemer Industries.

As soon as Harris departed her office, she removed the Hammelburg telephone directory from her desk drawer and began looking for the phone number of the Paul Heider residence. After locating the number, she got up from her desk, closed her office door, returned to her desk, and dialed the number.

Ruth Heider answered the phone. Mary visited with her briefly before asking if Will was available to speak with her. A few moments passed before Will got on the phone.

The conversation was very brief. Beth reminded him that they had met at The Bavarian on Saturday night and told him that Mary Rieff had suggested she call him and arrange an informal meeting to discuss Wiemer Industries' labor relations. Will did not appear surprised by her inquiry. He agreed to meet, and stated his concurrence that it was to be an informal meeting.

They agreed to meet at Beth's office at nine the following morning.

Had a third party been monitoring the telephone conversation, it would have been evident that neither party was enthusiastic about the communication or the purpose of the call. Both parties were civil, but the tone of voice and brevity of the conversation reflected the fact that both were apathetic regarding a meeting.

The following morning Will awoke to a slate grey sky and a light snow shower. He had breakfast with his parents, but said nothing more about the forthcoming meeting with Beth Brinson. He had informed them of the meeting immediately following the phone conversation with Beth. During the 20-minute drive to Wiemer Industries' corporate offices, his misgivings about the meeting grew more intense. He was disappointed at his own inability to convince his mother that it was inappropriate for him to become involved in the Wiemer labor dispute. He'd reminded her that at the end of his second year of law school, he had informed the family that he would not return to Hammelburg to practice law. He was quite specific about his negative reaction toward what he described as "the petty, parochial issues that dominate most local law practices."

However, Mary Rieff's intervention had suddenly swept him into a conflict that he had struggled to avoid. His mother's past relationships with, and respect for Mary were too strong for his counterarguments. He also regretted ever agreeing to meet with Jimmie Hudson and his colleagues. The phone call from Mary Rieff had to be connected to those meetings. There was

229

no other reasonable explanation. No one else was aware of the meetings. Moreover, Beth Brinson's demeanor during their brief phone conversation seemed unusually stiff and formal. He sensed that she wouldn't have been disappointed had he declined her invitation.

It was as if all the reasons that he had avoided returning to Hammelburg had suddenly emerged in a three-day period. He had a sudden desire to turn the car toward the interstate highway and return to Chicago, to the anonymity of life in a large city, to the protective formality of Cutler Earl and Levin, to the impersonal and unemotional discussions with partners and clients. He wanted to flee the disturbing issues surrounding job relocation, the IMU, Hammelburg and Juarez, its impact on families and communities and society. This was not his skill set. He was a legal specialist, not a therapist, not a mediator, not even a litigator. He specialized in the interpretation of labor law and environmental regulations, not people, not communities, not social problems.

By the time he arrived at the Wiemer Industries corporate offices, his mood was dark. He parked his rental car in the designated visitors' parking area and walked to the main entrance. He was dressed informally in slacks, a sweater, and a nylon jacket that he borrowed from his father. He didn't carry the familiar lawyer's briefcase. It remained in the car. After entering the lobby, he identified himself to the guard at the security desk, informed him that he had an appointment with Beth Brinson at nine, and signed the visitor's register. As he completed the registration, it suddenly dawned on him that this was his first visit to the headquarters of Wiemer Industries. Despite the fact that the initial 18 years of his life were spent in Hammelburg, he had never had occasion to enter the building.

As he waited to be escorted to Beth's office, he studied the portrait of Jacob Wiemer and reflected briefly on the intertwining of more than 150 years of the history of Hammelburg, Wiemer Industries, the Wiemer family, and his own family roots.

Within five minutes, Beth Brinson appeared in the lobby dressed in an elegant dark green pants suit. Despite her short, naturally graying hair and absence of cosmetics, she appeared much younger than a woman who had recently celebrated her 47th birthday. After greeting Will, she suggested that they meet in a small conference room adjacent to her office on the second floor. She had walked down to the lobby, but offered to use the elevator to return; Will declined her offer. As he followed Beth up the flight of stairs, he noted that she had retained a youthful, almost athletic figure. His mother had given Will a detailed description of Beth's background and the breakup of her marriage to Ted Brinson. Ruth Heider admired Beth, particularly her ability to successfully raise twin sons while maintaining an executive position with Wiemer Industries. Will was a bit puzzled by his mother's generous praise of Beth. He suspected it was indirect criticism of his former wife's decision to abandon their marriage to pursue her career goals.

Upon reaching the top floor, Beth walked directly to the conference room without passing through her office. As they entered the small, well-appointed room, a secretary was arranging a decanter of coffee and two cups in the middle of the conference table. The secretary smiled and spoke to Will. He suddenly realized that she had been a high school classmate, but he could not recall her name. Beth thanked her and suggested that Will occupy a seat directly across from her. She purposely did not occupy the head of the table.

After they were both seated, Beth attempted to establish some dialogue. "Did you enjoy the evening with your family at The Bavarian?"

"Oh yeah. I haven't been to The Bavarian in years. It's my mother's favorite restaurant. We use to go there frequently when I was a boy. Except for being somewhat larger, it hasn't changed very much. I enjoyed being there again."

"Do you return to Hammelburg often?"

"Only a couple of times a year when the sailing season is over. Otherwise, my weekends are spent on Lake Michigan attempting to prove I know how to sail a boat."

"My father use to sail on the Ohio River when we lived in Pittsburgh. I assume the Ohio River doesn't compare with Lake Michigan. I loved going out with him, but he had a very small boat."

"Lake Michigan has swamped some pretty good sailors. Ocean sailors often assume it's a piece of cake and get into real trouble. Coast Guard helicopters are busy during the summer, rescuing people who underestimate the Lake.

"How long have you lived in Chicago?"

"Since I graduated from law school, about 20 years."

"Have you always been in private practice?"

He realized that she was attempting to explore his credentials. He wanted the meeting to be short and inconclusive, thereby giving him an opportunity to escape any further involvement. He elected to accommodate her with a long answer that would satisfy her and allow them to move forward to the real purpose of the meeting. He already knew most of her background from the conversation with his mother.

"I joined Cutler Earl and Levin as a summer intern between my first and second year of law school at the University of Illinois at Champaign. I've been there ever since as an intern, associate, partner, and finally a senior partner. Labor law and environmental law are my primary pursuits. We're not a big firm like Jenner and Block or Kirkland and Ellis, but we have a solid corporate practice. The firm was formed in the late forties. We have about 150 employees. No offices other than Chicago."

Beth recognized the purpose of his extended answer and elected to move directly to the primary purpose of the meeting. "As you know, Mary Rieff, a member of our board of directors, recommended I call you … "

Will interrupted. "Beth, before we go any further, let me explain how I became involved in this issue. As you know, my mother is a close friend and avid admirer of Mary Rieff. To my surprise, she called my mother yesterday morning, requesting that I become involved in the Wiemer IMU negotiations. I didn't talk with her, but it appears that she was responding to a request from a third party. Obviously, I can't represent the IMU and I assume that Wiemer Industries already has adequate legal counsel

Beth pondered Will's response. She was sure that he had not revealed all of the details that led to Mary Rieff's phone call.

"Let me clarify one issue for you," she said. "We no longer have legal representation. The firm that represented us in the negotiations with the IMU has been discharged."

Will's face revealed his surprise. "I wasn't aware of that."

"I know. It hasn't been announced publicly, and it occurred only yesterday afternoon. I suggest you buy today's *Wall Street Journal* or *New York Times* and the read the story about a hedge fund and the SEC subpoena. It involves illegal insider trading by three members of a prominent New York law firm who managed the hedge fund. It explains why they no longer represent us."

"An SEC subpoena sounds like a serious problem," he said.

"It is," she answered.

There was a awkward pause in the conversation. Finally, Beth asked "Will, are you familiar with Jerry Bentenhausen?"

He suddenly realized that he was unsure of the direction or the purpose of the meeting. But he sensed that the lady across the table knew where it was going. "Yeah, I met Jerry Bentenhausen this weekend for the first time."

"Well, as you are probably aware, Jerry is a member of the IMU executive committee and a friend of Mary Rieff. Apparently, Jerry requested that Mary assist in attempting to persuade you to become involved in the negotiations. That's the reason Mary called your mother. I told Mary that I was puzzled by Jerry's request, as you had informed me that you didn't represent unions."

She looked directly at Will, expressionless, awaiting a reply.

Will took a deep breath, exhaled slowly, but audibly. "Obviously, you'd like and deserve some clarification. Let me first explain that I had no idea that Jerry Bentenhausen intended to contact Mary Rieff, nor did I ever encourage him to do so. If fact, I actively discouraged him from ever considering that I would somehow become involved in the negotiations. Jimmie Hudson introduced me to Bentenhausen. I've known Jimmie Hudson since I was a student at Hammelburg West. We weren't close friends, but I admired him. I hadn't seen Jimmie since we were teenagers. That's why I was totally surprised when he called me last week to ask if I would assist the IMU with their negotiations. I explained why I couldn't. Jimmie asked if I would meet with him informally. I told him if he wanted to have a beer and reacquaint ourselves, I would be in Hammelburg for the holidays, but I would not act as legal counsel. He agreed. We had a beer on Saturday afternoon. Frankly, it should have ended there, but for some inexplicable reason, I've always admired Jimmie, so I agreed to quickly read the existing IMU contract before returning to Chicago."

Will paused to give Beth an opportunity to respond. She remained silent, expressionless. "He called Sunday," Will continued. "I assumed he wanted my impression of the contract. Instead, he wanted to meet again, informally, and asked if I would object if two other members of the IMU—Jerry Bentenhausen and Norma Landis—attended the meeting. It was clearly understood that I was a friend of Jimmie, but in no way was I acting as legal counsel to the IMU. In retrospect, the second meeting was a mistake; clearly, my mistake. I should have declined. I assume that Jimmie doesn't know that Jerry called Mary Rieff. If he did, he would have contacted me"

Beth sat motionless watching Will as if she were attempting to evaluate his explanation.

As he awaited her response, it occurred to him that she'd really missed her calling; she should have been a prosecutor, or at least a trial lawyer. She was attractive, smart, and tough... dissecting defense witnesses with precession. . He considered offering a brief apology and leaving. Bring this goddamn travesty to an end. She had his explanation. He'd done nothing wrong. No harm, no foul. Get up, walk out, and put it behind him. It would become one of those stories that you share with close friends when you're comparing episodes of self-induced stupidity. Besides, she had a bigger problem: There was a high probability that the SEC would want to investigate the stock registration records of all the corporations who had retained the lawyers accused of securities fraud. If that happened, Wiemer would be searching for more than a labor lawyer. But she was smart. She wasn't going to talk about it. She made it clear; let him read it in the paper.

Suddenly, she began to laugh. "I'll bet Jerry pushed you pretty hard to represent the IMU. He's an old tiger, but a good judge of people. He was a 1960s radical; went to Vietnam, came back; joined the protestors and started raising hell. He joined the IMU and continued to be in the forefront of other hot issues in the community: housing, race relations, education, women's rights. Lots of courage for a high school dropout in a conservative Indiana community. He doesn't have a lot of friends, isn't married, but he's earned a lot of respect; even among those who don't like him. He and Jimmie make a great team. I don't know Jimmie very well, but I understand he was a high school hellraiser. Nevertheless, he's earned enormous respect among the IMU members. Norma Landis I know very well. She's smarter than hell."

Less than five minutes into the meeting, Will was caught off guard for the second time. Again, he had no idea where this lady was taking this conversation, but he was keenly aware that she knew where she wanted it to go. He decided to tag along for a little longer. He was fascinated by her tactics.

"Do you know Byron Hinkle?" she asked.

"No, I've never met him."

"But you know who he is?"

Will wanted to tell her he knew goddamn well who Hinkle was, and she knew he did. This cross-examination approach was going to end.

"Yeah, I know who he is. We discussed Byron Hinkle. Jimmie and Jerry wanted me to replace him as counsel for the IMU. I explained why I couldn't. I've never met Hinkle and know nothing about his law practice."

He paused for a moment. He thought again, maybe now was the time to terminate this conversation and extricate himself from this entire issue.

"Beth, I think any questions regarding my involvement with the IMU have been resolved. Its time for me to as gracefully as possible, untangle myself from a situation I should've never allowed myself to become... "

She interrupted. "Before you decide to make your exit, let me discuss another issue with you... The management of Wiemer Industries is facing a dilemma. For the past few years, all of our labor negotiations with the IMU have been conducted by an outside law firm. Before that, all the negotiations were conducted directly between representatives of management and the IMU bargaining committee. When the previous management elected to hire outside counsel, the IMU, in turn, hired Byron Hinkle to represent them. Our labor relations have been in turmoil ever since those two events occurred. Moreover, management has failed to exercise sufficient oversight. The vice president of personnel sits in the bargaining sessions, but is never consulted by outside counsel, and doesn't have a clue as to what is being discussed or agreed to. The only member of management who has direct communication with the outside counsel is our chief financial officer, Bruce Kramer. I don't even see the labor contract until it has been signed by both parties."

She paused momentarily in an attempt to evaluate Will's reaction. He provided no clues. He continued to be puzzled about what she was attempting to accomplish.

"So following yesterday's revelation that the two attorneys who were conducting our labor negotiations have received subpoenas from the SEC, our CEO elected to discharge the entire law firm, and we are now attempting to decide how and who will conduct negotiations with the IMU."

"I can understand your CEO's reaction. The SEC subpoenas cast a shadow on the entire firm, but you could retain another firm," Will responded.

"Yes, we could. But there's another matter that needs to be clarified. The IMU believes that the last contract was altered by our counsel without the knowledge of Byron Hinkle or the bargaining committee."

"I know about that wording, Beth. Jimmie Hudson told me about it and I read it. It certainly has a major impact on how the relocation settlement is fashioned, and there has to be a question about who did or didn't know about the insertion of those words in the contract."

"Well, if you know about it, you must also recognize that until the issue is clarified, it may be difficult to hire another law firm to conduct negotiations. Certainly, the news of the subpoenas is going to increase the IMU's suspicion of foul play. Moreover, I suspect that the SEC is going to want to take a look at our stock registration record to see if there was any illegal trading in our shares. If that occurs, we will be required to make a public announcement and further increase the lack of trust. I'm not sure any law firm will want to take on that task."

"What's your alternative?" Will asked.

"Return to our previous method of direct negotiation," Beth replied.

"Who do you have inside that can conduct negotiations? You've already indicated that the VP of personnel can't handle it."

As he finished speaking, he suddenly realized that he hadn't withdrawn from the issue; he was becoming more deeply involved, but from another perspective.

"I've volunteered to assume the responsibility for negotiations," she responded.

Will's voice revealed his surprise. "Why the hell would you do that? That appears to be the least attractive alternative. I would, at least, try to hire another firm, first."

"There are several reasons," she replied. "First, although I've no experience in labor negotiations, I've been with Wiemer Industries more than 20 years, and the members of the bargaining committee know me, and I believe they trust me. Second, if management elects to bargain directly, the IMU may decide to get rid of Byron Hinkle. Finally, without Hinkle and Perkins involved, we may be able to reach a reasonable compromise regarding the meaning of that phrase 'impending financial hardship.' I'm not sure we will ever discover how it got included in the contract."

"What do your CEO and board of directors think of this idea?"

"Our CEO has temporarily agreed to avoid the introduction of another law firm in the negotiations, and I think he can gain approval of the board, given the recent revelations regarding Perkins and Baker"

Will removed his glasses and placed them on the conference table, leaned forward and placed both arms on the table and squinted at the ceiling.

"O.K., how do I fit into your plan?" he said slowly.

"If I'm going to conduct the negotiations I'll need someone who can coach or tutor me. It'll be no secret that I'm receiving assistance. In my opinion, you're the perfect candidate. You are a seasoned labor lawyer; you grew up in Hammelburg and understand the community. Three members of the IMU executive committee know you and had enough confidence to attempt to hire you."

"Even if I agreed to such an arrangement. I'm sure all of them would feel betrayed after my having met with them and discussing the negotiations. I think that would only harm your efforts."

"Will, I have spent most of my adult life in Hammelburg. Even more than you have. I'm well acquainted with its culture and customs. You haven't lived here for many years, but your family has, and people associate you with your family. Your family is respected and, most important, trusted by a very large segment of this community. You're not a stranger from New York or Chicago. You come back, maybe not frequently, but you do come back to the community. That makes an incredible difference to these people."

She paused and looked directly at Will before continuing. "Whether you do or not, Will, they assume you care about them and Hammelburg."

"Well, I do care," he said quietly, "but I don't understand what role I would play. You can obtain legal advice from lots of reliable sources."

"It's not just legal advice I'm seeking. I'm attempting to re-establish a relationship between Wiemer Industries, its employees, and the community; a relationship that perished in a plane crash. After J.W.'s death, Adam Fulton assumed control of the company, and it changed dramatically. J.W. nurtured an enormous affection for the company and the community, as did his mother. All the affection that Adam Fulton could muster was spent on himself. Even his wife was part of his narcissism. She was only one of many ornaments that he collected in his quest for success. In very short order, the only measures of importance were the quarterly earnings report and the stock price. The quality of life in Hammelburg, the relationship between labor and management, the adoption of sustainable long-term goals for the company were suddenly dismissed or given superficial attention. Labor relations became a game in which each side attempted to extract as much from the other side as possible, with no consideration of the long-term consequences for the company or the community."

"Unfortunately, a total focus on quarterly earnings and stock price is the norm for most of corporate America today," Will said.

"I'm sadly aware of that, Will."

"All right, I admire your convictions and objectives, but I don't see any particular role for me in these negotiations that couldn't be obtained from another law firm," Will said.

"I'm not suggesting that you become directly involved in the negotiations. What I need is someone I can trust to give me honest advice and someone the IMU respects; someone who knows and appreciates Hammelburg. If we can accomplish that, maybe and only maybe, we can put these negotiations back on track."

"And what is 'back on track'?" Will asked.

"It's achieving an agreement that respects the rights and the integrity of all the stakeholders in the company: the owners, the employees, the community, the environment."

She paused to pour more coffee for both of them. "I suppose my statement about stakeholders sounds a little fuzzy and vague."

"Maybe a bit over the top, but not too far," he smiled.

She placed the coffee decanter on the tray and used a paper towel to wipe up several drops of coffee that had spilled on the table, then sat back in her chair. Her voice softened as she continued.

"Will, I'm convinced that your willingness to meet with Hudson and Bentenhausen and Norma Landis reflects much more than merely the wish to accommodate an old high school friend who wanted a little free advice. I sense that you're caught between some deep feelings about this community and the specific policies of your partnership regarding representing unions, and I think I can satisfy both of your objectives"

Will remained silent for what seemed like several minutes. He finally responded. "Well, my partners would probably raise no objection to my agreeing to represent Wiemer Industries; notwithstanding the possible SEC and labor problems. It's my hometown and a company with an outstanding history. But how would it go down with Jimmie Hudson and his colleagues? I wouldn't think about accepting your proposal without first disclosing to them our conversation and obtaining their agreement."

"I agree," Beth responded, "and if they object, I will accept your refusal without question."

"What about the CEO and your board of directors? Where do they stand regarding this proposed arrangement?" he asked.

"Harris Stevenson is aware of our meeting, and I believe he will endorse my proposal. We already have one member of the board of directors who strongly favors your participation. She assumed that you might represent the IMU, but I'm sure she will not object to my proposal. I believe the rest of the board members will follow the lead of Mary Rieff and Harris."

"I don't want to sound contentious, Beth, but I think it is important that I meet with your CEO to be sure we're all in agreement with the proposal."

"There's nothing contentious about that suggestion. It is perfectly appropriate, and I'll arrange it, but I assume that you'd prefer to discuss it with the IMU representatives beforehand."

"Yeah, I need to talk with the IMU and my senior partners as soon as possible. I want to talk to Jimmie Hudson first. No need to talk to my partners until I have the IMU agreement."

"Will, we need to resolve this rather quickly; I assume you know that?"

"Yes. I'll try to talk to Jimmie this afternoon and be back to you by tomorrow."

Beth accompanied him to the lobby. They shook hands, and Will exited the Wiemer headquarters. He smiled to himself and thought how different his attitude had been when he entered the building, compared with his feelings upon leaving. Maybe there was something to all this discussion of feminine mystique and persuasion. She was charming, attractive, and smart.

Chapter 18

Following the meeting with Beth, Will returned to his parents' home. He spoke briefly with them and immediately called the IMU office to leave a message for Jimmie Hudson to return his call as soon as possible. The receptionist told him Jimmie usually came to the office during his lunch break at 11:30. Twenty minutes later, Jimmie called. Will explained that he needed to meet with him that afternoon, if possible. Jimmie was obviously surprised by Will's call.

"Sure, Will, I can meet with you after my shift ends at four this afternoon. Should I ask anyone else to come along?"

"No, I think it would be best if it were just the two of us," Will responded.

"Is there some problem, or have you changed your mind about representing the IMU, I hope?" Jimmie laughed.

"It's a bit complicated. I think I'd best save the explanation for our meeting. Where should I meet you?" Will said.

"Well, I don't think we should go back to The Hammelburg Inn; Art may become suspicious. Let's have a beer at The Second Shift. It's an old bar about three blocks from the plant on Wabash. Your Dad knows where it is. It's been a Wiemer employee hangout for years. They all know me, but

I'm sure they won't recognize you, but they know your Dad," he chuckled. "I'll meet you there at four-thirty."

Following his amusement at Will's request for directions, Paul Heider told him precisely how to locate The Second Shift. At approximately four-thirty, he parked his car in a small lot adjoining the bar. The building appeared to be pre-WW II vintage, as were all the buildings in this section of Wabash Avenue. Most were vacant; a few were occupied by small retail establishments and a family restaurant.

The Second Shift was a working man's saloon. A red and white hand-painted sign hung over the sidewalk directly in front of the single entrance, "DeAchilles Second Shift." Large glass windows were located on both sides of the entrance. The entire lower halves of the windows were laminated with a red and white DeAchilles scroll. Neon signs advertising Budweiser and Miller Lite occupied the upper half of each window. The door was solid wood with a small round window in the upper half. It was impossible for anyone outside the bar to identify anyone inside.

Upon entering, Will immediately encountered a dark wooden bar on the left side that extended half the distance from the front to the rear of the large rectangular room, equipped with nearly 20 chrome-plated bar stools with well-worn cushioned seats. On the immediate right were several small wooden tables and chairs. The rear half of the room contained five large tables that would seat as many as eight customers. Along the far right wall, several booths occupied the entire length of the room. A swinging door containing a round window was located in the middle of the back wall. It was the entrance to the kitchen. The lighting was minimal, except for a series of neon signs located along both side walls and the rear wall of the room. Each light displayed a different brand name of an old Midwest brewery that had either been acquired or closed: Hofbrau Ale, River City, Falls City, Pabst Blue Ribbon, Stroh's, Falstaff, Old Milwaukee, Fox Deluxe, Schlitz, Carling Black Label.

An array of liquor bottles equipped with dispenser tops, occupied a tier of shelves at the base of the long mirror behind the bar. TV sets were suspended from the ceiling at each end of the bar and over the entrance. All three were tuned to ESPN, and the audio was muted. A rerun of a NASCAR race was the feature on ESPN. The odor of fried food and cigarette smoke dominated the room. Behind the bar were two husky-looking middle-aged bartenders filling drink orders for customers at the bar, as well as those being delivered by weary-looking older waitresses dressed in black slacks and white blouses. The Second Shift was enjoying a brisk late afternoon business. All but two of the stools at the bar were occupied.

A few seconds after adjusting his vision to the darkened room, Will recognized Jimmie standing and talking to two men seated at the bar. As Will approached, Jimmie saw him and immediately motioned to a booth at the rear of the room. Jimmie was dressed in a dark blue cotton shirt and pants with a Wiemer Industries logo embossed above the pocket of the shirt. A dark brown bomber jacket was draped over his shoulder.

Both of them arrived at the booth at the same time. As soon as they were seated, a waitress appeared and took their order.

"Well, what's up?" Jimmie asked.

"A lot since we met on Sunday afternoon," Will answered.

Jimmie looked puzzled, but didn't respond.

"I've a lot to cover so I'll make it brief. Apparently, sometime yesterday morning Jerry Bentenhausen called Mary Rieff, who is a member of the board of directors of Wiemer Industries, and asked her to assist in helping convince me that I should represent the IMU. Mary and my mother are very close. Mary immediately called my mother to see if she could influence me. She knew that I was at home."

Jerry closed his eyes and shook his head. "Oh, for Christ's sake, Will, I'm sorry. I had no idea Jerry would do that. He said nothing to me after the meeting, other than he thought you would be an outstanding counsel for the IMU, and he was sorry you couldn't accept the offer. He gave no hint that he intended to do anything else. I'm really sorry, and I apologize. I never should have invited Jerry to attend Sunday's meeting."

"Did you know that he was an acquaintance of Mary Rieff?" Will asked.

"No. I know who Mary Rieff is and a lot about her activities in the community, but I've never met her. I met her husband one time when he was walking through the plant. I knew she was a member of the board of directors. But why would a member of the Wiemer Board be involved in recruiting a lawyer for IMU? That's kinda strange. But I feel awful, and I apologize that we broke our word to you."

Will smiled. "Well, I'm not sure that Jerry technically violated our agreement. He apparently never informed Mary Rieff that he had actually met me or talked with me. He apparently made no mention of our meetings."

"Well, I'm glad to hear that, but he still had no right to make that call and impose on you and your family," Jimmie said.

The waitress arrived with the beer order. Jimmie, again, insisted on paying the tab.

As he was pouring his beer into his glass, he continued. "Jerry's a very unusual and dedicated guy. Sometimes too dedicated. A lot of people call him a radical. He's been in the middle of nearly every public debate in Hammelburg in the past 20 years, whether it's union rights, race relations, education, you name it."

"So I'm told," Will said rather caustically.

Jimmie paused a moment before continuing. "What some of his critics don't know is the personal tragedy that Jerry lugs around. I don't think he has ever recovered from it. Only a few of his oldest and closest friends have ever heard him discuss it. I've never heard him talk about it. He was in Vietnam... saw a lot of action. He married a Vietnamese woman. When he was shipped back to the States, he made arrangements for her to follow him. She was scheduled to leave and decided to pay a last visit to her family in a small Vietnamese village. While she was there, she was killed, her entire family murdered. She was pregnant. He's never been able to find out who did it, the Viet Cong or the South Vietnamese army. He never remarried."

Both men remained silent for a few moments.

Finally, Will broke the silence. "Well, Jerry was partially successful. After Mary Rieff called my mother, I became the target of some pretty intense persuasion. To make a long story short, after explaining God knows how many times that I couldn't represent the IMU, I finally reached a compromise with my mother. I offered to meet with the general counsel of Wiemer Industries to explain the situation."

Jimmie looked surprised, but didn't respond.

"Beth Brinson, Wiemer's general counsel, called me yesterday and invited me to meet her at her office this morning. I assumed that Mary Rieff, who is an elderly woman, had somehow become confused and I needed to explain my position and disentangle myself from the entire issue."

"Is that what happened?" Jimmie asked.

"No, and that's why I asked to meet with you this afternoon."

Jimmie's expression became more serious. "Go ahead."

"Are you aware that Wiemer Industries has fired Jack Perkins' firm? That they are no longer representing Wiemer Industries?"

Jimmie suddenly sat back in the booth. "When in the hell did that happen?"

"Yesterday afternoon, after they were informed that both Perkins and Baker had been served with subpoenas by the SEC... The story is they violated federal securities laws by engaging in illegal insider tradind.

"I'm not sure what that means, but it sounds serious."

"It is," Will responded. "It's a violation of a criminal code. If they're convicted, they could serve some time in a federal prison and probably lose their right to practice law."

"Does Byron Hinkle know about this?" Jimmie asked.

"I don't know, but I would be surprised if he didn't."

"Well, he sure as hell hasn't told me or other members of the bargaining committee. What the hell is Wiemer management going to do now about the negotiations? Christ, I can't believe they would let Fenn Sullivan take over. That poor bastard doesn't have a clue."

"I found out that's what Beth Brinson wanted to discuss."

Jimmie stared at Will for a moment. His eyes narrowed, and his face flushed with anger. "You mean they wanta hire you," he said.

"Wait a minute, Jimmie. Let me finish before you reach any conclusions."

Jimmie rested his chin on his fist and glared at Will. "O.K. go ahead, tell me."

"They aren't going to hire any outside counsel to conduct negotiations. Beth Brinson is going to represent management."

"Beth Brinson! What the hell does she know about labor negotiations? I've met her. I coached one of her sons in Little League for two years. She's smart, but I don't think she's ever even attended a bargaining session."

"You're right on both counts. She's smart and she has no experience in labor negotiations, but the management believes that their relationship with the IMU has deteriorated so badly that they need to negotiate directly rather than hire another outside counsel. They believe the allegations regarding Perkins and Baker will heighten the suspicions of the IMU regarding the way in which the current contract was written, and they want to try to remedy that."

Jimmie's face continued to register his suspicion of Will's intentions. "O.K., I think I understand that, but why Beth Brinson?"

"She believes that she's trusted and respected, and that is the first big hurdle to get over in establishing a better relationship with the IMU, and apparently the CEO—whom I've never met—agrees with her."

"So when in the hell did the management decide that they ought to come clean and admit they hired those bastards so they wouldn't have to negotiate directly with us?" Jimmie asked.

Will elected not to respond.

"So she sent you to deliver the news, right?" Jimmie continued.

"No. It's more complicated than that. Beth understands there's a lot about labor law and negotiations that she's not familiar with. She wants some coaching and counsel, but doesn't want any outsiders involved directly in the negotiations."

"She wants to hire you, right?" Jimmie insisted.

"Correct, but I explained to her that I had met with you and discussed the negotiations and, therefore, I had to declare myself unavailable unless the IMU didn't object and the senior partners in my firm agreed I wasn't violating legal ethics."

Jimmie's laugh reflected his skepticism. "Jesus, talk about flim flam. You can't represent the IMU, but you can be a consultant for Wiemer management. Is that right?"

Will paused long enough to take a long drink of his beer. "Look, Jimmie, from the outset, I've told you I can't represent a union. I know it sounds strange, but conceivably, I could serve as a consultant to Wiemer, but only—and I repeat, only—if you and the IMU agree. Which means you and the rest of your bargaining committee don't object to my working with Beth Brinson. Finally, I don't know what my senior partners are going to conclude after I lay all of this out for them."

"You mean all I have to say, right now, here at this table, is no, and you'll tell Beth no, and go back to Chicago?"

"You got it," Will answered quickly, "and my life would be a hell of a lot less complicated," he added.

"Then turn 'em down," Jimmie barked. "Or tell them your partners won't agree. Why ask me to get you off the hook?"

Will gazed at the back wall of the tavern for a moment before refocusing on Jimmie. "That's a reasonable question, but I can't give you a good answer. When I walked into Beth Brinson's office this morning, I intended to explain to her what had occurred over the weekend and put this entire issue behind me. It was going to be a short meeting. I was even cursing myself for getting involved... "

Jimmie interrupted. "But if the IMU and your partners say O.K., you will. Is that right?" The tenor of his voice reflected his skepticism.

Will was focused on a cardboard coaster embossed with an old Pabst's Blue Rbbon logo. "I guess, during the past three days, I've seen and heard things that reminded me that I have several reasons to care about Hammelburg. My grandparents started their business here during the Depression. They were Jewish immigrants from Germany. My mother was born in Munich. They came to Hammelburg a few years after arriving in Chicago, and the community accepted them and helped them build a small business, and it continued to help my parents. My brother, sister, and I benefited from growing up in an exceptionally progressive and generous community. We were exposed to ideas and attitudes that we wouldn't have experienced in other small cities in the Midwest. I took it all for granted, and I left. I never realized, until I saw more of the world, how unique it was to have grown up here. But now the community is starting to fade. Hammelburg is headed down the same path as many other industrial cities in the Midwest. I'd like to help keep it unique a little longer. It probably can't be saved, but maybe preserved for a few more years."

Jimmie stared at Will, attempting to measure the sincerity of his last statement. He finally responded "I guess you got that part right, if you mean it."

He looked around the room for a moment before returning his focus on Will. "You know, I don't understand how the hell you can express those feelings about Hammelburg and at the same time attempt to explain that it's O.K. for you to represent Wiemer Industries, but the IMU is off limits. If you and your firm base those decisions on some code of conduct, how do you square the fact that you'll work for a corporation that hired and paid lawyers who are accused of violating the law and probably included a few extra words in a labor contract on the sneak? How can you sit there and tell me that you can't work for a union for some ethical reason? We've all heard that pious bullshit about codes of conduct and ethical behavior. But when push comes to shove, none of that crap means a thing. When it comes time to report the numbers, lie and cheat is O.K., if you don't get caught."

Will's face was crimson. He wanted to try to explain to Jimmie that there were valid reasons for his decision, but he couldn't find the words.

Jimmie poured the remainder of his beer in his glass. "I'll talk to the bargaining committee. They won't object. It's better to have you advising Beth than those goddamn crooks in New York."

He finished his beer in two swallows, and looked directly at Will. "Are you going to do it pro bono for Wiemer?" he added sarcastically.

Will smiled and responded softly, "No."

Jimmie stood up and put on his jacket, shook hands with Will, said nothing more, turned, and walked toward the exit.

Will sat in the booth for a few minutes, attempting to rid himself of the sting of Jimmie's rebuke. His immediate reaction was that of a well-trained lawyer: What alternatives were available to gracefully recuse himself from this community imbroglio? Rather than carefully executing the resolutions he had made while driving to meet Beth, he had actually immersed himself more deeply. What could he tell Beth was his reason for refusing to accept Wiemer Industries as a client? If he told her that the IMU objected, she was sure to learn the truth about his conversation with Jimmie. If he withdrew without a valid reason, Jimmie would assume that his accusations were valid and Will's description regarding his feelings about Hammelburg was nothing more than a cheap, emotional sham. If he told Beth that his partners were unwilling to agree to the proposal, what would be the reaction of the partners if they learned that he had turned down a client without first discussing it with them? How had he managed to involve himself so deeply in something he had intended to avoid and quickly dismiss?.

Finally, he rose, without finishing his beer, and walked toward the exit. As he was passing the men seated at the bar, someone gripped his arm and spoke to him in a loud voice. "Will Heider, what the hell are you doing in here?"

Will turned to see a heavy-set, middle-aged man with a beard, green baseball cap, and dark blue sweatshirt smiling at him.

There was a moment of silence as Will attempted to recognize the man.

"You don't have any idea who I am, do you, Will?" the man laughed. "Three years together on one of the worst football teams in the history of

Hammelburg, and you don't remember an old teammate." He stuck out his hand. "Dean Tyler, number 26, free safety."

"My God, Dean, I didn't recognize you. I apologize."

"Apologize, for what? Not recognizing a fat old bastard that can't run 20 yards? Who the hell would recognize me as the guy who gave up two touchdowns to St. Ignatius in the final game of our senior year?" he laughed again. "I think the last time I saw you was when you were home from college workin' in your old man's store. I was drivin' an 18-wheeler for Yellow Freight. Came in to buy some work boots. God knows how long ago that was."

"A long time ago," Will responded.

"What are you doin' now, Will?" he asked.

"I live in Chicago."

"Doin' what in Chicago?"

"I'm a lawyer."

"A lawyer in Chicago," Tyler repeated. "Jesus, that's pretty impressive. You were smart. You got the hell out of this town before you got trapped with the rest of us."

"How about you?" Will responded.

"Well, I'm sure as hell not a lawyer or a doctor or a corporate big shot, or I wouldn't be sittin' here payin' too much for this beer!" He winked at the bartender.

Tyler turned on his barstool and motioned for Will to take the vacant seat beside him. "I'm a first shift foreman at Wiemer. Been there for nearly 20 years. Got the hell out of long-distance truck driving when I got married. I married Loretta Johnson. She was in our class. You probably don't remember her. She died three years ago. Breast cancer. I've got two kids; both about ready to go to college. Now they want to move my job to Mexico. No job, no insurance. Great timing, huh?"

Will nodded, but made no comment. He was still reeling from Jimmie's final comments.

"What the hell are you doin' in here drinking beer with Jimmie Hudson?" Tyler asked.

Will was puzzled as to how to respond. It was also apparent that the bartender and several other customers were interested in hearing his answer. Jimmie had miscalculated when he assumed no one would take notice of them at The Second Shift. It was obviously Jimmie who drew the attention until Tyler recognized Will and called out his name.

"Just having a beer together," he answered, sounding unconvincing.

Tyler smiled at him and winked again at the bartender. Will realized that his disingenuous answer had only sharpened their interest. He hoped Tyler would not inquire any further about the meeting.

Will wanted to leave, but felt compelled to engage in a brief, polite conversation with Tyler. He recognized that their conversation was being monitored by several men at the bar, and the bartender.

"Jimmie's one hell of a guy," Tyler said. "We came to work at Wiemer about the same time. You remember him in high school; tough as hell, and still is. They've tried to promote him to foreman several times. He wouldn't take it. He was smart. I was stupid. Foreman can't belong to the IMU. The labor contract won't allow it. Foremen are considered part of management. It's a goddamn joke. We live in no man's land. No union representation and management treats us like we were hourly employees, except we have no bargaining power. Jimmie's a master machinist and a union member, makes more money than I do. The only difference is, I earn a salary and Jimmie earns an hourly wage. Foremen are eligible for a bonus when Wiemer Industries makes enough profit to pay bonuses. The last one was three years ago. Medical benefits are the same, union or nonunion, thanks to the IMU."

Will said "I'd thought you'd have more protection in the event of a layoff or plant closure?"

"A temporary layoff; yeah, I'd probably stay on salary unless it becomes a permanent layoff," Tyler responded. "But a plant relocation, no; we get the boot along with everyone else if they move operations to Mexico. All we can hope for is the same settlement they give the IMU members. But the IMU doesn't negotiate for foremen or any other salaried staff. That's the rub; if they move machining and assembly to Mexico, it's not just the IMU members that lose their jobs, it's foremen, secretaries, accountants, even some engineers, a big slice of the salaried staff. They aren't going to move them to Mexico."

"But aren't your salary and benefits adjusted when a new contract is negotiated with the IMU?" Will inquired.

Tyler laughed sarcastically. "Oh sure, they toss us a bone, but we never see the kind of increases that the IMU gets. In fact, lots of salaried people get little or nothing. We get the medical insurance improvements only because we're on the same plan as the IMU."

He paused for a moment. "You know, Will, Wiemer started getting fucked up about 15 years ago when the union and management decided to see who could screw each other at the bargaining table. The hourly wage rates and benefits skyrocketed because the IMU thought they had management over a barrel. The IMU insisted on having a lot of stupid work rules that probably cost more than wage and benefit increases. A machine operator can't make a simple adjustment on his tooling. He has to stand and wait until a union mechanic is available. They stand there idle for 15 or 20 minutes. A foreman can't move a box of materials, a union member has to do it. It all started with the CEO. He was an asshole who only cared about getting his name in the *Wall Street Journal* and landing a better job. He paid the IMU too much and the shareholders too much. There wasn't enough left to invest in new equipment to reduce cost. Now they want to go hire Mexican workers for a couple bucks a day and leave Hammelburg. The IMU says it's management's fault and management says we're too expensive and they have to look out for the shareholders, whoever the hell they are, but both of them made this mess together. The only way to salvage it is for both sides to sit down at the table, quit trying to screw each other, and find a solution."

Will asked, "You think that will happen?"

Tyler shook his head. "We're a hell of a long way from that point and time is running out. The goddamn shame of it is that lots of people who never belonged to the IMU and never worked for Wiemer are going to lose their jobs."

"Is there a solution?" Will asked.

"Let me ask your question a different way: Do I believe people are willing to find a solution? I know there's a solution. No management in its right mind wants to walk away from an experienced group of employees who understand their products and how to make 'em; pay to move all that equipment thousands of miles; pay the cost of training people in a different language. And the IMU knows there ain't any jobs in Hammelburg or Indiana that come close to paying half of what we're makin' at Wiemer, and most of those jobs have no benefits. Yeah, there's a solution if you eliminate one issue on both sides of the bargaining table… greed."

"Is it possible after all the bad feeling?" Will said.

"If you put the right people on both sides of the table and take a hard look at how this company use to be managed… yeah, I think it's possible. Do I expect it?" Tyler turned both palms upward. "Who knows?" he concluded.

Will stood up and shook hands with Tyler before continuing his exit. Just as he was about to depart, one of the bartenders leaned over the bar and briefly held Will by the arm. "Tell your old man that Lou DeAchille said hello, and tell him I'll buy the beer the next time he comes in. It's been too long. I got a world of respect for that man" he said.

Will took the long way back to his parents' house. How could he word an honest evaluation of the Wiemer offer and at the same time achieve a negative reaction from the managing general partner? A few minutes after arriving and a brief conversation with his parents, he called his office from the privacy of an upstairs phone. It was four-thirty in Chicago, one hour earlier than Hammelburg. He told Shirley Kovac that unless there were critical messages for him, he wanted his call to be transferred to Miles Royston, the managing general partner. Shirley told him all his messages could wait, and immediately initiated the transfer. Royston was on a conference call. Will asked his secretary to have him return his call as soon as possible. Approximately 15 minutes later, the phone rang. His mother answered and called upstairs to inform him that the phone was for him.

Miles Royston had been selected as managing general partner because he was better at administration and attracting new clients than practicing law. His specialty was environmental law, but he failed to maintain an understanding of the technical aspects of new environmental legislation.

Will blandly outlined the series of events at Wiemer Industries, including his informal meetings with Jimmie Hudson. Royston was surprised about his contact with Jimmie; however, given the fact that Wiemer Industries was a well-known and respected Midwest industrial firm and, more important, a significant new client, Royston saw no reason to object to Cutler Earl and Levin accepting the offer. He was already aware of the news of Perkins and Baker and the SEC subpoenas. He made a brief but unflattering comment about Perkins' reputation. Will wondered if Royston really knew Perkins, or was just repeating legal profession scuttlebutt.

Will concluded the call with the full realization that his last chance to gracefully disengage himself from the Wiemer IMU dispute had been lost.

About the time Will was completing his conversation with Royston, Beth Brinson entered Harris Stevenson's office to brief him about her meeting with Will. She carefully reviewed what she had learned about his connections to Jerry Bentenhausen and his meetings with Jimmie Hudson and Norma Landis. Despite the unusual nature of those contacts, she recommended that Will be retained as a consultant to assist her with the contract negotiations, but not be involved directly in the negotiations. Initially, Stevenson challenged Will's exclusion, but Beth pointed out that Will had established an ethical precondition that the IMU not object to his participation as a consultant. She was sure that direct participation might create a problem. Harris finally agreed and requested that he have an opportunity to meet briefly with Will before the arrangement was finalized. It was agreed that Beth would attempt to arrange a meeting the following day, albeit the day before Thanksgiving.

As Beth departed Stevenson's office, she encountered Bruce Kramer. They spoke briefly. She noted that when Kramer entered Stevenson's office, he closed the door. It was unusual for Stevenson's door to be closed, unless he requested it.

Stevenson had not expected Bruce and was surprised to see him at such a late hour in the afternoon. Kramer was a stickler for dispensing all incoming mail and phone calls before leaving his office, and usually devoted the last hour of each day to those tasks. He was compulsive about having no paper on his desk at the end of the day.

After closing the door—which also surprised Stevenson—and seating himself, Kramer began speaking. His voice still reflected some of the emotion that had been aroused the previous day. "I called Perkins' firm, as you insisted, and told them they could no longer represent us. They were offended, as I anticipated, but there were no counterarguments. There are outstanding invoices that will have to be paid," he said tersely.

"Not offended or embarrassed enough to forget about those invoices," Stevenson quipped.

Kramer frowned. "I wouldn't expect that. After all, the firm did nothing wrong. It was three partners out of several hundred, and they haven't even been indicted."

"What do you think they're going to do, Bruce, if they find out that Perkins and his cronies' illegal trading activities includes our stock?" Harris asked.

Kramer's response was quick and sharp. It was evident that the question angered him. "Even if they are guilty of illegal trading, which I doubt, I would be astounded if it included any of Wiemer Industries' shares. But if it gives you any satisfaction, I will look into it the first thing in the morning."

Stevenson, who normally avoided confrontation with his subordinates, appeared to derive some pleasure from irritating Kramer.

"Well, I'm surprised you haven't already made that call, but you needn't bother. Beth has already placed calls to the specialist and the registration agent to see if there is any evidence of their trading in our stock."

Kramer's eyes narrowed and his voice stiffened. "That's not the responsibility of the general counsel. It's my responsibility, and I resent Beth doing that without first discussing it with me."

"What the hell are you talking about, Bruce? You have a phone in your office. Furthermore, Beth is the chief legal officer of this corporation, and these guys are accused of violating federal law, which may include illegal trading in our shares, It's sure as hell a legal problem, as well as a financial issue."

Kramer's anger was growing more obvious. He struggled for a moment, attempting to control his response. "I'm really offended by the events of the past two days, Harris. First, you insist on firing an outstanding law firm that has successfully represented us in labor negotiations for several years, and then without discussing it with me, Beth elects to call the financial community to inquire about our stock trading patterns."

He didn't wait for Stevenson's response; he continued, "I'm responsible for those inquiries. I have a personal relationship with the stock specialist and vice president of the bank that handles our stock registrations. This is a delicate issue. It needs to be handled with finesse. I wouldn't have made those calls until the issue settled down."

He paused momentarily. Stevenson said nothing.

"I've already made some inquiries about selecting the law firm that will replace Perkins. I called some friends at Morgan Stanley who recommended several New York-based firms that have excellent reputations in labor law."

Stevenson responded in his slow steady Midwestern monotone. "I've decided that we're not going to use outsiders in labor negotiations. We've already created a lot of turmoil over the wording of the current contract, and the fact that those two guys are now accused of stock manipulation isn't going to generate much confidence in anyone we choose to replace them. I've asked Beth to assume responsibility for negotiating with the IMU. She may select an outside law firm to act as consultants, but they'll have no direct involvement in the negotiations."

Kramer stood up abruptly, walked behind his chair, gripped the back of the chair firmly with both hands, his face flushed, head thrust forward. "Jesus, Harris, that's insane!" he barked "First, we fire outstanding legal counsel, then we elect to replace them with someone who has zero experience in labor negotiations. Hell, as dense as he is, I'd pick Fenn Sullivan before Beth. In fact, I'd pick myself before Beth, despite my limited knowledge of labor relations."

"Sit down, Bruce, and cool off." Stevenson's tone suddenly become sharp.

"First of all, we didn't make the decision, I made it. I'll be held responsible for it, not you. Second, I appreciate your input, but with a little less heat."

Bruce sat down again, slowly; he appeared to have regained control of his emotions. His tone shifted from confrontation to appeal. "Look, Harris, this is a life and death matter with this company. If we don't successfully negotiate the relocation of the machining and assembly to Juarez, this company is headed for bankruptcy. If the 'street' gets word of your decision, they'll drop our stock like a bad habit. The banks aren't going to renew loans if they conclude that we aren't taking a tough line on labor negotiations and cost reduction. We can't survive if that happens."

"I guess you're assuming that Beth can't or won't take a tough line with the IMU?"

"She's compromised. Like Jon Pertoski, and everyone else that's been with this company for 20 years. They're all infected with that damn paternalism and community support crap. It's handicapped this company for years. She won't sit across the table from the IMU and protect the shareholders. She'll buckle under. That's the reason Jack Perkins was successful. He never let anything else influence his negotiations. He understood that it was purely a question of economics. Philanthropy has no place in labor negotiations."

"Philanthropy, paternalism, community support crap— that's strong language, Bruce—do you really believe that until Jack Perkins arrived on the scene, Wiemer Industries' labor relations had been misguided?"

"That's not my point, Harris. That's all in the past. Today, we're competing in a world market. We can't isolate ourselves any longer from the rest of the world. We either lower our costs, or we get eliminated. The IMU either meets our labor cost requirements or we manufacture somewhere else. We can no longer protect Hammelburg. Our primary responsibility is our shareholders and creditors."

"And you assume Beth doesn't understand enough about world markets and current economics to negotiate a good agreement?"

"No. Beth understands it, but she's not tough enough to make it happen."

"But you assume that you are tough enough—you'd sit across the table from our employees and tell 'em, 'Tough shit, guys, you're out of a job, you can't cut it in the world market.'"

"No, Harris, I'm not suggesting that. I'm arguing that we've got to hire someone to represent us at the bargaining table that has those skills."

"Those skills," Stevenson repeated sarcastically. "Someone tough and honest and forthright like Jack Perkins—someone who may have engaged in illegal stock trading—someone who may have attempted to bury a couple of words in our labor contract to permit us to avoid a contractual obligation.--Now, Bruce, before you take my head off; remember, I said 'may have.'"

Kramer sat back in his chair and folded his arms across his chest. He was angry, but attempted to reason rather than argue. "Look Harris, I've been here for more than six years. My salary doesn't come close to what I could be earning on Wall Street. Wiemer hasn't paid an executive bonus in three years. I was given a 50,000-share stock option when I came aboard and 100,000 more over the past three years. One hundred and fifty thousand shares in stock options that, today, aren't worth a dime. The Wiemer stock price would have to double before I would make one cent on those options. I'm probably in the lower half of my Stanford MBA class in terms of income. I wanta be able to make some real money. I'm not interested in preserving historical relics. The Wiemers made plenty of money, Adam Fulton made a bundle. How about us? When do we get our turn?"

Stevenson leaned forward and thrust his face as close as possible to Kramer. An ex-Marine would have recognized the similarity between his demeanor and that of a drill sergeant correcting a recruit in boot camp. His tone was sarcastic, a low growl.

"Well, Bruce, I think it's safe to assume that the Wiemer family, with perhaps the exception of Gus Arnholt, earned their rewards. They built and managed an outstanding company. On the other hand, Adam Fulton was primarily responsible for the decline of this company. Rather than investing our capital in new equipment and manufacturing methods that would improve productivity and reduce labor costs, or in new products that generate earnings, he pissed it away on nitwit acquisitions, large salary increases for himself and two other idiots, and expensive schemes to promote his public image, including an outrageously expensive contract with the IMU, from which we have never fully recovered. The board of directors sat there with their thumb up their collective ass and watched him do it; despite the fact that every hourly employee on the shop floor knew Fulton was a two-bit hustler. When his next big opportunity came by, he stuffed our money in his pockets and jumped aboard. He's a goddamn conman. He was before he came here, while he was here, and he still is. But somehow those bastards never get exposed. They move quickly enough from one company to the next to avoid detection... So don't talk to me about the Wiemer family and Adam Fulton in the same breath... It's one of my hot buttons."

Kramer was obviously unsettled by Stevenson's remarks and his manner. "O.K., Harris, but that's water over the dam. We can't recapture those losses, but we can start making corrections by restructuring our business and lowering our labor costs."

Kramer failed to recognize the reservoir of suppressed anger and frustration he had punctured. Stevenson came forward in his chair again, his face red. "Are you suggesting that since the previous management really messed this company up, we should fuck over the employees to correct the problem?" Stevenson growled. "Is that what they taught you at that goddamn business school? Is that the playbook solution to our problems; screw the employees to save Wall Street's ass and collect our undeserved fortune?"

Kramer was visibly shaken by Stevenson's angry response, even frightened that he might come across the desk and grab him. "No, I'm not suggesting we do anything of the sort, Harris. But I am suggesting that we recognize that Wiemer Industries is a publicly owned company, no longer a family owned company that can afford to have philanthropic or paternalistic goals that supersede our primary responsibility to protect our shareholders' investment."

Stevenson's growl grew more intense. "How the fuck do you know that the Wiemer family set philanthropy and community ahead of the shareholder's interest? You don't know a goddamn thing about how this company was managed when it was family owned. You and all those assholes on Wall Street assume that those objectives are incompatible, because some financial wizard said so."

Kramer elected not to respond. He recognized that further discussion could only result in more anger and emotion from Stevenson.

But Stevenson continued. "I'll ask you again, Bruce: What do you think the market is going to do if they discover that Jack Perkins and his friends did a little illegal trading in Wiemer Industries stock? If the SEC discovers that they used inside information to make a few million dollars in our shares... do you think they'll pat us on the ass and say 'That's O.K., fellas; we understand that those things happen'?"

Kramer's response was restrained: "I'm sure that won't happen."

"How the hell do you know it won't happen? You haven't even bothered to call the people who may know. I assumed it was one of the first phone calls you made after learning about this mess."

He stood up and moved quickly toward the door. Without turning to face Stevenson, he opened the door and spoke quietly. "I'll call them tomorrow."

"I suggest you talk with Beth before you call. She may already have the information," Stevenson snarled.

Kramer turned and faced Stevenson for a moment, but said nothing. His face was pale.

Stevenson was suddenly aware that Kramer was frightened, but assumed it was a reaction to the angry interchange between the two men.

Chapter 19

As soon as Beth arrived at her office the following morning, she placed a call to Will Heider to inquire if he had spoken with his partners and Jimmie Hudson regarding her proposal that he serve as a consultant to Wiemer Industries. He informed her that he had, and that neither party objected, though Jimmie Hudson was probably suspicious of management's intentions. She was surprised to learn that Jimmie Hudson had not been informed about Perkins and Baker before meeting with Will. She also asked if Will could return to the Wiemer headquarters before lunch for a brief meeting with Harris Stevenson. Will agreed, but cautioned her that he would be wearing casual clothes. She laughed and assured him that Harris Stevenson was not a proponent of a strict dress code.

At approximately 10:15, Beth met Will in the lobby of the corporate headquarters and escorted him to Stevenson's office. Again, they walked to the second floor. Beth wore a dark wool suit comprised of a well-tailored straight skirt and jacket. Will again noted her trim figure. On the way to Stevenson's office they encountered Bruce Kramer in the hallway. Beth spoke to Bruce. He passed them quickly, without acknowledging Beth or returning her greeting. Will noted that Beth looked surprised by Kramer's lack of response.

Upon entering Stevenson's office, Beth introduced Will to Stevenson's secretary. She was about to tap on Stevenson's open door when she realized he was on the phone. It was unusual for Stevenson to keep anyone waiting for a scheduled appointment. But five minutes passed before he ended the phone conversation and invited them into his office. Stevenson was in his standard uniform: shirt sleeves rolled up, white button-down collar shirt, tie, and collar unbuttoned. He paused momentarily to slip into his loafers which he had removed while sitting at his desk; then walked around his desk. Not waiting for a formal introduction by Beth, he momentarily caught Will off balance by offering his left hand for the obligatory handshake. He apologized for delaying the meeting, and invited them to join him at a small round conference table that seated four people.

Will noted that his office was not the elaborate facility that he had observed in other CEO quarters. Other than his desk—which was reasonably untidy—a standard leather-bound desk chair, two straight-back upholstered chairs in front of his desk, and a small conference table with four chairs, there was no other furniture in the room; no leather couch, coffee table, or bookshelves lined with unread books and personal trophies. With the exception of an aerial photograph of the Hammelburg manufacturing facilities, the walls contained no pictures or art. There were no family photographs or personal memorabilia on his desk or conference table. His secretary entered with a decanter of coffee and several Styrofoam cups. One cup contained packets of sugar, cream, and plastic stir sticks.

Once seated and coffee distributed, Harris asked Will several questions about his past association with Hammelburg and about his family. He related that he had been in Bernie's several times when he was a young manufacturing executive. He had purchased steel-toed shoes and outdoor clothing. He then asked several questions about Will's experience as a labor lawyer and inquired about specific clients that his firm represented, but his demeanor was relaxed. He was neither challenging nor examining. Will was surprised how quickly Stevenson asked for his opinion regarding the existing labor contract and state of negotiations between Wiemer Industries and the IMU. Will crafted his response carefully, referring to the fact that he had read the contract only once, but had some questions regarding the definitions of pending financial hardship.

Stevenson asked Will how long he had known Jimmie Hudson and their relationship. Will replied that Jimmie was a high school classmate, but he was careful not to provide any information that Jimmie had conveyed in his recent conversations with Will.

A pause in the conversation suggested that Stevenson did not intend to pursue that subject any further.

Stevenson looked puzzled for a moment before he asked the next question:
"Do you know Byron Hinkle?"

"No, I've never met him and know nothing about his practice," Will replied.

Stevenson looked at Beth following Will's response. "Well, it probably isn't important. As of this morning, he no longer represents the IMU."

Beth's reaction reflected her surprise. "When did this happen ?"

"Bruce Kramer walked in here about 45 minutes ago and told me that Hinkle had called him last night, at home, and told him that he had decided to resign as counsel for the IMU."

"Do we know why?" Beth asked again.

"Bruce said he didn't offer any explanation. He simply asked Bruce to inform the management of Wiemer Industries that he no longer represented the IMU... I've known Byron for several years, and I knew his father-in-law when he was still practicing law. Byron is a strange guy, but much easier to deal with than Tom Damich. Tom's a crusty old bastard... still pursuing his senile, right-wing political agenda."

"Do you think the IMU fired him?" Beth asked.

"Stevenson shook his head. "I don't know. Bruce was rather tight-lipped about his conversation with Byron."

Will was about to ask a question regarding Hinkle's replacement when Stevenson continued. "The only other thing I learned from Bruce was that when Hinkle told the IMU, they decided they no longer wanted outside counsel. They're going to ask someone on the IMU negotiating committee to assume the lead, and Byron thinks it'll be Jimmie Hudson."

Will was amused. He was sure that Jimmie had pounced on that opportunity the minute Hinkle made his announcement.

"That's all right," Stevenson continued. "Maybe we can achieve an agreement more quickly with direct negotiations."

Will glanced at Beth; she was obviously puzzled by this recent turn of events.

Stevenson continued, "I also had a rather strange conversation with Cyrus Brown this morning." He turned to Will. "Cyrus is a longtime member of our board of directors and the retired vice chairman of the National Bank of Chicago. You may know him." He paused. "I probably should discuss this with Beth in private, but if you're going to act as our advisor, you may as well be aware of it."

Stevenson again grimaced and shook his head. "Cyrus got a call from a securities lawyer in Boston inquiring about Wiemer Industries' involvement with Jack Perkins. Apparently, Urban Partners wasn't just a cozy little hedge fund. The securities lawyer told him that Perkins and his cronies solicited limited partners all over Wall Street. The SEC turned over more rocks, and some big bugs crawled out. Cyrus believes once the entire story is out, it's going to be a real barn burner. It sounds like another big story about illegal insider trading. Cyrus wants our auditors to conduct an independent investigation to make sure there is no Wiemer Industries involvement."

"That on top of a difficult labor negotiation," Beth lamented.

"After I finished talking with Cyrus, I had a conference call with all the other members of our board of directors to tell them about this mess. That's who I was talking to when you arrived," Stevenson said.

He turned to Beth. "Has anything come back from those calls to the stock specialist and the transfer agent?"

"Not yet. It takes a few days for them to search through the information, and the SEC is probably standing right beside them, watching. I'll call them again this afternoon,"

"No," Stevenson replied, "I think it's best for you to concentrate on the negotiations with the IMU. We need to get back to the bargaining table. Without the outside lawyers on both sides of the table, it's like starting over. After Bruce told me about Hinkle quitting, I ask him to contact our auditors and start looking closely at our recent stock trading patterns."

Beth recalled Bruce's strange behavior in the hallway. He seemed to be totally unaware of their presence or his surroundings.

Stevenson suggested that Beth call the president of the IMU, explain her role in the negotiations, ask who would represent the IMU and establish a place and time for another meeting as soon as possible.

As they departed Stevenson's office, Beth suggested to Will that they have lunch. She wanted to discuss Will's interpretation of the pending financial hardship clause in the labor contract. She was convinced that this issue would become the primary focus of the IMU following Hinkle's departure.

Will agreed and Beth suggested the restaurant at the Marriott near the interstate exit. She volunteered to drive.

After informing her secretary of her lunch plans, they took the elevator to the parking garage beneath the corporate office. Exiting the elevator, Beth walked directly to a dark blue BMW convertible sports coupe. Will was surprised. As they entered the car, he jokingly commented on her sporty automobile.

Before starting the engine, she turned and looked at Will with a teasing smile. "We all have our weaknesses. Some of us love expensive cars, others love expensive boats."

Will laughed. "Touché. I guess I set myself up for that."

Twenty minutes later, they were seated in the restaurant at the Marriott Hotel.

After giving their order to the waitress, Beth inquired about Will's availability the following week. She thought it would difficult to try to schedule a meeting with the IMU on the day after Thanksgiving. Under the IMU agreement, Thanksgiving and the following day were paid holidays.

Will explained that he had intended to return to Chicago on Saturday to avoid the Sunday travel congestion. He would need to call his office and inquire regarding his schedule for the following week.

"I gather you're not married," Beth commented, surprising Will with the sudden, direct question.

"No... I'm divorced."

Beth nodded. "I'm also divorced. As you probably gathered from our conversation Saturday night, I have twin sons. I met my ex-husband at Yale Law School. He's a venture capitalist in California."

Will was surprised. He pictured Beth as an "iron lady" who probably revealed little of her private life to anyone.

"No children?" she asked.

"No," he responded.

She smiled. "I am being a bit nosy about your personal life."

He shrugged and smiled.

She laughed. "It's my style. I like to know as much as possible about people I work with. It must be the result of studying both science and law. But I'm not offended by reciprocal inquiries."

"Unless I've overrated your investigative skills, I suspect you have learned most of what there is to know about me," he said.

She suddenly displayed a flirtatious smile. "Oh no, but we'll leave that for another time... you practice environmental as well as labor law?" she continued.

"I practice both, but my primary field is labor law."

Beth nodded but did not respond.

"Speaking of environmental issues, I suspect you have some environmental problems associated with the old foundry and forge shop," he said.

Beth was clearly caught off guard. Until now she had controlled the conversation. Suddenly, it appeared that Will had assumed control. "I'm not sure what you're referring to," she said.

"How many years did Wiemer Industries pour molten iron, brass, and aluminum castings in that old foundry and dump the residue on the ground outside the building? They must have done the same with forge waste. I'd imagine a soil sample would attract the attention of the EPA."

"What's your point?" she replied, rather defensively.

Will leaned forward in his chair, placed his elbows on the table, and spoke very quietly. "Well, you mentioned environmental and labor law. There are some instances when they've become intertwined in relocation negotiations. The cost of cleaning up environmental contamination can be very expensive. It may cost a lot more than any savings from relocation. The issue is usually pursued by the community rather than the union. It rarely happens, but a threat to call in the EPA has influenced the outcome of a few relocation negotiations."

Beth laughed. "Who are you representing, counselor?"

Will smiled. "You were inquiring about my background. I played football in high school, right here in Hammelburg. I was a defensive back. I learned to concentrate on what the other team was going to do on offense. I've incorporated that technique in my law practice."

"So you're suggesting that the community or the IMU might threaten to call attention to the environmental pollution at our old foundry as a means of blocking the relocation?" she said.

Will paused for a moment, looked directly at Beth. "Yeah, I might adopt that strategy if I were representing the IMU or the city council."

"Well," she responded, "that kind of makes the whole issue of resolving the meaning of pending financial hardship look insignificant, doesn't it?"

"It could probably change the direction of the negotiations rather quickly," he said.

"Are you suggesting that it's an issue that's going to be raised?" The tone of her question was slightly accusatory.

Will recognized the intent of her question and laughed. "No, Beth. I haven't mentioned my observations to anyone else." He paused a moment before continuing. "But when I drove by that abandoned building last Saturday morning, I thought, if there is contamination in there, Wiemer can't escape that liability, even if they sell the property. Moreover, any potential owner is going to insist on environmental testing before the sale.

He smiled. "I guess I'd take the For Sale sign down until I knew if there was a problem."

When their food arrived, Beth appeared to have little appetite. She picked at her food. Her cheerful mood had disappeared. After a few moments, she resumed the conversation.

"I have an undergraduate degree in metallurgy. I know a bit about environmental issues associated with foundries. For several years, I've been concerned about the potential contamination at the foundry and forge operations. But I haven't convinced management that we should examine the problem. Our CFO damn near becomes hysterical every time I mention it. He claims that it could bankrupt the company. He talks about the enormous financial disasters experienced by companies involved with the asbestos cleanup."

"What about Stevenson and your board of directors?" Will inquired.

"Harris has a big bark, but little bite. He really detests management disputes. When they occur, he becomes angry and attempts to shut them down rather than resolve them. The board meets once every three months for one day. With the exception of Mary Rieff, the board lets management establish their agenda. It's never been discussed at a board meeting."

"Have there been any soil tests?"

"No. I suggested it after we closed the foundry, but the CFO went ballistic, and Harris deferred to him."

"What's their solution?" Will asked.

"I don't know, but I suspect it's political."

"A political solution?" Will responded.

"Yes," she said, "make the problem go away by political persuasion."

"I wouldn't bet on that as a long-term solution," Will observed.

Beth took a sip of coffee and slowly replaced the cup in the saucer before responding. "We don't spend time discussing long-term problems or solutions at Wiemer Industries," she said, sardonically.

By mid-afternoon, few employees remained at Wiemer Industries' corporate headquarters. Most had departed to prepare for Thanksgiving or commence their holiday travel. Harris Stevenson was also preparing to leave, but decided to first visit with Bruce Kramer to learn what he had arranged with the outside auditors regarding Cyrus Brown's request.

To his surprise, Kramer's office was dark. Despite his penchant for leaving a clean desk before departing, a clutter of papers remained on his desktop. His secretary, Mary Rose Keener, was preparing to leave when Stevenson inquired about Kramer. Mary Rose, a tall, handsome woman, had worked for Wiemer Industries for 35 years, joining the company the week after her graduation from Hammelburg Central High School. Her husband had worked in the foundry, but lost his job when the foundry was moved to Juarez. He had secured a job with a roofing repair company. Mary Rose had worked her way up through the secretarial ranks to executive assistant. She was highly regarded by the office staff and the executives she served, including Gus Arnholt.

Where's Bruce?" he asked

She shook her head, and looked perplexed. "I don't know, Mr. Stevenson. He left about an hour ago. He had no meetings scheduled outside the office. He turned off the lights, put on his overcoat, and walked out. I wished him a happy Thanksgiving, but he didn't say anything. He never leaves before me, unless he's traveling, and I know that he plans to stay at home for Thanksgiving. He even left papers on his desk."

"Well, it's been a hectic couple of weeks," Stevenson said. "Maybe he decided to go someplace and put his feet up for a while."

He smiled. "Anyway, Mary Rose, I'll wish you a happy Thanksgiving."

"Thank you, Mr. Stevenson, and you too."

Harris returned to his office, retrieved his coats, and briefcase, and took the elevator to the parking garage. He noted that Kramer's Mercedes was gone. He was amused by the contradiction between Kramer's complaint about his inadequate income and his expensive car.

He drove home to help prepare for the hour-and-a-half trip to his mother's home in northern Indiana. He and Ellen planned to spend Thanksgiving with their two adult children, their spouses, and his widowed mother. Ellen had prepared most of the Thanksgiving dinner in advance. He was loading the carefully-wrapped segments of the meal in the trunk of his car, when Ellen came to the door of the garage and told him that Nancy Kramer wanted to speak to him on the phone. As he passed her to go to the phone, she caught his arm and whispered that Nancy's voice sounded unnatural.

He picked up the phone. "Nancy?"

There was a long pause, a brief sob. "Harris… I'm at the hospital… Bruce is here… I came home this afternoon and found him lying on our bedroom floor… unconscious… I called 911… They came immediately… I thought he'd had a heart attack or a stroke… They just told me that he swallowed an enormous amount of some drug and is in a coma. The children are still at home. Oh dear God, I don't know what to do."

Stevenson's reaction was immediate. "Listen to me, Nancy—we're getting in the car right now. We'll be at the hospital in ten minutes. Hold on sweetheart, we're on our way."

He hung up and called to his wife. With a minimum of conversation, they both walked directly to his car. On the way to the hospital, Stevenson called the Pertoski residence. Maureen answered. He explained what had happened, and asked if she could go to Kramer's house, pick up the children, and take them to her home. Maureen never hesitated. Jon was not home yet, but she would drive to Kramer's immediately. She would call Jon from her car.

In the past, The Hammelburg Regional Health Center had received national awards and recognition for the quality of its service and advanced health care facilities, but with the elimination of the WI Foundation, the decline in the assets of the Wiemer/Rieff Foundation, the economic demise of the community, and the increased cost of health care, the quality of service and facilities had declined. It was evident in the condition of the emergency room. The staff had been reduced and the furniture in the waiting area needed replacement.

As the Stevensons entered the emergency waiting room, they saw Nancy Kramer sitting in a chair near the registration desk, her face white and tear-stained. She was dressed in a pair of gray wool slacks and a heavy blue cable knit sweater. Her bleached blond hair, which was beginning to darken at the roots, was worn in a careless ponytail.

Upon seeing the Stevensons, she immediately stood up and moved toward them. Ellen reached out and took her in her arms. She sobbed and talked incoherently about drugs and comas and her disbelief. Harris patted her back, attempting to console her. He did not ask any questions. A few minutes later, he suggested that Ellen remain with Nancy while he made some inquiries.

He walked to the registration desk; the nurse recognized him. "Mr. Stevenson, I'm sure you want to know about Mr. Kramer's condition. I'm sorry, but I can't tell you very much except that he was in a coma when the emergency response team brought him in. The ER medics pumped out the contents of his stomach. He had ingested a large amount of sleeping pills and tranquilizers. The ER doctor has administered what he believes is the appropriate antidote. He remains in a coma and is listed in critical condition. I'm sorry, but that's all I know. The ER doctor may be able to see you within the next half hour."

Stevenson thanked the nurse and turned to return to join Ellen and Nancy. Nancy was now sitting on a bench between Ellen and Jon Pertoski, who had arrived while Stevenson was talking to the nurse. Jon was holding Nancy's hand and speaking to her softly. Stevenson sat down next to Ellen.

Nancy was responding to Jon in a low, trembling voice. Her speech was broken by frequent sobs. "I have no idea what happened… no idea… He's not been himself for several days… He was very agitated when he came home last night… He didn't eat with us… He made several telephone calls… I think to people in New York… he became very angry at whomever he was talking to… He was using the phone in his study… but I could hear him shouting at someone about borrowing money… He also called Byron Hinkle… he had a long conversation with Byron… he was still angry… angry about something that had happened to them… something about investments they'd made with someone in New York."

Jon glanced at Stevenson. Harris was staring at Nancy, listening closely to what she was relating.

Jon continued to speak to her quietly. "Did he tell you anything after he was done with the phone calls?"

"Yes... he sat at the kitchen table after the children were in bed and talked about a big problem he had... a big problem with a big investment that he had made with some people in New York... he said he was sorry he hadn't told me... but he had borrowed a lot of money... he kept repeating... a lot of money."

Nancy grasped Jon's hand tightly and sobbed, "I told him not to worry... he seemed so upset... he seemed to be talking to himself... I'm not sure he even heard what I said... He kept saying he didn't know what was going to happen... he kept saying that he was only trying to catch up... I asked him what he meant... All he would say was he was trying to catch up... catch up with the rest of them... he'd fallen behind... way behind."

Jon again looked at Harris; his expression had changed from concentrated attention to anger.

"He came to bed about midnight," she continued. "I think he got up a couple times during the night... this morning he seemed to be all right... he didn't say much... He had breakfast... stayed at home a little later than usual and talked with the children... They didn't have any school today... they were playing at friends' houses when he came home this afternoon... I was shopping for Thanksgiving dinner."

Suddenly, Harris was aware of a tall man, well-built, short black hair, standing next to him. He wore a light blue shirt, gray tweed jacket, and dark corduroy pants. Harris thought he recognized him, but could not remember his name.

He quickly positioned himself between Harris and the others. His back was turned to them. He spoke in a low voice, attempting to avoid drawing attention to himself. "Mr. Stevenson, I'm Detective Rick Hudson from the Hammelburg Police Department. I would appreciate an opportunity to speak with you privately, before I interview Mrs. Kramer."

Harris immediately stood up and shook hands with the detective. "Sure... but I'm not sure how much I can help."

"Let's go over to the other side of the room and sit down for a few moments and let me ask you some questions," the detective responded.

They selected a bench seat, well out of hearing distance of Nancy, Jon, and Ellen. As soon as they were seated, the officer showed Stevenson his police identification.

"I'm a homicide detective, Mr. Stevenson. The homicide squad is required to investigate all suicides and suicide attempts. Under the law, they are considered homicides. I've already talked with the ER medical staff. The medical staff believes that Mr. Kramer will survive, but they're unsure what permanent damage may have occurred before he arrived at the ER, and if and when he will become coherent. Obviously, Mrs. Kramer has suffered an emotional shock. Could you give me any information that would help me make my questioning more effective and less painful for her; any idea why he attempted suicide?"

Harris shook his head. "I don't know."

"Has he given any hints? Any personal or job-related problems?"

Stevenson responded quickly. A little anger resonated in his tone. "Well, I assume you live in this town and you know that Wiemer Industries is having some problems; labor negotiations, plant relocation, and financial performance. Bruce is the chief financial officer. It's not an easy job right now."

"So, it could be work related," Hudson surmised.

Harris sat silently for a few moments. When he responded, he looked directly at the officer and spoke softly. "I can speculate, but that won't help much." Harris studied the detective momentarily. "My guess is that it may be a personal problem."

The detective nodded. His face registered no reaction. "Does his wife have any idea why he did it?" he asked.

"From the brief conversation she just had with Jon Pertoski, the man sitting beside her, she has no knowledge of why he did it. She discovered him on the bedroom floor this afternoon when she returned from shopping. I guess the medics must have some idea of what time he swallowed the pills. He left the office early this afternoon, which is unusual for him."

"But you believe it may be a personal problem, is that right?"

Stevenson attempted to retreat a little from his earlier speculation. "Well, I could be dead wrong, but I won't know until I have a chance to ask some questions of other people."

"Any chance of telling me who those other people are?" the officer asked.

Stevenson's response reflected his frustration. "Not until I have a chance to talk with our corporate counsel and ask those other people some direct questions."

Both men remained silent for a few moments. Finally, the detective stood up and placed his hand on Stevenson's shoulder. "Thanks for talking with me; I know it's tough to talk about. But you've given me some direction. It'll help me with Mrs. Kramer. If you have anything you can share with me later, I would appreciate it."

Harris stood up and looked directly at the officer. "Before you go over there, let me ask you... have we met before?"

He smiled at Stevenson. "I don't think so... but I look a lot like my younger brother, Jimmie... Jimmie Hudson... and I'm sure you've met him."

The detective walked toward Nancy Kramer, Jon Pertoski, and Ellen. He introduced himself quietly, squatted in front of Nancy, expressed his concern regarding the tragedy, inquired about her condition and whereabouts of her children, and began asking questions in a quiet, deferential fashion.

Harris did not join them. He walked outside and called Beth Brinson on his cell phone. Following a brief description of what had occurred, he related Nancy Kramer's comments about Bruce's telephone conversations with someone in New York and Byron Hinkle.

"I can understand the calls to New York, but the call to Hinkle doesn't add up. He told me this morning that Hinkle called him. Why the hell would he call Hinkle? And why would Hinkle tell Bruce that he had resigned as counsel for the ISU? Why tell the CFO? I would've expected him to call Fenn Sullivan, or let the IMU tell us. And he resigned the day after all that crap came out about the hedge fund and the subpoenas."

Beth said, "I don't know, Harris, but we've got to get some answers Luckily, tomorrow is Thanksgiving and the markets are closed, so we don't have to make a public announcement until Friday, but we have to have a press release first thing Friday morning, before the market opens. Most of Wall Street won't be at work on Friday because of the holiday, but we'll still get questions, and we need answers. The downside is that no one is going to be available tomorrow or Friday to help. But maybe Byron can tell us something."

He was surprised at her response, not even an obligatory expression of remorse; the immediate transition to the impact on the market, a cold professional reaction. She was even tougher than he had assumed.

"Yeah, I could even call Byron tonight," he said.

Beth responded carefully. "Harris, it might be better if I called him."

"Why?" he snapped.

"Because he might be less intimidated by me," she said.

There was a long silence. "O.K., but I'm not going north tonight. Ellen and I need to stay here with Nancy. I don't know what we'll do tomorrow. Maybe we can get the kids to come down here and we'll take our dinner to Kramer's house. It's in the truck of my car, right now. Jon and Maureen are helping. If you need to talk to me at any time, you can get me on my cell phone."

Immediately after hanging up, Beth grabbed the phone book and began looking for Byron Hinkle's residential number. It was unlisted. She looked for his office number and called. The phone rang three times; she expected an answering machine. Suddenly, a woman answered the phone. She spoke English hesitantly, with a heavy Hispanic accent. Beth asked to speak to Byron Hinkle. There was a long pause.

"I clean offices, but lights on his office. If he here, I tell him someone wants talk," she said slowly.

"Thank you. Tell him that it's Beth Brinson from Wiemer Industries and it is very important that I speak with him."

"Beth Brinson... Wiemer Industries," the woman repeated slowly.

"Yes, and it's very important that I speak with him. Thank you."

"O.K.," she responded. There was a short pause. Beth could hear a conversation, and then a man's voice on the phone.

"Hi Beth, what can I do to help you at this late hour?"

"I have some very bad news, Byron."

"Well, I'm sorry to hear that. I should have left earlier," he laughed.

She paused momentarily. "It's worse than that, Byron. Bruce Kramer attempted suicide this afternoon. His wife, Nancy, found him. He apparently swallowed a large number of tranquilizers or sleeping pills. He's in the hospital. His condition is critical."

There was no immediate response. Finally, he cleared his throat and spoke. His voice was weaker. "My God, I can't believe Bruce Kramer would attempt suicide." His response sounded like a conversation with himself.

Again, there was a prolonged silence before he continued. "Does anybody know why?"

"No. He's still in a coma and they don't know if and when he'll regain consciousness. But Nancy told Jon Pertoski that he made several phone calls last night. She thought one of them was to you. We hoped maybe you might help us answer that question," she said.

Beth heard Hinkle suddenly inhale. He cleared his throat again. "Beth, I'm not sure what you're talking about. I talked with Bruce last night, but there wasn't anything in our personal conversation that would explain an attempted suicide. I deeply regret this tragedy, but I've nothing to relate to you that would shed any light on the cause."

Beth hated carefully crafted lawyer responses. They reminded her of conversations with Ted Brinson when their marriage was ending.

"Byron, time is short, so let me describe our problem as concisely as possible. You must be aware that yesterday Jack Perkins and Trent Baker were accused of illegal insider trading, possibly including client companies. It's the big news on Wall Street and CNBC. All those client companies, including Wiemer Industries, will be questioned by the SEC to see if management was involved. This afternoon, the CFO of Wiemer Industries attempted suicide."

She paused momentarily. There was no response. She continued. "On Friday morning, Wiemer Industries will be expected to make a public announcement about Bruce, and there's going to be a hell of a lot of ugly speculation and questions to answer. If we don't have any answers, some enterprising investigative reporters are going to try to tie some loose strings together, and on the end of those strings they may discover some intriguing connections. I think we would be wise to sit down and discuss it before all of that starts."

"I understand what you are saying, Beth, but I don't see how I'm involved. I'm sorry, but it's clearly a Wiemer Industries problem."

"You may be correct, Byron, but it was Bruce who told Harris that you had resigned as counsel for the IMU. Frankly, we were a little surprised that you chose Bruce to pass on that information. We didn't know that you and Bruce had a close relationship." She intended her tone to be slightly accusatory.

There was a long silence before Hinkle responded. "Beth, I'm already late for a family dinner. I'd like to help, but I don't know how I can be of any assistance," he said.

"Well, how about sitting down and talking about it?" she said.

"About what?" He was growing increasingly irritated by Beth's persistence.

"About you and Bruce and what you may know that would help us understand what happened," she answered.

Again, there was a lull in the conversation.

"O.K., when do you want to meet, Beth?" His tone reflected both sarcasm and irritation.

"How about tomorrow morning in your office, about nine o'clock?" she suggested quickly.

"Tomorrow is Thanksgiving," he snapped.

"Just give me an hour in your office, Byron. I have to be able to make some sense of this by Friday morning."

"Beth, I don't know why the hell you think I can be of any help, but O.K. I've always had a good relationship with Wiemer Industries. I'll meet you here at nine in the morning, if you insist."

"I'll be there, Byron. Thanks."

After his lunch with Beth, Will Heider returned to his parents' home. His mother was in the kitchen preparing several large pans of sage dressing. He commented on the pleasant aroma and her willingness to prepare a Thanksgiving meal despite her disdain for cooking.

"Oh, this isn't for us. It's for the community dinner. I've already convinced your Dad that we should have a late Thanksgiving dinner at The Bavarian." she said.

He recalled that for many years, his parents had helped to prepare and serve a community Thanksgiving dinner for the homeless and destitute families in Hammelburg. The food was donated by individuals and merchants. The meal was prepared and served by volunteers in the kitchen and dining hall of Purdue University while the students were away for the holiday; a few special dishes were prepared by volunteers in their homes.

She turned away form her task for a moment. "I have a favor to ask of you, Will."

He immediately recognized from her smile and tone of voice that whatever the request, she expected a positive response.

"Your father has begged off of helping with the community dinner tomorrow, and I would like you to take his place." She continued to display her expectant smile.

He frowned as he responded, "I've never done that, Mom."

He was aware that his lame excuse was only going to encourage her.

"Yes, I know, but your brother and sister have, and this is your big opportunity," she laughed.

"Dad not feeling well?" he asked suspiciously.

"No, he's feeling fine," she smiled. "We begin serving at eleven o'clock" she continued. "We should leave here by ten o'clock to help with the setup. It will all be over by four o'clock. We can come home, clean up and go to The Bavarian with your father. Don't wear good clothes. You'll serve lots of food to hungry people."

"I feel like a teenager who's been assigned a task," he muttered.

She turned and smiled at him. "You're right; I should have done it much earlier."

"You know, during the last four days I've seen more of the inner workings of Hammelburg than I did during my initial eighteen years."

"Yes, isn't that fortunate," she responded cheerfully as she refocused on the preparation of the sage dressing.

He shook his head and laughed. "Ten o'clock and old clothes, is that it?"

"That's right," she responded cheerfully but firmly.

The following morning, a gray sky and cold wind greeted Will as he carefully loaded several large pans of sage dressing covered with aluminum foil in the trunk of his rental car. His mother placed two of her large aprons in the back seat. Will eyed the aprons cautiously, fearing one of them might be intended for him; she then occupied the right front seat beside him. By 10:15, they were on their way to the Purdue University campus. The traffic was light, and nearly all the commercial locations were closed, with the exception of several large grocery stores that remained open until noon for the convenience of last-minute shoppers.

As they past the Kroger store, Ruth Heider looked at the nearly empty parking lot. "I hope we have enough food for everyone," she said.

"It's really that big a deal?" Will asked.

"You wait and see. It's a real reflection of the economic decline of this community. You'll see how many people are living on the bottom rung. Last year was the largest attendance I've ever seen."

Ruth Heider had participated in the community Thanksgiving dinner for nearly 40 years. The event was started by Anne Wiemer Rieff during the late 1930s. It was originally held at the First Lutheran Church and financed entirely by Wiemer and Rieff family contributions. Within a few years, attendance became too large for the church and it was transferred to a high school gymnasium, and finally to Purdue University. Attendance began to decline after the war, and although it was never abandoned, it continued to be a rather small event until the late 1990s, when large numbers of homeless people, poor rural families, and Hispanic workers began to appear. The previous year, they had run out of food, and to assure that everyone received a Thanksgiving dinner, they solicited cash contributions from the volunteers and called a Kroger store manager and asked him to reopen his store to allow them to purchase more food. The last meal was served shortly before eight o'clock that evening.

"Are you sure that all of them are charity cases?" Will asked, attempting a little humor.

His mother stared at him for a moment before responding. "If you see anyone that you think doesn't deserve a Thanksgiving dinner, please let me know. I haven't seen anyone like that in 40 years, and we refer to them as our guests, not charity cases."

He glanced at his mother. She was frowning, staring straight ahead. "I'm sorry; that was a bad joke," he said.

"That's why I wanted you to come with me this morning," she replied.

When they arrived at the campus, his mother directed him to the parking lot near the university food center. There were already several cars in the lot and a line of people had begun to form outside the entrance. Many of them appeared to be families with young children.

As they made their way toward the entrance with Will awkwardly balancing several pans of sage dressing, a young woman holding a small child spoke to Ruth Heider. Ruth stopped momentarily, talked with her briefly, and patted the child. As they reached the entrance, they encountered a large sign stating that the Thanksgiving Day dinner would begin at 11:00 A.M. and end at 4:00 P.M. A police officer opened the door and allowed them to enter. Will noted that the officer recognized his mother and spoke to her.

Once inside, Will marveled at the preparation that had already occurred. The dining hall contained a large number of tables that seated four, six, or eight. A Thanksgiving decoration had been placed in the center of each table, along with settings of decorated paper placemats and napkins. Several men and women were setting up the cafeteria line, stacking plastic trays, paper plates and cups, and plastic knives, forks and spoons at the starting point; inserting large black plastic bags in trash barrels located throughout the dining hall. Tray recovery wagons were already stationed at the exit. Several Amish women wearing handmade aprons atop long dark dresses and white bonnets were busy preparing large trays of turkey, mashed potatoes, and sweet potatoes. Others were slicing pumpkin pies, placing servings on small paper plates, and transferring them to large trays.

Ruth Heider greeted several people as she showed Will where to deposit the pans of sage dressing. As soon as he unburdened himself of the pans, his mother handed him one of the two aprons she had placed in the back seat of the car. He protested—he did not want to wear an apron.

Before his mother could respond, an attractive, elderly woman with short gray hair laughed and spoke to him. "You'd best take your mother's advice or you're going to be a mess by four o'clock."

Ruth Heider immediately embraced the older woman, took her hand, and turned to Will. "Will, I don't believe you have ever met Mary Rieff."

Before she could formally introduce them, Mary smiled and spoke to Will.

"I suspected you were Will Heider when I saw you come in with your mother. You look a lot like your brother. As I remember, he also objected to wearing an apron."

Will laughed and put the apron over his head and tied it in the back. He was pleased that his mother had chosen a solid blue model. He feared he would be given one with prints of flowers or birds.

Will's assignment was the food line. He was asked to help serve the turkey. Mary Rieff was stationed next to him, serving the dressing.

They rotated every 30 minutes. Many of the volunteers were older people who needed to rest their legs after a half hour of standing and serving.

The serving began promptly at eleven o'clock. There were no gaps in the line. It was a constant stream of people, and the end of the line was not visible. It extended beyond the entrance to the building. Will noticed that many of the adults he served avoided eye contact with him. The children were less self-conscious. Will greeted each person as he placed large pieces of white and dark meat on their paper plates. A few smiled and responded; many thanked him; a few merely moved to the next serving point, never acknowledging his greeting. Many adults and children appeared to be inadequately clothed for late fall weather; faded, but not fashionable blue jeans, cotton shirts, cotton sweaters, old Nikes or the equivalent. Only a few women wore dresses. Many children were dressed in clothing that was either too large or too small. Several people resembled the homeless people Will encountered while walking to work in the Chicago Loop. They clung to large, tattered shopping bags stuffed with clothing and other personal items. The Hispanic guests spoke Spanish while standing in the line, but many attempted to express their appreciation to the servers with a few English words. Several young Hispanic and African-American men wore dark stocking caps pulled down below their ears. Some resonated resentment with their body language.

After the first 30 minutes, even Will was ready for a break. After being relieved by an older man, he retreated to the rest area, a line of aluminum lawn chairs behind the food line. As he sat down, Mary Rieff occupied the seat beside him. "First time at the community dinner?" she asked.

"Yeah" he responded "I'm the last member of the Heider family to participate in this event."

"Any surprises?"

Will considered the question before responding. "I guess I'm surprised at the number of people who appear to he homeless. I see a lot of them in Chicago, but I didn't expect to see them in Hammelburg."

"Oh, I recognize most of them," she responded without hesitation. "Indiana, like many other states, has closed most of its mental hospitals, and many of the patients have no family, so they end up on the street. They're supposed to have availability to clinics and receive medication," she shrugged. "Many of them live at the women's shelter. We have a growing number of young and old women and families living there. But there are many I don't recognize because the number increases each year. No jobs or not able to work because of mental or physical impairments, no income, reductions in welfare benefits, no health insurance, reductions in Medicaid. The need for private assistance is accelerating, while public and private support is declining. We used to assume that homeless people were a big city phenomenon. Not any more."

Will was surprised by her direct, matter-of-fact response.

After a moment, she continued. "Your mother and I have been involved in the community dinner for many years, but it was started long before we volunteered. Like so many things that make Hammelburg unique, it's a community tradition."

She glanced at Will. "You know, communities are like pieces of delicate china passed down from generation to generation. If they're not protected and cared for, they crack and crumble. The willingness of each new generation to maintain and preserve the quality of life in a community is dependent upon a large and generous middle class; those who've remained in the community for generations. But now they're disappearing, and so is the quality of life. Like so many communities in the Midwest, Hammelburg has become a way station for many of those who might assume leadership roles. It's a misconception that the generosity of the wealthy defines a community. After all, wealth is nomadic. We can retain our quality of life without the very wealthy, but we can't without the middle class."

She was looking directly at him, awaiting his reaction. He suddenly had the sensation of being interrogated, the same reaction he had at his first meeting with Beth Brinson. He was puzzled as to how to respond. He attempted to make a slight adjustment in the direction of the conversation without being too obvious. "I'm also surprised by the large number of Hispanic families."

"Well, poverty in Indiana is probably better than poverty in Mexico," she quipped.

Will looked at her, attempting to determine if she had intended to be humorous.

"We have small rental homes in this town that house as many as four Hispanic families," she continued. "Two-bedroom apartments that are occupied by as many as 12 Hispanic men. They come here, legal and illegal, and work long hours for low pay and no health benefits. Some leave their families behind and send money home; others bring their families so that both adults and older children can work."

"Who hires them?" Will asked.

"Small manufacturing companies, restaurants, big retail stores, maintenance and cleaning companies."

"What about the immigration laws? I thought they were getting tougher about undocumented workers?"

"Well, the INS comes through Hammelburg occasionally and makes a few arrests. But they're quickly replaced. Some businesses treat them like commodities... always available and cheap."

Will sat silent, amazed at this petite, elderly lady. Perhaps his initial reaction was correct. She was trying to evaluate him; knowing that he was a labor lawyer who worked exclusively with management. Despite having grown up in a moderately liberal family, with parents who occasionally supported ideas and policies that offended a predominantly conservative community. Maybe she was trying to find out where he was located on the spectrum of economic and social policies.

"It appears that the jobs are going in two directions," he said, "manufacturing jobs to Mexico, and lower-paying service jobs to Hispanic immigrants."

"Of course," she responded, "that's how we achieve lower labor cost."

"Is that bad?" he asked.

"There's nothing wrong with lower labor costs," she responded, "but the real issue is how the cost reductions are achieved. You can reduce cost by making the labor force more productive, by investing in new technology and new products, or by lowering pay and medical benefits, eliminating pension plans, and avoiding environmental regulations. There's also the question of who benefits from lower costs."

He was surprised by her articulate familiarity with economics issues.

"I guess, you could argue that the consumer benefits," he said.

"Really?" she smiled. "Do you believe the lower prices offset the cost of poor health, lower standards of living, and increased environmental pollution?"

Will avoided her question. He considered it rhetorical.

"Than you would object to Wiemer Industries relocating jobs to Mexico?" he asked.

"No. I'm not a protectionist, but I object to moving jobs to Mexico if the result is a reduction in the standard of living for both countries and increased damage to the environment. I believe there's an important distinction between the meaning of fair trade and free trade," she declared.

They both sat silently for a few moments, observing the seemingly endless number of people in line for Thanksgiving dinner.

She spoke softly as she focused on her small, wrinkled hands, laid flat on her patterned apron, fingers spread wide apart. The only ornamentation was a well-worn gold wedding band on her left hand. "The real issue isn't relocation. That's only a visible manifestation of a far larger problem: the slow, almost unnoticed, daily deterioration of small, productive, generous, creative societies. We're losing them, Will, We're losing Hammelburg. And it will take far more than retaining jobs at Wiemer Industries to save it."

Chapter 20

Beth Brinson arrived at Byron Hinkle's law office shortly after 9:00 A.M. on Thanksgiving morning. The office of Damich, Damich and Hinkle was located in the center of Hammelburg, near the Alamost County Courthouse. The building was a renovated two-story brick building that had been built in the early 1900s by a local bank, which failed in the early 1930s. The original name, Farmers' Bank & Trust Building, was still visible, engraved in a limestone block above the windows on the second floor. The building remained vacant until the mid 1950s, when a real estate broker remodeled and occupied it. It was vacated again when the real estate company built new facilities on the north side of Hammelburg. Tom Damich bought it in the late 1960s to house his law practice. A vacant lot bordered one side of the building. A retail store had occupied the property for 40 years before it was closed and the building razed. It now served as a parking lot for the law firm's employees and clients. The lot had curb cuts and a thin gravel surface. A building on the opposite side housed a small, family owned office supply business, barely surviving following the recent establishment of an Office Max superstore on the outskirts of Hammelburg. Two commercial buildings across the street were vacant.

When Byron Hinkle joined the firm, following his marriage to Damich's daughter in 1973, the first floor was remodeled, but the second floor remained vacant.

The original entrance to the building had been preserved—large, oak double doors with full-length window panes. Once inside, it was obvious that no remodeling had occurred for several years; other than desktop computers, printers, and other electronic equipment, it was a well-worn facility with gray metal office furniture. Being a holiday, no one occupied the small reception area. A narrow hallway at the rear of the reception area led to several private offices. One of the rooms was illuminated; Beth assumed it was Byron's office. She knocked on the open office door before entering. Hinkle, dressed informally in blue jeans and a blue woolen V-neck sweater pulled over a yellow cotton turtleneck, rose from his chair, smiled, and greeted her.

Hinkle was pear-shaped—narrow shoulders, wide at the hips, with a clear beginning of middle-age spread. The snug fit of his sweater and blue jeans suggested that he had become larger since acquiring them. His graying hair had grown very thin on top. He attempted to disguise it with an exaggerated combover. He wore black-rimmed glasses, which he removed and replaced frequently during conversations. It was an affectation.

The son of an iron mine foreman in Duluth, Minnesota, he graduated from the University of Minnesota at Duluth, and worked at a Minneapolis insurance company for two years before enrolling at the University of Notre Dame Law School, where he met Virginia Damich, who was an undergraduate at Notre Dame. Following graduation, he joined a large law firm in Milwaukee as an associate. Three years later, he married Virginia and became a full partner in Damich and Damich, later renamed Damich, Damich and Hinkle. After settling in Hammelburg, they became active members of the Alamost Country Club and Byron joined the Rotary Club, the local Bar Association, and took an active role in the local Republican Party. Both worked hard to gain acceptance in Hammelburg's prosperous social establishment. Tom Damich's past experience as an ultra-conservative state legislator and member of Congress was beneficial, but somehow the firm never ranked among the top tier of local law firms. It achieved its current size of five partners in the late 1980s, including Damich, his son Roger, and Hinkle. It was considered a modestly successful law practice, not a large income producer for the partners.

Hinkle's office was small, modestly furnished, and smelled of recent cigar smoke. University of Minnesota and Notre Dame diplomas hung on the wall behind his desk in narrow, black wooden frames. An early picture of his wife and two young daughters rested on a shelf behind his desk, along with a gold football embossed with a blue ND.

John T. Hackett

Beth occupied a seat across from Hinkle and thanked him for his willingness to meet with her during a holiday.

"No problem," he said, "but I was really shocked to hear about Bruce. How's he doing?"

"I haven't received a report this morning, but when they left the hospital last night, he was still in a coma," she said.

"Well, like I said, I'm just shocked. Bruce and I have been friends ever since he and Nancy arrived in Hammelburg. We play golf. Virginia and Nancy worked together on several committees at the club. We get together during winter vacations in Sarasota. Bruce is a pretty straight guy. I can't figure this out."

Beth nodded in agreement, but detected a lack of sincerity. She hesitated a moment before responding. "Nancy told Jon Pertoski that the night before Bruce attempted suicide, he talked with you on the phone, and she thought he was very angry about something. Not angry at you, but angry at someone else. She said he also had an angry conversation with someone in New York. Can you help us understand any of that?" she asked.

Hinkle shifted in his seat, removed his glasses, and frowned at Beth. "Bruce and I talked about my decision to stop representing the IMU, but I don't know that I would call that an angry conversation. Bruce was probably surprised, but I don't think he was angry."

"I assume you know that we've fired Jack Perkins and his colleagues, and I have been assigned the task of negotiating with the IMU."

"Bruce told me about that," he said as he replaced his glasses.

"Was that what he was angry about?" she asked.

He laughed. "Well, he didn't think it was a good idea, but he wasn't angry about it."

"Is that the reason you decided to stop representing the IMU?"

"Oh, hell no," he replied abruptly. "That had nothing to do with it. I'd decided to give it up before Bruce even told me that you were going to be involved in the negotiations."

"Well, why did you decide to quit?"

He exhaled loudly, raised his eyebrows, and removed his glasses. "I thought we got together this morning to discuss Bruce, not me," he snapped.

There was a long pause.

"Maybe Nancy misinterpreted what she heard," Beth continued, "but she told Jon Pertoski that Bruce made two telephone calls after he got home night before last. During both calls, he talked about losing lots of money. After he was done with the calls, he also talked with her, rather incoherently, about losing money."

Hinkle slowly reached down and opened a bottom drawer of his desk. Suddenly he smirked like a naughty boy. "Would it bother you if I smoked a cigar?"

"I guess not," she replied reluctantly.

She detested cigar smoke. Her father occasionally smoked cigars in the family car. During the winter months, when the windows were not opened to vent the smoke, she frequently suffered severe headaches or became carsick.

Hinkle carefully removed the cellophane wrapping from what appeared to be an expensive cigar, opened the middle drawer of his desk, retrieved a device to clip the end of the cigar, and a box of wooden matches. After making the necessary preparations, he lit the cigar and puffed several times to ensure that it was alit.

He then sat back in his chair, appearing satisfied and confident, and perched his glasses on the end of his nose.

"I've no idea what Nancy was referring to. I'm sure she's distraught and probably confused," he said rather glibly.

She paused momentarily, purposefully waved cigar smoke away, stared at Hinkle, and lowered her voice. "Twenty-four hours from how, I'm going to have to tell the world that the CFO of Wiemer Industries attempted suicide. There are going to be lots of questions. Particularly, after the media focuses on the fact that this tragedy occurred shortly after it was announced that the labor negotiator for Wiemer Industries was accused of violating federal securities laws and the counsel for the IMU resigned."

He thrust the cigar in the middle of his mouth, drew in both cheeks, lowered his head, and glared at Beth over his glasses before removing the cigar and exhaling a large puff of smoke in her direction. "Are you suggesting that I know why Bruce attempted suicide?" he challenged her.

"I'm not suggesting anything, Byron. I'm attempting to get some answers to questions that I may be asked tomorrow or soon after."

"Why is it necessary to answer stupid questions?" he snapped.

"I don't have to answer them. I'll just let them print their speculations, or suggest they call you," she replied without a trace of emotion.

He moved forward in his chair, placed his elbows on his desk, brought his hands together while holding his cigar between two fingers, pursed his lip and looked at the cigar smoke as it curled toward the ceiling.

"O.K., let me speculate." He took a long drag on his cigar and exhaled a cloud of gray smoke in her direction. "Remember now, this is speculation. I'm not recalling any conversations I ever had with Bruce or anyone else."

Beth's expression signaled neither acceptance nor rejection of Hinkle's proposal.

"Let's assume that somehow Bruce made some very large, very large investments with some friends," he continued, "and he recently discovered those investments had been improperly managed, and he lost all of his money, including all the money he borrowed."

She was annoyed at his clumsy attempt to be deceptive. "That might explain his actions," she said, "but it would probably result in some questions about possible connections between his bad investments and Jack Perkins's hedge fund."

"Who said anything about Perkins's hedge fund?" he barked. "It could have been anything. The recent plunge of Wiemer Industries' stock could have done him in."

She was losing patience with his shallow attempts to confuse the conversation. "Byron, in time, Bruce will probably recover and be able to talk about why he swallowed all those pills, and we can ask him about his phone call with you and others and really get to the bottom of it. So, we can talk about it now, or wait until Bruce recovers and let it all spill out… No need to speculate."

His face grew red; he tapped cigar ashes into a large square ashtray on his desk and cleared his throat before responding.

"O.K.… so Bruce and I talked night before last… but he called me. Bruce invested in Perkins's hedge fund; a lot of money, big money. Perkins talked him into making a lot bigger bet than he should have. Everything went great for the first couple of years, and Bruce decided to double up. He reinvested all his earnings and borrowed more money, several million… put it all in Urban Partners."

He coughed and cleared his throat. "Now, with the subpoenas, the fund is busted, and Bruce is probably staring at bankruptcy. Not a nice place for the CFO of a big company."

Beth showed no reaction to this revelation. "So why did Bruce call you?" she inquired.

"What do you mean?" His face grew darker.

"Why call you?" she repeated. "I assume you're not Bruce's lawyer, given all his connections on Wall Street. Maybe a golfing buddy, but not his investment advisor."

He carefully placed his cigar in the ashtray, removed his glasses and placed them on his desk, closed his eyes momentarily, and took a deep breath. He then leaned forward on his elbows, brought his hands together, interlocked his fingers, and held them to his forehead like a sun visor, avoiding direct eye contact with Beth.

"All right... I also invested in Urban Partners... not nearly as much as Bruce, but more than I should've," he said in a voice that was barely above a whisper.

He suddenly pulled his hands away from his face and glared at Beth. "And so did Gus Arnholt," he hissed, "and a lot of other smart money guys. I got some of mine back because I didn't reinvest it all, like Bruce did. We made big money, for a while."

He paused, picked up his cigar, took a large puff and exhaled, before continuing. "Despite his current problem, Perkins is a very smart guy and a real mover on Wall Street. A few years ago, when he was putting his hedge fund together, he flew down to Sarasota to meet with Bruce and Gus Arnholt. Gus came over from his home in Palm Beach. Bruce invited me to tag along so that we would have a foursome for eighteen holes. After golf, we had dinner at the Club. Perkins started talking about hedge funds and how much money was being made, and all the smart money that was imvolved."

"So that's when you invested?" Beth asked quietly.

"Sure, how many times does a small-town lawyer get a chance to play along with the smart money? Perkins was talking about rates of return that were staggering. He showed us the incredible record of that big hedge fund, Long Term Capital Management; that was before it went bust and the Fed bailed it out. They had Nobel Prize winners helping them invest."

He gazed at his cigar as he rolled it between his thumb and forefinger. He lowered his voice, again, to a near whisper. "The minimum amount you could invest in Urban Partners was one million, but Jack told us he would let us in for 500,000, because we were friends. Gus and I decided to do it. Gus was able to come up with 500,000. I had to do some borrowing to make it, but Jack helped me get it at a New York bank."

"What about Bruce?" Beth asked.

He cleared his throat again. "Bruce wasn't sure, but Jack really wanted Bruce to invest. He let Gus and me in, but he was really after Bruce. He offered to arrange a big loan for him, a couple million dollars. Perkins really worked on him; told him that he was wasting his time at Wiemer Industries, making peanuts; how his old buddies on Wall Street were way ahead of him. He told Bruce he'd help him get back on Wall Street and make big money."

"So he invested?" she persisted.

"Yeah, the two of them had breakfast together the next morning. I played golf with Bruce a few days later and he told me that he was in. I think he initially put in about two million. I was surprised by the amount. Jack must have arranged a big loan for him."

"What did they invest in that was so successful?" Beth inquired.

Hinkle shook his head and stared at the ceiling. "All kinds of deals," he said. "Trent Baker's wife was the chief investment officer. She ran it. She has a Ph.D. from M.I.T.—a math genius. They were located in some town in Connecticut. She hired a couple of computer gurus who created a model that was supposed to spot short-term investment opportunities in all the world markets; stocks, bonds, currencies, commodities, puts and calls. The first year, they made a 37 percent return on our capital. The second year, they scored again, over 45 percent."

"Did they tell you specifically what they were investing in?"

"No, hedge funds don't do that. They aren't regulated like mutual funds. They play it real close to the vest. The only thing they tell you is how much money they make and give you an accounting statement at the end of the year, but they don't tell you where they made the money."

"How did they distribute the earnings?"

"The general partners, Perkins, Baker and his wife, and a couple of the computer gurus, got 20 percent of the profit. But they only put up five percent of the capital. The rest of us, the limited partners, were entitled to the balance, but everyone had to agree to reinvest at least 50 percent of our earnings for the first three years."

"Then, in a short period of time, you must have recovered your original investment," she said.

Hinkle shrugged and displayed a sardonic smile. "Yeah, we should have, but something happened last year. They had one hell of a loss. Damn near sunk the fund. I don't know how Bruce knew, but he told me they bet the farm on Argentine bonds. They said they were doing a lot better this year."

Beth moved forward in her seat. She spoke softly and slowly. "According to the SEC, they were also involved in insider trading... securities fraud. Did you or Bruce know anything about that?"

His head jerked up, and his face radiated anger. "I don't know a goddamn thing about that that. I did nothing wrong or illegal. A lot of smart money is gone, but we didn't know what the hell Perkins and Baker were doing. Shit," he sneered, "even the chairman of your board of directors, Quentin Phillips got in, and he convinced his firm, Puritan Securities, to invest."

"How do you know that?" she asked quietly.

He suddenly appeared frightened. His voice became higher and louder. "Bruce told me. He talked to Phillips about it. He and Jack got him in."

Hinkle appeared to sink in his chair; he placed the cigar in the ashtray. His face reflected his sudden realization that he had said more than he intended. His tone changed from combative to conciliatory. "You know, Beth, I've shared all this with you in confidence... I trust you."

Beth didn't respond. She sat quietly with her hands folded in her lap, looking at Hinkle.

"Nobody, nobody but Perkins and Baker did anything illegal," he continued, "and we don't know if they did. A subpoena is not an indictment."

Beth drew a deep breath, leaned forward, her head cocked slightly. "I'm puzzled, Byron. Why did you elect to resign as counsel to the IMU the day after the news about Perkins and Baker was announced?"

Suddenly, he was angry again. "That issue again. That really pisses me off. I've been gracious enough to come down here on Thanksgiving morning and meet with you and try to help you understand why Bruce Kramer attempted suicide, and you sit there and suggest that maybe I'm involved in that goddamn mess in New York."

"I haven't suggested any such thing, Byron. I'm merely interested in why you've elected to no longer represent the IMU."

"First of all," he snarled, "it's none of your goddamn business who I choose to represent. I don't work for Wiemer Industries. Second, maybe I didn't want to sit across the negotiating table and have to negotiate with a company lawyer that doesn't know what the hell she's doing."

Beth choked back her anger and said nothing.

Hinkle crushed his cigar in the ashtray. "This goddamn discussion is over. I'm going home to Thanksgiving dinner. I guess you know the way out," he said.

Beth stood up to leave, but hesitated for a moment. "I'm sorry I've angered you, Byron. It was not my intention. Nor did I mean to imply that you were involved. But let me clarify something. You did say that Puritan Securities was an investor in Urban Securities?"

Her apology had little impact. "Have you forgotten that your chairman runs that company? Ask him," he snarled.

Shortly after Beth drove out of the parking lot at Hinkle's office, she turned onto a side street, stopped her car near the curb, and dialed Harris Stevenson's cell phone. It rang several times before he answered. He was talking with the head nurse in the section where Bruce Kramer was recovering. He had returned to the hospital after making arrangements to host the family Thanksgiving dinner at his home. Nancy Kramer had remained all night at the hospital. The Pertoskis had taken the Kramer children to their home.

Beth and Harris spoke briefly and agreed to meet in the main reception area of the hospital as soon as she could arrive.

Approximately 15 minutes later, Beth parked her car in the hospital parking lot. As she was walking toward the entrance, she was suddenly reminded that she and her son were expected at the Brinson household by late morning to celebrate Thanksgiving. She called to alert her son that she was unsure when she would arrive, and suggested that he meet her at his grandparents' home.

When Beth entered the hospital, she saw Harris sitting on a couch in the reception lounge. She was relieved that Nancy Kramer had not accompanied him. Leaning forward, arms resting on his legs, staring at the floor, he looked tired and depressed. She knew what she was about to relate to him regarding her meeting with Hinkle would only intensify his concern.

"How's Bruce?" she asked, while removing her coat.

"Not good. He's conscious, but unable to communicate," Harris responded.

"And Nancy?"

"Not as bad as last night, but the poor woman is absolutely devastated. Jon and Maureen have their kids. Jesus, what an awful thing for a family on Thanksgiving."

She sat down beside Harris and gazed around the room to be sure no one could overhear their conversation. "I met with Hinkle this morning at his office," she said quietly.

"Could he shed any light on what happened?" he asked.

"Yes... and it isn't good."

Harris didn't respond; he waited for her to continue.

"What I was finally able to squeeze out of Hinkle is that Bruce initiated the phone conversation with him night before last... Bruce wanted to commiserate about the Perkins fiasco."

She measured Stevenson's reaction before continuing. "Hinkle, Kramer, Jack Perkins, and Gus Arnholt had a golf match in Florida a few years ago. After the game, Perkins rolled out his hedge fund proposal and convinced the other three to invest. He arranged bank loans for Hinkle and Kramer, but Bruce—with Perkins' encouragement—went in much heavier than either Byron or Gus. The first couple of years, the hedge fund made some money and the investors got some back, but not a lot. Bruce reinvested all his earnings and invested more, with borrowed money. According to Hinkle, Bruce may have invested several million dollars."

Stevenson shook his head and stared at the floor. "How many millions did he put in it?" he asked.

"Hinkle wasn't specific, but it could be as much as three to five million," she said.

"That's equivalent to six to ten times his salary. How the hell could he borrow that much money? Even a second mortgage on his home wouldn't support that big a loan." Stevenson's face reflected his disbelief.

"According to Hinkle, Perkins arranged the loans with a New York bank."

"What about collateral? The bank must have had some security?" he said.

"All Hinkle said was Jack arranged the loans with a New York bank. Maybe they took hedge fund shares as collateral."

"God, that's hard to believe. A bank loaning money against a hedge fund investment, with no other collateral... hard to believe."

"Hinkle said there was lots of smart money in the fund, and that's what attracted him."

"Smart money," he repeated. "Jesus, I hate that term."

"Well, according to Hinkle, some of the money came from other people we know."

"Who else?"

"Puritan Securities and maybe Quentin Phillips," she responded.

He raised his head and looked at Beth. He studied her for a few moments."What are you trying to tell me?"

"I've told you all I learned during a short, smoky meeting with Byron Hinkle. But if he told me the truth, I suspect we're going to receive a lot of attention from the SEC and maybe the F.B.I."

"Do you think he told you the truth?"

"Yes, but not all of it. On the other hand, he may not know all of it."

"What do you think he didn't reveal, or doesn't know?"

"I want to be careful, Harris. But I have a feeling Bruce's involvement with Urban Securities may extend beyond a bad investment and a loss of a lot of his money."

"According to Nancy, he only talked about losing lots of their money," he said.

"I know, but Hinkle told me how aggressive Perkins was about getting Bruce in his hedge fund, and how he arranged big loans for him. Why was it so important for Bruce to invest? Hinkle had plenty of sources on Wall Street. Why the CFO of Wiemer Industries?"

"What about Hinkle?" he asked. "Is he just a poor, dumb cluck, or was he more involved than he admits?"

"I don't know. On two separate occasions, I attempted to raise the subject of his resignation as counsel for the IMU, and each time, he flamed. He really flamed the last time. He got very nasty and asked me to leave. I never got an answer."

"Well, I guess all we can do is wait for Bruce to recover and answer some questions," he said.

Beth leaned back and placed her coat on the arm of the couch before responding. "I'm not sure Bruce will answer any questions, Harris."

"Why not? He may be the only one who can explain this bizarre set of events."

"If I were Bruce's lawyer, I would probably advise him and his wife to refuse to talk to anyone about his suicide attempt, his investments in Urban Securities, relationships with Jack Perkins, or anything else that is remotely related to any of those subjects," she said.

His response was much louder. "My God, Beth, what are you trying to say? You think Bruce was somehow involved with Perkins in securities fraud?"

Beth leaned toward Stevenson and lowered her voice to a whisper. "Harris, I don't subscribe to conspiracy theories, but stop a moment and focus on what Hinkle told me. With Perkins's assistance, Bruce borrowed millions of dollars to invest in the hedge fund. The chairman of our board of directors and the retired CFO invested; and Puritan Securities, the company that manages Wiemer Industries' employee pension fund and savings plan may have also invested in Urban Securities."

Stevenson slid forward, extended his legs, crossed his ankles, rested his head on the rear of the couch, shoved his hands in his pants pockets, and focused on the ceiling of the hospital reception room. He remained in that position for several moments, contemplating what Beth had just told him. At the other end of the couch, Beth sat erect, hands in her lap, looking straight ahead, awaiting Stevenson's response to her last remark. Knowing his distaste for bad news and corporate politics, she was uncertain as to how he would react.

He finally spoke with a quiet voice. "O.K. Beth. As we used to say in the Corps, 'Shit happens.' Where do we go from here?"

She turned and looked at him. "Tomorrow morning, you'll have to make an announcement about Bruce. I'll start an internal investigation, before the SEC calls us. I'll need help. I don't think I can use anyone inside the company because of possible leaks. We don't have any outside counsel except Will Heider. If you agree, I'll call him and ask him to meet me in the morning, explain my concerns, and enlist his help."

Harris stood up and looked down at Beth. "I'm going back upstairs to check on Nancy and then go home and have dinner with my family... I guess the fun starts in the morning... Happy Thanksgiving."

As he walked away, Beth noticed that his normally erect shoulders were slumped. From her perspective, she watched a tired, old man walk toward the hospital elevators.

Chapter 21

Early Friday morning, Beth called the hospital and inquired about Bruce. He was still listed as critical, but they reported that his ability to communicate had improved. She had an early breakfast with her son and immediately drove to the office. With the exception of her car and Harris Stevenson's Buick, the parking garage was empty. For many years, Wiemer Industries had declared the Friday after Thanksgiving a paid holiday.

She went directly to her office and called Mary Rose Keener at her home and requested that she meet her as soon as possible at Bruce Kramer's office, and then phoned Will Heider at his parents' residence, briefly described what had happened during the intervening 36 hours, and asked him to join her at her office as soon as it was convenient. Her last call was to the security staff to alert them regarding Will's pending arrival. As she walked to Bruce Kramer's office to meet Mary Rose, she passed Stevenson's office. He was talking on the phone.

A few minutes later, Mary Rose arrived, looking bewildered. Beth ushered her into Bruce's office and closed the door. As Beth described what had happened to Bruce, Mary Rose stared at her in disbelief and then began to sob. Beth waited patiently for Mary Rose to recover her composure before inquiring about Bruce's behavior during the past few days.

"He's been a little edgy for several weeks. Lots of phone calls from bankers, lawyers, people from New York. But on Monday morning, he got a call from Jack Perkins's office, and that really upset him. Later that day, after a meeting with Mr. Stevenson, he was angry; and he spent the rest of the day on the phone with his door closed. When I left, he was still on the phone."

Mary Rose took a tissue from a box on Bruce's desktop, wiped her eyes, and gently blew her nose before continuing. "I took several calls from Mr. Phillips and Gus Arnholt Monday afternoon, but Bruce was never off the phone long enough to return them. He always returns Mr. Phillips's calls immediately, regardless of how busy he is, but he didn't call him back until Tuesday. Fenn Sullivan came over a couple of times, wanting to talk with him, but his door was always closed. On Tuesday morning, he came back, but Bruce was still busy. Fenn told me that Mr. Perkins was in some kind of legal trouble… Is that right?"

"Yes," Beth replied, "he received a subpoena from the SEC."

Mary Rose blew her nose gently again, before responding.

"Well, I don't know what that means. It doesn't sound good. But to tell you the truth, I've never liked him. He calls Bruce a lot, and he's very rude on the phone. If Bruce isn't available, he gets real ugly with me."

"Jack Perkins calls Bruce frequently?" Beth asked.

"Yes, and I know when Bruce takes his call, it's going to be a long conversation. He always shuts his door and never uses his speakerphone, like he does on other calls. During the last couple of months, he's traveled to New York a lot, and I know from his itinerary that he spends time with Mr. Perkins and Mr. Baker. I've always wondered why, since Bruce isn't really involved in union negotiations, and that's what we use Perkins and Baker for, isn't it?"

"Yes," Beth said.

"The day before Thanksgiving was the worst of all. After he came in, he went straight to Mr. Stevenson's office for a few minutes. When he came back, he looked like he was in a trance or something. It was like he wasn't even aware of what was going on around him. He was pale and acted funny. I was afraid he was having a heart attack. He stayed in his office with the door closed and made his own phone calls. He didn't come until out about three o'clock, not even for lunch. When he finally came out, he had his overcoat on and left without saying a word."

"Did he receive any calls on Wednesday?" Beth asked.

"Well, Gus Arnholt called him a couple of times, but he was always on the phone. Since his door was closed, I sent him a couple of e-mails telling him that Gus wanted to talk to him. I don't know if he called him or not."

She frowned. "I had to work for Gus before Bruce came."

Suddenly, someone tapped on the door. It opened slowly, and Harris Stevenson appeared. He looked tired and sad. He smiled at Mary Rose, walked to her side, and patted her gently on the back. Mary Rose began crying softly.

He looked at Beth and spoke quietly. "I've made some phone calls, and as soon as you and Mary Rose are done, I need to speak with you in my office." He patted Mary Rose again and departed.

Fifteen minutes later, Beth walked to Stevenson's office. Harris was sitting at his desk, looking at a yellow legal pad filled with handwritten notes. She sat down on the opposite side of Stevenson's desk and began talking. "All I was able to learn from Mary Rose was that Bruce has been acting very peculiar the last few days. He spent Tuesday and Wednesday on his phone with his office door closed. He received phone calls from Quentin Phillips and Gus Arnholt. She believes he returned Phillips' call, but doesn't know if he called Gus."

Stevenson frowned and massaged the back of his neck before responding.

"I called all the outside directors this morning. To save time, I arranged a conference call. All I told them was that Bruce had attempted suicide on Wednesday afternoon, that he is still critical but recovering in the hospital, and we haven't found out why he did it."

He shook his head and sighed before continuing. "Very different reactions from individual directors... Cyrus Brown insisted, again, that we bring in the outside auditors and hire a law firm that specializes in securities regulation... Mary Rieff had questions about Bruce's family... Clay Emerson said nothing... Quentin Phillips' reaction was the strongest. He insisted that Bruce would have a lawyer, now, today. His whole focus was legal representation for Bruce. He objected to Cyrus Brown's suggestion that we bring in the auditors and hire a securities lawyer; thought it was premature."

"Did Phillips, or anyone else, say anything about Urban Securities?" Beth asked.

"Not a word," Harris said, "but he repeated that Bruce will have a lawyer. He cautioned Cyrus several times about being too quick to call the auditors and securities lawyers; that was it."

"Did he explain why he thinks Bruce needs legal counsel?"

"No," he responded.

"No mention of Puritan Securities?" she inquired again.

"No... but while I was on the conference call, a vice president of Puritan Securities called me and left a voice mail message... Asked me to call him as soon as possible... He'd tried to reach Bruce earlier this week, but they never hooked up."

"That's bad news," Beth stated bluntly.

"Oh, we can't be sure. We won't know until I talk with him," Harris said.

"Did he leave a number?" Beth asked.

Harris cleared his throat. "Yeah ... I'll call him Monday."

"Harris, we need to know as much as we can about this mess as fast as we can. If the man called you today, he's probably still in his office this morning."

"It can wait till Monday," he insisted.

"I'm not sure it can wait. We need to learn as much as we can today, before our press release goes out and the phone calls start pouring in," Beth argued.

He hesitated for a moment, turned and secured a piece of note paper from the table behind his desk, and placed it beside his phone.

"O.K., I'll call him today, after we've finished with the press release and the other issues."

"Harris, I don't want to sound like a bitch, but I think you should call him now, and I should also listen to what he says. I think it's going to be bad news. It may require another press release. Puritan Securities manages our employee pension fund and savings plan. Together, they total more than two billion dollars."

Stevenson's jaw muscles rippled. His face grew dark. He took a deep breath, leaned forward, punched the speaker phone button, and dialed the number written on the note paper.

The phone rang twice before it was answered by a rather effeminate male voice, "Bradley Franklin."

Stevenson frowned at the sound of the voice, leaned forward again, and spoke. "Mr. Franklin... this is Harris Stevenson, CEO of Wiemer Industries. You called me earlier this morning."

"Yes, yes, thank you for returning my call."

"As you can probably detect, I'm on a speakerphone. Beth Brinson, our general counsel, is here with me," Harris said.

"Fine, fine, hello Ms. Brinson. I'm the chief investment officer for Puritan Securities. I'm calling about a problem we've encountered regarding your employee pension and savings plans. I've tried to reach Bruce Kramer several times this week, but he hasn't returned my calls."

Harris glanced at Beth. Her eyes were closed. She was prepared for bad news.

"You may have heard about some problems with a hedge fund called Urban Securities, and a SEC investigation."

"Yes," Stevenson responded.

"Well," Franklin continued, "as near as we can determine, the current book value of the entire Urban Securities fund is less than 20 percent of its original value, and following the announcement of an SEC investigation, the market value is probably much less than that."

"Why are you calling me regarding that issue?" Stevenson asked suspiciously.

There was an exaggerated pause before Franklin responded. "Unfortunately … as I'm sure you're aware… Wiemer Industries' pension and savings plan had a substantial investment in Urban Securities."

Harris Stevenson stared at the phone for a moment, stood up, placed the palms of both hands on his desk, and leaned over the phone. "No, I wasn't aware of that… Mind telling me, Mr. Franklin, why Puritan Securities elected to put our money in a risky investment like a hedge fund?" Stevenson growled.

There was a momentary pause in the conversation.

"Mr. Stevenson, surely you're aware that Puritan Securities was directed to make that investment by your CFO, Bruce Kramer, and it was approved by the compensation committee of your board of directors."

"I've no idea what the hell you're talking about!" Stevenson exclaimed. "Our CFO and compensation committee don't make investment decisions regarding our pension and savings plan… That's why we hired you."

Franklin's reply bristled with formality, which accentuated his effeminate tone. "Mr. Stevenson… my staff and I initially refused to make that investment on the grounds that Urban Securities did not meet the investment standards required for an employee pension or savings plan. But despite our appropriate due diligence and warning, Mr. Kramer insisted that we make the investment… Nevertheless, we continued to refuse until he provided documentation assuring us that the investment had been approved by the compensation committee of the board of directors of Wiemer Industries. We also insisted on receiving a copy of the committee resolution."

Stevenson dumped his large body in his chair. He looked at Beth. "Do you know anything about minutes of the compensation committee and investments in Urban Securities?"

305

"No," she answered quietly, "and my staff and I prepare and retain all the minutes of the meetings of the board of directors and the committee meetings."

The silence in the room and on the phone was ominous. Stevenson elected not to argue about the authenticity of the investment approval. He and Beth both sensed what had occurred.

"How much did we invest?" Stevenson asked.

"We were specifically directed to invest ten percent of both funds in Urban Securities... nearly 200 million dollars," Franklin replied.

"How much have we lost?" Stevenson asked.

Franklin exhaled audibly "If we were able to sell it, we might be able to recover 30 or 40 million dollars, but no one will buy any part of Urban Securities with the SEC problem hanging over it. I fear it is a total loss."

"Any other of your pension or savings plan invested in Urban Securities?" Stevenson inquired.

Franklin's reply was cold and formal. "Puritan Securities adheres to strict ethical procedures regarding our clients. We never reveal client names or the nature of their investments."

"That wasn't my question," Stevenson barked. "I didn't ask you to reveal a name. I only asked if there were other pension funds invested in Urban Securities."

"As I said, I cannot respond to those questions, Mr. Stevenson."

"O.K., I think you've answered my question," Stevenson said sarcastically. "But you know, of course, that Quentin Phillips, your chairman, is also chairman of our board. Does he know anything about this investment?" Stevenson asked.

Franklin's response was short and formal. "I can't comment on that, Mr. Stevenson. Best you ask Mr. Phillips."

"You can't or won't?" Stevenson replied angrily.

"As I said, I suggest you ask Mr. Phillips."

"Did you consult Quentin Phillips about the investment before you made it?"

"We adhere to a specific policy that prohibits public discussion of internal communications."

"Your message is that we've lost 200 million dollars of our employees' money and Puritan Securities is not at fault. Is that it?" Stevenson snapped.

"I'm sorry Mr. Stevenson. We deeply regret this loss, but I can assure you that Puritan Securities fulfilled its fiduciary obligations. We informed Mr. Kramer that it was not an appropriate investment, but despite our counsel, he insisted, and your compensation committee approved it."

Stevenson sat in his chair, his eyes closed, his lips compressed.

Beth suddenly joined the conversation. "Mr. Franklin, when did Bruce Kramer request that you make the investment?"

"At the time the hedge fund was being organized," he replied.

"How were the managers of the fund compensated?"

"They received an annual fee of two and a half percent of the original value of the fund and were entitled to twenty percent of final profits," Franklin said.

"How large was the fund?" Beth inquired.

"Approximately 2 billion dollars."

"So the management received 50 million dollars a year for five years for managing the fund, even though there was no profit, only large losses?" Beth asked.

"Well, they made money during the initial two years."

Beth rephrased her question. "But they've lost nearly all the original investment?"

"That's correct," he answered quickly.

"Well, the management fees account for 250 million dollars. How was the rest of the money lost?" she asked.

"As near as we can determine—and we don't receive much information from them—they lost an enormous amount of money investing in Argentine government bonds. They bought them a few months before the peso was devalued. The last two years, they incurred big losses on large long and short positions in common stocks of several U.S. companies. It was some of those investments, according to the SEC, that involved illegal insider trading."

"Any information regarding the specific stocks involved in illegal trading?" Beth asked.

There was no response from Franklin. Beth thought they had been disconnected.

"Are you still there, Mr. Franklin?"

"Yes" he replied.

"Did you hear my question?"

"Yes." He hesitated. "Only rumors."

"What are the rumors?" Beth asked cautiously.

"Have you been contacted by the SEC?"

"No," Beth answered.

"Well, I'm sorry to tell you that among several other allegations, one of the rumors involves illegal trading of Wiemer Industries shares," he said.

Neither Harris nor Beth responded.

"According to our contacts inside the SEC, Urban Securities made a short sale of 2 million shares of Wiemer Industries, before the stock price began to decline sharply, earlier this year. At the same time, they placed a large buy order with a small investment firm in Hartford to repurchase 4 million shares at a significantly lower price; they wanted to buy twice the amount required to cover their short sale. The buy order price was set very low. The SEC believes the buy order would have expired early next year, a few days before a deadline for the settlement of a Wiemer labor contract regarding manufacturing job relocation. It's assumed that Urban Securities thought that news of a favorable labor settlement would drive up the price of the stock. The SEC alleges that two of the general partners of Urban Securities were involved or had inside knowledge regarding Wiemer's labor negotiations."

Stevenson suddenly leaned forward and placed both hands over his face. "Jesus Christ, this has to be a nightmare. This can't really be happening," he muttered.

Beth decided to terminate the phone conversation, but she had one additional question: "Mr. Franklin, is Adam Fulton still a member of the board of directors of Puritan Securities?"

There was another long pause before Franklin finally responded: "Yes... I believe he is."

At the end of the phone conversation, Beth and Harris sat silently, contemplating the information they had just received.

Stevenson finally stood up and walked to office window, which looked out on Hammelburg's rapidly deteriorating city center. The day after Thanksgiving, a bleak cloudy day, the day that most retailers experience their busiest day of the year, Hammelburg's downtown was quiet. Most of the remaining stores were open, but traffic was light. The desolate asphalt parking lots, which once contained retail stores, were less than half-full. Several city employees were hanging badly-worn Christmas decorations from streetlamps, preparing for the holiday season. As he stood looking at the bleak city center, he tried to remember what it looked like more than 30 years earlier when he had joined Wiemer Industries: a bustling downtown, sidewalks crowded with holiday shoppers, a scarcity of parking spaces, colorful holiday decorations on all the storefronts, a vibrant local economy. He recalled bringing his children downtown on the Saturday before Christmas to visit with Santa Claus at Kimberly's Fashion Store and watch the annual Christmas parade.

Without turning away from the window, Stevenson began speaking. "I read an article in the *Sentinel* that local requests for emergency food assistance increased nearly 20 percent this year and applications for public shelter jumped nearly 15 percent, and that is about in line with the national trend. Christ, if we're no worse off than the rest of the country, who the hell is realizing the benefits of an economic recovery?"

Beth ignored his rhetorical question. She knew he was engaged in a brief period of denial regarding what he had just learned. She had witnessed this many times.

After a few moments of continued silence, he returned to his desk and reoccupied his chair. Beth noticed, as she had the night before, that his physical stature had changed. He looked older and slightly confused.

He sat staring at the back of his large left hand, which rested on his knee, unable to extend his right arm that far. After a few moments he spoke, without shifting his focus. "How do you tell a group of employees and a community that we wish you a Merry Christmas, but you no longer have a job, and it appears that some of the corporation's officers and directors misappropriated a large portion of your pension and savings fund, and lost it, trying to get richer than they already are?"

Beth delayed her response until she was sure he was done. "I don't know, Harris, but I think we need to start preparing a press release regarding Bruce and then confirm what Mr. Franklin told us before we talk with our board of directors and the SEC."

Harris gave a derisive laugh. "I think what I ought to do is get a pad of paper and pencil and go over to the hospital and hand 'em to Bruce and ask him to write down why he swallowed all those pills, why he decided to borrow several million dollars, and help himself to a few hundred million dollars of our employees' savings, and invested it all in a high-class scam."

Beth said nothing.

He suddenly looked directly at Beth, his face red with anger. "You know what he'd say?" he continued in a demonstrative, mocking fashion. "He'd say, 'Harris, I didn't swallow those pills 'cause I borrowed more money than I could ever repay or because I screwed the employees out of their savings. I just got real depressed because all my buddies on Wall Street are getting real, real rich, and I'm not. I'm falling behind. I look like a loser. I'm only making a few hundred thousand bucks a year, that's chump change, Harris. I was just tryin' to catch up. You probably don't understand, Harris, you've never been on the fast track or played with the all-stars.'"

She studied Harris for a few moments as he returned his attention to his extended left hand. "I don't know, Harris. I'm not sure that's what Bruce would say. Maybe that's how Jack Perkins would explain it. On the other hand, Jack Perkins would never attempt suicide, and I think we know why Quentin Phillips wants Bruce to have a lawyer, and it isn't to protect Bruce or his family."

She paused. There was no response. She continued. "Despite all that, during the next few days, we're going to have to explain to our employees and the community what happened to their jobs and their money. And a lot of people in this community, regardless of how angry they are, they'll feel some sympathy for Bruce, and they'll try to protect Nancy and those kids."

Harris continued to remain silent, staring at his left hand.

"I called Will Heider earlier this morning and asked him to come down and help. He's probably in my office now."

"O.K.," he replied quietly, "I'll be here."

As she walked toward her office, she saw Will and Jon Pertoski standing in the hallway in front of her office. They were talking.

She invited both of them to join her in her conference room and briefly explained what she had learned from her conversations with Byron Hinkle, Mary Rose, and the telephone call with Bradley Franklin.

Will appeared embarrassed, as if he were listening to a description of a lurid family scandal. Jon Pertoski shook his head slowly in disbelief.

After Beth completed her synopsis of the events, Will was the first to react.

"After we talked this morning, I called one of my partners, a specialist in securities law. He has good contacts inside the SEC and several large New York-based law firms that specialize in securities litigation. I asked him to make some inquiries about the Urban Securities case and call me here at your office. It may take awhile. Lots of people on vacation today."

Jon Pertoski waited until he was sure that Will was done speaking. He leaned forward and rested his arms on the conference table, unsure as to how to proceed in Will's presence. He was acquainted with Paul and Ruth Heider, and Tom, but Will was a stranger. During their brief conversation, before Beth arrived, Will had informed him that he was working with Beth and she had asked him to come to her office this morning.

He finally spoke, slowly and quietly. "My real reason for coming down here this morning was to talk with Harris. I wanted to share something with him that's been troubling me. But given all he's experienced for the last two days, I probably ought to hold off."

He hesitated and again studied Will for a moment, still evaluating whether he should proceed. He elected to continue.

"I wanted to talk to him about our earnings reports." He paused, then spoke very quickly. "I've been concerned about our last two quarterly reports."

He crossed his arms and sat back in his chair. "I really don't know, I'm only speculating, but I think we've understated our actual profits for the past six months."

Beth and Will appeared confused, but neither responded.

He compressed his lips and stared at the table for a moment. "I've talked with Bruce several times, but he always assured me the reports were correct. He claimed that the losses were caused by nonrecurring special charges— write-downs, or reductions in the value of assets on our balance sheet. I had a lot of trouble understanding it. There was just too big a difference between our operating earnings and the earnings we reported to the shareholders. I can't believe we lost that much money. I even talked with some of the people in accounting, and they were kind of confused and 'squirrelly.' They seemed to be satisfied because the financial statements were approved by the auditors."

Will raised his eyebrows. "Did you talk to the auditors?

"Well... no... that's not my area of responsibility."

Will looked at Beth. "Did anyone on the board of directors or members of your audit committee question the financial statements before they were released?"

"They don't review the quarterly reports, only the annual report," Beth said.

"Doesn't management review the numbers before they're released?"

Beth and Jon exchanged glances before she responded. "Will, you need to understand, Harris isn't a numbers guy. He's a very good manufacturing executive, but he doesn't have an affinity for accounting statements. He may believe Bruce is a bit stuffy, but he trusts him. So, if Bruce tells him those are the numbers, Harris doesn't challenge him. Moreover, as I have suggested to you before, he avoids controversy."

"So, the numbers could have been cooked," Will declared.

Beth laughed. "I thought you were a labor lawyer, not a securities expert."

"I'm not, but I don't have to be to a CPA to smell a problem with an understatement of earnings coupled with a simultaneous short sale and buy order."

Their facial expressions reflected their skepticism.

"Really, I'm serious," Will protested. "The intentional understatement of earnings immediately following a short sale, that could depresses the stock price and lock in the short seller's profit. When the price seems to have reached bottom, they buy a very large number of shares, cover their short sale, and still own shares as the price rises."

Beth said. "I'm not following you."

"Stay with me for a moment," he continued. "The poor earnings reports support an argument of pending financial hardship, which eliminates the need for a large payout to IMU for job relocation; they correct the earnings reports after the labor settlement is signed. The stock price increases in response to better earnings and a favorable labor settlement. They've already covered their short sale and made that profit; but they make more money on the shares, or call options, they own as the price rises Urban Securities makes a lot of money, and the managers get 20 percent of it."

"But why would Bruce get involved in something like that? He knows the law regarding insider trading," Jon said.

"Maybe the managers of the hedge shared their 20 percent with some other people," Will responded.

"Are you referring to Bruce?" Beth asked.

"Yeah, and maybe others, like Byron Hinkle."

Jon shook his head.

"I really have trouble believing Bruce would do something like that, and why would he put our employee pension and savings money in the fund? That would increase his risk of exposure."

Will's response was immediate. "A bigger fund means bigger management fees. A bigger fund could also generate bigger profits, assuming they made good investments. They take 20 percent of a much bigger profit pie, they put the pension and savings fund money back, and everyone gets rich. If it isn't profitable, they still keep the management fees; 50 million dollars a year for five years; that's a lot of money to divide up between a few people."

"But the Wiemer pension and savings plan didn't invest 2 billion dollars," Jon responded. "Beth said they invested ten percent of the total in the hedge fund. That would be about 200 million. Where did the rest of the money come from?"

"Probably other pension funds and high net worth individuals. That's where most of the hedge fund money comes from," Will said.

"Since we appear to be speculating about other investors in the hedge fund, there are some likely candidates," Beth declared. "Hinkle hinted that Quentin Phillips was an investor. Bradley stonewalled Harris when he asked if Phillips knew about the Wiemer money in Urban Securities. Then there's Adam Fulton, our ex-CEO, who sits on the Puritan Securities board. His high-tech company probably has a large pension fund, and I'll bet it's also managed by Puritan Securities."

"If you're right, the SEC is going to have a field day," Will said.

The room was silent for a few moments as all three occupants considered the ramifications what had been said.

Beth finally broke the silence. "Well, that's not our most immediate problem. We need to prepare a public announcement regarding Bruce and our involvement with Urban Securities."

"Do you know how much was lost?" Will asked.

"No, but we know approximately how much was invested, and it's probably a safe assumption that it's all gone," she replied. "So we need to decide how we inform the IMU about Jack Perkins's role in Urban Securities; his subpoena; the involvement of Kramer, Hinkle, and Arnholt; and maybe, and dear God I hope not, the chairman of our board of directors."

Jon was about to suggest a meeting with the IMU, when the phone rang in Beth's office. She walked from the conference room to her adjoining office to answer it. She returned immediately and informed Will that one of his partners wanted to speak to him. As Will entered her office, she shut the door between the office and the conference room and returned to talk with Jon about informing the IMU and the community about the events of the past two days. She was convinced that Harris Stevenson could not offer much assistance. In her opinion, he was emotionally unprepared to engage in any public dialogue. Jon volunteered to assist in establishing communicationt with Jimmie Hudson and the IMU. He recommended that they meet with Jimmie before any public statements were issued. Beth insisted that an announcement regarding Bruce could not be delayed, but the problems associated with the employees' pension and savings fund could be temporarily deferred while the auditors evaluated the size of the loss. Jon was about to place a phone call to Jimmie Hudson's residence to arrange a meeting, when Will returned to the conference room.

He reoccupied his seat at the conference table, looking perplexed. "That was the partner I referred to earlier this morning. He made some calls to New York and Washington… Everything he was told should be considered unsubstantiated rumor… But according to his contacts, the Urban Securities mess is the hot topic all over Wall Street… Lots of rumbling about a possible SEC announcement on Monday implicating prominent Wall Street names and large corporations."

"Any specific names?" Beth inquired anxiously.

"Not yet, but the market already knows about Bruce Kramer's attempted suicide, and I assume Harris Stevenson's phone is ringing a lot."

Without any explanation, Beth rose from her seat and exited the room. She walked directly to Stevenson's office. His office lights were still on. She knocked, there was no response. She entered his office. It was vacant. The voice mail message light on his phone was blinking.

Chapter 22

Harris Stevenson decided to leave his office immediately following a call from a *Wall Street Journal* reporter inquiring about Wiemer Industries' involvement in the Urban Securities scandal. His refusal to comment fueled the reporter's assertiveness. Less than two minutes after receiving the call, Harris pushed the disconnect button on the speaker phone, grabbed his parka, and walked to the elevator. It was then that he began to imagine what would appear in the *Journal* on Monday. After exiting the building, he stood motionless for a few moments in the small plaza at the front of the building, hands jammed in the pockets of his parka, staring at the near deserted streets, attempting to dispel his emotional imbalance.

Sensing that the security officer posted in the lobby was observing him, he walked away from the building with no specific destination in mind. A few minutes later, the anxiety that he experienced following the phone call was replaced by despair; the realization that the organization and business culture that he had been part of for nearly 30 years was about to collapse. He was seized by anguish greater than anything he had experienced since Vietnam. How could he explain his lack of knowledge regarding what had occurred? Was it that well disguised? Would he become the quintessential CEO called to account for a corporate scandal, pleading lack of knowledge, satirized and scoffed at by the media?.

He knew he should return to the office and assist Beth in the preparation of a public announcement regarding Bruce, and inform the directors of his conversation with Bradley Franklin. But he could not bring himself to retrace his steps. He needed time to clear his mind; a temporary escape, a brief refuge, even for an hour or two. Home was not an option. His home phone was listed in the local directory.

Art Fiester unlocked and entered the Hammelburg Inn bar at approximately 11:30 A.M., turned on the bar lights and half the fluorescent ceiling lights, removed all the chairs from the tabletops, walked the entire length of the crescent-shaped bar to be sure the stools were properly aligned, and casually examined the floor, tabletops, and ashtrays for anything he had overlooked at closing the previous night. There had been few customers on Thanksgiving Day; therefore the beverage the coolers and ice maker were well stocked. He turned on the exhaust fan to circulate the stagnant air— which became even more oppressive when the bar was closed— unlocked the cash register and checked the contents, tuned the television to CNN, and muted the sound. Confident that the Friday after Thanksgiving business would be slow, he arranged his stool behind the bar and began reading yesterday's edition of the *Sentinel.*

A few minutes later, Harris Stevenson walked slowly through the lobby of The Hammelburg Inn and entered the bar. He could not recall the last time he had visited the inn. He knew it was long before he became the CEO of Wiemer Industries.

Art Fiester looked up from his paper as Harris entered. He recognized him immediately, and watched in silence and disbelief as Stevenson occupied a stool on the far side of the bar. During seven years of bartending, he had never seen Stevenson at the inn. During his tenure at Wiemer Industries, Art had watched Stevenson rise from manufacturing director to the president and CEO of the company. He was a familiar face on the factory floor. He rarely talked to anyone in the forge shop. It was noisy, and it was rumored that Stevenson had a hearing problem. But he was popular. They were comfortable with him. Everyone knew he had been in the Marine Corps, and not an officer. On several occasions when Stevenson made an appearance, one of forge operators, an ex-marine, would shout, "You can eat the apple, but don't fuck with the Corps!"

Stevenson would never respond, but there was always that quick smile.

Art folded and placed the paper on the bar, got off the stool and walked toward Stevenson. He noticed that he had not removed his heavy winter parka.

"What can I get you... Mr. Stevenson?" The inquiry reflected his recognition and surprise.

Harris observed Art as he approached, but he didn't recognize him. "How about some Jack Daniel's in a short glass with a little ice."

"I can do that," Fiester responded.

They both remained silent as the drink was prepared. After placing the glass in front of Stevenson, Art extended his right hand, the hand with the partially missing forefinger, and introduced himself.

"I'm Art Fiester; I worked 15 years in your forge shop, before you relocated it."

Harris looked directly at Fiester and thrust his open left hand toward him.

Fiester was caught off guard and grasped Stevenson's left hand awkwardly.

"Sorry, my right arm doesn't work very well," Stevenson explained.

"Too much golf?" Fiester inquired.

Stevenson frowned. "I've never played golf, Fiester. How about you?" he snapped.

Fiester laughed. "Hell no... and the customers call me Art."

Stevenson picked up his glass, took a long drink, placed it back on the bar, and shoved it toward the bartender. "I think I'll do it again," he said.

Art took the glass, refilled it with Jack Daniel's and fresh ice, and placed it in front of Stevenson. There was a long silence as Art returned to his stool and picked up the paper. No sooner had he sat down when Stevenson spoke.

"Fifteen years in the forge shop. That's tough work. You probably don't miss it," Stevenson remarked.

Without looking up from his paper, Art said, "Oh no, I miss it."

John T. Hackett

"You mean you miss the money, not the work."

Fiester got off the stool, placed the paper on the bar, picked up the bottle of Jack Daniel's and returned it to its place on the shelf behind the bar, then turned to face Stevenson. "That's what most of the world thinks... but it's a hell of a lot more than just money. It's having a job you're proud of, where you make things that people need, that requires some skill. You miss the guys you worked with and the things you done together."

Harris could feel his face burning. It was like a sucker punch, an unexpected blow. Art Fiester had struck a raw nerve.

"Well, when we relocated the foundry and forge shop, all I heard was bitching about the loss of money and benefits. I didn't hear the union talk about anything else," Stevenson replied defensively.

Fiester walked toward Stevenson, stopping directly in front of him. "That's true, and that's the problem. Unions and management only talk about money, and benefits, and work rules. Nobody talks about things that can't be put in numbers."

He picked up the 20-dollar bill that Stevenson had placed on the bar, walked to the cash register, returned with a receipt and change and placed them in front of Stevenson.

"My job was a big part of my life. Wiemer was my company, drop forging was my skill; the guys I worked with, I played with. When they took all that away, they took a hell of a lot more than money; they took our pride, our community, and messed up some families. Those things can't be put into numbers or contracts. Everyone knows they're important, but we don't know how to talk about 'em."

"So you think relocation is wrong?" Stevenson asked nervously.

Art shook his head. "I don't know if it's right or wrong. I guess it ain't that simple. But I do know that moving a lot of good jobs out of Hammelburg is like taking a big cement block and throwing it in the middle of a small pond. A lot waves go in all directions for a long time. People need to understand a lot more about those waves and what they hit."

"What waves are you talking about?"

320

Art moved closer to Stevenson, and leaned toward him as he placed both hands, palms down, on the bar. "Mr. Stevenson, this place is a hell of a long way from the most popular bar in Hammelburg, but we have some regulars and I listen to a lot of conversations... One of the most important things that got hit was community trust and respect. That may sound pretty philosophical, but it's damned important. When I hired on with Wiemer, the workers, the company, and the community trusted and respected one another. We didn't always agree, but we trusted each other." He paused momentarily as he looked directly at Stevenson. "That's gone now... that got hit by one of the big waves."

Stevenson stared quietly at his half-empty glass. What Art had said stuck in his gut like a dull knife. How the hell was he going to explain to the community and the employees that management not only took their jobs, but also lost a portion of their savings and pension fund?

He quickly finished his drink and thrust his empty glass toward Art. "One more and I'm done," he said.

Art was surprised. Three drinks in less than 15 minutes. He had been a bartender long enough to recognize when someone was trying to drown a problem.

A few minutes later, he returned with a fresh drink. He had decided to go light on the Jack Daniel's and heavy on the ice.

Stevenson recognized the difference with the first sip.

Without being asked, Art took some of Stevenson's money off the bar, walked to the cash register, and returned with some change.

"I think you were a little stingy with the Jack Daniel's," Stevenson said, holding up his glass and looking at it.

"Yep," Art responded. "A good bartender always takes care of his customers, and I have no idea where you're gonna go after you finish that drink."

Stevenson laughed. "Neither do I, Art."

The conversation stopped when a small Hispanic man entered the bar and occupied a stool directly across from Harris. He wore a brown leather jacket over a dark blue cotton sweatshirt, blue jeans and a bright orange and black baseball cap decorated with a NASCAR logo and the number 32.

He lit a cigarette. "Hey man, I'm startin' early today. Gimme a Budweiser longneck and a couple packages of Beer Nuts."

Art moved to the beverage cooler, withdrew a bottle, removed the cap, grabbed two packages of Beer Nuts from a box beneath the bar, and placed the order in front of the customer.

"Need a glass, Tino?" Art asked.

"Nope, I drink too damn fast when I have a glass," he said, exhaling cigarette smoke.

Tino studied Stevenson as he opened a package of Beer Nuts.

Harris avoided eye contact with him, hoping he wouldn't recognize him.

After observing Harris for a few moments, Tino looked at Art. "Heard the latest shit about Wiemer Industries?"

Art shrugged, signaling disinterest, hoping to avoid the conversation, but Tino persisted. "I guess one of the big shots tried to kill himself a couple of nights ago. They took him to the hospital, pumped out his gut, and saved him."

Art turned and looked directly at Harris. He showed no reaction as he stared at his drink.

Tino placed a handful of Beer Nuts in his mouth and chewed on them while continuing to talk. "My neighbor's wife is a cook at the hospital. She says the poor bastard swallowed everything he could find in his medicine cabinet. He must a been in some deep shit trouble."

He lifted the bottle, took a long drink, and put the bottle back on the bar.

"Man, all kinds of rumors goin' round; he got caught with his hand in the company cookie bowl; he was screwin' some other woman; he lost all his money gamblin'. Seems like a lot of big shots are gettin' caught doin' stupid things. Damn near every day, there's another story about some big shot stealin' millions of dollars... "

Art didn't respond. He turned away from Harris, secured an ashtray from one end of the bar, and placed it in front of Tino.

"But, I don't give a damn what they do as long as they keep their hands off my money." Tino shook his head. "Hey man, imagine working 15 or 20 years for a company, they relocate or go broke, you lose your job, and they screw you out of your savings. What the hell is happenin' to this country?"

Harris quickly finished his drink, left two dollars on the bar, and said nothing as he prepared to leave. Art watched him as he walked quickly toward the exit, head down, hands plunged in the pockets of his parka.

There was a long silence after Stevenson departed. Finally Art spoke. "Any good football on TV today?"

"Yeah, I think Texas A&M is playin' someone down there this afternoon," Tino replied. "Hey, man, who the hell was that guy that just left? I never seen him in here before, but he looked kinda familiar."

Art was using the remote control device, attempting to find the football game on TV. "I'm not sure, maybe a Weimer exec. First time I've seen him in here."

Tino laughed. "Man, there's two places in this town you'd never see a Wiemer exec—here and The Second Shift."

Art found the football game and adjusted the sound on the TV set. He picked up Stevenson's empty glass, flipped the remaining ice in the bar sink, and wiped up the ring of water from the glass with a clean bar towel. He then folded the two dollars and placed them in his shirt pocket, quickly washed the glass, dried it, and replaced it back among the clean glasses.

He then responded to Tino's observation. "You're right, and the chances of that happening get more remote each year."

323

John T. Hackett

Art walked back to his stool, sat down, and recovered his newspaper.

Tino studied Art for a moment before he responded. "What do ya mean, man?"

Art lowered the newspaper. "Those guys don't own the company anymore, Tino. They work for people that work for other people that work for the owners. The owners don't know anything about Wiemer Industries; other than the price of the stock, and if the price goes down or doesn't go up fast enough, they sell it or get other management... They don't know or care anything about Hammelburg; the people that live and work here, all the history, doesn't mean a goddamn thing to them... If Wiemer Industries can make more money by moving out of Hammelburg, they move it. Don't fret about the people, the community, the history, that's not important, that confuses the system."

Art got off his stool, walked over to the bar, picked up Tino's empty Beer Nuts package and dropped it in a trash container beside the bar. He stared at the doorway through which Harris Stevenson had exited. "We're all strangers, Tino, a community of strangers," he said.

The hospital lobby was nearly empty when Harris Stevenson arrived. He had walked the entire ten blocks from The Hammelburg Inn to the hospital, too distraught to notice the cold wind and low temperature. The conversation with the bartender and the customer at the inn, and three consecutive Jack Daniel's had not provided any relief; his anxiety was accelerating. His emotional condition was dangerous, a combination of anger and despair resulting in a driving determination to confront Bruce Kramer and insist on an explanation of what had happened, regardless of Bruce's physical and mental condition. He needed to understand what happened before he could grapple with the consequences, and he needed to know now, today, before he returned to the office. He was going to learn the whole story regarding the theft of the pension fund, and the involvement of Quentin Phillips, Byron Hinkle, and Gus Arnholt.

He approached an elderly woman serving as a volunteer at the reception desk, and requested Bruce Kramer's room number. She seemed perplexed and informed him that he would have to speak with the head nurse on the fourth floor regarding permission to visit Mr. Kramer. She did not volunteer his room number. Stevenson was afraid that she had detected the smell of liquor on his breath and was unwilling to give him the information. He thanked her and walked quickly to the elevators.

After exiting the elevator, he walked to the nurses' station and ask to speak to the head nurse. She appeared to be waiting for him, a short, thin, black woman in a crisp white blouse and slacks and dark red knit sweater covering her shoulders. Harris requested permission to visit Mr. Bruce Kramer.

The head nurse looked at him suspiciously. Her demeanor and tone of voice left no doubt about her authority.

"I'm sorry, we have explicit instructions that he is to receive no visitors or telephone calls from anyone other than his immediate family and Mr. Robert Cornelius."

Harris pulled back the hood of his parka. "I understand, but I'm one of his closest associates at Wiemer Industries and it is critically important that I speak with him for just a few minutes."

She was unimpressed with his explanation. "I'm sorry, but I was given explicit orders by Mr. Cornelius and Mrs. Kramer that he was not to receive any visitors or phone calls from anyone other than his lawyer and his immediate family."

"His lawyer, you must mean his doctor?" Harris responded.

"No. Doctor Mann was not involved. Mr. Cornelius is his lawyer. Mrs. Kramer told us that he was hired to represent Mr. Kramer. They came in this morning and visited briefly with Mr. Kramer, and then requested a meeting with the hospital executive officer and myself. Mr. Cornelius told us that he represented Mr. Kramer and insisted that no other visitors or phone calls be permitted; it's all part of patient's rights. Even the police can't talk to Mr. Kramer unless Mr. Cornelius is present."

Harris stood mute, staring at the head nurse, trying to clear his mind and focus on what was happening.

"He gave me one of his business cards, in case anyone wants to talk with him. Would you like to see it?" She sounded less foreboding.

"Yes, I would. Thank you."

She turned, opened a desk drawer, withdrew a business card, and handed it to Harris.

Harris studied it closely:

Robert Sheffield Cornelius
Partner
Sticknet Cord and Fraim LLP
Attorneys at Law
Boston, Massachusetts

"May I have copy of this?" he asked.

"I'll make a copy for you."

She retrieved the card, walked quickly to an adjoining room, returned in a few moments, and handed Harris a Xerox copy of the business card.

Thirty minutes later, Harris Stevenson was sitting in his office, seething with anger and anxiety. He had walked directly from the hospital to his office. As he entered the Wiemer Industries building, the security guard in the lobby had spoken to him. Stevenson, uncharacteristically, neither responded nor looked at him. He took the elevator to his office, dropped his parka on a chair, walked to his desk, and before sitting down, leaned over his phone and pushed the programmed button that dialed Quentin Phillips's office.

The phone rang several times before Phillips's secretary answered. She immediately recognized Stevenson's voice. After the usual greeting, she explained that Mr. Phillips was unusually busy receiving and making phone calls. In fact, he had called her home at mid-morning and asked her to come in and screen his telephone calls, She suggested that she inform Phillips that Harris had called and wanted to speak with him and urge him to return his call as soon as possible.

"Is he on the phone now?" Harris snapped.

She was surprised by his tone of voice. She had always enjoyed brief, informal chats with Stevenson when he called to talk with Phillips.

"No, he isn't, Mr. Stevenson, but I'll be sure that he knows you want to speak with him."

"I'll stay on the phone. You tell him that he better take my call right now. I won't wait for him to call me back. I think he knows why I'm calling."

There was another long pause before she responded. "All right, I'll tell him, but I can't promise he will take your call. He's turned down several other calls this afternoon."

He heard her place the call on hold. He waited for what seemed like several minutes before he heard the phone reengaged on the other end.

"Hi, Harris, what's so urgent?" Phillips inquired in an artificially calm voice.

Stevenson's anger was fueled by Phillips's condescending tone. "Well, let me give you the short version," he said in a sardonic tone of voice. "About a half hour after I finished talking to you and the other board members, I returned a call from your guy, Bradley Franklin. He told me that Kramer ordered him to put a big chunk of our employee pension and savings fund in Urban Securities, and it went down the toilet with the rest of Perkins's hedge fund."

Phillips didn't respond. Stevenson continued. "And when I asked him if you knew anything about this, he was very, very careful and suggested I ask you."

Phillips maintained his silence.

"So, before calling you, I decided to take a walk over to the hospital and ask Bruce Kramer about this fiasco, but the head nurse told me that some high-powered lawyer from Boston got there ahead of me and told the staff that no one is permitted to talk to Kramer without his permission... So I walked back here and followed Bradley Franklin's advice and called you."

Phillips finally replied, "What is it you expect me to tell you, Harris?"

Stevenson's voice got louder. "I'd like to know, Quentin, when you knew about this illegal investment, and who the hell sent Robert Sheffield

327

Cornelius tearing out to Hammelburg, Indiana from Boston to be sure no one talks to Bruce."

"Now, tone it down a little, Harris. After all, you're talking to the chairman of the board of directors... Like you, I was shocked to learn about the losses in Urban Securities, but Franklin told me Wiemer's investment was approved by the compensation committee, and we have a copy of the resolution in our files. As you know, I'm not a member of the compensation committee, and I knew nothing about the resolution."

"That goddamn thing is bogus" Harris responded. "Beth tells me that all minutes of the board meetings and committee meetings are prepared by her staff and approved by her before they are signed, and there was never a resolution approving that investment."

Phillips's response was immediate and stern. "Beth's memory may be inaccurate."

"Beth has a damn good memory, Quentin. She also had a conversation yesterday with Byron Hinkle, the local lawyer who represented the IMU. He resigned after he heard about Jack Perkins's little problem. He admitted that he and Bruce and Gus Arnholt invested, and he and hinted that Puritan Securities and maybe even you were in Urban Securities."

Phillips's voice became even harder. "Well, if Hinkle's allegation regarding me is correct, I made a mistake, didn't I Harris, but that's my business and none of his or yours."

"C'mon, Quentin, stop playing games with me. It doesn't pass the smell test. Jack Perkins told Bruce Kramer he'd make him filthy rich if he'd just borrow one hell of a lot of money and invest in Urban Securities. Then Bruce tells Puritan Securities to invest a quarter of a billion dollars of our employees' money in Urban Securities. Your staff tries to talk him out of it, tells him it's too risky, not an appropriate investment for a pension fund, but Bruce insists. So, to cover their ass, your staff tells him they have to have a copy of a board resolution approving the investment, and Bruce produces a bogus board resolution approving it."

"Assuming your allegation is correct, what's your point, Harris?"

"I have to assume that if Bradley Franklin really opposed putting our employees' money in that sinkhole, he or some member of his staff must have said 'Hey, Quentin Phillips, our chairman, he's also chairman of Wiemer Industries, let's go ask him if we should do it.' I asked Franklin that question; but he didn't give me an answer. So I'll ask you: Did you know about it?"

"Are you attempting to interrogate me, Harris?"

Stevenson's voice became less shrill. "No, but there are several questions that I'm going to have to answer in the next 24 hours—the illegal trading of our stock, our employees' money flushed down the toilet, our CFO's attempted suicide, and the sudden arrival of a lawyer from Boston to muzzle him. I need some answers, Quentin."

Phillips cleared his throat. "O.K., Harris, here's one answer, I'm the chairman of the board of Wiemer Industries, and you're the CEO. You're responsible to me and the other members of the board for managing the company. Your performance has been abysmal. The recent financial performance reflects your inadequacies. You've created a significant problem with the union. The price of the stock has collapsed; now the SEC is investigating insider trading; there are allegations that management was involved. Therefore, I might decide that I have a fiduciary responsibility to call an immediate meeting of the outside board members to determine if you should continue as the CEO. Unless, of course, you elect to resign beforehand."

Stevenson remained silent as Phillips continued. "Now my second answer may be more appealing. You stop acting like a naïve schoolboy and get this situation under control. You tell the world that Bruce made a tragic mistake. Although you can't condone what he did, his intentions were honorable. He was misguided in his attempt to benefit the employees' pension fund. Confronted with the severity of his error, his suicide attempt reflects his depression and anxiety. Your sympathy and support is extended to his loving family. Nevertheless, corrective action will be taken, And in the event you're asked about Urban Securities, you know nothing about it, and suggest that they speak to whoever is defending Jack Perkins. Then you hire a good outside law firm to represent Wiemer Industries when the SEC shows up in Hammelburg and another one to deal with your employees."

Phillips paused before continuing. "Now, which one of those answers do you like best, Harris?"

"Neither one of them," Harris replied.

"Well then, I suggest that you spend the weekend preparing your *mea culpa* and release it to the board of directors, the employees, and the media on Monday morning," Phillips responded mockingly.

"You're assuming that I won't talk about Puritan Securities' involvement in this mess?" Stevenson said.

Phillips laughed. "What are you gonna tell them, Harris? Jack Perkins and Bruce colluded to siphon money from the employee pension fund into Urban Securities. Puritan Securities' management wisely objected. Bruce created a false document to override our objections; shame on the CEO for not being more observant?"

"Don't kid yourself, Quentin. If I make that speech, I'm gonna talk about Puritan's participation in this goddamn fiasco."

Phillips suddenly adopted a condescending tone. "Now, now, Harris, who's gonna believe your fairy tales? Even if we made an investment, it would have been channeled through a separate partnership with many other investors. Partnerships that invest in hedge funds attract a lot of well-respected organizations and individuals. Just like the smart money that got lost in Long Term Capital a few years ago. Nobody remembers, or even knew, who invested in that fiasco."

"Other people know about your investment."

"You really don't seem to comprehend how this works, Harris. You're exhibiting your naiveté, again. Perkins is too smart to talk about who invested in his fund. He wants to get back on Wall Street, after the SEC spanks him. Other investors aren't going to talk about it. My management team is certainly not going to brag about it. Maybe a hick lawyer like Hinkle blows off, but who's his audience? After we fire you, or you resign, it will be clear to everyone that you were a careless, incompetent CEO attempting to blame your failure on others."

"What about Bruce? He's going to have to do some explaining."

"Well, poor Bruce violated his fiduciary responsibility. But I'm confident that as long as he follows the advice of his new lawyer, he'll receive lots of support; and he'll receive lenient treatment. Of course Bruce will cooperate with the investigation, but be he won't tell the SEC anything they don't already know."

"What about the quarter of a billion dollars that's gone?"

"Oh, Harris, that will take a long, long time to clean up; lots of litigation, lots of lawyers, lots of negotiation, lots of compromises."

"I think you're kidding yourself, Quentin. You won't come out of this smelling like a rose."

Phillips's tone changed again from condescending to threatening. "I've never attempted to smell like a rose. But I've never smelled like you're going to if you don't take my advice."

"What about the rest of the board? You think they'll buy your story?" Stevenson countered.

"What story, Harris? I've served on lots of boards of directors and I've been around the financial world for a long time. Board membership is a selective, well-mannered club. We've all learned how to protect ourselves. The only one on the Wiemer Board that doesn't belong to the 'club' is Mary Rieff, and I don't think she'll make headlines."

Stevenson offered no response.

"Now, Harris, let me repeat my advice. Stop trying to be some kind of anti-establishment hero and recognize reality. You are one of those fortunate few that that is grossly overcompensated, and you need to cover your ass to keep your job and your reputation. Otherwise you can resign before you get fired. I need to know what you want to do. I need to know by Monday morning. If you don't make a decision, I will. … Go home and think about it. I'll call you first thing Monday morning."

Stevenson heard Phillips disconnect followed by a dial tone.

Chapter 23

Will sat with Beth and Jon until early afternoon while they prepared a draft of the news release regarding Bruce Kramer's attempted suicide. The absence of Harris Stevenson passed without comment, but they decided to postpone the release until Monday morning to afford him an opportunity to review it. Jon called Jimmie Hudson's home, but there was no response. He left a voice mail asking him to call his cell phone number as soon as possible. Beth attempted to reach the senior partner at Wiemer Industries' public accounting firm in Indianapolis. He was not in his office or at home. She also left voice mail messages at both locations, asking him to call her at her home before Monday morning.

After Will Heider departed the Wiemer Industries headquarters, he drove aimlessly about the city for 40 minutes. During the past five days, he had witnessed the final stages of a tragedy transpire—the destruction of a unique bonding and leadership of several generations of families, businesses and a community, destroyed by the intentional violation of a carefully-nurtured coexistence that permitted both to grow and prosper for more than a century. And now a blatant betrayal of that common bond for the financial advantage of a few, most of whom had little connection with the community.

Of all the cities and businesses that he had some familiarity with, Hammelburg and Wiemer Industries would have placed dead last on his list of possibilities for such an event. His earlier reaction to flee from Hammelburg and return to the anonymity of Chicago and Cutler Earl and

Levin was gone. His mind was flooded with recent conversations with Beth, Sam Thomas, Jimmie Hudson, Mary Rieff, his parents; the sudden lack of purpose in his own life: a failed marriage, childless, a successful but narrowly focused profession. Little else in his life other than a seasonal, solitary retreat aboard a sailboat. All of this had kindled an unexpected desire to protect the community and its heritage, if only for a short time.

After returning to his parents' home, he entered the living room quietly. His father was sitting in his favorite chair in front of the television, asleep, a football game showing on the muted TV.

He sat down on the living room couch, still wearing a heavy sweater beneath his father's black windbreaker, silently observing the room and its décor. A deep melancholy swept over him as he recalled the holiday celebrations and special family gatherings that had taken place in this room. The well-decorated Christmas tree, always positioned near the front window; the small display of Hanukkah candles that his mother placed on the mantle over the fireplace. Her elaborate preparation for holidays and family birthdays; the presentation of gifts; careful recording of who gave and received gifts; her relentless post-celebration reminders to write thank-you letters.

Observing the family pictures on the walls, he recalled his grandmother working as a seamstress at Bernie's long after his father and mother had become the owners; her quiet pride in their success; the love she radiated when her three grandchildren visited the store; the arthritis that disfigured her hands and forced her retirement. The faded photograph of Bernie's in the late 1930s—his maternal grandparents and their two children standing proudly but self-consciously in the entrance; their struggles to become assimilated in a small city in a new country, to speak a new language; careful avoidance of too much fraternization among the relatively few Jewish families; guarded discussion of the infrequent trips to Fort Wayne to attend services at the synagogue.

Their experience was symbolic of the struggles of generations of families of diverse religious and cultural backgrounds, but together they created and nurtured the exceptional ambiance and quality of life in Hammelburg. In other communities, the financially successful citizens frequently took their wealth and moved on to more exciting, culturally attractive locations. Somehow, Hammelburg had been spared the loss of its leadership and wealth, until recently. Now, with the growing allegiance to global theocracy, the ensuing epidemic of corporate greed, and anemic leadership, Hammelburg was also descending the economic ladder.

Although he may have given it some thought in the past, it was here, today, in his family home, surrounded by old photographs; that he was experiencing a full realization of the strong links between his life, his family, and Hammelburg.

He heard the phone ring once, and his mother answer it in the kitchen. A few moments later, she entered the living room quietly and whispered to him that Beth Brinson wished to speak to him.

He followed her to the kitchen and picked up the phone. "Hello, Beth,"

"Will, I apologize for bothering you, but Harris has asked that we meet with him tomorrow morning at nine o'clock at his office to discuss the labor contract and the recent events surrounding Bruce and the pension fund… Are you available?"

"Yeah, I guess so. I was planning to return to Chicago, but I can delay it until Sunday… "

Beth said, "Thank you. I have no idea how long the meeting may last. Harris called me a few moments ago. He also requested that Jon Pertoski attend the meeting."

"O.K., Beth, I'll see you tomorrow at nine."

After the call, Will returned to the living room. His father had awakened, turned off the television, and was talking with Ruth Heider. They both looked at Will as he entered the room.

His father spoke first. "It sounds like your involvement with Wiemer Industries is more extensive than you anticipated."

His mother was sitting on the edge of the couch. She looked troubled, but said nothing.

Will shook his head and sat down beside his mother before responding. "Wiemer Industries, as of today, is a client of Cutler Earl and Levin… I guess I have to leave it at that."

Will's mother spoke quietly without looking directly at him. "We know about Bruce Kramer. It was reported on the local radio at noon today. What a tragedy."

Will looked puzzled. "How could they learn about that? Wiemer Industries has made no announcement."

Paul Heider said, "Local reporter looks at the police logbooks every morning. A suicide is a homicide. It has to be investigated and reported by the police."

Saturday morning was bright and cold, a typical late autumn day in northern Indiana. The traffic was light; Indiana University and Purdue University pennants were fluttering from car windows. The traditional Indiana - Purdue football game, marking the end of the college football season, was scheduled at West Lafayette, a one-hour drive from Hammelburg. Neither team was expected to be invited to any postseason bowl games. As usual, the Michigan - Ohio State game dominated the media attention. The winner would play in the Rose Bowl on New Year's Day.

Will parked his car in Wiemer Industries' visitors' parking lot and walked to the security desk in the lobby. As soon as he identified himself, he was informed that he was expected in Mr. Stevenson's office. He elected to take the stairs and stop at Beth's office before proceeding to Stevenson's office. Her door was open and she was having a quiet conversation with Jon Pertoski. They both looked troubled.

Jon was explaining to Beth that he had left several messages for Jimmie Hudson, but he had not returned his calls.

"Jimmie's smart. If he learns the whole story regarding the episode with Bruce before we meet with him, he'll be doubly difficult to deal with," Jon concluded.

No one disagreed, but it was time to gather in Harris Stevenson's office.

As they entered his office, Harris was standing with his back to the entrance looking out the office windows at the activity on the street below. The only light in the office was natural; the fluorescent lights had not been turned on. Upon hearing them enter, he turned and suggested that they meet in his adjoining conference room.

He sat down slowly in his usual place at the head of the conference table. Although the natural light in the room was inadequate, he made no effort to provide any artificial light. The shadows in the room accentuated his appearance of fatigue and aging. The lines in his face seemed to have deepened in the past three days.

As soon as everyone was seated, he began speaking without making direct eye contact with anyone in the room. He appeared to be looking at some distant object that appeared through the window located at the other end of the room.

"I assume that Beth has informed you about the loss of a large portion of our employee pension and savings fund in a hedge fund, and Bruce Kramer's involvement."

Both Will and Jon nodded acknowledgment.

"I tried to talk to Bruce yesterday," he continued, "but an attorney from Boston got to the hospital before I did and instructed the hospital staff that Bruce is not permitted to receive visitors who are not approved by him."

Beth registered her surprise. "An attorney from Boston?"

"Yeah, Boston." Harris pushed the Xerox copy of the attorney's business card in front of Beth.

Beth read aloud the name of the law firm: "Sticknet, Cord and Fraim."

Will recognized the name. "It's an old Boston firm, corporate law and litigation. Lots of jokes about the founding of the firm dating back to the *Mayflower*... It's an Ivy League law firm," he added.

Beth frowned.

The room grew quiet for a few moments before Harris continued. "I suspect that they were hired by Quentin Phillips to protect Bruce and make sure he doesn't talk to anyone about the flimflam that he and Jack Perkins concocted."

Jon Pertoski shook his head. "Why would Phillips do that?"

Harris hesitated for a moment before answering, "Because he and God knows who else may have been involved in this scheme."

Jon and Will appeared puzzled by Stevenson's response.

"That's a serious accusation, Harris," Jon responded cautiously.

"Jon, I'm a country boy, but I'm not stupid. After a nasty conversation with Quentin on the phone yesterday afternoon, I'm convinced that the Boston lawyer was sent to Hammelburg by Quentin to make sure that Bruce doesn't talk to anyone. Phillips made it clear that if I want to keep my job beyond Monday, I'll tell the world that Bruce overruled the good advice of Puritan Securities and put the money in the hedge fund for the good of our employees. When he realized the gravity of his mistake, he tried to commit suicide."

There was a long silence before Jon Pertoski responded. "Assuming you're correct, what do we do about it?"

Stevenson laughed sarcastically. "That depends on who you define as 'we', Jon."

Pertoski looked confused.

"I would guess that by Monday afternoon or Tuesday morning—however long it takes Phillips to arrange a teleconference with our board of directors—I will no longer be the CEO of Wiemer Industries." He paused momentarily. "Perkins offered me three alternatives: stonewall this whole mess with the public and the employees, resign, or be fired. I've decided to accept his second alternative."

"You're going to resign?" Beth exclaimed in disbelief. "I don't think Phillips can get the board to go along with firing you, once they know the whole story."

"Oh yeah, he can get it done. He even explained to me how members of corporate boards of directors protect each other. The only member of our board who will challenge him is Mary Rieff, a little old lady full of weird liberal ideas."

Jon Pertoski shook his head. "Even if you believe he can pull if off, why not make them fire you and then make a public statement?"

Stevenson's answer was weak and defensive. "I thought a lot about that, Jon. I don't want to be fired. I'd have to answer a lot more questions if they fire me. If I retire. it's less disruptive."

Beth said "What about Bruce? Isn't the public going to get the entire story from him sooner or later?"

Harris picked up the Xerox copy of the lawyer's business card he had received at the hospital, and studied it briefly before responding to Beth.

"I'm sure that Robert Sheffield Cornelius has convinced Bruce that he will be best served and carefully protected if he follows his specific instructions: Keep your mouth shut and let me do the explaining."

"What about the employees? Who tells them what happened?" Jon asked.

Stevenson's response was weak. "I don't know, Jon. What do we tell them, other than Kramer and Perkins created some kind of a scam to get the employees' retirement money into Urban Securities and lost it, and we don't know how to get it back?"

Beth was angry with Stevenson's lack of courage. She glanced at Jon. He was staring at Harris in disbelief.

"I assume Jon hasn't had time to share with you his concerns about the possibility that we've underreported our earnings during the last several quarters?" Beth asked.

Stevenson looked surprised and turned to Jon. "Underreporting of earnings. What earnings? Hell, we haven't had any earnings."

Jon described his concern about inaccurate cost information included in the earnings report during the past three quarters, and the unsatisfactory response that he got from Bruce and the accounting staff when questioning them about the reports.

Stevenson said "What about the auditors? If we understated earnings, wouldn't they catch it?"

Beth replied, "I've called the senior partner at his home in Indianapolis. I left word for him to call me. But I know what he's going to tell us. The auditors only review the consolidated financial statements; management is responsible for internal accounting."

Harris shook his head in disbelief. "Christ, this story gets worse by the hour. Why would Bruce intentionally overstate our losses? He owns stock in this company. Why would he intentionally do something to drive down the price of his own stock?"

Jon and Beth looked at Will.

Beth said, "I think Will came up with a plausible explanation yesterday. I had trouble believing it at first, but given what has transpired in the past 24 hours, I think it makes sense."

Will reflected discomfort at becoming the focus of attention. He proceeded to explain to Harris that what he was about to relate was pure speculation.

Harris mumbled something about careful lawyers and urged Will to continue.

He quickly outlined his suspicions regarding the relationship and timing of underreported earnings, illegal short selling of Wiemer shares, inclusion of the "pending financial hardship" clause in the labor contract, and Bruce's illicit funneling of pension funds into the hedge fund.

As he concluded, Harris stared at him silently for a moment. His eyes narrowed, large jaw protruding, face flushed.

He finally spoke in a low growl. "Take me through that story one more time Heider. I want to be sure I understand what you just said."

Will cleared his throat. "Let me repeat, I have no evidence... "

Harris interrupted him. "Skip the caveats. I understand. Just give me the story one more time."

Will repeated the allegations, including a more technical explanation of illegal insider trading, short selling and call options.

Following his explanation, the conference room was quiet for several moments, with an absence of eye contact. Stevenson finally responded in a tight, quiet voice: "How do we prove it and prosecute those bastards?"

Beth was the first to respond. "That's the SEC's job, and it appears they're already involved. They've gone after Jack Perkins and his accomplices. Cornelius has probably warned Bruce that he will be served a subpoena in the next few days. Cornelius will be standing by his bedside when the U.S. Marshal appears, to assure that Bruce says nothing."

Stevenson appeared to disregard Beth's comments. "How long will it take?" he asked.

"How long will what take?" Beth replied impatiently.

Stevenson raised his voice. "How long will it take to put those bastards in jail?"

Will's sudden intervention surprised both Beth and Jon. "A long time, if ever... a long, long time to gather evidence, structure the criminal and civil charges, get a trial date, negotiate pleas, interview witnesses, combat a whole series of defense attorney maneuvers, and select a jury, on and on and on... "

"You're telling me they won't go to jail," Stevenson barked.

Will looked slightly amused. "There's a whole lot less chance of their going to jail than some kid who robbed a liquor store for the first time."

Will's cynical remark didn't amuse Stevenson. "What about Phillips and Puritan Securities?" he snapped.

Will didn't hesitate. His response was brimming with skepticism. "Forget it. Even if they were involved, they'll never touch 'em. The SEC backlog on white collar crime is huge. They concentrate on high-profile sure things. They've got the evidence on Perkins, and they'll make an example of him. He may lose his right to practice law and he may be banned from securities trading. But he'll have lots of opportunities to make a good living after he completes probation and does a little public service. They'll probably leave Kramer to twist in the wind for several years, but he won't go to jail."

Stevenson was visibly unhappy with Will's conclusions. "You sound like a tough defense lawyer, Heider. Maybe they should hire you."

Will was annoyed, but not intimidated, by Stevenson's sarcasm. "Nope, I'm not a litigator or a trial lawyer, but I've watched the system work for 20 years. Rich people who can afford to hire the likes of Cornelius and his colleagues rarely go to prison."

Stevenson's sarcasm continued. "You sound like you're O.K. with the way the system works."

Will frowned and glanced at Beth. She recognized his anger before he even replied. "Harris... let me explain something to you: The money available to pay defense lawyers in white collar crime prosecutions makes the total SEC budget look like petty cash; plea bargaining saves time and money for the SEC, and good defense lawyers are adept at bargaining for their clients."

"It stinks," Stevenson growled.

Will was sitting on the edge of his chair, his hands clenched tightly, resting on the table. "Sure it stinks... Perkins and Kramer hire a strong defense team. There's no incarceration. The judicial process crawls on for months and years... But the kid who popped the liquor store... can't make bail... a couple of days later, he gets a public defender who tells him to plead guilty so he'll get less time in Pendleton. Now, how do you propose to change the system?"

He sat back in his chair, placed his hands in his lap, watching Stevenson, waiting for his rebuttal. Beth and Jon were quiet. They had never witnessed anyone confront Stevenson so strongly. Even Kramer was more circumspect when he argued with Stevenson.

Stevenson shook his head. He looked at Beth and then Jon. "O.K., how do we deal with the employees, how do we tell them about this mess? Got any suggestions?"

Neither of them responded.

But Will's sudden aggressiveness had not been spent. He jumped in again.

"Someone has to sit down with the IMU leaders, explain what happened, be prepared to have some skin taken off their backside, and propose some solutions. The bargaining committee may decide that they'll inform the membership or they'll insist that management take the heat and tell the employees directly."

Stevenson turned to Beth. "Who do we talk to? Byron Hinkle resigned."

"Jimmie Hudson is now the spokesman for the IMU." she said.

Stevenson rested his jaw on his left hand and growled, "Does anyone know Hudson well enough to call him and get a meeting before the damn *Sentinel* prints the whole story on Monday morning?"

Will was on a roll. "I can guess what Jimmie will do."

Stevenson was surprised; he looked at Beth and Jon in an attempt to measure their reaction. Both wore puzzled expressions.

Stevenson was skeptical. "O.K., what do you think his reaction will be when we lay this whole mess out in front of him?"

Will's answer was immediate and strong: "Jimmie's tough and smart. Even before all of this crap hit the fan, he was suspicious of Hinkle, detested Perkins, and didn't trust the management of Wiemer Industries. Therefore, I assume he will not be kind and reasonable."

Stevenson challenged him. "How do you know that?"

"I've met with him twice in the past week. Beth must have told you that he wanted me to represent the IMU."

"Yeah, she did," Stevenson snapped.

Stevenson placed the palms of both hands on his cheeks, elbows on the table, and focused on the window at the end of the room before making his proposal. "O.K., Heider, do you think you could meet with him again and explain our mess?"

Will was momentarily stunned by Stevenson's question. He looked at Beth. She was seething.

Stevenson continued. "I think it would be easier for someone who knows Hudson, but not a member of management, someone who never negotiated with the IMU."

Will struggled to refrain from revealing his true reaction to the proposal. Notwithstanding his intention to resign, how could a CEO who had just discovered that one of his key staff members had swindled money from the employee pension and savings fund suggest that anyone other than himself make the confession and apology to the victims? Despite his bluster and anger regarding the failure of corporate integrity and weakness in the judicial system, Stevenson appeared to lack the courage to talk to his employees. Did he understand the intertwining of authority and responsibility?

Beth attempted to disguise her contempt for Stevenson's proposal with a modest suggestion: "Harris, I don't believe anyone other than a member of senior management will have much success in explaining and resolving this mess with the IMU."

Stevenson continued to focus on the window at the end of the room.

"I don't agree. Heider has a better understanding of what took place. He can explain it. He knows Hudson; he wasn't involved. He understands labor contracts and... "

Beth interrupted. "Wait a minute, Harris, Will can't discuss any speculation regarding the circumstances of the misappropriation. It's only a guess. It may appear logical and prove to be factual, but it can't be discussed outside of this room until we can confirm it."

Jon Pertoski intervened cautiously. "Harris, wouldn't it be more appropriate for you to meet with Hudson and explain what happened, and talk about solutions?"

The tone of Stevenson's reply revealed his frustration. "Goddamn it, Jon. I'm not going to be the CEO of this company after Monday. My resignation is going to be effective immediately. If Hudson is as smart as Heider thinks he is, he sure as hell is going to come after me about remuneration and contract concessions. I can't negotiate with him in good faith and resign 24 hours later."

Beth's rejoinder was sharp: "Then don't resign."

Stevenson took a deep breath and exhaled dramatically. "Beth, let me lay it out for you one more time. Phillips made it crystal clear that I have three options: stonewall the media and SEC, resign, or be fired... I won't stonewall... And regardless of which of the two remaining alternatives I select, by the middle of next week, I'll no longer be the CEO." He paused, cleared his throat and concluded, "After 30 years... I prefer to resign."

Beth was angry. "And who assumes your responsibilities following your resignation?"

"That's a decision for the board of directors," he snapped.

He turned and looked directly at Will. "Are you willing to meet with Hudson before Monday?"

He recognized that Harris was correct on insisting that a meeting be arranged with Jimmie Hudson before Monday. He thought Stevenson's argument that his resignation disqualified him from attending the meeting lacked credibility, but he was sure that he could not be persuaded otherwise. He concluded that he was not violating any ethical guidelines by assuming responsibility for informing the IMU of the misappropriation. It was fact. It had happened. Beth had clarified the impropriety of any mention of the speculation of what might have transpired. He had been hired to act as legal counsel for Wiemer Industries. Therefore, he would be representing a client. Finally, he aclnowledged that he probably had a closer personal relationship with Jimmie Hudson that any other person in the room. Given the sensitivity of the meeting, that relationship might prove valuable for both parties. He might better serve the process as an arbitrator.

He looked directly at Beth before responding to Stevenson's question. Her eyes were narrowed, lips clamped tightly between her teeth. Somehow her neatly coiffured hair had become slightly tousled. It struck him that she was even more attractive with her hair slightly disheveled.

Jon Pertoski was watching Will carefully, but dispassionately, awaiting his reply.

Will spoke slowly. "I'm willing to attend a meeting with the IMU, but not alone, not without senior management representation."

Stevenson didn't hesitate. "Who do you suggest?"

Will was surprised by his concurrence. He realized that Stevenson was abdicating his executive authority without hesitation, but he wouldn't let him walk away so quickly.

"As long as you're the CEO, I believe that decision is your prerogative."

"O.K., Beth has responsibility for negotiating the labor contract and Jon knows the hourly employees better than any other member of management. But I want you to do the explaining about the pension fund losses."

Beth made no attempt to disguise her anger. "What the hell are we supposed to say after we tell them about Bruce's little malfeasance? Somebody may be smart enough to ask what the hell we're going to do about it."

Jon Pertoski intervened, never looking at Harris, speaking directly to Beth. "Let's try to solve that problem when it arises. I won't even speculate on Hudson's reaction… Will's right; he's tough, smart, a strong leader. I've watched him on the shop floor. People respect and listen to him. After we tell them about the losses, the IMU is gonna be holding a strong hand."

Chapter 24

Late that afternoon, Gloria Hudson returned home from her Saturday morning errands and weekly beauty parlor appointment. She entered through the back door after parking her Ford Tempo in the driveway. Jimmie's pickup truck was parked in the single-car, unattached garage.

When she entered the kitchen, she found Jimmie sitting at the breakfast table reading the *Sentinel*. As he looked up to greet her, she was surprised by his worried expression. It was out of character. Jimmie enjoyed weekends; working on the house, transporting the girls to their various activities.

"Bad news in the paper?" she inquired.

"Lots of bad news today," he replied.

"Want to talk about it?" she asked cautiously. Jimmie was inclined to avoid discussing work and union problems at home. The physical abuse that his father dealt out to Jimmie, his brother, and mother was often triggered by a combination of Teamsters Union issues and job insecurity, fueled by heavy alcohol consumption.

He folded the paper carefully and placed in on the corner of the table. "Yeah, maybe we better talk about it while the girls are out of the house."

Gloria recognized the warning sign. Anything to be discussed in the absence of their daughters was usually serious and troubling.

Although there were groceries in her car that needed to be brought in the house, she removed her parka, hung it on a hook near the back door, returned to the table, and took a chair directly across from him. She sat quietly, waiting for him to continue. It was obvious that he was deeply troubled about something.

When he finally spoke, it was in a quiet tone. "Will Heider called me a couple of hours ago. He wants to meet with me tomorrow afternoon at the union office. Beth Brinson and Jon Pertoski will be with him. They want to talk about some problems at Wiemer and discuss the labor contract."

"Is that good or bad?" she asked.

"It's a mess," he declared.

She made no comment, waiting for him to continue.

"I think they're going to tell me about some management problems."

"How do you know they want to talk about that?"

He shook his head and smiled ironically. "Will's lived in Chicago too long. He's forgotten how quickly the word gets around in Hammelburg."

"Bruce Kramer, the CFO... " He paused for a moment and motioned toward the newspaper resting on the corner of the table. "He attempted suicide the night before Thanksgiving. It's in the paper. Rick's assigned to the investigation. He called me this morning. They think Kramer was involved in some kind of financial scandal, but they can't interview him; his lawyer won't permit anyone to talk to him."

"That's serious, but is that what they want to talk to you about on Sunday afternoon?"

"I'm afraid it's a lot more than that. I called Norma and Jerry and ask them to come to the meeting... Jerry's been very busy the past few days... Yesterday, he decided he wanted to know why Byron Hinkle resigned so quickly. As usual, Jerry went directly to Byron without talking to me or anyone else."

"Did he find out?"

"Hinkle told him he had a conflict of interest. Jerry pushed him pretty hard; told him it wouldn't be good for his law practice if the IMU didn't understand. All Hinkle would say was that he and Perkins had done some investing together that disqualified him from continuing to represent the IMU."

Gloria said, "That's not much of an answer. Investment in what?"

Jimmie shrugged his shoulders. "Jerry agreed it wasn't much of an answer, so he called a friend of his who is close to the Wiemer management and asked what the hell was going on."

"What friend?"

"I'm not sure, but I think the same person that was with him when he went down to Juarez and took those pictures. It wasn't another IMU member; Jerry would have mentioned it if it was."

"How do you know that?"

"Jerry was in a couple of the pictures. Someone else took them... Anyway, that person told him that the senior management and the board of directors believe that Kramer invested one hell of a lot of his money in the Perkins deal, lost it all, and attempted suicide. They also know about Hinkle's investment with Perkins."

Gloria was skeptical. "So that's what they want to tell you tomorrow? I don't think so. That's an ugly story, but that could wait until Monday."

Jimmie rubbed his jaw with his right hand. His mood seemed to darken. He shook his head, abruptly stood up, walked across the room, and leaned against a countertop. He folded his arms across his chest, his muscular arms stretching the sleeves of his dark green T-shirt. He stared at the ceiling for a moment before speaking.

"Jerry also has a friend in the accounting department. He called him this morning. A few weeks ago Jon Pertoski came into the accounting department a couple of times and asked a lot of questions about how they calculated some cost figures... Pertoski thinks the company reported less profit than they actually made."

Gloria smiled. "Well, if that's true, it puts a big question mark over the financial hardship story, doesn't it?"

To her surprise, her remark was not received as a welcome revelation. Jimmie looked directly at her. His expression reflected the anguish he was experiencing over what he was about to divulge. "The accountant also told Jerry that a big part of the employee pension and savings is invested in Perkins's fund. The auditors called and told them, yesterday… "

"Told them what?" she asked.

He stared at the ceiling, his voice faint. "They believe it's a total loss."

Gloria was stunned. She shook her head in disbelief. "My God, Jimmie, that's our money, my dad's money, the whole town's money. They can't do that. There are laws that restrict where they can invest our money."

Jimmie attempted to recover his composure. He inhaled loudly and unsteadily, coughed, cleared his throat, and closed his eyes.

"We've been sloppy and stupid… really stupid. We haven't insisted that management tell us where the pension and savings funds are invested."

He stopped momentarily, lowered his head, and placed the thumb and forefinger of his right hand over his eyes.

"When J.W. Rieff was CEO, the corporate treasurer met with the IMU Board once a year and reviewed all the investments and the rules. When Adam Fulton became CEO, that stopped, just like all the other financial information got shut off. Norma asked for a list of the investments several times, but never got 'em. She asked Hinkle to get the information. He kept stalling… told her as long as Puritan Securities was managing the money, she didn't need to worry."

Gloria's voice reflected her alarm. "Who are these people, Jimmie? I mean, they come in here from God knows where, take the big jobs, get big salaries, fire a lot of people, reduce pay and benefits for the rest of us, now they've screwed up our pension funds and savings. Where are we living… Argentina… China? This isn't the same town you and I grew up in. For more than 30 years, my dad trusted and respected the management; didn't always agree with them, but never mistrusted them. My grandfather earned a 40-year service pin at Wiemer. He told my dad he wanted it pinned to his lapel when they buried him"

Jimmie didn't respond. He continued to lean against the countertop, arms crossed, still struggling to control his emotions.

There had been only one time during their married life that Gloria had seen Jimmie cry: his mother's death.

She stood up, walked to him, and placed her arms around him, resting her head on his chest. He immediately embraced her. She could feel him shaking as he attempted to regain his composure.

She spoke to him softly. "Maybe all these events will make it easier to get a new labor contract, stop the relocation, and the company will pay back all the money to the pension and savings fund."

He held her more tightly, patted her back gently, raised his head, and stared at the ceiling.

"That would be a happy ending, Gloria, but I'm afraid we've used up all the happy endings at Wiemer Industries."

Still embracing him, she said, "What about Will Heider? If he's involved won't he try to help? You've always said you like and trust Jon Pertoski. Won't he be in the meeting tomorrow?"

"Oh, I'm sure they'll try. Management's pension and savings went down the tube as well. But where is Wiemer Industries going to find hundreds of millions of dollars to repay us? They can't borrow it. Perkins can't repay it. If we sue the company, they'll probably declare bankruptcy, sell the company, and the banks will take all the money. Even if they agree not to relocate, we'll take a cut in pay and benefits, and it will take years to restore the amount they lost in the pension and savings funds."

Gloria had no response.

They continued to embrace each other.

"You know, Gloria, something important and vital has broken; something that made Hammelburg a good place to live. Whatever broke, took a long time to build, and it's gonna take a long time to fix it... if ever.

She looked up at him. "What broke, Jimmie?"

His response was soft, as if he were carefully evaluating her question. "I am not sure. It's hard to define. It's all involved with trust and respect and sharing. I'm not even sure how we'll fix it. Maybe we have to start by thinking about how we value ourselves and how we value Hammelburg."

About the Author

During his career the author has served as a venture capitalist, chief financial officer of a multinational corporation, university administrator/ faculty member, Federal Reserve economist and member of the board of directors of several corporations and public service organizations. A frequent contributor to business and financial journals, **Race to the Bottom** is the author's fictional depiction of the social and economic devastation suffered by a Midwestern community as a result of corporate relocation and corruption. The author is a native of the Midwest.

Printed in the United States
21208LVS00002BB/7-18